THE BEFORE AND THE AFTER

Catherine Sequeira

This is a work of fiction. All of the characters, organizations, and events portrayed in this novel are either products of the author's imagination or are used fictitiously.

THE BEFORE AND THE AFTER

Copyright © 2023 by Catherine Lamm

Cover design by Tyler Dryden

Cover copyright © 2023 by Barcelos Publishing, LLC

All rights reserved.

Published by Barcelos Publishing, LLC, Sacramento, CA, USA

The Library of Congress Cataloging-in-Publication Data is available upon request.

ISBN 9798988723103 (trade paperback)

ISBN 9798988723110 (ebook)

Our books may be purchased in bulk for promotional, educational, or business use. Please contact your local bookseller for more information.

First Edition: October 2023

Printed in the United States of America

*To anyone who has ever felt lost or alone.
We're in this together.*

—

When looking back on the Before and the events leading up to the After, it was impossible to say precisely when everything went to shit. There were just two points in time, with a hazy space in between, leaving the carcass of the Before to be picked over by those in the After.

CHAPTER ONE

Trader made one last pass around the house before leaving it all behind. The place suited him just fine for three-quarters of the year, but the empty period between the trading seasons was excruciatingly long. He was eager to get back out on the road again.

He whistled for Sasha, and a *merf* sound responded as a gray ball of kitty floof dashed through the closing door. Remembering her feline dignity, she then sauntered over to the wagon, rubbed her face against the wheels, and hopped into her cat bed in the driver's seat. With the door closed behind her, he walked away without locking it. Trader was born in the After, and locks weren't needed in a city that boasted a population of less than ten.

Grabbing the lead rope, Trader waded through the abandoned backyards to collect Boxer, spotting him snoozing beneath a sycamore. He ran his hands along the Clydesdale's back and gave his mane a scratch. Boxer replied with a soft nicker and lazily swished his tail. Trader pressed his forehead against Boxer's neck and inhaled the rich horse smell.

He went through the familiar motions of hitching the horse to the wagon. Boxer held his breath to keep the harness loose, and Trader gave him a light nudge in the girth. It was a game the two friends played. Like an old couple teasing each other. With a huff, Boxer relaxed, and the harness was cinched just right. Boxer bobbed his head, conceding the match and signaling that he was ready to go.

The wagon was Trader's home away from home and looked like it was straight from a western frontier exhibit at Sutter's Fort. Trader had built it five years ago with scrap wood from the house next door and wheels that Rat had scavenged. The wagon made the trading route every year just fine, rolling as smoothly as possible on the crumbled roads and keeping the contents dry during storms.

Earlier that morning, Trader had loaded the wagon with goods. He'd been busy this winter growing and canning winter crops to trade. Kimchi was the most valuable thing he produced himself. The tools, nails, and screws had come from one of Rat's scavenging runs. The needs of each settlement on his route differed, and he would also be picking things up on the way to trade later down the road. He liked helping the settlements. Not many people ran the Nor Cal circuit, and it felt good to be starting another season.

After one last wagon check, Trader patted his pockets to make sure everything was in order and hopped into the driver's seat. He scratched Sasha under the chin, and she responded with a purr, eyes closing happily. He clicked his tongue and flapped the reins. Boxer nickered in reply, pulling against the harness.

The sound of clopping hooves echoed in the quiet as the wagon rolled out into the street. Though Trader enjoyed the period of relative solitude between runs on the circuit, he was ready to be around groups of people again, sharing a meal and hearing their stories. He wondered how the settlements had changed over the last year, hoping that the births had outpaced the deaths from Weeps.

THE BEFORE AND THE AFTER

Trader's place was pretty isolated, even for the After. His home sat southeast of downtown Sacramento in the Oak Park neighborhood. He only had one neighbor, Carla, who lived a few blocks over and had been a middle school teacher in the Before. Though she kept mostly to herself, she was his only friend in this ghost town. Last night over dinner, they'd said their goodbyes for the season, with Carla promising to look after his garden until he came back. He'd miss her, but he also trusted that she'd do just fine in his absence; she was a tough cookie.

Trader turned the wagon onto Martin Luther King Jr. Blvd. and took the on-ramp to the 99, dodging a large pothole. At this height, he could see the tops of the downtown high-rises piercing out of the Sacramento Bay. The waters made a comforting lapping sound, and sludgy waves pushed against the western side of the highway. Amorphous plastic waste and brown foam bordered the water. Carla was always grumping about how the once-crystal-clear Sacramento River was now a murky mess of a bay. Sure, it would be nice to have a clean water source nearby, but Trader didn't know anything different. And, even if he let it bother him, there wasn't much he could do about it. The damage had long been done.

The 99 would take them along the banks of the Sacramento Bay through Modesto where they would turn west just north of the inland desert. Since everything up to the Oakland Hills was underwater, they would turn north at Walnut Creek. The Benicia Bridge was still passable, or at least it was last year, and would give Trader a path to loop through Vacaville and back east to Sacramento. Depending on the weather, he might make a short trip further east into the Sierra foothills. The After being the unpredictable beast that it was, he would have to play it by ear and make a decision about heading into the foothills later. For now, it was one step at a time, and his first stop was Forty Two.

* * *

The first leg of the journey was thankfully uneventful. Some low spots in the highway were partially flooded, but there was still enough room to navigate the wagon around any questionable bits. He definitely wouldn't be taking a lunch break in the shade near any of the stagnant pools of cloudy water. The risk of Weeps was too high. Just because he'd made it this long didn't mean he could let his guard down.

Being in his early twenties, Trader only had a conceptual idea of how packed the highway used to be before Weeps hit. Carla shared stories of the 99 in the Before; the lanes stacked with cars for as far as the eye could see, moving an inch at a time. It spooked him to think of being boxed in with hundreds of other cars lined up like metal coffins. Trader enjoyed these vast empty spaces between settlements and couldn't imagine it any other way.

Outside of Elk Grove, two people were out on a boat in the bay, fishing poles hanging over the side. They were pretty brave, or hungry, to eat anything they might catch out of the oil-slicked water. When the wagon passed, the sound of Boxer's hooves clopping on the asphalt drew their attention. They both turned to look and waved. Trader didn't know them but waved back anyway. His mom had taught him that it never hurt to be friendly, especially in a world with so few people left. Relationships with wanderers, Singletons, and settlements were critical for survival. Plus, it just made Trader happy to put some good out into the world.

It was early afternoon and the trio was nearing the city of Galt when Trader saw a woman riding a pedal bike north on the 99. A shopping cart filled with supplies was rigged up as a trailer. She was slim, likely in her early twenties, and had dark brown skin. She wore a loose-fitting, patched dress that fluttered in the breeze. Trader pulled the wagon to a stop, curious.

"How's it going?" he asked amicably. "I'm Trader. This here's Boxer and Sasha." He gestured to his traveling companions. Sasha deigned to peek over the rim of her bed at the sound of her name.

The woman stopped and smiled, setting her feet down and resting her elbows on the handlebars to catch her breath. She grabbed a canteen and took a sip before answering.

"I'm Natalia. Nice to meet you." She used her foot to drop the kickstand and headed over to the wagon to shake his hand.

"Is that a cat riding with you?" she asked, eyes wide.

"Yep, Sasha comes with us everywhere," Trader said proudly.

Most people didn't have pets in the After. Feral cats were tolerated, especially since they didn't get Weeps. Plus, cats tended to fend for themselves and, more importantly, kept the rats away. To Trader, Sasha was more than a means of rodent control though. She was family, and he couldn't imagine life without her.

"That's super cool. How'd you train her to do that?"

"I'm not sure you can train a cat." Trader laughed. "Honestly, it wasn't love at first sight. When I'd try to call her over, she'd respond with a big, fat, feline nope. I wasn't able to get close to her until I started sharing my dinner. After a while, she got more comfortable around me. A big storm brought her meowing at my back door, and…." He shrugged and gestured to the content cat-loaf in the driver's seat. "Here we are."

"That's so fricking cute." She shook her head, smiling.

Trader smiled back and scratched Sasha under the chin.

"Where're you headed?" he asked. He didn't see people on the road often, much less with a rig for trading.

"I'm on my way back to Jackson. I just dropped off some pork jerky at Forty Two and picked up some tools. You?"

"We're headed south on the circuit. We're from Sac. Oak Park actually."

"Originally from there?" She shaded her eyes and rested her other hand against her lower back.

"Nope, originally from the foothills. When my mom died, I took Boxer and headed down into the valley. Oak Park was as good as anywhere else. Randomly crossed paths with Jesse several years ago, and they got me into trading. Been running the circuit since. How about you? You originally from Jackson?"

"Born and raised." She nodded.

"You thinking about running the full Nor Cal circuit?"

"I used to bring stuff back and forth between Forty Two on foot. It was a miserable two-day walk, and the pack was hella heavy. So, I didn't go very often. This is my first run with the bike, and it's going pretty good."

"Planning on hitting any other settlements and widening your circuit now that you have wheels?"

"Thinkin' about it. What's up in Sac?" She nodded north up the highway.

"The city is pretty much flooded. Not many of us left up there. You could head up the 50 to Gold Bug or west on the 80 to the Machados'. If you want to expand slowly, your best bet is hitting up Rat. He has lots of tools and scavenge items. Just bring lots of food to trade. The dude can't grow anything for shit and is always looking to keep his pantry full. Take Folsom Blvd. off the 50. He's in an old recycling center. Rat can be a little gruff. Don't let that fool you, though. He's a good guy."

Natalia pursed her lips, thinking, and nodded her head. "I might do that. Test drive the bike on a longer stretch. Think he might have spare bike parts for me?"

"Yep. But, if you're looking for bike parts, you should also visit Les and Rodger. They live outside Davis in an old greenhouse tucked off the 80. Take the Kidwell exit and then turn on Olmo. They know bikes best out of anyone."

"Gotta get these trades back home first," she said as she gestured back to the grocery cart. "I'll see if I can get to Sac after. There's still some time before the heat sets in. Maybe I'll try Davis next year."

She sighed. "Whelp, it's getting late. My biscuits are burning from the bike seat, and I got a cushy chair at home callin' me. Thank you for all of the tips. I appreciate it. Nice to meet you. Looking forward to crossing paths with you again; maybe we can even share a meal next time."

"Sounds great, and happy to help. Travel safe." Trader nodded and smiled.

Natalia took another sip from the canteen, waved goodbye, and leaned into the pedals to get the contraption rolling again.

Trader was pleased to see a new person carrying goods between settlements. A settlement that didn't trade wouldn't last long. Between the Before and the After, there had been a gradual, almost imperceptible creep of desolation that built on decades of natural disasters and economic contraction. Weeps was just the nail in the coffin, a plague to pick off what was left. People who passed goods between settlements were rare, but they were desperately needed in the After. Without people running the circuits, many of the settlements wouldn't survive. Trader hoped Natalia's new rig would allow her to do some more serious trading.

Impatient to get his own first trade of the season under his belt, Trader made a clicking sound and flapped the reins lightly. The wagon lurched forward south on the 99 towards Forty Two.

CHAPTER TWO

The city of Galt was fairly typical of those in the After; it was a husk of its former self. A sprawl of abandoned buildings straddled the highway and stretched out to meet the adjacent open spaces. In the Before, Galt had boasted a modest population, enough to support a single Wal-Mart. Now, only twenty-eight people called Galt home.

The city was already flooded when the Weeps hit thirty years ago. When everyone started dying, a small group of survivors took over a local golf course and established a settlement, naming it Forty Two. The settlement grew as refugees and wanderers happened by. A steady supply of food, a reliable water source, and solar power made it an attractive place to put down roots.

Rosa was the closest thing they had to a mayor at Forty Two. She ran a tight ship; everyone knew their job and did it well. Despite the rigid organizational structure and no-nonsense attitude, everyone was welcome at Forty Two, and the people within the community were content. Trader always enjoyed his time there and was looking forward to hanging his hat up for the night.

The wagon rolled through the orchard bordering the settlement. One of the community's founders, sensing the end times, had collected potted trees from the nurseries and kept them alive, knowing they would come in handy later. Roughly twenty-five years later, the settlers could now enjoy lemons, oranges, apricots, apples, almonds, and walnuts.

On the other side of the orchard, the immaculate lawns, ponds, and sand traps of the golf course had been replaced with rolling farmland. Ground crops were rotated under the protective semi-shade of a solar farm. There was also a native grass pasture for the horses and cows. The bay was cleaner near Galt, and water for the crops was brought in via an underpass using large irrigation pipes. The water was crap for drinking, but it would do for the fields. As the wagon passed by, Boxer whinnied softly, and the two resident horses whinnied back.

Sasha woke up as soon as they turned into the settlement and sat up to watch. Trader saw a few people working the farms and moving between buildings, many of them raising a hand as he passed, recognizing his wagon. Trader smiled inwardly, cheered to see the settlement doing so well. Boxer picked up his step, eager to be with the other horses, and the trio soon made their way to the country club. Excitement built in Trader's chest. This was the first big group he'd seen in nine months, and it'd be nice to be around the hustle and bustle again.

As soon as the wagon stopped, Sasha leapt out of the driver's seat with a quick *merf* of a cat goodbye and disappeared around the back of the building. The chicken hutches were back there, which attracted mice. Trader knew she would find plenty to eat.

Trader hopped out of the wagon, stretching his legs just as Rosa came outside to greet him.

"Hello, stranger," Rosa said as she wiped her hands on a towel tucked into the waist of her pants.

Rosa was short, stout, and solid as a rock. Her long dark hair was braided beneath a beanie. She wore patched cargo pants and a handmade knit sweater. Trader was shocked to see that she was also sporting a fine pair of boots. The shoes looked too nice to be anything but newly made.

"Nice to see you, Rosa." Trader hugged her.

"Those're some kickass boots you have." He nodded down to her shoes. "Where on Earth did you find those?"

"We got really lucky. A shoemaker, Samson, joined us over winter. He knows his leather and does a fine job crafting shoes. He figured out a trick to build the soles out of a combination of tire rubber and wood. Pretty damn sturdy." She stuck one foot out, turning it this way and that to show off her kicks. "We may have a chance to hook you up with a pair while you're here."

She looked down at Trader's shoes with a smirk. He wore what looked like the afterbirth of a chimera crossed with a palm tree on his feet. Desperate to keep his feet warm last winter, he had cobbled them together with what was around his place. Sadly, his version of Uggs had turned out pretty sorry looking. They hadn't kept his feet very warm either.

It was amazing how hard it was to find shoes from the Before. If ninety percent of the population had gone in a flash bang, there would have been plenty of footwear for Trader's lifetime. But it hadn't happened like that. Layer after layer, things had just seemed to wash away. Long before Weeps hit, the severe weather events and supply chain issues meant that less stuff was produced and stores closed one by one. Eighty years later, it was virtually impossible to find a halfway decent pair of shoes, especially sturdy boots like Rosa's.

"New shoes would be fabulous. I've got some fair trades for them if there's a pair my size."

"I'm sure we do. Come on in. We'll feed you before we start sniffing through your goods." Rosa gestured with a thumb over her shoulder back into the country club.

"Sounds like a plan. Let me get Boxer situated first."

A few others started wandering up from the farms and a

couple of kids came from around the back. People started peeking in the wagon, curious to see what he had this season. A small girl chased Sasha from behind the country club and tried to catch her, without any luck. An older boy came up to Boxer, offering his hand to Boxer's nose. After a sniff, Boxer licked his lips, a sign that the horse accepted the boy. The boy reached up to scratch Boxer's mane. Trader's heart swelled seeing the kids still around and a year taller.

"Nick here can unhitch Boxer for you and get him some water if you want," Rosa suggested.

"That would be great. Thanks, Rosa, and thanks, Nick." Trusting the older boy to take good care of the horse from there, Trader followed Rosa inside.

The country club was surprisingly homey, all trappings of starched privilege faded away. Old throw rugs crisscrossed the floor. Couches and chairs covered with quilted blankets formed three small clusters by the windows. The windows were all intact, with thick curtains thrown wide to let the sun in. It was a veritable wealth of cloth that was in good condition. During the day, the lights were off to save power. But, with house batteries, the room would be warmly lit when night settled in.

The country club had a cafeteria-sized kitchen off to the left with an adjoining dining hall. The kitchen equipment had survived fairly well, and plenty of fine meals were made there for the inhabitants of Forty Two and their guests. Scents of fresh cornbread and baked beans trailed out from the kitchen. Trader's mouth watered. Though he was a fairly good cook, the folks at Forty Two had access to fresh ingredients that he didn't. And it was just nice having someone else cook something different for a change. He always looked forward to sampling the varied flavors along the route.

Speaking over the sounds of cooking, Rosa leaned into the kitchen and asked, "I know it's early, but can we get a couple of plates?" She turned to Trader. "Let's go grab a seat."

Trader followed her into the adjoining dining hall. Six picnic tables filled the room, each with bright yellow spring flowers in a cup. Rosa grabbed a seat at the closest one, setting out two glasses of water. Trader sighed with contentment after a long drink. The water was fresh, cool, and tasted crystal clean, having come from well-maintained water barrels. The water from his barrels back home always had a slight plasticky aftertaste. He made a note to ask Rosa how they managed perfection at Forty Two.

"Tell me about this new shoemaker," Trader prompted. "I am surprised that the craft made it into the After, honestly."

"Me too," Rosa replied. "Especially since Samson used to be a Singleton."

"Really?" Trader asked, unable to keep his eyebrows from raising.

"I know, right? He's a highly skilled hunter, and leatherwork came naturally after that. He started with deer moccasins and experimented quite a bit with different materials before getting what you see here."

"Yeah, but how did you manage to get a Singleton to settle here?" Trader asked, still perplexed.

"He used to trade fairly regularly with Gold Bug. He said he thought about settling there but heard about Forty Two and decided to check us out."

"Wow."

"I know, I know. They usually don't come down from the mountains. I think he just started to get lonely up there. He came to see what it was like and decided to stay. He still keeps to himself. But I think he likes having meals cooked for him and eating something besides game and berries."

A young man brought them plates filled with cornbread, baked beans, collard greens, and fresh carrot sticks. Trader inhaled the spicy aroma before taking a bite. The food was delicious. A warm meal made at Forty Two was always a treat. As he

13

savored a mouthful of cornbread, he began to understand why a Singleton might want to settle down here.

"How'd the last year treat you?" Rosa asked between bites.

"We got by just fine. There was enough rain to keep the raised beds growing. I'm feeling grateful to have a full belly and lots of food left to trade. How about you all?"

"Our drinking water ran low last summer. We almost didn't make it," Rosa answered, pausing to reflect. "Crazy, right? One minute we're hoping for rain. And the next, we're dreading it with the flooding and Weeps and everything. We lost three this year."

Every settlement had to weigh the perks of having a steady water supply against the risk of Weeps. And, depending on what fell from the sky, the pendulum could swing one way or another. Even though he was young in the whole scheme of things, Trader felt like humanity had been running a marathon with the Weeps nipping at their heels. It was hard leading people and losing some, and he didn't envy Rosa's position.

"Sorry to hear that," Trader said, watching Rosa as she pushed the beans around with her fork.

"In early winter, there was a nasty fire about ten to twenty miles south. The smoke up here was so bad that we had to stay inside for a few days. Where's the rain when you need it, right?" She finally took a bite of the beans.

"Was it the Silvas'? Any idea how bad it was?"

The Silvas' was more than twenty miles south, but the flat land of the valley could be deceptive. Estimating distance was difficult. He hadn't expected to start the circuit finding one settlement laid to waste.

"Oh geez, I hope not," Rosa chewed on her lower lip. "I assume we would've got some refugees if it was their place. Plus, the fire seemed closer than that. I hadn't even thought it could be them until you said something."

"I'm sure they're okay," he said, trying to reassure himself as much as he was her.

He took a sip of water before continuing. "I met Natalia on the way down. Looks like you have yourselves another recurring visitor. I bet it's good to see a regular circuit with Jackson set up."

The idea of trade helped pull Rosa out of the shadows, and a slight smile spread across her face. "It is, indeed. Once Samson gets cranking, we should have more shoes to trade too."

"Speaking of which, I've got some good stuff this season. Rat hooked me up, and I have lots of tools this time. Might be some in there to help your shoemaker. If not, let me know what you need, and I'll keep an eye out. I do have meds, but they're all expired." He scooped the last of the garlicky collard greens in his mouth.

"Weeps meds or other stuff?" Rosa asked hopefully.

"Both. Gen 2 Proxleep, Ibuprofen, some Keflex, and other random things I grabbed from Kuldeep last year. No clue where the Keflex has been hiding all these years…it expired ages ago. Doesn't hurt to try though, right?" He offered a smile.

"Yep. Doesn't hurt to try." She smiled back. "We're glad to have you here, Trader. Hope you'll stay the night after the trade."

Rosa reached over and gave his arm an affectionate squeeze. Trader gave her another big smile around a mouthful of cornbread soaked in baked bean sauce. Rosa was a genuinely kind person. Though Trader enjoyed his space, it felt good to be around Rosa and to be able to help Forty Two. Moments like these drew Trader back to the settlements each year like a lonely comet pulled into the gravitational field of a tight-knit community.

15

CHAPTER THREE

Trader and Rosa finished their meals, chatting companionably about gardening and debating how hot it might get this summer. With the last crumb licked away, they bussed their dishes and headed outside. Word of Trader's arrival had spread throughout the settlement, and a line of people stood by the wagon. With only Trader and Jesse running the full Nor Cal circuit, his arrival was always a big event. He knew the people of Forty Two would be anxious to see what he had this year and hear any gossip.

Trader made a point of always trying to give people what they needed. Sometimes the trades were fair, and sometimes he took a hit. At the end of the day, the communities he traded with always welcomed him, which made it worth it.

He stationed himself at the back of the wagon, open for business. On request, he dug out meds, a knife set, a half-dozen metal tools, a metal bucket, and several jars of kimchi. In exchange, he received pork jerky, several quilts, four novels in fairly good shape, some writing charcoal, and several jars of fruit and vegetable preserves.

The *coup de grâce* was a pair of handmade leather cowboy boots with a low heel that just happened to be available in his size. Grateful for the amazing start to the trading season, he immediately donned them. The smooth leather caressed his skin and didn't chafe like the Uggs. They'd be hearing "Taps" playing tonight when he buried those sorry things. He walked a few steps in the new boots, pleased to notice that nothing pinched his toes and his ankles didn't rub in the back. Never before had a pair of shoes fit him this well, and he was delighted.

Trading finished just as the sun was starting to set, a cool breeze coming in from the bay. Trader secured his new items in the wagon before joining Rosa by a large firepit. He was looking forward to sharing stories and feeling like a part of something again.

The earthy smell of campfire smoke filled the air. The pit was about five feet wide with a low, stone wall. A couple of buckets of water and an old shovel sat nearby. Even though it was usually safe to have an open fire this time of year, one could never be too careful in California.

Ten or so people of various ages were gathered in seats around the fire, talking quietly in friendly tones. They sat on a hodgepodge of old metal benches, fancy dining room chairs, and plastic patio furniture. One lucky winner was gently rocking in a rocking chair. Some folks ate from heaping plates from the cafeteria, and others were already finished. Unable to resist the pull, Trader grabbed a seat.

Rosa turned to him as he sat down next to her. "Great haul today. How're the boots?"

Trader stuck his leg out and pulled his pant leg up. "They're pretty awesome. You lucked out with that Singleton."

"We sure did," she replied, smiling, gaze shifting back to the bright light of the fire. "Jerome and Naomi started apprenticing with him. Samson was kinda pissed about it. He likes his space. But he eventually warmed up to the idea. We're hoping to have more shoes to trade next year. The leather will be the hardest thing to get."

Though Forty Two had cattle onsite, the animals were used for milk and fertilizer. It was rare that they would kill one of them, even for meat. The animals were simply too precious.

"Might be able to use horses," she mused.

Horses were immune to Weeps, but the same mosquitoes that carried the Weeps also carried West Nile and Equine Encephalitis. Despite the threat of viral infection and the dangerous, unpredictable weather, the number of wild horses still increased every year. Trying to catch them would be tricky though. Time would tell if Forty Two would have horse-leather shoes to trade next spring.

"The Nakamuras might have leather for you. If I cross paths with Jesse early enough, I'll ask them to bring some for you. Otherwise, I'll get you some for next year," he promised.

"Thanks for thinking of us. We appreciate your visits, Trader." She paused, looking into the fire. "Stayin' the night, I assume?"

"Yep, if that's okay," Trader replied. "No need to set me up in a room. I'll sleep in the wagon. Can Boxer stay out in the pasture overnight? He likes visiting."

"Sure. You three are welcome anytime, and you can stay as long as you like." She paused, letting the silence settle between them for a beat. "If you ever wanted to, Forty Two would be privileged to have you on permanently. Our doors are always open."

Trader smiled slightly in response and looked down at his new shoes uncomfortably. His bootheel rocked side-to-side in the dirt, creating a flat C shape.

Rosa watched him closely as if she could read him weighing the pluses and minuses. Seeing his discomfort, she changed the subject and said, "Thank you again for coming, Trader."

A companionable silence settled between them.

The sun was fully set now, and the light from the fire danced across their faces. He let the warmth sink into his bones. Sasha sauntered up, rubbing against his leg. She looked up at him and meowed questioningly. Trader patted his lap. She jumped up and quickly got to making biscuits.

He sat quietly listening to other conversations and taking in the stories that moved around him. Next to them was an elderly couple snuggled close together on a bench, soaking in the warmth of the fire and relaxing after the meal. A thread-bare quilt was stretched across both of their laps.

"Ji-Min is about six months along," one of the women said. "I wish Molly would just stay here. We need a good nurse."

"I think what she's got with Danny may end up lasting. They've been rolling in the hay whenever the Fosters come by. With a bit of nudging, I bet we can get ourselves a nurse!" The other woman snickered.

"It'll be nice having a baby around. It's been a while. After the Weeps took George's boy, people have been spooked. There's a big difference between surviving and prepping the world for a future that has people still in it. It's hard to bring a critter into a world like this one." The first woman sighed and snuggled closer to her partner. They both watched the fire as it crackled and sparked.

Loud laughter boomed from the group directly across the fire, startling Trader. He reflexively smiled in response, pleased to see people having fun. After being egged on by friends, a large man with a beard stood up. He started singing a rendition of "Take Me Home, Country Roads" in a deep booming voice. The lyrics, having shifted over time, now told a story of longing for the Before and all of the bloody tears shed over a land now gone. Trader felt himself swept up by the music, a tightening in his chest.

At the chorus, others joined in. Even Trader started singing softly about halfway through. The sound of everyone's voices coming together made his skin prickle. Everyone was smiling sadly, including the two old women. After the song, the bearded man returned to his seat, his friends patting him on the back, and conversations resumed. Trader had no clue what triggered the outburst but appreciated it all the same. It warmed his heart and made him feel, just for a moment, like he was part of something bigger.

Rosa glanced over at him. "I'm worried about you, Trader. You look down this season."

Trader stared at the fire, collecting his thoughts.

"If I'm being honest, it's always hard coming out of winter." He looked down at Sasha curled in his lap and started petting her. Her soft purr comforted him. "All around me are empty houses and skeletons of the Before. There's nothing new. There're less and less people around. It's just...." He paused and sighed. "It's just hard to have hope; to feel like anything that we are doing even matters."

Rosa stared at him for a long time. Trader kept his head hung, eyes on Sasha and avoiding Rosa's gaze. Rosa reached over and put a hand on his leg and squeezed.

"It's okay to feel that way. Honestly, anyone who says they haven't felt that way at one time or another is a damn liar."

Trader sighed deeply and leaned back in his seat. "I do appreciate being welcomed. These stops mean a lot."

"They mean a lot to us too. People like you, Natalia, and Jesse, you connect the few of us who are left. We need you and appreciate what you do for us. If you ever need anything, just ask."

Trader let Rosa's words settle around him. He tilted his head back, staring at the endless bright twinkling starlight. The stories about cities being so bright in the Before that the stars were not visible sounded crazy to him. Even sitting close to the large fire, the stars twinkled brightly in the sky like shattered glass. The dark shapes of bats flitted above, hunting the insects attracted to the firelight.

Forty Two was his first stop on the circuit each year; his first chance to be around a group of people again after several months. It was like the first sip of fresh, cool water from a canteen after a long hike. It felt good, filling something in him that he didn't realize was empty until he stopped to breathe for a moment.

Trader and Rosa sat comfortably together as people drifted off to bed in twos and threes. Feeling heavy-lidded, Trader eventually said goodnight and headed back to the wagon. He gave Rosa an extra-long hug, trying to impart his appreciation for the companionship in the gesture.

Once tucked into his bedroll, Sasha purring at his side, he rolled the fireside conversation over in his head. Rosa was right when she talked about how important the circuit was to the survival of the settlements. People were counting on him and the trades he brought. He knew that, with each stop, the winter loneliness would ebb away. With these encouraging thoughts swirling in his mind, he fell into a deep, dreamless sleep.

* * *

Trader awoke the next morning to the hubbub of people moving about. Though he wasn't used to all of the noise in a settlement, the sounds of others always reassured him when he was on the road. The air was crisp, but he could already feel the warmth moving in. In a couple more months, nights would be so hot that it would be hard to sleep. Right now, it was a gorgeous time of year. Songbirds chirped in the nearby trees, and the smell of freshly blooming flowers filled the air.

As Trader climbed out of the wagon, he shifted his weight quickly to avoid stepping on the three small decapitated mammals lying in a neat row on the ground. Sasha liked to leave him these as presents. Tired from a busy night massacring the local wildlife, she was now sleeping in a tight ball nestled in Trader's bedroll. He picked up the carcasses and tossed them into the compost pile. At various points in his life, he had been hungry enough to consider eating even those sad little things, but not today. He could afford to recycle the meat.

Trader went to the outhouses for his morning piss, admiring the settlement's approach to waste management. Wooden outhouses sat in a line over holes in a flat trailer that was parked over a large ditch. When the ditch was three-quarters full, the remainder would be backfilled, and the trailer would be pulled to a new site. Golf flags were placed to avoid an unpleasant foray into a sewage pool. After a year, crops would be rotated over the site. This process closed the loop and put the essentials right back into the soil.

After completing his morning constitutional, he topped up the water jugs and readied the wagon. He fussed about, making sure everything was secure after the busy day of trading. With a carrot in hand, he lured Boxer from the pasture and hitched him to the wagon.

As he was finishing up, Rosa came out with a package in her hand.

"Morning. Sleep okay?"

Trader nodded.

"Here." Rosa handed him the bundle. "I know you want to get on the road. It's breakfast to go. Kinda like those old fast food drive-thrus." She laughed.

"And, here." She pulled a book out of her back pocket and handed it to him. "I know how much you like books. I think you'll dig this one. The main character reminds me a lot of you. Might help you a bit on your journey."

The book was *The Last Cuentista* by Donna Barba Higuera. A picture of a sleeping woman was on the cover. Trader thumbed the yellowish pages of the paperback, eager to start reading. Books were treasures, offering a way to be around people in a world where so few existed. Similar to the stories that people told along the road, books were a way for him to feel connected.

"Thank you, Rosa."

Rosa studied his face.

"I appreciate the hospitality and the generosity. And…I can't thank you enough for these bad boys." Trader stuck one foot out to show off the new boots one last time. He grinned at her.

Rosa kept her smile for a flash and then her face got serious. "Trader, I know I've said this before. But, should you ever want to settle or if things get bad up north, you always have a place here."

Trader's smile softened, and his eyes said all the "thank yous" that he couldn't sufficiently verbalize.

"One step at a time." She gave him a rough pat on the back. "See you next year." They waved to each other, and she headed back into the country club.

Trader climbed into the wagon, stashing the small meal and the book between him and Sasha's bed. After a light flap of the reins, the wagon started moving away from Forty Two and back onto Highway 99. Leaning out to peer behind him, he soaked up one last look at the settlement before turning forward and heading out into the empty stretches between here and the next stop. His heart twinged a bit at leaving these good people so soon, but he had a long way to go and many more stops on the circuit to fill him up.

CHAPTER FOUR

It was usually an easy run down the 99 to the Silvas'. Not today. Life had other plans.

Waving native grasses straddled the highway, stretching east to meet the faded purple crags of the Sierra Nevada mountains and west to where it abutted the Sacramento Bay. The sea of pale green grass was interrupted by swathes of yellow wintercress flowers. Clusters of orange poppies crowded the edges of the highway. Except for a female American kestrel perched on a fence post, the vista was fairly empty of wildlife, and Trader didn't meet anyone else on the road. This was the calm before the storm.

As Trader reached the outskirts of Lodi, all of the pleasant feelings from the first leg of the trip were briskly whisked away. A barricade hunkered across the highway on the north edge of the city. Dilapidated, rusty cars, paint faded with time, were arranged perpendicular to the 99, blocking all but a narrow passage. Trader's stomach flopped, and the hairs on the back of his neck went up.

"Whoa there, boy," Trader said softly. He pulled on the reins to stop the wagon.

This had most assuredly not been here last time Trader had come down the 99. He surveyed the empty road, confirming no one was around. He didn't know if this was supposed to be a checkpoint, a warning, a way to keep people out, or even a way to keep people in. He had read about barricades in books but hadn't seen one before. There was no reason that something like this would be set up in the After, and it spooked the living shit out of him.

All the rampant violence postulated in just about every post-apocalyptic novel didn't happen when the four horsemen made their stop on this little planet. Most people were just trying to get by and knew the power of a healthy relationship. Instead of forcing people apart—the Weeps, the floods, the fires, the economy dying a slow and painful death, the intermittent famine —all of that actually brought everyone closer together as the population quickly declined. The people left behind couldn't survive alone. Plus, there were just so few human beings left that it changed the way people thought about each other. Every remaining life had become infinitely more valuable in the After.

Sure, there were the occasional bad apples. But the small communities kept those folks under control, and hardly anyone ever came to blows over anything. All the bloody tears shed with the Weeps were enough, and people could not bear to see another sanguineous drop lost.

Trader sat still, assessing the situation. The only sounds were a light wind in the trees off to the left and the chirping of birds. Otherwise, it was a ghost town. A light layer of dust coated the highway, with no evidence of any tracks. Trader could tell he was alone, even though he really couldn't explain how. Goose-bumps broke out on his arms.

Despite the creepy vibe, Trader pressed forward, navigating the wagon around the barricade. Boxer swished his tail irritably. Sasha sat up, watching intently from her bed, whiskers moving as she sniffed the air. The oppressive silence followed them as they headed deeper into the city, the empty highway stretching ahead of them and the battered empty shells of buildings from the Before crouched on either side. About a mile into town, Trader once again pulled the wagon to an abrupt stop, muscles tense.

The city had been obliterated.

Remains of destroyed and burned-out buildings pierced the sky like bones from a half-eaten carcass rising from a thick layer of ash. The wind shifted and the acrid smell of burning chemicals hit him. Everything was still eerily silent, and he hadn't come across a single person. In fact, he had not come across a single *anything*, other than the birds singing their hearts out when he first entered town.

"What the fuck?" he said quietly.

Trader had seen his fair share of burn scars in fields and across hills. But it was damn hard to burn down this many buildings from the Before. The fire had to have been exceedingly hot and fast to cut through an urban area. Boxer flicked his ears back and swished his tail. With a click from Trader, Boxer reluctantly continued pulling the wagon at a slow pace through the desolate city.

The destructive effects of the fire worsened the further they ventured south. Just beyond the Kettleman exit, Trader pulled the wagon to a stop for the third time since reaching Lodi. He stayed in the driver's seat with the reins clenched in his hands.

On the side of the road, nine charred bodies were laid in a neat row. Bits of white bone played peek-a-boo through cracked and leathery layers of black material.

Someone burned the bodies, Trader thought to himself with a sinking feeling.

Trader looked over his shoulder back towards Lodi. There was a blackened path of destruction beginning where the bodies were laid out and stretching north and east back into the depths of the city.

At least it looks like they were dead before they were burned, he thought, startling himself for even contemplating that. What would the alternative be? Burning people alive? Why in the world would he think someone would burn people alive?

Because it happened in the Before, and it could happen in the After, a small voice in his head answered.

Trader looked down at the blackened corpses. Of course, bodies needed to be disposed of properly to prevent disease from spreading. But California was a fucking tinderbox. The dead were buried, not burned.

What idiot would light a fire in the middle of a dry field? the small, awful voice in his mind chimed in again.

Whatever had hit this group must have been something damn awful. The Weeps had done a pretty good job weeding out the weak genes. Sure, the sickness would pick off one or two every year, but not nine people. *Nine.* Trader shook his head in disbelief.

Was this a new and especially deadly disease? Was it something so bad that the bodies had to be burned? What had they done to get the fire to burn so hot? And, more importantly, what did they do once they realized the fire was racing toward the city? Unanswered questions whirled through his head.

There was no sign of who had neatly arranged these bodies and lit this fire. Trader was not aware of a group in Lodi the last time he had come this way. They could have laid low and not announced themselves, but Trader found that unlikely. There were so few people in the After that those who were left needed connections with other settlements to live comfortably. It nagged at him that he didn't know where these people had come from, and, probably more importantly, where the survivors were now. They certainly weren't at Forty Two. Rosa would have said something. Trader's stomach clenched again.

Unsettled, Trader urged the wagon forward. Boxer was more than happy to oblige, obviously discomfited as well. Sasha continued sniffing the air, now scrunched down and peering over the edge of her bed with her ears flat. The animals felt it too and were just as eager as Trader to have Lodi in the figurative rearview mirror.

***

Three hours later, the trio approached Stockton, the smell of acrid smoke still lingering in their noses. Because of the nearby inland tributaries, most of the city was now under oil-slicked water. Garbage from the Before floated in large rafts and formed thin rims along the waterline.

With the disturbing images from Lodi fresh in his mind, Trader was disquieted and felt vulnerable out on the open highway as it arched over the flooded city. He thought about just pushing through to the Silvas' without a break. After consideration, he decided it was best to give Boxer a quick rest and a drink despite how anxious he felt.

On one of the drier stretches of road, Trader stopped the wagon. After pouring Boxer and Sasha some water, he took a few chugs for himself. He pulled out some dried apples, walnuts, and a bit of Rosa's cornbread. The break would need to be short to get to the Silvas' before nightfall.

After lapping up some water, Sasha meowed for a treat. Trader held a walnut out to her. She sniffed it, and her tail swished. *Seriously?* Trader laughed quietly, relaxing just a tad.

Sasha decided to have a go at the walnut anyway, leaving nut bits on the driver's seat. She looked up at him, batting his hand. He gave her a couple more walnuts before dusting his hands off. The short break and Sasha's shenanigans distracted him a tad. Once Boxer had a moment to rest, Trader packed everything up and got the trio moving, wanting to put more distance between himself and the ruined city of Lodi.

CHAPTER
FIVE

Thankfully, the remainder of the trip down the 99 to the Silvas' was relatively uneventful. Grasslands stretched east and west. A small herd of wild cattle grazed in the distance. At some point when the world was falling apart, a brave—or crazy—soul made a point of cutting gaps in all of the fencing in the valley. It must have taken years in oftentimes nasty weather to ensure every bit of pasture land was opened. But there were enough wild herds to know someone had done something right. Livestock moved freely to find food, water, and safety. The dumb ones ate their pasture out, died of dehydration, died in wildfires or flooding, or became food for someone. The genetic cream of the crop had survived into the After; generations of struggle making them super flighty. Best to leave them alone at this point, unless leather was needed for shoes.

Trader huffed a laugh.

The trio took the E. Lathrop exit in Manteca and headed down to the church just as the sun was setting. The Silvas' was smaller than Forty Two, just a handful of folks, some related and some not. There was no official leader or council, but Gilberto ran the place for all intents and purposes.

Between the church and the highway were acres of well-tended fields bordered by mature fruit trees. Several rows were lush with winter crops, mainly leafy greens that fared well in the cooler weather and would struggle in the upcoming heat. Freshly planted tomato and pepper seedlings peeked from the ground. The biggest of the plots next to the church was plowed into neat rows. Soon, cotton would be planted here, which was what the Silvas were known for. Trader's fingers and toes were crossed that the Silvas would have bolts of cloth available. New cloth was rare and exceptionally valuable.

The church boasted a well, which was one of the reasons it had been chosen as a place to settle. The well produced enough to irrigate the fields and provide clean drinking water. Trader wasn't sure how long it would take for the well to run dry or become unsafe to drink. The Silvas would have to move or start trying to hunt down rain barrels if that ever happened.

The church was surrounded by suburban homes from which the few residents of the settlement had their pick. Everyone gathered at the church to process the cotton and sort the other harvested crops. But the homes served as a place to lay their heads at night with an added bit of privacy.

As Trader turned into the church driveway, a large dog came bounding out from around one of the buildings, barking deeply. Sasha decided the cacophony was too much to handle and jumped in the back of the wagon. Boxer swished his tail and licked his lips but did not flinch or stop.

"Oh, hush now, Gunther," Trader said to the dog.

When Trader first stopped here, he was surprised the Silvas kept the large brindle pit bull mix at the church. Dogs could get Weeps, and anything that got Weeps could technically give it to something or someone else. In contrast, cats were immune to Weeps. They also kept the rat population down. Given that rats also carried Weeps, people were usually more than happy for a cat or two to roam around a settlement. Dogs were another story.

THE BEFORE AND THE AFTER

The first time he had traded here, it had taken him only a few moments to understand why the Silvas kept Gunther on. The dog was sweet as could be and fiercely loyal. Gunther's devotion and companionship afforded him a spot here despite the zoonotic risk.

Gunther, recognizing a non-threat, slowed down and started wagging his tail. He continued to bark, but more of an alert bark rather than a threatening one. The front door of the church opened, and Liluye walked out. Her hand rested on the gun at her hip. She saw it was Trader, and her hand quickly dropped by her side.

"*A'ho*, Trader." She greeted him with a slight nod.

Liluye was in her late forties with long, straight black hair laced with gray and light brown skin. She was tall and well-muscled. She wore homemade loose cotton pants, a threadbare t-shirt, and flip-flops. Her usual confident and cheerful presence was replaced with slumped shoulders and a furrowed brow. Trader was glad to see her but couldn't get past the fact that she was packing. He didn't even know she had a gun until now.

"Nice to see you, Liluye," he answered.

Gunther stopped his barking and circled the wagon, nose down. Boxer shifted his weight and sniffed Gunther when he came by the front of the wagon. Boxer licked his lips and bobbed his head slightly. Gunther wagged his tail. Peace was made, and all was good.

Trader hopped down from the wagon to grasp Liluye's hand in greeting. No one else had come out yet, including Gilberto, and Trader was a bit nervous. Liluye's hand was rough and calloused from working the cotton, her shake firm but friendly.

Liluye coming out with her hand on her gun made him nervous, and it was a situation he wasn't used to dealing with. The fact that he hadn't seen hide nor hair of the others also triggered alarm bells. Something was off at the Silvas', and it nagged at him that he couldn't put his finger on it. A dozen unspoken questions hung in the air between them. Trader chewed on his lower lip as his unease started to build again.

"Come on in," Liluye replied. "I don't have anything ready to eat, but let me see what I can whip up."

Trader relaxed a tad. Breaking bread was the universal peace offering and part of the usual ritual when he arrived at the smaller settlements. He tried to shake the uneasy feeling.

"I am a bit hesitant to ask...but where is Gilberto?"

Liluye sighed and hung her thumbs in her pockets. "He's inside. He was out working the fields a couple of weeks ago and fell. His ankle got twisted pretty good, and he said he heard a pop. It swelled up all purple and black. We wrapped it and elevated it. The swelling has gone down a lot, but I'm pretty sure he broke something."

"Oh no," Trader replied.

An injury like that could mean death in the After. He'd heard stories of Singletons found starved to death in the mountains with similar injuries. Gilberto was lucky to be part of a group. Trader would have been up shit creek without a paddle with a similar injury.

"Yeah. It pretty much sucks. He can hobble around with a cane, but...." She shrugged.

With Boxer settled, Trader followed Liluye and Gunther into the church. The sun had just tipped over the hills to the west, and it was dim inside.

"¡*Qué onda*!" boomed a loud voice from across the nave as soon as they entered.

Gilberto sat on the left side of the room, deseeding the cotton by hand. He grabbed his cane and hobbled over. Gilberto was in his sixties, with a stocky build, dark gray hair, and light brown skin. Despite the perky façade, Gilberto seemed to have aged significantly over the last year and a deep permanent crease marred his brow. Trader's concern for his friend deepened.

"Speak of the devil," Liluye said.

"I thought I heard Gunther barking. You shouldn't be going out alone, *mija*. Gunther doesn't count." Gilberto gently shook a finger at her.

Gunther wagged his tail, happy to hear his name.

"I had Mol'-luk," she answered, patting the gun at her side.

Gilberto sucked his teeth in reply. He reached out to shake Trader's hand, then pulled him in for a one-armed hug.

"*¿Qué pasa, vato?*" Gilberto said, releasing him and patting him on the back. He shifted his weight to the cane and waved him through the room. "Let's go grab some food and sit down."

All of the cotton processing happened in the nave. On the left side of the room, plastic bins filled with seeded and deseeded cotton bolls sat on tables separated by space to prep the cotton for spinning. In the middle of the room, baskets of deseeded cotton and homemade wooden drop spindles rested next to a couple of old, blanket-covered, cushioned chairs. On the right side of the room, two adjacent tables held small looms. One loom had a partial length of cloth dangling from it. Every step in the cotton processing was done by hand, which took a shit-ton of time. But time was one resource folks had during the winter in the After.

Gilberto's cane thumped and Gunther's toenails clicked on the floor as they navigated through the back hall into the church's small eating area. The church's old breakroom served as the kitchen and larder. The sink was non-functional, as were all of the electrical outlets that may have supplied power to a coffee pot and toaster oven back in the day. The counter was now populated with a few old cutting boards, kitchen knives, and a handle-crank nut butter machine. Next to the equipment sat some freshly harvested jicama, carrots, and greens.

Old metal shelves stacked with baskets of potatoes, onions, and garlic sat on one side of the room. There was also a ton of jarred food, which surprised Trader. Usually, at the end of winter and going into spring, the preserved food was almost all gone. Something was undoubtedly up, but he was hesitant to ask.

"Have a seat," Liluye said. "I'll put something together real quick. Put your foot up, Gilberto."

Gilberto and Trader obliged, settling into chairs across from each other. Gilberto propped his injured foot on the chair next to him with a grunt. Gunther laid down under the table, head resting on Gilberto's other foot.

Liluye grabbed plates, forks, and a butter knife from one of the drawers. She pulled a jar of almond butter off the shelves, placed it on the table, and stabbed the knife into it. This was joined by a jar of pickles, a jar of olives, and some sun-dried tomatoes. She grabbed a couple of tin camping cups, filled them with water from a jug, and placed them on the table.

Trader was afraid to ask where the others had gone, especially Liluye's brother. It was rare for family members to make it so long. *It's unusual for anyone to make it so long,* Trader thought glumly. Even though Gilberto and Liluye had both been welcoming, they were tense. He coughed uncomfortably, trying to think of what to say around the *chop, chop, chop* from the cutting board.

To Trader's relief, Gilberto filled the awkward silence. "How's trading?"

He jumped right in, grateful to be talking trade. "So far, so good. Picked up some great stuff from Rat before I left. Also, have an excellent batch of kimchi this year. Forty Two is doing good, too. They have a shoemaker now." Trader kicked one foot out from underneath the table, proudly showing off his new boot.

Gilberto whistled.

Liluye looked over. "Damn, those are nice."

"Yep. Worth every pill I traded for them. Rosa hopes to have more shoes next year. I'll bring some along if they do. They're also sharing a nurse with the Fosters. Rosa is hoping to nab her full-time and start training other people."

He paused to drink some water as the *chop, chop, chop* continued.

"I got tons of good stuff from them. I'd like to stay the night and trade in the morning if that's okay."

Trader usually stayed the night at the Silvas' and never had to ask before. Until he knew more about what happened here and where everyone was, he was going to play it safe and be extra polite.

"*Sí.* Happy to have you." Gilberto cleared his throat. "We're living in the church *ahora*. We have a spare room if you want a real bed over the wagon."

"That would be nice. Thank you," Trader said, trying to hide his surprise.

Liluye, her brother, and her brother's boyfriend used to live in one of the houses in the adjacent subdivision. Gilberto and Gunther had resided in another. The last person, a woman whose name Trader couldn't recall, lived on her own next door to Gilberto. The church had always been just for working cotton and storage, not sleeping.

Liluye brought over plates and bowls filled with jicama, carrots, and chopped lettuce. They each spread almond butter over the sliced roots and ate their salads. The occasional carrot disappeared under the table followed by the sound of Gunther crunching. The lack of conversation spread uncomfortably between them until Trader finally worked up the nerve to speak.

"Hey, I gotta ask…," Trader's voice trailed off as he noticed Gilberto's brow furrow and Liluye tense.

"Umm…I just…," Trader stammered.

"Where the fuck are all the *gente*, and why we packing?" Gilberto asked.

Liluye huffed a bitter laugh.

"I don't mean to pry. I just…It's weird only seeing the two of you. Is everything okay?"

"Shit's fucked, *wey*." Gilberto paused, fighting tears despite his gruff exterior, and reached under the table to pet Gunther. Trader stopped eating and fidgeted with a carrot stick.

"We lost my brother to Weeps," Liluye filled in, her face wracked with anguish. She sighed and leaned back in her chair.

"Oh, Liluye. I am so sorry." Trader rested a hand on her arm. Gunther shifted under the table and put his head on Liluye's lap.

"Crazy how that shit still eats away at us, even though most of us have survived so long, and there's hardly any standing water around here for those fuckers to breed in. It feels like we keep getting kicked when we're down." Liluye shook her head, pressing her lips together.

"Molimo's *amor* went *loco* after he died," Gilberto continued sadly. "He nursed him to the end. He and Maria left with a preacher who passed through a few months later. Now, it's just *nosotros*."

Gilberto gestured down to his ankle. "Only makes this shit more fucked up."

"We've made it this far. We'll be fine." Liluye reassured him. "It's just rough. Losing Molimo and then having Bryson and Maria take off." She shook her head again.

"Did you say they left with a preacher?"

Trader had read about preachers but never actually met one. In the After, no one practiced traditional religions anymore. The idea of a religious leader in a world without organized religion was even more perplexing.

"Yep, Preacher came by selling his snake oil, brainwashing Bryson and Maria, taking them away right from under us. After losing Molimo…." Liluye crossed her arms, eyes filled with frustration.

"Where on earth did a preacher come from?" Trader asked, still confused.

Gilberto shrugged. "Preacher appeared out of nowhere right before winter looking like a skeleton. The *chingado* was all dirty, barefoot, and had a weird symbol on his forehead in blood and ash. He was saying it was his purpose to raise people into the God's light or some shit like that. Fucking *pendejo*." Gilberto shook his head in distaste.

"He had nothing, not even a canteen or anything. He seemed harmless and, hat in hand so to speak, asked for help. We took him in, fed him, and got him cleaned up. We even set him up in one of the less worn-down places on Harvest Mill. Every life matters now, you know?" Liluye added.

Trader nodded. He did know.

"At first, all was fine and dandy," she continued. "He helped in the fields, with prepping meals, and with the cotton work, mainly removing the seeds and spinning. Bryson took to him immediately. The two of them would spend a ton of time talking. Bryson had been seriously messed up after Molimo died. He kinda went through the motions, but he never laughed and hardly ever talked." Liluye sighed. "It was hard on all of us. But it just sucked the life out of Bryson. We essentially had him on suicide watch until Preacher came."

Trader blew out a low breath in sympathy. Everyone thought about suicide sometimes. They were liars if they said it had never crossed their minds before. There were just so few people now, though. Suicide was yet another way for nature to keep whittling away at them, making the loneliness worse by taking even more people away.

"I don't know what Preacher said to him when they'd go off for one of their long chats," Liluye said. "Bryson went from being a depressed suicide risk to wanting to be with this dude constantly. He was mesmerized by him. There was a bit of life in him again, for which we were initially grateful."

"About a week in, Gilberto and I realized something was up. I mean, Preacher always felt a little off, but we could deal. Every person counts, and he was kinda helping Bryson in his own weird way. First, he insisted on having Bryson make him a long sleeve shirt and loose pants in all white. Bryson obliged and sewed them with care. That's all the dude wore. Like, *always*. Then, Preacher started putting that fucking weird symbol on his forehead again—in blood and ash—*all the time*. A few days later, Bryson also had the symbol on his head." Liluye paused, pursing her lips.

Gilberto continued the story. "Then, Bryson just up and moved out of the place he had with Molimo. No word, nothing. *Pero* you do you and all. If it was helping him, *es bueno*. Bryson didn't leave Preacher's side after that and always wore that fucking symbol on his head. Few days later, Maria moved in with them, and just cut us off. They kept their heads down, *pero es gacho*. We both felt it." He gestured between Liluye and himself. "We couldn't get none of them apart. Maria and Bryson worshiped the *pinche madre*...it was creepy as fuck. They would've gouged their eyes out for him.

"Whenever one of us talked to Preacher, he would go off about the only way to live a blessed life was to follow him. Blood and Ash. God's pure white light. God would bring purpose." Gilberto waved his hand dismissively and snorted. "Stupid *pendejo*."

Trader shifted in his seat. Many of the books from the Before had a god or gods in them in some form or fashion. But he just couldn't believe that there was a real God. If there was, they were some kinda messed up for all of the punishment they'd laid down on the planet. He couldn't imagine that simply following Preacher would bring him eternal peace.

Gilberto took a sip of water and continued. "About a month in, they spent most of their time praying while they worked the cotton. Preacher did most of the talking. The *tarugo* would never shut up. They just looked at him like he was all that and a bag of chips."

"His rambling was how we found out that he'd been part of another group. He'd gotten them all killed," Liluye interrupted flippantly.

THE BEFORE AND THE AFTER

"What?!" Flabbergasted, Trader leaned forward.

"Dude's a whack job," Liluye said. "He was boasting about the disaster like it was a gift from God. Turns out everyone in his old community got sick and died—sounded like dysentery but don't know for sure. I can't even imagine thinking that's a gift. Then, said he lit a fire, the fire spread, and he barely escaped with his life. He said he rose from the ashes or some shit. Said it was his mission to start fresh and bring God's light to his acolytes. Who would think shit like that? That's when I started to worry about him, and mostly for Bryson and Maria. They're good people. Not like that Preacher."

Silence spread between them as they all considered Liluye's words. Trader's stomach clenched as the pieces started falling into place.

"Holy crap," Trader blurted out as he put two and two together. "I passed a row of burned bodies on my way down. I bet that was them. Caught the whole damn town on fire with that bit of stupidity. It's creepy as hell there now. Even Boxer was nervous. There were a lot of bodies. I mean *a lot* of bodies."

Gilberto and Liluye exchanged glances, eyebrows raised.

"They had these barricades on the highway," Trader added. "I wondered if they were to keep people in or keep people out. Or both. That was some spooky shit." He started fidgeting.

"It got worse day by day," Liluye continued. "Tension started building between us and them. They started doing their own thing, eating meals apart, and would barely talk to us. Even Bryson."

"Preacher kept pushing to join him," Gilberto said. "He said the only way we could live bountiful lives was together with his *familia*, underneath his wings and the eyes of God."

Liluye laughed mirthlessly. "Yeah…bountiful. Now we have all this food, and it's just the two of us."

"Did they leave town? They didn't take any food? What happened?" Trader's mind was racing. This was new territory for

41

him. A slow gnawing began to build in his gut, and he felt a sudden urge to make sure Sasha and Boxer were okay outside.

"A few weeks back, before Gilberto's ankle broke, Preacher came to try to recruit us one last time. He kept going on about how the only way to achieve true community was to join his flock and follow God. He was so fucking convinced that, after rising from the ashes, God would protect anyone who joined him. He said that non-believers wouldn't be tolerated, and basically said it was our last shot." Liluye caught Gilberto's eye with a questioning look and continued after he gave her a resigned nod.

"For a minute there, we thought he was going to get violent when we told him, 'No thanks'," Liluye continued. "I think he was thinking about taking the place by force. But he just walked away. The next day, they were all gone—him, Bryson, and Maria. Didn't say nothing, didn't take nothing. Just left. I guess they figured their God would provide," Liluye said wryly.

Gilberto snorted.

"We haven't seen him or the others since. He's a snake, that one, selling false hope to innocent, depressed folks like Bryson. I don't trust him. That's why I keep Mol'-luk on me, and why Gilberto is worried like a mother hen. Plus, it's just the two of us now with a lot of resources. I know the fighting days are pretty much over. But it still makes us nervous, especially with Gilberto's ankle all fucked up."

Gilberto huffed. "The dude is *loco*. We don't know which way he went or if he's just hiding out in Manteca somewhere. *Ten cuidado*." He shook his head.

"Damn, you guys," Trader said sympathetically. "That's crazy." After a pause, he asked, "Anything I can do to help?"

"We're all good," Liluye answered. "Thanks for offering, though. There's just a lot of work and not enough hands."

"Do you plan on staying here? You're pretty isolated now."

"*Es chido aquí*," Gilberto answered. "And we have each

other. It'd be nicer with a small group, *pero* we've got you and Jesse. *Todo está bien.*"

"This is our home," Liluye added. "We built this whole place up. It's hard to just walk away."

"What about joining another settlement? Like Forty Two?" Trader asked. "They have a nurse that comes by every so often. She might be able to help with your ankle."

"It's nice to be around other people. But those big settlements like Forty Two are almost too big. You know?" Liluye caught Trader's eye, and he nodded in agreement.

Those settlements were nice to stop at and then move on. Quick visits were best. Trader couldn't imagine living around all of that noise and all those people all of the time, no matter how lonely he got. He liked everyone there. He just didn't want to be around them all of the time.

With that, Liluye got up to clear everything away, and the conversation died. Trader quickly joined her to help. As he dried the dishes that Liluye handed him, he rolled the story over in his mind. Preacher reminded Trader of the *yakubyō gami* from the ancient manga books that Earl had scrounged up from who knows where. Like the evil Japanese spirits, Preacher left a path of calamity in his wake. People like that just didn't pop up in the After, and a disquieted feeling settled around him.

CHAPTER SIX

By the time they finished tidying the kitchen, the sun had fully set and the stars were starting to pop in the sky. Trader went out front to get the animals settled and move the wagon, thoughts of Preacher racing in his mind. The moon gave off enough light that everything was faintly visible in shades of gray. As a general rule, he wasn't nervous outside at night. But the memory of Lodi in ashes and the story of Preacher gnawed at him.

"Sorry, bud," Trader said as he patted Boxer.

Boxer had his head down and appeared to be asleep. After petting him gently to wake him, Trader hitched Boxer to the wagon and drove it around the back.

Boxer whickered softly. *Really?*

Trader scratched Boxer's mane sympathetically.

Sasha disembarked from the wagon and wove around Trader's legs as he worked. After a friendly *merf*, he reached down to pet her, and she started purring. She then perked up, hearing something off in the grass, and trotted off to find a late-night snack. She'd be pissed to come back and find him and his bedroll gone when she was done hunting. Trader moved the cat bed from the driver's seat to the back of the wagon, trying to make things as comfortable as possible for her.

He was nervous leaving them outside on their own. In the past, he'd never thought twice about it at a place like the Silvas'. But it wasn't the same place he'd visited before. The ominous cloud of Preacher still hung in the air.

Trader grabbed his bedroll, the book Rosa had given him, and a few other items from the wagon. Following the glow of the small lamp flashing from the church windows, Trader made his way back to the eating area. "I'm gonna hit the hay early. Where'd you like me to camp out?"

"Let me show you." Liluye hopped up.

Though Gilberto and Liluye both could navigate the church in the dark and the moon was pretty strong coming in through the windows, Liluye knew Trader was not used to the place. With an old solar lamp in hand, she led him down a short hall to a private room. The room was small and sparsely furnished. On top of an old metal bed frame, there was a hand-sewn mattress filled with cotton. After the unsettling day, Trader was thankful for a soft bed indoors.

Liluye left the lamp on an old metal table next to the bed and headed out with a wave.

He unrolled his bedroll, kicked his boots off, and undressed down to his undershorts. The bed was amazingly soft and hugged him as he snuggled in. Out of habit, he reached to pet Sasha for comfort, before regretfully remembering that she was outside. His mind swirled with thoughts of the nine bodies and horrible burn scar in Lodi before a restless sleep finally took him.

* * *

The next morning, Trader woke to bright dancing beams of sunshine pouring through the curtainless windows. He snuggled further under the covers, enjoying the warmth. The church was eerily quiet, and he guessed that Liluye and Gilberto were probably still asleep. Resting on the table next to his bed was *The Last Cuentista*, offering a distraction from what he had learned yesterday. Despite the allure of a yet-unread book, he was too worried about Sasha and Boxer to start the book without checking on them first. He quickly threw some clothes on and hustled outside.

As soon as the wagon was in sight, he knew that all was well. Boxer was still close by, languidly chewing through the grass. Two decapitated treats were left on the ground at the back of the wagon by the ever-generous Sasha. The *dame de la mort* was absent, likely off doing cat things. But the present she left told him that she was around. It surprised him how relieved he was that everything looked in order. He didn't realize how much the story of Preacher was worrying him.

Reassured that all was well outside, he settled in with the book. Trader made it to chapter four before his grumbling stomach forced him to put it down. The book hadn't fully hooked him yet. It was the idea of a completely new story that kept him flipping the pages. This was the first one he'd read since last summer, and it was a treat. He had picked up a few books last year in Walnut Creek, but they hadn't even held him through the end of spring. Rereading books was common in the After.

Gilberto was already in the eating area, quietly reading a battered old book with an empty plate sitting in front of him. Gunther was laying under the table, the sound of his tail giving away his location.

"*Buenos días.*" Gilberto looked up and smiled.

"Good morning. Liluye up yet?" Trader sat down with his food.

"She's sleeping. She's been pulling the weight around here

'cause of my damn ankle." Gilberto looked begrudgingly at his foot that was resting up on a chair.

Trader opened the container of nuts and held it out to Gilberto. Gilberto reached in, grabbed a handful, and started crunching away at them. Trader got up to grab two forks, popped the container of preserved peaches, and offered Gilberto a fork.

"I was thinking," Trader started around bites of breakfast. "What do you think about me staying on a few days to help you and Liluye get your feet back underneath you? It doesn't feel right just leaving you here after trading is done."

Gilberto leaned back in his chair and rubbed his neck with one hand. "*Estás bienvenido aquí.* We could pay you in cloth, *también. Pero* I don't want to mess up your schedule or nothing. Or make you skip us next year 'cause we aren't big enough to make it worth it."

"I would never skip seeing you two on the circuit." Trader reached across the table and gave Gilberto's arm a gentle squeeze. "I know I only see you once a year, but I like our time together. It gets lonely sometimes up in Sac. Stops like these keep me going. Recharge my battery for next year."

Gilberto smiled and nodded once. "I'll give Liluye the low down when she wakes up. We can always use help with the cotton. We can teach you to spin if you want."

"That would be great," Trader said.

He was actually excited about the idea. Learning how to work cotton would be a good skill to have. He might even be able to trade for a spindle and teach others on his way. If other settlements could learn to spin and weave, Gilberto and Liluye could also trade raw cotton if they didn't have time to work it all.

"Rosa gave me a book. One I haven't read before. Staying a bit will also give me a chance to enjoy it. I've been itching to read it since she gave it to me. I just started it this morning."

"What's it called?" Gilberto asked.

THE BEFORE AND THE AFTER

"*The Last Cuentista*," Trader said. "Not far enough into it yet to know where it's going. Supposed to be about a girl traveling through space. But so far, they haven't even left Earth yet."

"*The Last Cuentista*, huh? The last storyteller...," Gilberto translated and paused. "Let me know if it's any good?"

"Will do," Trader answered. "If I finish it in time, I'll leave it here for you. Otherwise, I'll bring it back around for you next year."

Gilberto was also an avid reader, and Trader suspected he was equally hungry for a new book to read. Like other things from the Before, books were hard to come by. Over eighty years of sequential disasters had snuffed production out. If anyone was lucky enough to find a bookstore that survived the digital age and wasn't flooded, it was probably sitting empty, someone thoughtfully having packed everything neatly away before the doors closed for the last time.

Libraries, however, had made it into the After. Being a public institution, they stayed open through the crazy weather, assuming the buildings weren't flooded, burned down, or torn to shreds by a freak tornado. The libraries also kept going after the economy ground to a halt, the last vestige of a dying world. New books stopped coming in, but they were still open for business with what was already on the shelves. Then Weeps hit, and there weren't enough people to work the libraries anymore. One by one, the libraries were also shuttered and stayed that way, sheltering the books as if they were frozen in time.

As the population slowly ebbed away, the normal rules of breaking and entering went to the wayside. Most stores were empty anyway, and mass looting just wasn't a thing. It was little things, like needing to figure out how to build a loom. Or looking for a book to escape the loneliness of the real world. Or looking for a story to bring joy to a little one born into the After. Those were the reasons people got over their inhibitions and

49

finally broke into the libraries to peruse the books on offer. Thanks to those people, books were still around today. Maybe, someday, they might start writing new stories again.

Gilberto and Trader continued chatting companionably about books until the peach preserves were all gone and about half the walnuts were left. Trader scooched his chair back with a heavy scratching sound and stood. He grabbed the dishes to scrub them in a tub of soapy water resting in the sink.

"Since we're staying for a bit, I'm going to get Sasha and Boxer settled. Mind if I bring Sasha inside?"

On every previous stop at the Silvas', Trader had only slept overnight in his wagon before moving on. He was unsure of the routine or the rules around here. He wanted to be a good guest.

"*Sí, es chido*," Gilberto said. "Gunther might chase her, *pero* he won't hurt her."

Gunther's tail went *thump, thump, thump* under the table when he heard his name. Gilberto reached under and gave his soft airplane ears a scratch.

"I'm gonna find a better place to park the wagon and bring some things in. Is there a good spot to keep Boxer?"

"We don't have no paddocks or nothing. If he won't wander, just leave him out there. Even if he gets into the crops, we have more than enough this year." Gilberto answered, waving his hand absently.

Trader fidgeted a bit before asking, "Should I worry about that Preacher guy? I can't lose Boxer."

"My guess is you'll be okay. That *pinche* preacher could be holed up in Manteca. *Pero* I gotta feeling he took off to find more worshipers. You're more likely to meet him further down the road."

"Gotcha," Trader said, slightly relieved. Deep down, he felt like he was only putting off the inevitable, but he was still glad for a few days of respite to get his head straight.

"Be back in a bit," Trader said, nodding as he headed out.

"I won't be going nowhere." Gilberto laughed, tapping his cane on the ground a couple of times.

CHAPTER
SEVEN

The gorgeous morning sunshine greeted him outside the church.

Sasha glided out of the tall grasses, meowing. Trader picked her up, cuddling her. She rubbed against his face, purring, and made biscuits on his arms, tiny claws pricking his skin lightly through his shirt.

"Yeah, yeah," he said affectionately. "I know. Sorry I left you alone last night. Gilberto said you can sleep inside from now on."

She answered him with a deep throaty purr.

With Sasha shifted to one arm, Trader reached into the wagon, pulling out her cat bed. He brought it inside the church and placed it at the bottom of his bedroll, which conveniently happened to be in the sun. He gently put Sasha down on her bed, petting her from nose to tail. She was so happy that she started to drool. She kneaded the bed a bit before settling down. He continued to pet her for a while and then headed back out to let her sleep in the warm sun.

Now to deal with the wagon. He scouted around the church for a good place to park and found a nice location that was relatively hidden from the road and slightly sheltered should they get any rain. Boxer was resting nearby, with one back leg cocked, snoozing with a full belly. Trader gave his mane some scratches. Boxer whickered in greeting, slightly swishing his tail.

"Hey, buddy. I need you for just a sec. After that, you get a couple of days off." Trader ran his hand along Boxer's neck and down to his flank.

Boxer whickered softly again and licked his lips.

After working the wagon into its new parking place, Trader unhitched the horse. Boxer gave him a slightly annoyed look, licked his lips again, and swished his tail once more.

"I get it. But just think of all the grass you get to eat!"

Boxer didn't appear appreciative.

Trader got an old wooden bristle brush and started grooming Boxer. He should've done this last night. But everything about the day before had put him off his game. The anxiety that had begun as a small flicker in Lodi built into a tight ball of dread at the Silvas'. Seeing Liluye packing a gun, learning that Gilberto was injured, and hearing the stories of Preacher had overloaded him.

With Boxer taken care of, Trader focused on keeping his stuff safe. Though the canvas covering was water resistant, he preferred not to test fate if he was going to be here awhile anyway. He grabbed some clean clothes and food to share before he tightened the canvas flaps closed. That would be enough to weather a mild storm.

On impulse, he unlaced the flaps to go back in to get his large hunting knife. He had never once used it to threaten or hurt a human being. But after what he saw in Lodi and the fact that even seasoned Liluye was spooked, he figured he couldn't be too cautious. After lacing the flaps back up, he headed inside and dropped off his load, leaving the knife under his pillow.

Trader wandered around the church until he found Liluye and Gilberto in the nave. Gilberto was back to deseeding cotton with

Gunther asleep at his feet. Liluye sat next to them, eating her breakfast and chatting. She had Mol'-luk back on her hip again.

"*A'ho*, Trader. Sleep well?" Liluye asked when she saw him.

"I did indeed." Trader grabbed a chair and sat, forming a circle with them. "Did Gilberto fill you in?"

"Yep," she answered. "We're super grateful to have you staying on a couple of days, even if just for the company. I gotta go deal with the waste ditch today. We also gotta start picking some of the veggies out there and get them preserved. Willing to pick this morning? Once I'm done with the ditch, I can work on preserving them and you can work with Gilberto on the cotton." She paused to look up at him and then added, "Seriously though, you don't have to work at all. I kinda feel bad asking."

"I am happy to help," Trader replied truthfully. It felt good to be part of something; to have a purpose. It also felt good to help people. If everyone worked together, human beings might still be around in fifty years.

"What do you want picked?"

"I am thinking we harvest the kale for sure. We should pull up the rest of the potatoes, too. I can show you where they're hiding. And dig up the jicama to store. Let's harvest about seventy-five percent of the carrots too. We'll pickle those." Liluye paused, thinking through what was out in the fields. "You may not get to it all, and that's totally okay. Please don't overwork or anything."

"Sounds easy enough. I'm on it." Trader nodded.

They passed the time casually talking until Liluye finished her breakfast. She took her dishes into the eating area to clean them and came back with several baskets for harvesting. Trader joined her, grabbing his straw sunhat. They headed outside with Gunther following close behind, nose to the ground. Liluye showed Trader the sections that needed to be harvested, dropping baskets along the way. She went into a small building behind the church and brought out a wooden stool and a potato hood rake.

"It is really nice having you here. Not just to work either. That stuff with Preacher and then Gilberto's ankle...it left a black cloud over this place. You helped bring blue skies again."

Trader smiled bashfully. Though the settlements appreciated his trade and said he was always welcome, it wasn't often that people thanked him for his company. He was surprised at how good it felt to know that just him being around brought joy to them.

"I am gonna go mess with those nasty-ass ditches. I'll come in for lunch in a bit and then start working on the stuff you pick. Just leave everything by the well. Feel free to stop whenever you want."

Trader dove immediately into the work. He liked having stuff to do. Idle hands and all. The fact that it also helped out two people he liked made it all the better. As he dug up potatoes and jicama, pulled carrots, and harvested the kale, he felt his muscles loosen up. The work was relaxing, and the quiet of the fields was soothing. He always liked working outside, but there was something about helping others that made the work more meaningful.

Gunther had decided to stay with him, sprawled out on his side and snoozing in the dirt. Trader appreciated the company and gave the dog an occasional scratch on the head. Gunther would keep an eye out for snakes which he appreciated. Rattlesnakes were no joke.

Gunther will also keep away creepy preachers, said the voice in his head as Trader's stomach knotted.

Trader managed to harvest everything that Liluye had pointed out to him, filling all six of the baskets. It was good to see so much food. It felt even better knowing that he could pitch in a little. He brought the baskets back in from the field, taking trips and placing them by the well to be washed.

He leaned the rake against the small building and placed the stool next to it. He thought about going in to put them away, but

THE BEFORE AND THE AFTER

he didn't want Liluye to feel like he was nosing around. Some people were particular about the order of things.

He brushed his hands on his pants. There was dirt under his nails and dried smudges on his palms. That was okay. He would wash them when he needed to. Sometimes it felt good to have a bit of earth on him for a while.

Trader walked around the church and checked near the privy ditch, looking for Liluye. She was nowhere to be seen, but her work was clearly done. The existing native grass in the ditch had been moved over to the compost pile. Fresh-cut grass lay in neat piles. The pre-existing pooper spot was also filled in, a new ditch had been dug, and the commode was moved several feet. A pile of dirt sat next to the new hole with the courtesy scooper stabbed in it.

With his stomach growling, Trader headed back inside with Gunther following. He peeked in the nave first and saw Gilberto spinning cotton.

"Gonna grab a bite to eat if that's okay," Trader said as he lifted a hand in greeting.

"*Sí, sírvase.* I'll be there *en un minuto.*" The spindle danced as he spun the last bit of cotton boll.

Trader headed towards the eating area. Gunther decided to stay with Gilberto, laying down at his feet and resting his head on his paws. Trader found Liluye already sitting down, all washed up from her adventures ditch-digging. She had a plate of food in front of her.

Trader smiled a greeting. "I left the rake and stuff by the outbuilding for you. Didn't know if me going in the shed was a problem or not. Didn't want to mess up any system you may have."

Liluye laughed. "You are free to go wherever. We trust you. Also, there's definitely *not* a system in there."

Trader gave her a thumbs up. Joining her at the table, he took his hat off and started on his meal.

57

"How was ditch duty?"

"Uh-mazing. I wish I could do it all day every day." She snorted. "Seriously though… glad it's done. On to better things now. How'd harvesting go?"

"Got everything done. It's all waiting for you by the well. Let me know if you need a hand with washing and getting everything ready to store. Otherwise, I'll join Gilberto for the afternoon."

"I'll be good," Liluye answered. "It shouldn't take more than an hour or so. It will give me time to make us a warm meal tonight." She leaned back in her chair, stretching her arms over her head.

"Cool. I am actually looking forward to learning to work cotton. Think I could grow it up in Sac?" Trader asked.

"Maybe…but you need a lot of space to grow enough to make it worth your while." Liluye pursed her lips. "How about we teach you what to do and send you with seeds? You can let us know how it goes when you come back next year?"

"Sounds like a plan."

There it was, resting quietly between them: her promising that they would still be here next year and him promising to come back. These small promises built up like bricks along the circuit, giving them all a reason to keep on going. One step in front of the other, despite crazy Preachers and broken ankles. The times they shared sustained Trader, and he suspected it kept Liluye and Gilberto plugging away as well.

CHAPTER EIGHT

With his meal finished, Trader headed to the nave and grabbed a seat next to Gilberto. Gunther wagged his tail in greeting. The deseeded cotton sat in baskets next to the chairs like large, fluffy clouds. Trader picked up a boll and rubbed it between his fingers, surprised at how coarse it felt.

"Grab a spindle and I'll show you," Gilberto said as he passed a spindle to Trader.

The spindle was a long thin piece of wood, almost like a large knitting needle. About an inch or so from one end, there was a flat, circular piece of wood that resembled a thick washer. At that same end, there was a small metal hook at the tip. It looked pretty simple and easy to make.

"Grab some cotton and follow along," Gilberto instructed. He used his fingers to pull on one edge of the cotton boll. He looped this around the hook and spun the two ends together. In one hand, he pinched the cotton about four or five inches from the hook and spun the spindle. He stretched the boll out another six inches or so from where it was pinched off. He let the pinched fingers go. The high tension in the twist spun the cotton into a string towards the unspun boll. He repeated this effortlessly until he had about a foot of string, and then wrapped it around the long end of the spindle.

At first, it was frustratingly tough for Trader to get the hang of it. After a few tries and some coaching from Gilberto, Trader was able to spin his first section of cotton with a *whoop* of delight. Loop after loop of cotton string began to fill up his spindle. The repetitive nature of the pinching and spinning was oddly hypnotic. He was starting to feel confident that he could bring this skill home. Now, all he had to do was to get those promised seeds to harvest.

Trader and Gilberto sat in companionable silence as they pinched, whirled, and wound the cotton. This year on the circuit was already so different from those that came before. There had been highs, like the new shoes that graced his feet, as well as pretty dramatic lows, like all the stuff with Preacher. With a mixture of anticipation and apprehension, he wondered what the rest of the season would hold.

Sasha roused him from his musings with a purr-meow as she wandered in. Gunther picked up his head, airplane ears perked, but didn't chase her. Sasha rubbed against the chairs. Her loud purring could be heard over the silence. She scoped out Trader's lap and realized it was a no-go with the spindle whirling about. She decided to lie on one of the empty cushioned chairs next to him and promptly went to sleep.

As Trader continued spinning, he realized that he didn't know much about the Silvas. On previous visits, he had spent the night in his wagon, traded in the morning, and headed to the Nakamuras' right after. The Silvas had been at the church as long as he had been trading, but that was about all he knew.

"How'd you end up at the church?"

"Don't even know where to start, *hombre*." Gilberto pursed his lips. "I was born in Manteca sixty-three years ago. *Por lo menos*, I think I'm *sesenta y tres*? Time's weird in the After.

"*Papá* died when I was a kid. Don't know why. It was fast,

THE BEFORE AND THE AFTER

and it wasn't the Weeps. It wasn't around yet. *Mamá* and I used to live on the other side of town in a housing tract when there were lots more *gente aquí*. I don't have no brothers or sisters."

The spindle spun in Gilberto's deft hands as he continued to work the cotton in a steady rhythm. Trader kept spinning as well, slower now that his attention was focused on Gilberto's story.

"I don't know exactly when we left. Everything happened so slow. One business would close, then *un otro*. *Supermercados* got emptier and emptier. The farm stands were the last to go. We got some food from the garden. Once *Mamá* lost her job, we started picking stuff from other people's trees so we wouldn't starve. Schools had closed by then, and she spent a lot of time teaching me how to read and write and stuff.

"The drought got real bad when I was like twenty or thirty, and we went to one of those emergency shelters that was like a camp. We walked all the way to Stockton, *pero* the city was flooded when we got there. We had no power and no news in Manteca. So, we didn't even know that the city *era muerto* until we got there. We saw the church walking back. We were hella tired and *mi mamá* didn't look so good. I kinda thought she wasn't gonna make it. We saw some *gente* working the fields and...." He shrugged. "We were lucky it was the Silvas *aquí*."

Trader could tell by his expression that Gilberto had come to terms with so much loss, but he still wore his past like a heavy backpack over slumped shoulders.

"I always thought you were a Silva. Didn't the name come from you?"

"*Nel.*" Gilberto shook his head. "Donny Silva, his wife Mary, and his daughter Elsa lived here first. Their place had flooded, and they moved here. Over time, people came and people went. *Mi esposa* was a refugee from the western shore of the San Francisco Bay."

"You were married?" Trader asked.

"*Sí, por muchos años.* Weren't able to have no kids. The

Weeps took her before you started trading on these routes. She left a bleeding hole in my heart when she died," Gilberto answered sadly. He cleared his throat as he fought tears.

Trader did the mental math. He hadn't been trading very long; this was his seventh run on the full circuit. He could still see the pain on Gilberto's face.

"When did you meet Liluye and Molimo?" Trader asked.

Gilberto paused his spinning, laying his hands on his lap, to consider. "*No sé exactamente*. It was long before Carmen died. A while ago." He resumed spinning, his deft hands filling up the spindle quickly. "The fires chased them out of Yosemite Valley. They started down south, *pero* anything past Modesto is a constant dust storm. They decided to go north on the 99 until they arrived *aquí*. I guess we just clicked. Carmen loved having Liluye around. It was like having our own *hija*."

Gilberto took a deep breath, still fighting back tears. "We're used to people coming and going. *Pero* losing Molimo and having Bryson and Maria take off with that preacher *cabrón*... It's been rough, *hombre*." He reached down to pet Gunther. The loyal dog's tail thumped softly on the floor.

"I don't like big groups," Gilberto continued. "*Pero* I do like having a bit of company. There are so few *gente* around. We only see you and Jesse in the spring. Any other time, it's the dead zone. We don't even see refugees no more. I think people have settled for good."

Trader paused his spinning, reflecting on the last few trading years. "I hadn't really thought about it, but now that you say it... there *are* a lot less people on the road. The folks I do see are just moving stuff between settlements.

"On the plus side, the settlements are fleshing out a bit," Trader continued. "Forty Two has power, water, and even livestock. With the new shoemaker, trade will only get better and better. Definitely not the Before, but we may be more comfortable if Weeps will stop picking us off."

THE BEFORE AND THE AFTER

"*Es la verdad.* It's *not* the Before." Gilberto huffed.

His face looked troubled, wrinkles forming as his eyebrows pressed together. Trader worried that all of this talk had made Gilberto even more depressed and lonely. He reached over to pat his arm. Gilberto harrumphed, but he had a slight smile on his face.

"*Gracias por* staying a few days," Gilberto said. Trader smiled kindly back. They resumed spinning in comfortable silence, just enjoying being in each other's company.

After he had spun three spindles-full of thread, Trader's hands felt sore, and the tips of his fingers were red. He'd done a lot, and he was proud to have put a dent in the baskets full of cotton.

"I am gonna call it a day with spinning if you don't mind," Trader said.

"*Por nada.* Go read and enjoy yourself. You've done plenty. *Gracias, wey.*"

Trader tipped his head and headed out. Gunther said goodbye with the thumping of his tail. Sasha woke to the sound of Trader rising and hopped out of the chair to follow him out of the nave. After a quick trip to the privy to empty his bladder and a stop at the eating area to grab a snack, he headed back to the sleeping area.

There was still plenty of light coming in through the windows, signaling that he had enough time to read several chapters of *The Last Cuentista*. His boots landed on the floor with a thud as he kicked them off. The soft cotton of the mattress embraced him as he settled in with the book. Sasha jumped on the bed and curled up next to him, purring.

The main character, Petra, was supposed to have been placed in a long hibernating sleep. The attendants had messed the process up, and her mind was awake for hundreds of years as her body remained in stasis. Petra's isolation was agony for him to read about. Her only connection to her world, to her

63

sanity even, were the stories that were doled out through her feed.

Trader empathized with Petra's plight. At the end of the day, he was also alone. The different stops at all of the settlements brought stories of different lives. He lived off those stories, stayed connected through those stories, and stayed sane by those stories, just like Petra. A few tears dripped down his cheeks as he let Petra's story fill his heart.

* * *

Trader woke up several hours later, the dim light of the setting sun visible through the window. All of the activity the last couple of days had tuckered him out, and he had fallen asleep reading without even realizing how tired he was. Thankfully, his thumb was tucked into the book on his chest, holding his place. Sasha had skedaddled off at some point, likely slinking around the church looking for her next victim.

With the place in his book saved with a piece of scrap ribbon, he slipped his boots on and headed outside. Muffled voices came from the back, where Gilberto was sitting by a large fire pit with his foot up. He was leaning forward, massaging his ankle tenderly.

"Rain's coming," Gilberto said to Liluye, who was working at a table next to the fire pit, preparing food. Gunther sat below her, eagerly watching her every move, hopeful that something would drop.

"You broke your ankle, and now you are a damn weatherman?" she laughed. Liluye noticed Trader walking over and smiled.

"¿*Qué pedo*? Have a seat. Liluye is pulling out all the stops tonight," Gilberto turned to face Trader and gestured to one of the chairs next to him.

The firepit at the Silvas' was the best he had seen on all of his travels, having been built in the Before. The pit itself was a large stone rectangle with the long end sitting parallel to the back of the church. On one side, there was a flat piece of metal to cook on with an adjacent spit. The other side was more for enjoying the fire itself and perhaps for roasting marshmallows during camp in the Before. He'd read about s'mores but couldn't imagine eating something that was described as sickeningly sweet and gooey. It wasn't the first time that he found himself shaking his head at some of the weird things people did in the Before.

Surrounding the pit was a large cement patio, which helped contain the fire. Cement benches with low backs formed a U-shaped border about twenty feet from the fire pit. A large picnic table with chairs was situated on the far side.

A fire had already been lit, and, to Trader's delight, Liluye was cooking corn tortillas on the flat metal surface. On the spit, there hung a steaming cast iron pot that smelled of beans. A bowl of fresh lettuce, sautéed onions, a few lime wedges, a jar of salsa, and some preserved bell pepper slices were laid out on the table. Three precious pieces of fruit were sitting in a small bowl in all of their black, wrinkled glory.

"Holy shit!" Trader blurted out. "Where did you get avocados!?"

"¿Sí, verdad?" Gilberto said, smiling. "Some homesteader from the Before planted some in their front yard a few blocks away. Found it when Carmen and I were mapping the fruit trees. *No sé* how they have made it this long without watering and the weather being so jacked, *pero* they did."

Trader was astonished that avocados grew around here. He was equally astonished that the fruit had lasted to spring. He could count on one hand how many times he had eaten avocados.

"You've been holding out on me," Trader said, still getting over his shock.

"Well, we typically don't share, and we always save them for a treat. I guess you're growing on us," Liluye teased him.

That little gesture of sharing something as precious as an avocado left Trader speechless.

As the sun set, they enjoyed a wonderful meal of tacos, After-style. The "gualsa", as Liluye called her version of guacamole, had chopped cilantro, thinly sliced red onion, ripe tomato chunks, and a hint of lime. Trader had never eaten guacamole prepared like that and savored every bite. After everyone ate their fill, Liluye wiped the guacamole bowl clean with her fingers. They talked and laughed. Gunther sat poised under the table, receiving his meal in bites from Gilberto. The fire crackled warmly next to them.

Once the sun fully set, Trader said, "Whelp, I am stuffed. That was amazing, Liluye. Thank you kindly." He leaned back and patted his stomach. "I am gonna check on Boxer and then hit the sack."

"Thank you for the help and the company," Liluye said. "It is nice having you here."

"Might want to make sure your wagon is buttoned up and Boxer has a place to shelter. Rain is coming *esta noche*," Gilberto advised.

"Good lord. You and that ankle!" Liluye teased. "Go to bed, old man." She lightly smacked Gilberto on the side of his good leg.

Earlier, there had only been loose fluffy clouds idly drifting over the hills from the west. The weather was unpredictable, though. One minute all would be calm, and the next there would be a massive dust storm or torrential rain. Even in the summer months, a rainstorm could decide to shuffle in, which was almost worse since lightning invariably led the charge, and the grasses were usually tinderbox-dry by then. Trader, never knowing anything different, was not surprised when a storm popped up out of nowhere. He did the best he could to roll with whatever nature threw at him.

Trader helped clean up from dinner and then checked on Boxer. The horse was already under the overhang where the wagon was parked, snoozing next to it. He perked up when Trader came over and whickered. Trader scratched his mane. After confirming the wagon flaps were still tightly secured and everything was tucked neatly in, Trader headed back inside just as the first drops of rain started to fall.

The rain quickly picked up, pinging on the roof and against the windows. As he was getting settled in bed, Sasha came dashing in, all wet. Trader laughed sympathetically and dried her off with a spare towel.

"Got caught outside, did you?" Trader asked her. She gave an annoyed *merf* in reply, tail twitching with irritation. She hopped on the bed and promptly started grooming herself. Trader laid back under the blanket, hands behind his head, staring up at the ceiling in the dark as the storm moved through.

CHAPTER
NINE

The short overnight rain had washed everything clean. The light brown haze typical of the valley was now replaced by a crystal clear, blue sky. The air was filled with a fresh earthy smell that always seems to follow the rain. Trader stopped for a moment, taking deep breaths and enjoying the heat from the rising sun as it danced across his face.

Boxer was already chomping on the wet grass, tail swishing languidly. Despite sheltering close to the church, the horse's coat was still damp with rain. The day would warm quickly, and Boxer would dry off soon.

In response to a tickling sensation, Trader looked down at his arm. He quickly smacked the mosquito feeding on him, leaving a smear of blood behind. He wiped it on his pants, brow furrowed.

Fucking mosquitoes ruin everything, he thought.

Rain was such a mixed blessing. In California, it was desperately needed to fill rain barrels, creeks, streams, and wells to survive. Rainwater was also critical for putting out the fires that raged endlessly in the late fall. On the flip side, little drizzles like the one last night also meant standing water and cool, still weather: the perfect condition for Weeps-carrying mosquitoes.

Like Malaria, Weeps never really went away as long as mosquitoes were still around.

Every time Trader was bitten by a mosquito, a small part of him worried he would start showing signs. Symptoms began with a fever and then red spots all over the body. Sometimes people coughed up or crapped out blood. Every once in a while, someone would live long enough that their joints would fill with blood. One symptom was universal though: everybody wept bloody tears at the end.

Trader wasn't too worried about this mosquito bite, though. The likelihood of someone or something else having Weeps around here at the moment was slim. Mosquitos had to feed on the infected before giving it to someone else. If Weeps was still around the Silvas', there'd be signs. Dead rats were the biggest clue, out in the open with dried blood crusted around their eyes, flies bobbing slowly around them. There hadn't been anything like that around here since he arrived.

When Weeps first started kicking ass and taking names, the powers that be had tried and failed to make a vaccine. The best they could do were various antivirals. Proxleep was one of many, and probably the most effective, especially Gen 2 or Gen 3. The only problem was there weren't enough people left to manufacture the drugs on a mass scale. The pharmaceutical companies in California were underwater. There were still rare, scattered manufacturing facilities hanging on by a thread throughout North America. Trade routes occasionally brought meds into Nor Cal, but not often. If Trader started getting a fever, he could take some of the Gen 2 Proxleep he had on hand and hope his genetics could hold him the rest of the way.

Feeling grumpy after the mosquito had snacked on him, Trader went inside and tracked down Liluye and Gilberto. They were seated in the eating area, Gunther in his begging spot under the table, his wagging tail playing its usual tune. Gilberto and Liluye were both enjoying leftover corn tortillas smeared with nut butter and jam. They both looked up and waved good morning.

"Is that any good?" Trader asked doubtfully, grabbing a cup of water and taking a seat.

"*Sí*, actually it is. Ain't like bread, but still pretty good." Gilberto slathered some nut butter and jam on a tortilla for Trader and handed it over.

"Wow," Trader said after his first bite. "That's actually pretty tasty. Call me converted."

The three of them chatted idly, enjoying breakfast together. Gilberto, staying true to form, snuck treats to Gunther under the table.

"We got a leak in the ceiling over the old bathroom," Liluye said, getting to business. "Up for climbing on the roof with me today to fix it, Trader? It shouldn't take too long. Maybe after that, you can help me drag in some of the piping from the fields? We won't be able to grow as much this season with just the two of us. I guess we won't really need to, either."

"Whatever you need help with, I got you," Trader responded. "Before we lose light though, I'd like to copy your loom designs and see how it works if that's okay."

After they tidied up, Liluye, Trader, and Gunther headed outside, leaving Gilberto behind to work in the nave. Trader thought he glimpsed Sasha slinking through the shadows inside and suspected that Gilberto would have some company today. Sasha liked the Silvas' and was quickly settling in.

Up on the roof, the sun beat down hard. Trader was glad he had decided to grab his hat and a loosely woven long-sleeve shirt to cover up. The old timers said it didn't used to be so hot in the Before. As the ozone layer leached away, the sun's rays became more destructive, bright, and just damn hot. Despite being all sorts of messed up in other ways, the dust storms and ash from fires usually settled in the bowl of the valley like a brown fog, offering a protective layer from the sun. A shower like the one last night cleared that haze away until it built back up again. The next few days would be blazing.

They had a surprising number of roofing tiles and nails available for the repairs. Liluye said Maria and Molimo had scavenged them from other places around town the last time the roof leaked. In the not-too-distant future, all the composition tiles would have long outlived their time, and they wouldn't be able to scavenge anymore. They'd have to switch to clay tiles or come up with another creative solution. For now, the scavenged tiles would do for the patch they were planning.

Up on the roof, Liluye quickly identified the loose and damaged tiles; they were deemed beyond repair. She pulled them off, tossing them on the ground, careful not to hit Gunther who was patiently waiting below, watching them with his airplane-ears perked. Trader slid the newer tiles in place, with Liluye following behind to nail them down.

Making conversation, Trader asked, "Gilberto said you joined the settlement from out of town. Why did you decide to come here?"

She finished hammering the nail before responding. "Molimo and I lived just outside of Yosemite. My *hama* raised us. She was a manager or something in San Francisco in the Before. When things went bad, she brought her family back to our ancestors' lands. She and grandpa rebuilt the old home when they still could buy stuff to do it. My mom hooked up with a refugee that was wandering the area with a few others. They had me and Molimo. My dad left when the Weeps took my mom and grandpa. It was probably for the better.

"My *hama* had learned how to live off the land from her own *hama*, and she passed it on to us. She thought it was the best chance we all had when everything started going to shit. My *hama* took care of us. She knew lots and taught us everything she knew."

Trader continued to line up tiles as Liluye followed behind to nail them in.

"Anyway, *hama* eventually died. Not sure from what, but it was slow and ugly. After she died, it was just me and Molimo, and it wasn't easy living. There was barely enough game, and we practically lived off acorn porridge." Liluye scrunched her face at this. "Molimo and I stuck it out for several seasons after that. We knew fires were chewing their way through the mountains. It was only a matter of time."

She shrugged after this, but her face was filled with pain.

"After one particularly bad fire season, we packed up what we could and moved west. It was a rough trip. There was no food or water across the valley. We almost didn't make it. I ain't religious or nothing like that crazy preacher fucker. But I tell you, man, when we saw that church with all them people, I cried.

"Carmen and Gilberto welcomed us like we were their own kids. It was nice to be taken care of. It was scary when it was just the two of us. I was always afraid I wouldn't be able to protect my brother." She stopped and tears welled up. "I guess I didn't end up protecting him after all."

Trader reached over and gently rested a hand on her shoulder, careful not to knock her off balance. A stillness settled between them.

"Last time I was here, Molimo looked happy. He had you. He had Bryson. He had a good life here." Trader pulled his hand away. "No one can shoulder the Weeps, Liluye."

Liluye wept softly and quietly, looking down. After a heavy sigh, she bit back the tears, wiped her face with her sleeve, and continued her work. Trader waited for her to start speaking again, giving her some space.

When she finished the last tile, she sat back on the roof with her arms draped over her knees, facing out towards the fields. "It's really fucking hard. Sometimes I wonder what's the point."

Trader joined her, sitting down and leaning back on his

hands. Up here, he could see rows and rows of empty houses off to the left, each representing lost lives stretching far into the distance. To his right, the rows of crops stretched to the road, ready to feed people who were no longer here. And beyond that, empty land extended to the foothills; land once harvested but now overgrown with endless oceans of native grass.

"At this moment and in this now, the point is to keep this place running and take care of Gilberto. Day by day, step by step. Once you're done with that, come see me." He caught her eye, trying to lend her strength.

Liluye smiled sadly and huffed.

"Come on, you. Let's get this done so we can relax." Liluye hooked the hammer in her belt, tossed the spare tiles over the edge, and clamored off the roof.

Trader followed her down to clean up.

In the After, no one threw anything away. At the Silvas', all non-compostable items were stacked in the outbuilding, even the damaged tiles. Each and every item might come in handy in some way in the future. Liluye tossed the used tiles in a random corner and searched around for the tools she'd need to fix the irrigation. The place was a mess, and it was several minutes before she swapped her hammer and nails for some wrenches, pipe cutters, and irrigation caps.

Liluye led Trader out into the far, unplanted field. Gunther and Sasha had since switched places, the loyal dog joining Gilberto inside. Trader spied Sasha enjoying the sun, sprawled out by the fire pit and grooming herself. He could see Boxer snoozing by the wagon, one rear leg bent and tail occasionally swishing.

"With just the two of us, we can cut our crops in half. Saves us water, I guess." Liluye pointed straight ahead. "That right there is for cotton. Next to that, you can see where we already started the tomatoes and peppers. Too late to back out of that now. We'll use that space where the greens are for the summer crops, like okra and stuff." She pointed to the left. "That area is where we would normally plant more food. We won't need it. So, I want to drag all that shit in and cap it by the lettuce back there."

"Easy peasy," Trader answered.

Moving together, they made quick work of it. Liluye capped off the last bit of pipe where the lettuce was planted. They brought the lengths of pipe back to the outbuilding for storage. Once done, they went inside and had a quick lunch with Gilberto.

"I'm going back to work the cotton. You two gonna join me?" Gilberto asked.

"Yeah, I'll weave some," Liluye replied. "The sun is baking me after that rain. This afternoon is gonna be rough."

"I gotta take care of some stuff," Trader said cryptically. "Give me a bit and I'll come and help. I really want to learn how to use the loom and get those diagrams."

"Oh yeah! I already forgot about that. Let me go grab the book. I'll have it by the looms when you get back." Liluye headed into the recesses of the church.

Trader left to tackle the messy outbuilding. After a couple of hours, he had it pretty well sorted. It felt good to do this for them and eased some of the guilt he felt when he thought about the two of them alone.

Trader cleaned up and grabbed some charcoal and paper from the wagon. Back inside, he found Liluye and Gilberto working cotton in the nave. Gunther welcomed him with his wagging tail but didn't get up from where he was laying by Gilberto's good foot. Sasha napped in a kitty loaf on one of the spinning chairs, her front paws tucked underneath her chest.

"Got the stuff right here for you." Liluye pointed to a table next to the loom. A beat-up old book with a tan cover sat on the table next to her. "You can build a simple wooden square loom from small pieces. But I am thinking you want something like this puppy." She patted the loom in front of her.

Trader investigated the loom at the station she wasn't using. The floor loom was large, about six by five by five feet, and solid wood. The wood would be easy to source, and the build looked simple enough. The hardest part would be finding the metal bolts and washers to hold the whole thing together. There were a few metal pieces that looked like gears on the inside and a handle crank on the side. He would undoubtedly need Rat's help tracking down the required metal pieces.

"Looks fairly easy to build," Trader said.

"Yeah, the design is in the book if you want to copy it down. The actual weaving is more complicated. The hardest part is getting all the strings set up. Once that's done, it's just passing the shuttle, working the pedals, and watching the fabric flow out." Liluye's hand passed a bobbin on a shuttle back and forth across the loom between the alligator mouth of the threads. The other hand pulled the beater bar down between passes while her foot worked the pedals.

"Have you ever thought of taking on an apprentice?" Trader asked.

"You gonna stay?" Gilberto countered. Trader couldn't help but notice the sliver of hope in his voice.

"Nah, just wondering. It might be nice for you to have company again with Maria and Bryson gone. I can pass the word on down the circuit if you want?" Trader offered.

Liluye stopped weaving and turned to Gilberto, eyebrows raised. "What do you think?" she asked.

Gilberto ruminated on it. "As long as they aren't like that Preacher, *soy bueno*. Might be nice to have some fresh blood around." After a thought, he added, "Not too many."

"I'll make sure they're cool before I pass the word," Trader reassured them.

Trader watched Liluye work, asking her questions as she

operated the loom. Worrying that he might ruin the beautiful half-woven cloth, he wasn't brave enough to try it this year. It would either take heaps of trial and error or some serious mentorship to be as good as Liluye was on the loom.

As late afternoon pressed in, Trader asked, "How about I cook tonight?"

"Won't say no to that," Gilberto said enthusiastically.

"Something wrong with my cooking?" Liluye chided, her lips quirked into a smile.

Gilberto held his hands up. "No, no. Just thought it would be nice to give you a break. You're always running around looking after me. This *pinche* ankle. *Me siento culpable.*" Gilberto glowered at his foot.

Liluye smiled and turned back to the loom. "That's right, old man. Don't forget what side your bread is buttered on." They all had a good laugh at that as Trader packed up and headed out to get started on dinner.

CHAPTER TEN

Just after sunset, the fire-side feast was complete. Plates of large freshly washed lettuce leaves sat to one side. There was an array of bowls filled with kimchi, spicy red beans, fresh bean sprouts, sauteed garlicky spinach, and pickled spicy cucumber salad. In the center sat a large plate of pork jerky that had been soaked and barbequed over the fire pit.

The smell of the cooking meat filtered into the church, drawing everyone outside by the fire. Thick trails of drool dripped from Gunther's lips. Shifting his weight and licking his chops, he was almost unable to control himself. Sasha, of course, pretended not to care, but Trader knew she was keeping a side eye out for anything that might drop.

Meat was a special treat in the After. If a settlement was lucky enough, there might be eggs or cheese. But to kill an animal meant to lose that animal forever. It wasn't taken lightly. Trader could get meat on the circuit from the pig farm in Jackson via Forty Two and from the cattle farm at the Nakamuras'. If the Machados had goat jerky, he could get that too, but that was all dependent on how many males they had the last year and how rough the winter had been. Trader figured after the feast with guacamole and fresh tortillas last night, it was his turn to share a rare commodity.

Trader showed them how to use chopsticks to place items from the bowls into the lettuce leaves and wrap everything up. The sauce on the pork was spicy and sweet from the dried peppers and honey he had brushed on before tossing it on the grill. The kimchi was particularly tasty this season, accenting the sweet pork.

"This is amazing," Liluye said, stuffing her face.

"I think Gunther likes it too," Trader said, laughing. "There is a legit pool of drool there."

Gunther shifted his weight, scooching closer to Trader at the sound of his name.

After stuffing themselves, they chatted idly by the fire, picking the last bits out of the bowls. Though the darkness had settled in, the smoke from the fire kept the mosquitos away.

"Reminds me of the time Carmen made that roast *jabalí*, remember that?" Gilberto asked Liluye.

"Holy shit," Liluye said, shaking her head and smiling. "That was ages ago."

They both burst out laughing.

"Okay, okay, you gotta share the story now," Trader said.

"Some of the *güeyes* around the church back then managed to catch a *jabalí*," Gilberto began. "I have no fucking idea why it was here, or how they managed to kill it. But they did. They hauled it back like they had found the *Santo Grail*."

"They had!" Liluye laughed.

"Carmen had this plan that, instead of cooking up carnitas or something, we would dig this big pit in the ground, throw a bunch of corn husks in there, and toss the dressed *jabalí* on top to cook it Hawaiian-style. Everyone thought it was *chido*. They dug this huge pit, like four feet deep. An *imu* I think it's called? Anyway, they put stones and wood at the bottom and lit this huge fire. When it was just hot coals, they added the corn husks, laid

THE BEFORE AND THE AFTER

the *jabalí* on top, put a sheet over it, and buried the fucker. They let it cook down there overnight. *Pero...,*" Gilberto started laughing so hard tears filled his eyes.

"The fucking coyotes dug it up!" Liluye bellowed, cackling.

"What?" Trader asked, shocked.

"Coyotes," Gilberto continued. "Dug the damn thing up. Must have burned the shit out of them. *Pero* I think they were so hungry it didn't matter. There was a trail of *jabalí* bits across the field. Carmen came out the next morning *muy enojado*. She didn't cry or nothing, *pero* she was fucking pissed. There was *nada* left."

"She decided to say 'fuck it,' and cooked a kick-ass Chinese dinner, complete with rice we'd been saving." Gilberto smiled softly to himself. "She liked her shit *caliente*. Everything had a ton of peppers in it. *Pero* she pulled out all the stops and it was *chido.*"

"Remember Molimo?" Liluye said, grinning. "He wasn't used to spicy food. He practically cried taking his shit the next day." Both of them started braying with laughter again, and Trader joined in.

The laughter slowly died down. Gilberto wiped at his eyes.

"Damn," Liluye said, taking deep breaths with a huge grin on her face. "I haven't laughed like that in ages."

She took another deep, full-body breath and stared into the dancing fire. Her smile slowly fell. "I wish Molimo was here."

"Me too, *mija*. Me too."

"He probably would have thrown food at us for telling that story." She smiled sadly. "I miss him so much it hurts."

"*Sí,*" Gilberto gazed into the fire. "At least we have these stories, these *momentos*. Nothing will fill those empty spaces. *Pero* Carmen would be happy knowing we got a good laugh out of that damn *jabalí* fiasco. I am sure Molimo would be, *también.*"

Trader, Liluye, and Gilberto sat by the fire long into the

81

night. Gilberto and Liluye continued telling stories of people lost. Trader kept his own council, giving them space as they shared their pain. He reflected on the spectrum of stories he collected on his journey and how similar he was to Petra in *The Last Cuentista*. Gilberto's words rang true; stories helped ease the pain and kept memories alive. For Trader, the stories also gave him purpose. By listening to those tales and collecting them like small treasures, he was building out the world around him. Even if the characters in those stories may not be around the next time he made the circuit, the memory of them would still burn strong.

* * *

Three more days ambled by in a similar fashion. Each morning, Trader would help Liluye outside, the bright sunshine and manual labor filling him with energy. In the afternoon, they would all work cotton together in the nave. Sometimes, Trader would stop a bit early to read more of the book before heading to dinner. None of the meals were as grand as those first two nights, but each meal was relaxed and companionable. The days passed slowly but joyfully, like a bubbling creek.

On the fifth day, Trader started to feel the itch. If he was being honest with himself, he might even be happy if he stayed there for a while, even permanently. But that damn *itch*. The road was calling him. He craved the empty silence and wide, open spaces that spanned the stretches between settlements, with just Boxer and Sasha for company. He was hungry for new stories, the companionship of old friends, and the fulfillment of bringing people what they needed.

As they were cleaning up from dinner that day, Liluye finally broached the subject. "I get the sense that this meal was your swan song, Trader. Thinking of moving on tomorrow?"

Caught off guard by Liluye's intuitiveness, Trader's reply

stuck in his throat. He looked down at the dishes he was carrying to the pump to be washed, glad that the evening darkness hid his face. He cleared his throat.

"Yeah. Was gonna do some last trades with you all in the morning and then head to the Nakamuras'." The cold water in the large bin under the well pump chilled him as he rinsed the dishes and handed them over.

"You and Gilberto gonna be okay?" He knew there was only one answer to that question, and he felt guilty framing it in a way where he would hear what he needed to hear.

"Yep. We'll be fine. Lasted this long, haven't we?" Her faint smile was barely visible in the dim light. "The company and the help were appreciated." She dried her hands on a towel hanging from her waist and patted him on the back.

They finished cleaning up in silence, which wasn't quite awkward but wasn't easygoing either. There was an air of faint sadness mixed with understanding and a dash of finality. They both knew that Trader needed to move on. They also knew that life would be very difficult for Liluye and Gilberto after he left. Once they finished the washing, Liluye gave him an extra-long hug.

The next morning, Trader woke just as the sun was starting to rise. He noticed that Liluye had not only washed his dirty clothes but had managed to dry them out on the line without him even noticing. She must have known he was going to leave before he himself had fully known, having done it when he was working the cotton with Gilberto before dinner and sneaking them back in sometime before he woke up. The clean clothes now sat in a neat pile in a chair across the room.

Trader packed up his bedroll, clean clothes, hat, book, and Sasha's bed, taking them out to the wagon. After one last look around the cozy room, he realized that he'd forgotten something. He pulled back the pillow and stared down at the knife that had rested there, unused, for the duration of his stay. He was leaving

83

a safe zone and would need to keep it handy. He stashed the knife within grabbing distance of the driver's seat of the wagon.

With the wagon ready to go, Trader joined Liluye and Gilberto for one last meal together. Breakfast consisted of dried apricots, walnuts, and freshly cut jicama. They talked companionably over the meal, not rushing it, aware it would be the last for the season. As usual, food was snuck under the table to the awaiting Gunther. Trader choked up, hearing the steady, friendly thump of Gunther's tail; he was gonna miss the dog. Gunther was a sweety, his love for his pack less fickle than the loner, Princess Sasha.

After breakfast, they went outside to trade. Before the bartering started, Liluye handed Trader three bolts of beautifully woven, soft, white cotton cloth. "This is a gift. Thank you for helping these last couple of days."

"Liluye, I can't take this without a trade. It's too much."

"Take it, *pendejo*," Gilberto said with affection.

Trader reverently took the bolts of cloth and said his thanks. He placed them in a safe spot in the wagon before continuing the trading.

"Funny, but after staying here almost a week, I still have no clue what you might be needing," he said.

"With everyone gone, there isn't much we need just now; unless you have a surgeon back there to fix his ankle?" Liluye asked, pointing to Gilberto's foot.

"What books you got?" Gilberto asked.

"Here, have a look. I wanted to leave you *The Last Cuentista*, but I'm not done yet." Trader pulled the flaps back to expose the long line of books in the wagon.

"*No hay bronca*. Just bring it next year." Gilberto smiled and patted Trader on the back. The idea of coming back here next year, and maybe even spending a couple of days again, made Trader feel good. Like he had something to look forward to. A promise to keep.

THE BEFORE AND THE AFTER

"*Pero*, you can only come back if you promise there'll be another Korean BBQ night," Gilberto added, grinning as he picked through the books, selecting a couple.

"Wanna swap these books for some of mine?" Gilberto offered.

"I'd love a gander at your bookshelf."

Trader followed Gilberto back into the church. A large bed layered with quilts sat in the middle of Gilberto's sunlit room. A plush beat-up old chair sat in the corner. A bookshelf covered one wall and was almost entirely filled with books.

Trader stood with his mouth open. "Holy crap, Gilberto. You've been holding out on me! Where did you get all of these?"

"Mostly from the library. Some were gifts. Others trades."

Trader perused the books, running his fingers affectionately along the spines. There were so many that he was slightly overwhelmed. The books appeared to be organized by subject. He dropped down to a squat to look at the sci-fi/fantasy section. It still blew his mind that Gilberto had enough books to even have sections.

Trader stood. "I can't decide, man. The only other place I have seen this many books is Earl's."

"Here," Gilberto awkwardly kneeled on the ground, trying not to tweak his ankle, and pulled out four well-worn books, three hardcover and one paperback. The top one was *The Gunslinger* by Stephen King. A cowboy holding a gun and a rose were on the cover.

"These are the first four in the series. It's a story about *un hombre* who wanders with a purpose, but it's kinda an empty purpose. The third book is meh; you gotta power through it. *Pero* the end of the story will be worth it. Remember, the journey itself is what matters the most. You can pick up the last four books next year. Give you a reason to come back."

Trader was gobsmacked. Not only did Gilberto have enough books to have actual sections, but he also had eight books in the

85

same series. There was nothing worse than reading a good book, and realizing it was the first or, even more terrible, in the middle of a series for which the rest of the books couldn't be found in the After. This was a treasure.

"Wow, Gilberto. Are you sure? This is…," Trader trailed off at a loss for words.

Gilberto nodded. "Just bring 'em back next year. You can borrow the last four then."

After handing Trader the books, he shakily leaned on the bookshelf to stand back up. They headed back to the wagon, where Liluye and Gunther waited. They stayed and chatted as Trader hitched up Boxer. Sasha, knowing it was time to go, curled up into her cat bed in the driver's seat of the wagon.

Trader got down on one knee to hug Gunther, rubbing his ears. "You take care of them for me, okay?"

Gunther licked Trader's face with his big tongue. Trader gave Liluye and Gilberto each a long hug. Trader surprised himself by choking up a bit.

"Watch out for that preacher fucker, got me?" Liluye instructed, chasing away her tears. "His symbol looks like this." She bent down to draw it into the dirt: three circles arranged in a triangle, topped with five vertical lines. "You see that, get the fuck out of there."

Trader gave a nod with a slight frown.

"*Nos vemos*, Trader," Gilberto said.

Trader made a clicking sound, and Boxer pulled the wagon out of the church parking lot. Gunther followed them to the end of the driveway. Trader looked back to wave one last goodbye, but Gilberto and Liluye had already made their way inside. Gunther stood a few feet away, wagging his tail slowly but not following further. Trader smiled sadly as the wagon rolled out onto E. Lathrop.

CHAPTER ELEVEN

The sun was high and bright, beating down hard on them. Trader hunched under his hat, not wanting to burn, and sweated heavily under his long-sleeve shirt. Sasha had abandoned her post in the driver's seat and was now undercover in the back of the wagon. Boxer was still steadily trudging along, though his tail was droopy.

The intense heat and clomping of Boxer's hooves echoing on the empty freeway threatened to lull Trader to sleep. He kept pinching his leg, trying to stay awake until he reached the Nakamuras'.

Liluye's parting words kept echoing in his head. *Watch out for that preacher fucker.*

Preacher spooked him; it was unfamiliar territory. He didn't want to get caught off guard and alone on the highway.

Just north of Modesto, the sight of two people sitting in the shade on the side of the highway startled him out of his half-doze. They looked relaxed, eating a meal. He approached cautiously. Though he didn't let his guard down completely, Trader relaxed slightly when he realized they were dressed in a variety of colors and didn't have anything painted on their foreheads.

"Howdy," Trader called out when he was within fifty feet or so, raising a hand. They both raised their hands back.

"Join us for lunch?" The man gestured to the food sitting between him and the woman.

They were both in their late twenties or early thirties. Their clothes were threadbare and definitely from the Before. Plenty of food sat in front of them, their packs looked nice, and they had full canteens.

Trader tried to shake off the wariness that had settled over his shoulders. These people were clearly not part of Preacher's group. He kept reminding himself that most people were nice, and that violence was rare. He shouldn't let Preacher scare him out of a friendly encounter and possible trade.

Packing the anxiety away, Trader answered, "Sure. Thanks for the invite." He stopped the wagon in the shade.

"Let me get my horse some water," he said.

Trader left Boxer hitched but gave him a bucket to drink from. He grabbed his canteen, some nuts, and preserved peaches to share. Preserved peaches were a trustworthy peace offering and always warmed people up.

Trader sat down with them on the highway, holding the peach container out. "Help yourself." They smiled and took a peach or two as the container was passed around.

"I'm Adam. This is my wife, Barbara."

"I'm Trader. That big guy over there is Boxer. Sasha's my cat, but she's hiding in the wagon. Where're you two headed? I'm going south and can give you a ride if you need one."

"We appreciate the offer, but we're headed north," Barbara said. "We heard about a nice settlement up in the Galt area. Hopefully, it isn't flooded?"

"It's still there and doing well, too," Trader answered. "It's called Forty Two, and it's run by a lovely woman named Rosa. They happily welcome newcomers."

Adam and Barbara turned to each other and smiled. A weight seemed to come off their shoulders with the news.

"The road is intact and passable. Some spots are partially flooded but easy to get around. On your way, there is a church off E. Lathrop in Manteca that will make a nice stop. Gilberto and Liluye will take you in for the night if you need a place to crash. Don't mind the dog, he's nice." Trader paused to take a drink of water. "Just north of that, Stockton is completely flooded and Lodi is a pile of ash, so you'll need to sleep on the road or walk into the night to make it to Galt from Manteca."

"That's great intel," Adam said. "Thanks. We don't have to rush but sleeping outside sucks."

"Where're you from?" Trader asked.

"We had a place east of here, just the two of us. It was a pretty sweet farm. The dust storms never got bad. There was a creek nearby that hardly ever flooded. We even managed to keep chickens despite the coyotes. We'll miss it," Barbara replied, stroking her slightly swollen stomach.

Trader started. The woman was pregnant.

"Forty Two is nice. There are quite a few people there, almost thirty folks. They have all the perks of a larger community. They even have power. You'll be comfortable. Best of all, they have a nurse who sometimes visits," Trader said, hoping to reassure them a bit about their choice to leave their home.

The couple turned to each other again. Adam reached over and half-hugged Barbara, leaning close.

"See?" Adam said softly to Barbara, resting his forehead on her shoulder. "It'll be okay. We got this."

Trader felt a twinge, not wanting to spoil the moment but also wanting them to be safe.

"Be cautious on your way north. There are roadblocks in Lodi.

89

And, as I said, the town is entirely burnt down. It looks scary, but no one is there. What you need to worry about is the guy who did that. There's a preacher wandering around. The people at the Silvas' in Manteca told me about him. Just...be careful."

After exchanging a surprised look with Adam, Barbara said "We'll watch out. Thank you for the warning. It's easy to get too comfortable. Most people are nice and just want to help. I guess that's one of the few good things nowadays."

Trader nodded in agreement. "Yep. Most people are awesome. You'll see that at the Silvas' and Forty Two. Nice folks there." He changed the subject. "Your packs look pretty full. Looking for anything to trade or need anything for the trip?"

"We're good, thanks for asking. Left anything worth trading back at the house to keep things light for the hike. Sorry about that. Barbara can work metal. I'm the farmer in the family. Hoping we can find a place to chip in and earn our stay at Forty Two," Adam said.

"You work metal?" Trader asked. That was a valuable and very rare skill in the After. "Forty Two would love to have you. Between you, the shoemaker, and the nurse who comes by, they almost have it all. Where'd you learn how to do that?"

"My mom was an artist who worked with metal. She and my dad had a farm. She would work in her shop in the back. When things went south, she taught herself how to cast stuff, like nails and screws. She could even make tools like knives. My dad would carve the handles for them." Barbara pointed to Adam's side, where a well-made knife sat on his hip. "She taught me the craft. It came in handy for repairs and pretty much set us up so we didn't need to trade or scavenge much for anything."

That explained why their clothes were threadbare despite looking well-fed and outfitted. It sounded like they had a great set-up out on that farm, and it probably killed them to leave it all behind. Trader understood why they had, though. Having a baby was no joke in the After.

THE BEFORE AND THE AFTER

"You'll fit right in at Forty Two," he said kindly.

After they finished up, Trader rose and started packing. "I should be on my way. It was nice meeting you both. Safe journey. Maybe I'll see you at Forty Two next season."

They both stood and shook his hand.

"Looking forward to it," Adam said, half hugging Barbara. "Hopefully, there will be three of us there to greet you."

Barbara put her hand on her stomach and smiled.

"Hope so," Trader said, smiling back.

He grabbed Boxer's water bucket and put it back in the wagon. In the cool shade of the tree, Sasha had decided to make an appearance. Trader mounted the driver's seat next to her. He made a secret wish that the couple would make it safely to Forty Two without a whisper of Preacher.

* * *

A short time later, Trader had made his way to the abandoned city of Modesto and turned west. The 132 was a two-lane, paved highway that had seen better days. It was pretty dilapidated now, with chunks of the road missing and a portion washed out as the canal passed under the highway.

Just outside of Modesto, the Nakamuras' perched on the south side of the highway squeezed between the canal and the road. In the Before, this region had been packed with farmland, with a mixture of vegetable crops, fruit trees, and dairy farms. In the After, most of the land consisted of long stretches of light brown, sandy, spent dirt with scattered scrub brush. As people started dying from Weeps or abandoning their farms for other settlements, the Nakamuras just expanded.

The decades of drought had hit this region fairly hard. The Nakamuras' was an oasis on the edge of habitable land, with dust storms blotting out most life in the southern part of the valley. They'd get dust storms here too, but not nearly as bad as Fresno.

A double row of trees bordered their property, providing a buffer.

The canal on the southern edge of the farm was their lifeline. The risk of flooding was moderate, and the canal would occasionally dry up in the summer months. However, having a somewhat steady supply of running water nearby reduced the mosquito risk and kept their farm going. If the canal dried out in the hot summer, they would drive their cattle to the nearby San Joaquin River and camp there for a couple of months. They could also move the cattle north if the canal flooded.

Trader turned south off the 132 and onto a bumpy dirt road. On his left, there was pasture, kept healthy by water piped from the canal. Several dozen still-domesticated beef cattle grazed peacefully. The far end of the pasture was planted with walnut trees. The settlement and adjacent crops were on the right side of the road.

The settlement consisted of three structures, raised on stilts six feet off the ground. The buildings formed a half circle around a large cooking pit. Adjacent to the buildings was an entire solar panel array built on another raised platform. Wires ran from the array high above the ground, connecting to the three buildings.

Trader pulled the wagon in and parked next to the chicken tractors. The chickens were housed in repurposed semi-truck trailers that were moved around the settlement for the chickens to forage. They could also be towed to safety if the area flooded. By the sounds of the soft, late-day clucking, the chickens were back home and locked in for the evening.

Behind the houses, there was a large barn flush on the ground with an adjoining pasture shaded by oaks. Through the gap between the houses, Boxer noticed the three horses grazing and whinnied loudly. One of the horses in the pasture whinnied back. As Trader climbed off the wagon, joyful singing spilled out from one of the buildings.

"Hello, Trader here!" he called out loudly.

THE BEFORE AND THE AFTER

The singing stopped, and the front door of the middle building opened.

"Well, well! Nice to see you," Akari said, wiping her hands on her apron as she stepped out on the porch.

Akari was in her mid to late twenties, short, and thin. Her long black hair was braided down her back. She wore a loose dress made from patched fabric covered by an apron and tattered house shoes.

From around the back of the house, her father appeared. Hiroshi was short and stocky. A battered cowboy hat covered his short, salt-and-pepper hair. He wore loose-fitting cotton pants, woven flip-flops, and a loose-fitting cotton shirt. Over his shirt, he wore a thin leather vest, pockets stuffed with small pieces of wood and a whittling knife.

"Hello, friend," Hiroshi said. "It's a pleasure to see you again. I know Yuki, Pochi, and Tadeo will be pleased to see Boxer, too. Come on in."

Trader got out of the driver's seat and began to unhitch Boxer. "Mind if I take Boxer out back and get him settled?"

"Not at all. I'll walk you back. The rest of the group is out mending fences and should return soon for dinner." Hiroshi joined Trader at the wagon.

"Back to work for me," Akari called from her front door. "Come on up when you're all settled."

After Boxer was completely unhitched, Trader quickly brushed him down and checked his hooves. The horse was fidgety and difficult to groom. He whinnied a couple of times, the other horses always answering back. Boxer tugged at his lead rope, prancing slightly, as Trader led him back to the pasture. Hiroshi opened the gate for them. As soon as the halter was off, Boxer joined the other horses. They touched noses, licked their lips, and swished tails, reacquainting themselves with one another.

93

Hiroshi closed the gate and led Trader back out front. "Will your cat be okay, or do you want to grab her?"

Trader glanced over to the wagon and saw she had already abandoned her bed, likely to go hunting.

"She'll be good for now. Thank you, though. I need to grab something from the wagon. Just a sec."

Trader trotted back to the wagon to grab a host gift. He had been mulling over what to give them the entire day, hemming and hawing over the various sundries available. A bolt of cloth might be too much. But something like a jar of kimchi wouldn't be enough. Throwing caution to the wind, he decided on the bolt of cloth.

He presented the cloth to Hiroshi, holding it with both hands. "Thank you for welcoming us."

Hiroshi was usually pretty good at guarding his expressions. But Trader caught a quick flash of surprise followed by a pleased expression on Hiroshi's face.

"This is a wonderful gift. Thank you." He bowed his head slightly as he accepted the gift with both hands.

Trader climbed the ladder to Akari's house, with Hiroshi passing the bolt of cloth to him so that he could follow. Once inside, they removed their shoes, setting them by the door. Hiroshi showed the bolt of cloth to Akari. She smiled appreciatively.

"That's wonderful, Trader. Thank you. Izumi is quickly outgrowing her clothes. Please sit. I'll make tea. Would you prefer mint or chamomile?" she asked.

"Thanks. I'll have what you are having," Trader answered.

Hiroshi and Trader took a seat while Akari prepared the tea. The front room consisted of a small open space. There was a living room area with two large plush chairs, a rug of woven scrap fabric, and a bookshelf with a small number of well-worn books and baskets with wooden toys. Next to this was a small dining table, where they all sat. A countertop with a sink and a

THE BEFORE AND THE AFTER

hot plate sat on the far wall. A single bedroom was in the back. Behind a curtain, there were composting toilets that drained down to a catch at ground level.

"What's the news from up north?" Hiroshi asked as they sipped their tea.

"Forty Two is doing grand. The settlement is growing. They have a shoemaker now. I met a couple on the way who was heading up there. One of them is a metalworker. They lived back east on their own but decided to join a bigger group because she's pregnant. Stockton is completely flooded. Lodi was burnt down by some crazy guy. The Silvas..." he paused, trying to find the right words. "They had a rough spell. It's just Gilberto and Liluye now. They're still focused on cotton production though, and looking for an apprentice if you have anyone interested."

He took a sip. It was a perfectly brewed cup of mint tea with a dollop of honey. It was delicious. He sighed happily, relaxing in their company.

"Things are looking great here. How'd the last year treat you?"

"The summer was rough," Akari said. "After you passed through, we had several big dust storms. There was grit everywhere, in our hair, in our food, in our beds. Yuck. We moved the cattle in the barn for the worst of it. The winds were so bad we thought the buildings would come down.

"The canal also dried up. At one point, we moved down to the river which was just a trickle at that point. We'd come back to check on the bees, bringing water for them and crossing our fingers. The rains finally came mid-winter, and we were able to come back. We lost some of the late winter crops. We're fortunate in that we didn't lose any of the hives or the livestock."

The Nakamuras' bees were a treasured part of the farm. Hiroshi had even taken extra care and put the hives on their own raised platform under the shade of a small copse of oak trees. Not many people kept bees, and Trader wasn't sure why. Wild bees had come back well enough to keep everything pollinated; their population rising as the human population fell, acting inversely to each other. However, kept hives meant honey. Trader always tried to negotiate at least a couple of jars on the circuit, planning on keeping at least one for himself as a treat. Beekeeping was another skill, like working cotton, that might be good to spread along the settlements.

"There'll be two calf crops this year," Hiroshima added. "We had four calves come in the fall, and all survived despite the summer killing the pasture. Not many, but enough. At least a dozen cows will calve in the next month or so."

"Wow, that's fortunate. Do you plan on growing the herd?"

"We'll see," Hiroshi answered. "Depends on how rough this summer is."

"Mommy?" a small voice called from the back of the house.

A young girl peeked around the corner. She held a small carved wooden horse in her hand. Akari's daughter, Izumi, had grown quite a bit since Trader had seen her last. He couldn't remember how old she was. Kids were so rare nowadays it was hard to place their ages.

"Have a nice nap, honey?" Akari asked.

Izumi rubbed her eyes and went over to her mom, hiding behind her. She peered around her mom's dress to stare at Trader.

"Don't you remember Trader? He's come to swap yummy things with us. He also brought us some cloth. I can make you some new clothes."

Izumi pulled her mom's apron over her face and peeked around the edge again.

"She's getting big. How old is she now?" Trader waved at Izumi.

"She just turned five," Akari said proudly.

Trader smiled. Akari *should* be proud. It was very difficult to get pregnant, much less safely deliver and then raise the child to the age of five. There were a multitude of reasons there weren't many kids around.

"Come sit and have a snack." Akari got up to fix Izumi a plate. Izumi shyly took a seat across from Trader.

"Would you like anything, Trader?" Akari asked.

"I'm fine, thank you. Had lunch just a bit ago. The tea is perfect."

Akari placed some fresh snap peas and sliced carrots on the table. Izumi, warming up a bit, started snacking away.

"Please stay to eat dinner with us if you have time after we trade," Akari offered.

"I would be honored. Thank you." Trader paused before asking, "Do you mind if I stay overnight as well? In my wagon, of course."

Trader usually made a quick stop just to trade at the Nakamuras' and moved on to camp further down the road. With Boxer flagging from the heat, Trader preferred to let him rest up before setting out again. That being said, he didn't want to impose on the Nakamuras either. Akari shared her place with her partner, Ben, and her daughter. Hiroshi had a house to himself and preferred it that way. The three other farmhands stayed in the third house. All in all, it was a tight fit.

"You're most welcome to stay," Hiroshi answered.

After the tea was finished, Hiroshi and Trader went outside to chat under the shade of a large oak. The weather had cooled just a bit with the setting sun, still warm but with a slight breeze. Small birds were high up in the tree, chirping. Off in the distance, the cows grazed. It was a peaceful spot. Trader closed his eyes and took a deep breath, letting the moment fill him.

CHAPTER
TWELVE

As the sun tipped over the hills in the west, the group working on the fencing returned home, with Ben leading three others. Trader was pleased to see things as they were from last year, including the little one still around and slightly taller. It meant that the Weeps hadn't taken anybody. It also meant that Preacher either hadn't passed through here or, if he had, he hadn't successfully recruited anyone.

After everyone greeted each other and the group washed up, the trading began. The Nakamuras were wealthy by Trader's standards, offering several prized items. He was able to secure several jars of honey, jerky, five tanned hides, and half a dozen bars of lavender-scented soap made from bee's wax. This gave him enough of the precious honey, soap, and jerky for himself with plenty to spare for trade further along the circuit. He would save the leather for Forty Two, bringing it to the shoemaker next year. One more commitment to help him stick through another year.

In exchange, the Nakamuras took a knife set, a bag of salt from last year's run, preserves, quilts from Forty Two, and one more bolt of cotton cloth. He now only had one bolt of cloth left from the Silvas', and he planned on keeping it for himself.

With the trading now done, they all settled around a freshly built fire. Akari began barbecuing several steaks and baking potatoes on a grill. Trader's stomach grumbled, his body craving the precious meat. Once it came time to eat, the steaks and potatoes were served with steamed broccoli and cool mint tea. Idle chatter died down as everyone started in, even little Izumi. Sasha, smelling the meat, also made an appearance. Trader passed her some of the steak to enjoy. This was the only stop they would get to enjoy freshly cooked beef, and he wanted to make sure she had a treat too.

During the meal, a cobbler sweetened with honey was cooked in a Dutch oven. Though Trader was stuffed after the steak and potatoes, he helped himself to a small portion.

With the sun fully set, darkness flooded the valley. The small group sat comfortably around the fire, relaxing.

"Tell one of your stories, Dad," Akari prompted.

Hiroshi was a talented storyteller, sharing tales passed down through the generations. His deep, melodic tone and use of different voices for the characters pulled everyone in. Since Trader usually passed through fairly quickly, he had only experienced Hiroshi's performances a couple of times. He was excited to catch one this year.

The conversation died down as everyone settled in for the story. To Trader's immense surprise, Izumi came over to him and climbed into his lap. He'd never had a child sit in his lap before, and he hugged his arms gently around her protectively.

As soon as everyone was comfortable, Hiroshi told the story of Momotaro, the boy born from a peach. He drew the audience in with his voice and the cadence of the story. He even got up, pretending to fight as Momotaro battled demons. Izumi stared, wide-eyed and entranced, with her thumb in her mouth.

Hiroshi reminded him of Petra in *The Last Cuentista*. Storytellers were like traders in a way, sharing their goods with others and bringing people together. At the end of his story, Hiroshi took a dramatic bow, and everyone clapped.

"You're an excellent storyteller," Trader complimented Hiroshi as he sat back down.

"These are the stories of my grandmother. I want to make sure they are passed on to Akari and Izumi. These stories are us." He lightly tapped his chest over his heart.

"Stories are a great gift," Trader said.

They talked a bit about the weather and the recent short rain. They shared funny stories about their escapades on the farm. They also talked about the cattle, chickens, and bees, including the yields this year and what they expected this coming spring and summer. Trader was hesitant to ruin the mood, but he needed to know if Preacher had been this way and what might be waiting for him further down the road.

After some internal hemming and hawing, he finally asked, "Has anyone passed through lately?"

The number of travelers in the After had diminished significantly in the last couple of years. Being a minor thoroughfare, Highway 132 was well off the beaten path. People only came to the Nakamuras' if they knew the settlement existed and had an explicit reason for visiting. However, Preacher had already turned the status quo topsy-turvy this year, and he might have taken this route.

"Jesse came through right before summer last year, heading east," Ben answered. "They brought some great trades from Walnut Creek. I think we cleaned all their salt out. Other than that, it's been pretty quiet."

Trader relaxed slightly.

"Sometime after the solstice, we saw two people on horses with large packs headed west on 132," Ben continued. "They stopped to have a meal, stayed the night, and moved on. They were sick of the fires in the mountains and were gonna go to the coast. Not sure it's much better there. I know they have tech there, but living in a flooded urban city? That's not my thing.

"A little over a month ago, three people on foot passed by on the 132, heading west. It was kinda weird. They didn't have packs or any supplies. The guy in the front was wearing all white. Hiroshi and I were on the horses out with the cattle. I know they saw us, but they didn't wave or anything. Not sure how they planned on surviving. They clearly needed food and water. It was very odd."

Goosebumps tickled down Trader's arms. "I think that might have been Preacher with Bryson and Maria."

Hiroshi turned to Trader with a questioning gaze.

"I've never met him," Trader cautioned, shrugging his shoulders a bit. "He stayed with Gilberto and Liluye, and all I know is what they told me. Preacher set the whole city of Lodi on fire when he was burning the dead bodies of his previous group."

Ben whistled softly in disbelief.

"Preacher showed up at the Silvas' talking about rising out of blood and ash or something like that," Trader continued. "Apparently, Preacher was pretty adamant that God's way was the only way to escape loneliness and find purpose. After losing Molimo to Weeps, Bryson was severely depressed, and Peacher's words swayed him."

"Oh no," Akari exclaimed. "They lost Molimo…Poor Liluye."

Trader nodded sadly. "Preacher's proselytizing bounced right off Gilberto and Liluye, though. They said Preacher was a bit off his rocker and warned me to stay away from him. Liluye was even packing. I haven't ever seen her carry a gun before."

Trader paused and chewed on his cheek. "If Preacher comes through here again for some reason, be careful. Not saying you should turn anyone away. Just…be careful."

Silence spread through the group. Ben reached out to grab Akari's hand. One of the farmhands fidgeted. Hiroshi looked deep in thought, staring into the fire. Warnings about other people just weren't a thing in the After, and everyone had to take a moment to process.

"I was pleasantly surprised that people took care of each other when things first went bad," Hiroshi said, finally breaking the silence. "Movies from the Before painted a fairly dramatic and desolate picture of possible futures. They assumed we would revert to warring tribes like chimpanzees. We should consider ourselves lucky that we've had only one aberration so far. I'm glad Preacher went his own way without any trouble."

Hiroshi crossed his arms confidently and looked over at him. "Don't worry about us, Trader. We've survived much worse with the storms. We'll survive this too. Thank you for the warning."

With this show of strength from their elder, the rest of the group relaxed. The conversation started again, drifting away from post-apocalyptic hypotheticals, and moving on to lighter subjects late into the night. Izumi had fallen asleep in Trader's lap, her small hand curled around his first two fingers. There was so much hope in the sleeping child, so much potential. With so few children in the After, this little girl was important to all of them, not just Akari and Ben. And not just those at the Nakamuras'. She was the future and one of the reasons why Trader needed to come next year, and the year after, despite the occasional bad seed in the bunch. These communities need to stay connected so the little ones could survive.

* * *

The next morning, Trader woke to the smell of campfire and cooked potatoes.

"Good morning," Ben said when Trader joined him.

Three cast iron pans containing steaming corned beef hash were set to the side of the fire. Ben was cracking eggs into a fourth skillet.

"If you want, there's a shower out back," Ben offered. "Sal built a mini-water heater and set it up last winter. As long as the solars are up and running and the house batteries stay charged, there's a hot shower waiting. There's soap in there too."

"I'll take you up on that. I have a couple days until I see civilization again. It'll be nice to wash up."

"Breakfast will be ready by the time you're done." Ben nudged the cooking eggs with a metal spatula.

Trader went back to the wagon, grabbed a change of clothes, and headed behind the houses. Hot showers were few and far between in the After, and he luxuriated in the warm water. Before this, the only hot showers he'd experienced were in Walnut Creek. Trader longed for a solar panel set-up with batteries to heat the water back at his own place. He would need someone with experience with electrical equipment, though, and he hadn't been able to pry Rat out of his scrap shack yet.

Now presentable and smelling of lavender soap, he dropped his dirty clothes off in the wagon and grabbed a jar of salsa and another of canned peaches. They'd be the perfect accompaniment to breakfast.

By the time he got back to the firepit, everyone was up and eating. Trader passed around his salsa and peaches to share. A plate of corned beef hash and fried eggs was passed back his way. After the salsa had made its rounds, he dumped some on top of the eggs. Between the warm shower and the delicious breakfast, he felt relaxed and ready to set out on the open road.

"What are you all up to today?" Trader asked, making conversation.

"All of us will be out in the fields planting more of the spring crops," Hiroshi replied. "This time of year is always busy."

Trader nodded. It was a busy time for every settlement. Everything needed to get in the ground and start producing before the hellacious summer heat settled in. Not much could survive the scorching summer, except corn, cotton, and okra.

"Have you ever thought of growing cotton?" Trader asked the group.

"We haven't," Akari said. "We have been mainly focused on growing food. Why do you ask?"

"The Silvas are sharing cotton seeds. They're also welcoming apprentices who want to learn to spin and weave. The looms they have look pretty simple to build. I have the plans if you want to copy them. Operating them is the tricky part. It might be easier to just go and stay a month or so to learn how to use it, maybe over the winter when things slow down a bit. You have lots of usable property here. If the water that you get from the canal can support another field, you may want to think about planting cotton, too."

Hiroshi nodded, thinking. "Interesting idea. We should consider that. Winter is always slow. It'd be nice to make our own cloth." He was always contemplating ways to make his little outpost more independent.

After everyone had finished up, Hiroshi said, "We need to get to work. Thank you for coming out of your way to stop here. We appreciate it." He shook Trader's hand.

Trader shook hands with the rest of the group. Izumi came up and hugged his leg. He took a knee to look her in the eye.

"Wait here a sec, okay?" he asked.

She nodded shyly and put her thumb in her mouth, her other hand clutching the wooden horse her grandpa had whittled for her. He jogged back to the wagon, rustled around, and trotted back.

"Here." He handed her *Oh! The Places You'll Go* by Dr. Suess.

Children's books were rare in the After. The books that had made it through had seen decades of love from other kids, and the cover of this book was a bit rough and ready. Trader tried to pick up a few kids' books every year from Earl's, always hopeful that they would find a home. Izumi's face lit up when he handed her the book. She popped her thumb out of her mouth and gently took the book.

"Fank you," she said softly, smiling.

She gave him another hug and ran to her mom, pulling on Akari's apron and asking her mom to read it to her. Akari gave Trader a smile of thanks before looking down at her daughter.

"Okay, just once, and then we need to go plant the veggies." She sat with Izumi on her lap and started reading to her.

After waving goodbye, the rest of the group headed to the fields. Trader went behind the houses, collecting Boxer from the pasture. Boxer was content with the other horses and reluctant to leave. Trader scratched his mane in apology.

"I promise we'll come back next year, buddy."

CHAPTER THIRTEEN

The trio headed west on the 132, leaving the lush farmland of the Nakamuras' behind and entering the desolate space beyond. It was a hot ride in the full sun, even with his hat on, and his shirt was damp with sweat. Sasha had retired in the back of the wagon, seeking shade. Trader had to stop to let Boxer rest and water him several times. It was tough going.

The road was empty and increasingly in disrepair. The only sound was the clopping of Boxer's hooves on the baking asphalt. Small dust devils stirred in the barren wasteland south of the highway. Though Trader typically enjoyed the empty spaces on the road, this stretch of the circuit was particularly depressing.

Around lunchtime, they reached a portion of the road that had been entirely washed away. Dry, cracked dirt littered with scraggly, dead weeds filled the stretch between the slabs of crumbled asphalt. The bridge over the San Joaquin River became visible in the distance, and Trader hoped it was still crossable. With a clicking sound, Boxer pulled the wagon onto the exposed dirt, trying to avoid any chunks of asphalt that had been left behind.

As Trader neared the bridge, he started to see the tall, wild grasses again, waving slightly in the breeze. The river made slow joyful sounds of bubbling water. A jackrabbit scampered across what was left of the road, starling Trader and Boxer. A large hawk circled in the sky above. They were small spots of life hidden away between the stretches of dry wasteland.

When they reached the river, they found the bridge sturdy enough to cross, having been spared any significant damage related to the flooding that had taken out the previous stretch of road. A thick layer of dried, cracked mud lay across one edge of the bridge, but it was otherwise in pretty good shape. The river was now well below the high mark, passing lazily below.

Boxer was flagging in the heat and would need to rest soon. Even though it was only mid-day, Trader decided to camp there rather than try to find something in the wasteland between here and the hills to the west. On the opposite side of the bridge was a relatively flat area lush with knee-high grasses that bordered a smooth slope down to the water's edge. It was a perfect campsite.

Trader perched on the wagon, snacking on dried fruit and nuts and enjoying the burble of the river and the peaceful solitude. A red-tailed hawk sat perched on an old fence post across the river. Trader glanced around for Sasha. The grass rustled, but he couldn't spot her. He'd have to keep an eye on her. She was a scrapper, but some of the larger hawks and owls would take down a cat if hungry enough.

Once his meal was finished, Trader headed towards the river with his dirty clothes and the lavender soap from the Nakamuras'. He took his boots off and waded in up to his ankles. The water was cool and gently danced over his feet. He wiggled his toes in the sandy dirt of the riverbed. He washed his clothes, lathering them up in soap, rinsing them off, and wringing them out. He hung the clothes on a line that dangled between the wagon and one of the oaks. With the chores done, Trader set up an old metal folding chair by the river under the shade of an oak

THE BEFORE AND THE AFTER

tree and continued to read *The Last Cuentista*. The book had been spinning in his head, especially after Hiroshi's story by the fire the previous night.

Hours slipped by as Trader devoured the book, only looking up every so often to get eyes on Sasha and Boxer. In the story, Petra was now awake, after years of isolation, and was sharing her stories with others to bring them hope. The further he got into the book, the more he felt a kinship with Petra. As the sun set, he reluctantly put the book down to make dinner.

Tonight's meal was a cold one. Though he enjoyed these interludes between the settlements, he did miss having a warm meal. Being around this much tall grass, he was nervous about lighting a fire. The last thing he wanted to do was burn down what little grass had been able to eke out an existence in this dust-torn valley. He put together a meal of preserved beets, pickled okra, and jerky.

After the sun fully set and the sky filled with stars, Trader decided to call it a night. Sleeping away from a settlement always held risks. Coyotes and owls prowled down in the valley. Up in the hills, bears and big cats were the ones to watch out for. And now, according to Gilberto and Liluye, he had to guard against Preacher and his merry band. Before he tucked into bed, he loosely tied Boxer's lead rope to the wagon. He called to Sasha, who heeded his command in a very un-cat-like way, joining him before he sealed the canvas flaps closed. His hand found his knife next to his bedroll, offering a modicum of comfort.

* * *

Trader woke up grumpy and stiff after a fitful sleep. Mosquitoes had buzzed around his head all night, waking him up repeatedly with their irritating noise. There must have been standing water somewhere nearby. The water of the San Joaquin River was moving too quickly for them to breed in. Several angry mosquito bites were scattered on his arms and around his ankles. Clearly, he had been scratching them in his sleep. His boots would be uncomfortable today. The ever-present threat of Weeps also nagged him.

He climbed out of the covers and started to get dressed in the wagon. Sasha glared at him from the end of the bed, looking irritated. He must have kept her up with his tossing and turning. He wondered if the mosquitoes had dined on her as well and thought it likely. Though cats didn't carry or get sick from Weeps, there were other diseases that they could get. Without the fancy meds from the Before, cats like Sasha just had to deal with fleas, ticks, and things like heartworm.

"Sorry, girl," he said, stroking her.

Trader rifled through his stuff and pulled out a small piece of jerky, offering it to Sasha apologetically. She gently ate the meat, minutely mollified. He fed her a few more pieces, knowing she had missed hunting last night. After the last piece, she looked up at him hopefully and licked her whiskers.

He laughed softly. "I feel bad, but not that bad."

The sun was just coming up as he went outside. A startled jackrabbit bounded away through the grasses as he opened the canvas flap. Boxer looked well rested, still dozing with his back leg relaxed, resting the tip of his hoof on the ground. Trader ran a hand down Boxer's side and scratched his mane. He removed his halter to let him graze before he hitched him back up again.

The clothes on the line were now dry, blowing slightly in the wind. The river gurgled in the distance. He folded his clothes, took down the line, and repacked everything in the wagon. Seeing the folding chair with the book lying on top, he was tempted to read a bit and get a late start. But it would be a long trek for Boxer today. The hills sat in the distance to the west, and Trader wanted to make it over the pass. On the other side sat

Live More, the cheekily-named settlement on the edges of what used to be Livermore.

After a cold breakfast and packing up, he climbed into the driver's seat, mosquito bites chafing against his boots. Sasha was already in her bed, still looking miffed. It was going to be an off day.

* * *

The river retreated in the distance as the trio headed west on the 132. The lush native grasses were slowly replaced by sandy, dry, cracked dirt and scraggly scrub brush. The wind picked up, forming small dust devils in the distance. The occasional tumbleweed scooted by.

To the south, past Mount Oso, he could see large, brown clouds rolling east down the hills and sweeping into the valley. It looked like someone had poured a bucket of sand at the top of the hills, with large billowing folds cascading down. The dust clouds enveloped the valley to the south of the highway, blocking everything from sight like a hungry beast. The sunlight reflected through the dust in a red glow at the top of the mountain. Trader half expected a large demon to rise above the peaks with pitch-black, spider creatures pouring forth from the red haze to wreak havoc.

The storm looked to be far to the south and was moving east rather than north. He thought they'd avoid the worst of it, but it wouldn't hurt to hustle and get further up the road. They still had a long way to go if they wanted to make it over the pass and out of the valley.

When they turned north on the 580 towards Tracy, the wind was getting progressively more violent, with large gusts of dust and sand whipping at them. Trader clicked and lightly flapped the reins, urging Boxer along. In the thick of it, those dust storms were severe enough to damage eyes, clog lungs, and scrape skin away like sandpaper. If they could get to Tracy and the lower edge of the foothills, they might be able to avoid the worst of the storm.

The gritty dust started to fill the air, turning it hazy and reducing visibility. Boxer was bobbing his head in irritation. As he wiped gunk out of his eyes for the millionth time, Trader realized that the storm was catching up to him faster than he had originally calculated. With a sinking feeling, he understood they couldn't outrun this one. They'd need to find shelter immediately and wait out the storm. A few miles ahead, there was an old, abandoned warehouse complex. He'd try his luck there and see if they could find a place to safely hunker down.

They made it to the W. Patterson Pass Rd. exit just as things were starting to get nasty. Sasha was already crouched back in the wagon. Trader had to pull a cloth kerchief over his nose to breathe better and squint to see. Boxer was practically trotting, sensing the urgency to find shelter.

The warehouse complex was an old Costco distribution center and meat packing plant. It had been stupidly built in a depression to the right of the highway between two parallel water canals: the Delta Mendota Canal and California Aqueduct. This led to regular flooding of the area. A thick layer of cracked, dried dirt had settled over the pre-existing asphalt. Many of the buildings were severely damaged and falling apart, often with dry mud caking the surfaces. Garbage and debris, carried there by the flooding, lay in heaps around the complex.

A couple of years ago, Trader had found shelter in one of the more intact buildings. He hoped it was structurally still safe enough to weather the dust storm. The storm had gotten so bad that he could barely see through the light brown haze as sand nipped at his exposed skin. He got out of the wagon and led Boxer through the structures, hunched over and face tilted away from the brunt of the biting wind. Fortunately, the building he had stayed in before was still standing and looked fairly intact.

THE BEFORE AND THE AFTER

The building had been a distribution warehouse in the Before, with a long loading dock. A large ramp, wide enough for the wagon, led from the parking lot to the dock. Rolling doors stood closed along its length, with thick layers of dried mud sealing them shut.

Trader led Boxer and the wagon up the ramp, kicking away any garage or debris as fast as he could as the wind picked up speed. Once on the dock, he got a short-handed shovel from the wagon to dig the caked dirt away from the rolling door. The dust storm was getting worse, lashing painful pinpricks against his skin and he had to squint to see. Boxer whinnied nervously. The light dimmed significantly, the dust reflecting any escaped rays and turning the sky scarlet. With the dirt seal broken away, he rolled the door up and led the wagon into the warehouse. The door clanged closed behind them and shut them into semi-darkness.

Despite being mid-day, the storm blocked most of the sun, and it looked like dusk inside the building. The sand made a scraping sound that echoed through the empty building as the wind scoured the exterior. Boxer whickered and shook his mane. Trader fumbled to unhitch Boxer in the gloom. The leather was gritty from the dust. He brushed his hand along Boxer, releasing thick layers of dirt from his coat. The wagon was going to be a mess.

Trader set out Sasha's bowl and Boxer's bucket, filling them with water from the wagon. He grabbed a few sips for himself. The wind was rough and had dehydrated him quickly. He fruitlessly tried to brush off his arms and his pants.

The damn dust is going to be everywhere now, he thought dejectedly.

Trader sat on the back of the wagon, staring out into the emptiness of the warehouse, and weighed his options. The warehouse was row after row of bare metal shelves, and every motion any of them made echoed loudly despite the raging storm

113

outside. The layers of dried mud on the floor did nothing to dampen the sound.

He wondered when the people of Before had decided to give up on this place. It was difficult to tell whether flooding or the chronic supply chain issues had turned these buildings into empty skeletons. He figured it was probably a death by a thousand cuts, like just about everything else in the After. The building depressed him.

Trader sighed; he'd have to stay until the storm was over. The last mile or so before they had found shelter had worn them all down. Even if the storm decided to stop right at this moment, Boxer would need to rest before attempting the Altamont Pass to Live More.

In the back of the wagon, there was a bag of oats that he reserved for emergencies just like this. Boxer whickered in appreciation, quickly gobbling them up. Brush in hand, Trader did his best to try to get the bulk of the dirt off Boxer. After Trader shook out his own hair, he then used the brush to have another go at the dust layered on his clothes. He knew it would take a dip in some water and a serious deep clean of the wagon to get the grit out of everything.

While he had been checking on Boxer, Sasha had wandered off to investigate the building. By the time Trader was done, she returned with a mouse in her mouth. Trader wondered how the creature had survived in this barren landscape. There was no way in hell he would ever stay here.

Sasha quickly ate the entire mouse in front of him and then gave him a look. *You didn't share all of your jerky and you dragged me through that storm so I'm not sharing.*

Trader laughed softly to himself. After a slightly resentful stare, Sasha hopped into the wagon, quickly brushed her tail against him, and proceeded to take a bath.

The gloom in the warehouse persisted with the wind whistling outside and the sand pelting the metal of the building.

THE BEFORE AND THE AFTER

Trader pulled out his book, but the light wasn't enough to read by. Frustrated, he decided to eat and then cursed himself as he crunched on grit in his dried fruit. His skin felt grimy, and his mosquito bites itched.

This fucking sucks.

He laid down in the back of the wagon, hoping to at least kill time with a nap. He tossed and turned. Having reached her maximum amount of annoyance, Sasha left the wagon in disgust. Lying uncomfortably with the wind wailing outside, Trader finally fell asleep.

* * *

After anindiscernible amount of time, Trader awoke with a start, surprised he had been able to sleep. His skin still felt gritty, his eyes were dry, and he was thirsty. The wind had died down, and it seemed brighter in the warehouse. He hopped out of the wagon, rolled up the door, and walked out on the dock.

The storm was over. A thick layer of fresh dust coated the complex, covering the tracks they had surely left on their frantic flight to the shelter. The sky was clear and everything was still. Unfortunately, the sun was just about to kiss the hills to the west. There was only a short window of daylight left.

"Fuck," Trader said quietly.

He was grateful that the warehouse had sheltered Sasha, Boxer, and him through the storm. But it was not a place he wanted to hang out and spend the night. There was no easy access to water, no food for Boxer, and it was creepy in that vast cavern of a building with just the three of them. He decided to cut his losses, try to turn in early, and leave first thing in the morning.

As he turned back to the building, he abruptly stopped short. To the left of the row of rolling doors was a smaller, pedestrian door. A large arc had been scraped out of the cracked dirt in the

115

ground at its foot. Only a very thin layer of dust coated the carved-out surface. Goosebumps tickled across his arms.

Trader didn't care about the simple fact that the door had been opened and closed. It was the symbol painted on the door that made the hairs stand up on the back of his neck. At eye level, there were three dots arranged in a triangle shape crowned with five radiating lines. The symbol had been painted in what looked like blood and ash. It was Preacher's symbol. He was sure of it. Trader had missed it when he was scrambling to get the wagon in the warehouse during the storm earlier.

You see that, get the fuck out of there, Liluye whispered in his head.

Trader's muscles tensed. He looked around the dock and out towards the other buildings. Warehouse skeletons glared back at him with no sign of life. But with the damn dust storm, it was possible that recent tracks had been erased and the group was hunkered down somewhere. Heart racing, he dashed inside.

Boxer was still standing lazily next to the wagon, relaxed as ever. Trader paused to listen and was answered with silence. As much as the sound bounced around this place, he expected to hear something if anyone else was in there with him. His gut still twisted anxiously.

Ben said that he had seen Preacher's group go by the Nakamuras' about a month ago. It was possible that Preacher had just passed through Tracy and moved on. There was fuck all here for them, and they weren't carrying packs. But Preacher had surprised Trader at every turn, often making risky decisions. For all Trader knew, the group could still be here.

Trader grabbed his knife from the wagon and paused again, listening. Only the sound of Boxer shifting his weight answered him. The large building was dim, and the far corners were hidden in darkness. He'd need to walk the perimeter of the inside of the building to completely clear it. As he neared the inside of the pedestrian door, the faint outline of a pile of ashes came into focus. He clenched the knife tighter.

It was obvious Preacher's group had been here. Trader hadn't noticed the smell of residual smoke when they barreled in earlier, and only a faint hint of it was present now. His mind whirled as his palms grew sweaty. How long ago had Preacher and his group passed through here? How the hell did they find any wood to light a fire in this fucking wasteland? Even if they found something to burn, what idiot would light a fire inside a building with no ventilation?

The same idiot who would burn the dead in the middle of a dry field, Trader thought glumly.

He moved closer to the ash pile to investigate it in the dim light. There were scuff marks and footprints of different sizes. The dirt on the floor near the ash pile was smudged, likely representing where they had rested. Trailing from the ash pile were several drops of dried blood that formed a path back to the door. Trader's stomach flopped.

Trader peered around the inside of the building again. The space still *felt* abandoned. He walked the remainder of the building just to be sure, footsteps echoing loudly. After circling back to the wagon, he hadn't found any evidence that the group had been anywhere in the building other than near the fire. Trader closed his eyes, doing one last sensory check. The place felt empty. He was pretty sure they had stopped at some point and then moved on.

It was going to suck enough as it was trying to sleep in the warehouse tonight, with grit grinding in every damn crevice of his body. Having the taint of Preacher on this place only made it worse. Trader decided to try to get a few hours of sleep and leave as early as possible in the morning.

After confirming that Sasha was back in the wagon, Trader buttoned things up for the night. The small pedestrian door had a push lock on the handle, which he engaged. Then, he closed the large rolling door with a rattling sound. There was only a useless key lock on the rolling door, but Trader was certain the noise of the door opening would wake him up at night.

    Though Trader was sick to his stomach, he forced himself to eat a quick, just-for-calories meal. He undressed, sick of the grimy clothes, and tried to get comfortable in his bedroll, grit still chafing against his skin. He fell asleep gripping the knife under his pillow.

CHAPTER
FOURTEEN

Trader woke up grumpy, scraping the crust away from his dry eyes. The grit on his skin and in his bedroll chafed. He had tossed and turned all night just waiting until there was enough light to get back on the road. As soon as he could see enough to move around, he got ready to go. He briefly debated putting on a fresh pair of clothes and decided to stick with the gritty ones from yesterday. Everything was already miserable this morning, and a fresh pair of clothes wouldn't change that fact.

He'd never before experienced a dust storm that severe. The storms usually built up in the dead zone of the San Joaquin Valley and pushed east. Any storm that happened to move far enough north petered down to a dim, yellow haze by the time it reached Sacramento, dampened by the bay and the city's tree canopy. The Nakamuras were veterans at making it through storms like this one. Trader was not, and all of the dry grit gnawed at his nerves. The threat of Preacher only made everything worse.

He stepped outside with his knife tucked in his waistband. A thick layer of sandy dust coated everything like snow, and a haze obscured his view to the south. However, the sky in Tracy was clear, and the air was still. Though the storm was over, Trader was still on edge. To get his head on straight, he needed a good rinse and a full night's rest away from the marked building. Eager to get to Live More, he hitched up the wagon and hit the road.

The 580 over the Altamont Pass was relatively intact, with minimal flood damage. There was minor wear and tear, but it was otherwise a smooth ride. Trader was thankful. After the stress of the dust storm, they could use a break. Trader walked next to the wagon, trying to make things easier for Boxer as he pulled the heavy cargo up the incline.

Gradually, the dry cracked earth and scrub brush of the valley transitioned to grassland spotted with old oaks. This time of year, the grass was a lush green. The Diablo Range lacked any visible burn scars on this side of the pass. This little patch of heaven had made it through the winter unscathed.

The sun's gentle rays trickled down on them. Jackrabbits occasionally sped across the road, white tails flashing. A red-tailed hawk sat patiently on an old fence post, waiting for the right moment to pounce. Hovering over the grass, a white-tailed kite swooped down quickly to catch its prey. A female American kestrel perched on an old barbed wire fence. There must have been plenty of smaller prey, such as deer mice and ground squirrels, rustling about in the grasses to support so many predators.

As Trader entered the lush hills, he felt the stress and anxiety of the dust storm start to ebb away. Despite the lack of restful sleep and the road being steep at some points, the exercise energized him. He loved this segment of the circuit, with its spectacular views and abundant wildlife. He wasn't going to let last night ruin it for him. He inhaled the fresh scent of the clear air. It was a serene passage, and he felt himself slowly recenter.

The tops of the hills were crowned by large windmills from the Before. Many of them spun lazily in the gentle breeze. With the grid down, the windmills spun without purpose, skeletons of a time when electricity was considered essential. A couple of the windmills were missing a blade; the fallen pieces lay crumpled at the base like amputated limbs.

As the trio crested the pass, they stopped for a late lunch. Trader rested Boxer, unhitching him to let him graze. He grabbed his canteen, some dried fruit, and some nuts and settled into the driver's seat, looking down into the valley and towards Live More.

This side of the pass was more verdant than the easterly side since the hills caught the clouds rolling in from the ocean and collected more water. Large oak trees were plentiful, forming multiple dense copses. To Trader's delight, he saw a herd of wild horses grazing in the distance. The caws of crows sounded across the hills.

At the base of the pass, the Before city of Livermore unfolded out into the valley, the taller buildings protruding from the still, murky water. Several creeks had carved ravines in the hills that led towards the spillways and retention ponds to control flooding in the Before. Now, the creeks fed the large lake that had enveloped Livermore and the nearby town of Pleasanton.

Just east of the old city and a tad up the hillside was the cozy settlement of Live More. The settlement consisted of a tight cluster of a dozen homes that sat adjacent to a nature preserve. Because they had ready access to water, the settlement was surrounded by lush farmland, including a vineyard. Live More boasted a population of fourteen and was run by a small council with a rotating membership. The people there were relaxed and friendly. Trader was looking forward to the company, a warm meal, and a chance to wash the last of the dust storm away.

Thinking about the storm led to the memory of Preacher's stain on the warehouse. Now looming in the forefront of Trader's mind, bitter thoughts of Preacher replaced what little peace he had found coming over the pass. Trader was fairly certain

Preacher's group had passed this way since it was the only direction to go without circling back to the other settlements. Would he find Preacher in Live More? Or had the group simply walked past the settlement as they had with the Nakamuras'?

Preacher and his followers surely needed water and food after reaching the other side of the pass. Live More screamed abundance to anyone heading that way, and the settlement was ripe for the taking. Trader would be surprised if Live More remained untouched by Preacher and his group.

His stomach clenched as his mind whirled with a myriad of plausible scenarios. Had Preacher converted the entire settlement? Trader didn't think that was likely given what he knew of the people there. Had he gathered just a few followers and moved on, his group bigger now? Possibly. Had he brought disease there? Also possible. The only thing that gave Trader a modicum of solace was the fact that he could see with his own eyes that Preacher hadn't burned the place down.

Trader was irritated that Preacher's taint was on everything. Ever since Lodi, this season had been off-kilter, and Preacher's influence was like a painful burr he couldn't get out of his sock. Not knowing what he would find at Live More just made him more irritated and anxious.

Restless, Trader decided it was time to finish up lunch and move on. He hitched the wagon back up and called Sasha. Now that the wagon was headed downhill and Boxer would have an easier go of it, Trader hopped back in the driver's seat. He chewed the inside of his cheek as they neared the settlement.

About five miles out, Trader noticed turkey vultures circling high above, riding the thermals. He slowed Boxer down, assessing the situation. Vultures could be seen circling above even the smallest of dead critters. However, they were definitely circling over Live More itself and not the adjacent farmland. The homes were visible through the surrounding trees and appeared undamaged. The surrounding crops also looked planted. Everything appeared normal, except for the damn vultures.

It wasn't until he got to the Laughlin Rd. exit that the truth of what happened became clear. Trader pulled the wagon to a stop. In the middle of the road leading to the settlement, the word "Weeps" was spelled out in fist-sized rocks, blocking the road and impossible to miss. Trader's stomach dropped. Now he understood why the vultures were circling.

Worry creasing his forehead, Trader weighed his options. The settlement was obviously off-limits. He didn't know if everyone was dead, or if there were survivors, if they had decided to stick it out or move on. Either way, he needed to put some miles between this place and himself. Pronto. There was a ton of standing water around here. With active Weeps cases in this area, his chances of picking it up increased a hundredfold.

One option would be to head back up the mountain and stay the night in the upper hills. Boxer had already dragged the wagon over the pass, and it would be a lot to ask him to drag it back up again. No easy roads led north or south from here. The only other option was to push west and try to get to the other side of Pleasanton before dark. That would take another three to four hours at least. If he pushed it, he could clear the flooded parts before dusk and camp on the highway in Dublin. He chose the lesser of the two evils and decided to press forward since he had to go that way anyway.

Trader clicked and swished the reins, urging Boxer westerly. He decided to hop out of the wagon to lighten the load and set a swift pace. Boxer, sensing that something was up, automatically quickened his gait. His ears flicked back, and his tail swished.

There was significant damage to the 580 along the stretch that ran through Livermore. Just inside the city, the Arroyo Las Positas flowed down from the hills and crossed under the highway. Though the road wasn't currently underwater, there was evidence of previous flooding and a mudslide. A layer of smooth, semisoft mud about a foot deep coated the bridge and adjacent asphalt. Animal tracks from an opossum or a raccoon dotted the edge of the mudflow on the near side of the bridge. Trader contemplated backtracking and taking an exit to go around this section of highway. But the city to the south sat in water about three to four feet deep, and the north was bordered by a steep hillside. He also needed to hustle to get through the wet parts before dusk hit and the mosquitos came out.

The best option was to slog through the semisoft layer of mud and hope nothing nasty was hiding beneath the surface. The last thing he needed was for one of them to step on something sharp. He couldn't risk Boxer going lame this far from any settlements, not to mention the threat of infection. Trader clicked and nudged Boxer to keep going, moving to the back of the wagon to push from behind.

It was a very slow slog through the mud, but they made it through the section without physical injury. Mud coated Trader's new shoes and was spattered up on his pants. Thick layers of mud also coated Boxer's legs to above the fetlock. As Boxer swatted his tail around irritably, mud from the tip of his tail flicked onto his flank. Sasha sat daintily in the driver's seat, clean as a whistle, watching them work.

After making it through the affected stretch of road, Trader quickly watered Boxer and drank from his canteen before pressing on. He anxiously followed the course of the sun as it tipped toward the western horizon. Right now, it was hot enough that the mosquitoes weren't out. There wasn't much time left, though.

Up ahead, Cayetano Creek passed under the freeway from the hills. Despite the surrounding city being flooded with a few feet of water, the road was mostly spared. Boxer's hooves echoed on the bridge, his gait uneven from exhaustion. Trader muscles were shaky, and he hadn't worked nearly as hard as Boxer. He was worried about him.

THE BEFORE AND THE AFTER

After another mile or so, a deep lake opened up to the south of the highway. Brown murky water spilled over into the road in some places, gently lapping at the edges. The surface was slick with a thick layer of oil, and it smelled of rotting plant material. Arcing rows of garbage formed a border. Fortunately, the highway remained passable, and they hustled past the lake.

On the western edge of the lake, Pleasanton and Dublin could be seen stretching to the south and the west. The last time Trader had been through here, he hadn't seen anybody. People could've been hiding out in the unflooded parts of either city. However, the chance of catching Weeps was too great being this close to a flood zone and standing water. He suspected any stragglers had gone to Live More or moved north or south up the 680. Further west was a wash. The sea levels had risen so high that most of the coast was underwater in that direction.

The road was empty and lonely, with the sounds of their passing echoing off the empty buildings that hugged the highway. It was like tiptoeing over a skeleton. Trader couldn't wait to get out of this place.

* * *

At the intersection of the 580 and 680, Trader was fairly confident that he was far enough from Live More and any standing water to be relatively safe. Or, at least, as safe as one could be in the After. The highway at this point sat flush with the surrounding ground. At the sweet spot where the two highways crossed, there was a small sanctuary to graze Boxer in the center of the loops formed by the on/off ramps. The light was slowly fading as the sun set, and they had made it just in time.

Finally having a moment to breathe, a wave of anguish hit Trader. He wouldn't know for sure what happened to everyone in Live More until next year, but the thought of losing an entire settlement to Weeps crushed him. The moments of joy, like

125

seeing Izumi a year older and meeting the pregnant couple on the 99, were always overshadowed by the constant loss of life. At moments like these, depression weighed heavy, and doubt crept in.

Why do I even bother, he thought.

Dejected, he stopped the wagon on the highway and went through the motions of getting Boxer brushed down. The mud had dried on his fetlocks like glue, and Trader couldn't get it off. Frustrated, he finally gave up. Taking care of Boxer usually grounded him. Not today. He couldn't shrug off the heavy weight of what he had seen at Live More.

Leaning his head against Boxer's neck, Trader scratched his mane.

"Thanks for your hard work today, old man."

Boxer whickered, bobbing his head slightly. Trader released him, and the horse headed over to the tall grass, his gait stiff. The rush over the pass and through the flooded city had been hard on the guy.

Trader contemplated building a fire to bring some comfort into what had been a fairly depressing and miserable day. Only having a small amount of wood in his wagon, he decided to suck it up and eat a cold meal of preserves and nuts. His thoughts wandered back longingly to the wonderful meal he had at the Nakamuras'.

After he finished up, he did his best to get out of his clothes and shoes without getting dried mud everywhere. The wagon was already filthy enough from the dust storm in the valley. He didn't want to make it any worse with clumps of mud. He looked sadly at his new boots, hoping that a bit of washing followed by some oil and TLC would get them looking new again.

He was fully settled in by the time the sun set. Once again, he kept Sasha in the wagon with him, and the canvas flaps tied closed. He was pretty sure Boxer would be safe. Mountain lions weren't seen this far into town. There were coyotes, though, and he could already hear them yipping. Along with the threat of great horned owls, he just felt better keeping Sasha inside. After feeding her a few pieces of jerky to keep her content, she snuggled in next to him purring. He quickly fell into an exhausted, dreamless sleep.

CHAPTER
FIFTEEN

The sunlight pouring in through the slim space between the closed wagon flaps woke Trader. After the hike over the pass and the race through the flooded areas, he'd slept like a log. He'd made it through the bog of a city by the skin of his teeth with no new mosquito bites.

Sasha made a *merf* noise as Trader stretched under the covers, trying to loosen his stiff calves and rotating his ankles. Loud purring rumbled from her chest when she noticed he was awake. He gave her a few pets, taking the time to be in the moment and enjoy her company. After sufficient snuggles, her ladyship was off to grab breakfast.

Trader dressed in his stiff, dirty clothes. With his feet hanging out over the wagon, he knocked his boots together. Clumps of dried mud rained down. It was an unpleasant reminder of yesterday. He closed his eyes, breathing deeply, trying to keep the ugly thoughts at bay.

Boxer whickered softly when Trader ran his hand along the horse's neck and down his back. He was relieved to see the horse more relaxed and looking less sore. He scratched his mane affectionately. Boxer shifted his weight, knocking one hoof up on the tip, and swished his tail.

"Should be a short run today, bud," Trader said. He was glad Walnut Creek was close. They would stay a night or two there, letting Boxer fully recuperate.

Breakfast was more nuts and preserves. The same food over and over was getting boring, and he was looking forward to having a warm meal again. He sat on the back of the wagon, munching away, swinging his legs, and watching Sasha stalk through the grass. She quickly pounced and proudly brought back a dead mouse.

Mer? Sasha meowed inquisitively around a mouthful of mouse, looking at Trader.

He laughed. "No thanks. All yours."

She proceeded to devour the mouse, finishing up right about when Trader did, and joined him in the wagon. He leaned back on his arms and looked out towards Dublin.

This was a depressing part of the circuit. With the repeated flooding and proximity to the retention ponds, the entire city had been vacated long ago. Coyotes now ruled the dilapidated buildings. Despite being canids, they were resistant to Weeps, unlike their domesticated cousins. Their populations had exploded as the number of people declined.

A tall, faded Target sign sat high on a building in a derelict mall. He wondered what it was like walking into places like that in the Before. Carla had talked about shelves overflowing with more than anyone could possibly want. Some of that stuff had traveled thousands of miles and across oceans in the Before. He couldn't even comprehend that distance. He also couldn't fathom not growing your own stuff, especially the simple crops like zucchini that actually took effort to kill. Why would anyone *buy* zucchini?

The idea of even buying something was a foreign concept. About thirty years ago, Weeps had hammered the final nail into the financial system's coffin, and people turned to trading instead. Having been born after the fall, Trader only had a theoretical understanding of money. Though he had read about the economy during the Before, it was hard for him to wrap his head around the idea that the action of doing work created digital numbers in some nebulous place. Those numbers could be moved around into another place so someone could just take stuff home from a store like Target. The idea blew his mind.

Shaking off the bemused feeling, Trader decided it was time to get going. Walnut Creek was the nicest settlement on his circuit. It would take him about half a day to get there with a lunch stop, assuming the 680 wasn't a mess. He was looking forward to his arrival. After seeing what he presumed was the fall of Live More, he was a bit nervous. But Walnut Creek was dialed-in to weather just about anything the After could throw at it.

Except for Weeps, Trader thought bitterly. *No place is safe from that shit. And maybe Preacher.*

Trader kicked himself for so easily slipping back to negative thoughts.

Trying to distract himself, he went about hitching Boxer up. Sasha was already in her cat bed taking a post-meal bath when he climbed into the driver's seat. He gave her a scratch, grateful to have her by his side, and flapped the reins.

The 680 was nestled between two tall mounds of hills. It would've been picturesque but, in the After, this place was a death trap. Because the highway sat in a valley, it routinely flooded. Large burn scars attested to the raging fires that regularly swept across the hills. Burned-out husks of mansions sat on hillsides like tombstones. Large chunks were missing from the hills, evidence of previous mudslides.

In spite of it all, nature kept pouring back in. The grass was starting to fill in over the burn scars. Yellow, orange, and purple flowers painted the hillsides with their spring blooms. The trees that had survived this year's fires and floods were now covered in leaves. As the trio moved north, yellow pollen dusted the roads and small, white flowers dotted the evergreen pear trees that stood in the old residential areas.

Off to his right, Mount Diablo stood tall and proud. Large oaks formed thick layers up the mountain, with pine trees and maples mixed in. Raptors were slowly riding the air currents off in the distance. On a clear day, Trader could see the mountain all the way from Sacramento. This close, it loomed before him.

Rumor had it that some of the roads up the large mountain were passable, and one could still get fairly close to the top. He often toyed with the idea of making a short side trip to do just that. He had never been up that high and suspected the view from the top was incredible. To make the steep trip, he would have to leave the wagon behind, and probably Boxer and Sasha too, which he just hadn't had the nerve to do yet. He certainly wasn't going to do it this year with traces of Preacher everywhere along the circuit. The trip to the peak stayed on his bucket list for another season.

Between San Ramon and Danville, he stopped the wagon to rest Boxer and have lunch. Once out of the wagon, he stretched his sore muscles before rooting around for food. As he pulled his provisions from the wagon, he noticed someone far off in the distance heading towards him on the 680. Based on the rig, he was almost certain it was Jesse. A huge smile stretched across his face.

"Hot damn!" Trader said with delight. Jesse brought sunshine with them everywhere. Trader thanked his lucky stars that they'd crossed paths today. He needed a dose of Jesse's cheer.

Jesse was astride their horse with a refurbished, single-person, pop-up camper trailing behind. The set-up was well-worn but otherwise in good repair and had served them well on their travels. Jesse ran roughly the same circuit that Trader did but in reverse, starting from Vacaville.

THE BEFORE AND THE AFTER

Working the route in opposite directions helped spread the goods more evenly between the settlements. It also reduced the need to store too many items over the winter. Trader looked forward to their time together when their paths crossed on the road. Especially this year. It had been a rough season so far.

Jesse was over six feet tall and lean with green eyes and blond hair pulled back in a low ponytail. Trader guessed Jesse was close to his age; about twenty or so. They were wearing a blue, cotton poncho and loose slacks. Jesse rode bare-back on a thickly woven horse blanket. Their legs were stretched wide over their horse's broad back with flip-flops dangling from their feet. Trader smiled to himself. Only Jesse could rock a pair of flip-flops when riding a horse.

Jesse's horse was a dark brown Belgian named Delilah. Boxer, recognizing his buddy, whinnied softly in greeting. Delilah whinnied back; ears perked forward.

"Whoa," Jesse said kindly to Delilah when they were side-by-side with Trader. Jesse hopped down to give Trader a big hug.

"Well met, Trader!" Jesse said with a broad grin on their face. "It's wonderful to see you!"

"Great seeing you too, Jesse. How's trading been?"

"It's been fantastic," Jesse answered. "I just came from Walnut Creek. Things are bopping along there. As per usual, they snatched up almost all of the food and just about cleaned me out. But don't worry, they'll still clean you out too, I'm sure. A lot of people to feed with not a lot of workable land around there."

"Yes, indeed," Trader agreed.

He stepped back, holding Jesse's shoulders affectionately.

"It's really great to see you."

They hugged again.

"How are things further up the circuit?" Trader asked, grinning ear to ear, happiness filling him at the sight of his good friend.

133

"Great," Jesse answered, grinning back. "Wild Bluff and Gold Bug did fairly well over the winter. Gold Bug lost a few, but they're still trucking. Les and Rodger are fab. The Machados…ohhh…" Jesse's eyes got wide, and Trader could practically see the lightbulb. They smiled conspiratorially with one eyebrow raised. "Have you eaten lunch yet?"

"Not yet, but just about to. You?" Trader answered, going with the flow. Jesse's happy thoughts often bounced around, racing between topics. It was part of their charm.

Jesse gave Trader a mischievous smile. They popped up the trailer, dug around, and reverently cradled a cloth-wrapped lump in both hands like it was the holy grail.

"I did save some stuff from the locusts at Walnut Creek," they said and flicked back the cloth with a flare to expose a perfectly baked loaf of wheat bread. The crust was golden brown and crispy. Jesse lifted it to their nose, taking a deep sniff, and letting out an exaggerated *ahhhhh* of contentment.

"Holy shit!" Trader exclaimed, eyes wide. "Where did you get *that*?"

"The Machados'," Jesse answered, swaddling the loaf back up and handing it to Trader. "If we'll be a bit, let me get Delilah out of that contraption. Give me a sec."

After placing the bread on the wagon seat, they both went about unhitching their horses, who greeted each other with friendly nose bumps and ear flicks. Sasha, recognizing Jesse, started circling their legs, meowing. Jesse picked her up, cradling her and scratching her head. Sasha headbutted Jesse's chin in affection and started purring so loudly that Trader could hear it. He smiled, happy to see one of his favorite people getting cuddles from his year-round buddy.

As Jesse continued cooing at Sasha, Trader grabbed some almond butter and strawberry jelly. He sliced thick sections of the precious loaf with his knife.

"I still can't believe you have bread." He shook his head, thrilled. "Thank you for sharing."

"Anything for you, sweetie pie." Jesse grinned again. They sat down in the driver's seat, squishing the cat bed between them. Jesse put Sasha down, petting her until she settled in a meatloaf in her bed. Trader handed Jesse some of the butter and jelly-smeared bread.

They sat companionably on the wagon seat, eating sandwiches and enjoying the sunshine. Trader couldn't remember the last time he ate a sandwich made with wheat bread. His mouth watered in anticipation of each bite, the earthy smell of the wheat combining with the sweet smell of the strawberry jelly. He sighed and smiled happily.

"It's great seeing you, Jesse. It's been rough this year." Trader was surprised to feel his eyes start to water. He blinked back the tears.

Jesse patted him on the leg reassuringly.

"Great seeing you too, bud."

A comfortable silence stretched between them as they ate. Sasha sat attentively at their side, snarfing down bits of the bread that Jesse snuck her. She was definitely spoiled. Jesse was always generous, and Trader appreciated every bite of the precious bread they shared.

"Thanks again. This is delicious."

Jesse grinned with their full mouth and cheeks puffed out. Bringing people joy made them happy, and Trader could see it written all over their face.

Curious, Trader asked, "How're the Machados making wheat bread?"

"They converted the space on the other side of the road from the goat pasture. They were grazing the goats on it for a bit and then thought about just turning it into a field to grow grain. After the harvest, they could turn the goats back out on it. I guess it was a bitch getting water to it and finding seeds and all. But Nari miracled it." Jesse took another large bite, leaving a small smear of jam on their cheek.

"It's a shit ton of work," they continued. "I guess they harvest, separate, and grind it all by hand. This was just a test year. Not sure if they'll ramp up production or not." Jesse pursed their lips, thinking. "Speaking of which, keep your eye out for any books on homesteading or wheat farming or whatever. I think they want to try to build some stuff to make it easier and all."

"Will do," Trader nodded. "Those kinda books are worth more than gold, but I'll try. The cotton is coming along at the Silvas' too. I took some drawings of the looms. They taught me to spin and weave a bit and even shared some seeds. Gilberto and Liluye are looking for an apprentice. Pass the word."

"On it," Jesse said, nodding slightly back. They looked up at the hills and swallowed another bite before saying, "Kinda cool seeing the settlements build up like that, ain't it?"

"Yeah." Trader sighed. "But it's been strikes and gutters this year. On the upside, Forty Two has a shoemaker now. A former Singleton."

"No shit?!" Jesse was gobsmacked.

"Yeah, I know, right?" He kicked his dirty boot out. "I know they don't look great. I got caught in a mudslide. But these boots are awesome. I'll give 'em a good wash and shine at Walnut Creek."

"Those are dope. I hope they have a pair my size. I love my flip-flops, but a pair of boots would be great for the winter." Jesse nodded appreciatively at his shoes.

"The Nakamuras are doing great. Grab some leather there for the shoemaker, and I am sure Rosa will love you even more than she already does. I plan on saving some to bring to Forty Two next year, but they would appreciate some sooner than that I bet."

"Thanks for the tip."

THE BEFORE AND THE AFTER

Trader paused, mulling over the best way to share the rest of the news. Jesse was a bucket of joy, and Trader always felt cheered after they crossed paths. Even though he knew it would dampen the mood, he still needed to warn Jesse about what awaited them further along the circuit.

"I don't want to be a total downer, but there's some bad stuff that I gotta tell you about."

Sensing the seriousness of what Trader was about to share, Jesse's friendly sunshine smile finally dipped and their shoulders drooped. "Oh no."

"I don't know if anyone is even alive at Live More or not. I didn't check. There's a Weeps warning there. I hustled through that spot pretty fast. You might want to stay the night just north of Dublin with a plan on pushing over the pass in one quick trip. There's a mudslide blocking part of the 580, too."

Jesse dropped their head, thinking, and started bouncing one leg up and down. "I can tell by the way you're talking that there's more."

"There was a pretty nasty dust storm reaching all the way up to Tracy," Trader continued. "I guess that's always a risk, but this time it was bad and set us back a day. Heading along the 132 is still worth it, in my humble opinion, because the Nakamuras are good people, have excellent trades, and have been sparse in the visitor arena lately."

Jesse liked helping people, running the circuit to be of service to others more than anything else. They would brave hellfire and brimstone to make sure the settlements stayed connected. He could tell by the resolute look on Jesse's face that they would be stopping at the Nakamuras' no matter what awaited them on the other side of the pass.

Trader took a swig out of the canteen, trying to buy himself a moment to collect his thoughts before he continued. "Look now, Jesse. What I gotta tell you next is just rumors and all."

"We live by gossip, dude," Jesse said, chewing on their lower lip. Their leg kept moving up and down, slightly shaking the wagon. Trader hated making them so uneasy.

"Gilberto and Liluye told me a pretty ominous story. I didn't see anything first-hand. But I trust them."

"No doubt. I trust them too."

"They said that late last fall, this Preacher guy showed up all skin and bones, with no supplies. They decide to take him in."

"Of course they did," Jesse interrupted. "Gilberto and all of them are awesome."

Trader nodded. "The story goes that Preacher had a group in Lodi. After being at the Silvas' for a while, it came out that everyone in Lodi had died. Preacher had tried to burn the bodies and ended up incinerating the entire fucking town."

Jesse sucked their teeth, looking up at Trader sharply. The bobbing leg stopped momentarily and then picked back up again.

"Yeah, I know, right? After he'd been at the Silvas' a bit, he started preaching. He was saying that he rose from blood and ash like a phoenix. Lonely? God has an answer for that. Feeling lost? God will give you purpose." Trader snorted and then shrugged. "I guess the message worked because Preacher left the Silvas' with Bryson and Maria in tow. The whole thing made Liluye nervous enough to be packing."

"Where did they go when they left?"

"The Nakamuras said they saw the group pass by without packs or anything. Preacher's group didn't even stop for water or food. They just walked right by the Nakamuras' without even a wave."

"Holy cow. That is crazy." Jesse shook their head in disbelief. "There's nothing out that way. Did they make it to another settlement?"

"No clue." Trader shrugged and sighed. "The next place was Live More, and well…I couldn't stop there to figure out what happened. Anyway, be careful out on the road. I haven't seen Preacher, but he has a symbol like this." Trader mimed drawing three dots arranged in a triangle capped by five vertical lines on the wagon seat.

"I've seen that!" Jesse blurted, back now straight and leg still again. "Just north on the 680 on an old road sign. Looked like it was drawn with ash mixed with blood. Never seen nothing like that. Freaked me out."

Trader went still, looking up at Jesse.

"Did you see anybody walking north on the road?" Trader asked. "How about someone dressed all in white with that symbol on their forehead in Walnut Creek or anywhere else?"

"Nah," Jess answered, leg picking back with the bouncing up again. "This year's been real quiet and lonely. I haven't seen hardly anyone on the road at all, much less this dude. Haven't seen no one like that in Walnut Creek or at the Machados' either."

"That's probably a good thing. Just be safe, all right?"

"I will," Jesse said with a serious tone. "You too. Sounds like you have a better chance of crossing paths with him than I do."

Seeing Jesse uncharacteristically stressed only amplified Trader's concern. It also made him feel bad for being the bearer of bad news. Jesse was such a wonderful person, he hated dimming their sunshine even a tad.

Jesse looked down, fidgeting with a piece of bread. After a lengthy pause, they asked, "Is he really that dangerous? I'm just kinda surprised. People don't do that kinda stuff no more. There aren't a lot of us left. We gotta work together."

"Having never met the guy, I can't say for sure. But I trust Liluye and Gilberto. They seemed worried and warned me. Plus, I saw Lodi with my own eyes. That was no joke. The dude burned down an entire city, leaving nine corpses behind." He felt a fresh flood of guilt for freaking Jesse out.

Jesse nodded, biting their lip again.

"Sometimes I wonder if it's all worth it. I love being on the road, talking to different people, seeing different places, and stuff. But each year there are fewer and fewer people, with almost no babies no more. It feels like one year, we'll go out, and there won't be nobody left." Jesse paused, looking out over the hills. "I didn't use to get so lonely, but this last year has been rough. I've been toying with the idea of joining a settlement. But I know that those same settlements need people like you and me moving between them. To, like, connect everybody and stuff."

Trader nodded slowly, chewing on his cheek. "After I saw Live More, I started asking myself the same thing. It's like we're swimming upstream."

Jesse took a deep breath and started petting Sasha.

Straightening their back, they said, "We gotta keep on going for them. Running these circuits. Connecting these places. Maybe, if we do that, we can start seeing more people again, like kids and stuff. Maybe we can crawl our way out of this crap hand we've been dealt by the people from the Before and keep the damn human race alive." Jesse paused, worrying at the edge of their poncho.

With a heavy exhale, Jesse slapped their hands on their legs. "Whelp, on that happy fucking note…want some more bread?" They held a slice out with a wide grin, trying to dispel the tension.

With the warning out of the way, Trader tried to put the thoughts of Preacher to the side and enjoy the last bit of time he had with Jesse before they parted ways for the season. The conversation shifted to lighter topics as they shared what was up for trade on either end of the circuit and what people were looking for. They swapped stories about Delilah and Boxer and shared some packing tips.

After a bit, Jesse said, "I wish I could stay longer, but I'm sure you wanna get up to Walnut Creek. And I'd like to get a bit further down the road and tuck in early before the trek on the 580 tomorrow."

Jesse picked up the last few breadcrumbs with their finger,

folded up the empty cloth, and hopped out of the wagon. Trader followed and reached out to pull Jesse in for a heartfelt hug. Trader felt himself relax with the embrace. Jesse was so positive and genuine. Hanging out with them was likely taking a sip from the happy well. He wished they'd been able to spend more time together. He always loved it when chance had them crossing paths at a settlement, and they could talk long into the night by the fire. He wished that had been the case this year; he needed more of Jesse.

"Be safe and wishing you many good trades," he said, smiling.

"Same to you, dude," Jesse said with a big grin. "Now, let's go tell our hooved mates that their time for making moony eyes at each other is over."

Once everything was safely packed away and the horses were hitched, Jesse vaulted effortlessly on the Belgian's tall back, flip-flops miraculously staying on their feet. Trader got back in the wagon's seat. After another exchange of goodbyes and a wave, they headed their separate ways. Trader felt a twinge of sadness as the sound of Delilah's hooves faded in the distance.

CHAPTER
SIXTEEN

Slightly more cheerful after breaking bread with Jesse, Trader started looking forward to the next stop. Walnut Creek was one of the few settlements that had assumed the name of the city from the Before. The settlement was nestled below the looming overpasses at the 680/24 split. In the Before, this had been a major hub, connecting San Francisco with the East Bay. In the After, the remaining wisps of the population had gathered in the Broadway Plaza Mall, and the area still served as a central location for trading on the west coast.

As Trader neared the settlement, the Berkeley Hills loomed to the west. Though he had never crossed them, he knew that the San Francisco Bay now reached the base of the western side of the range, flooding the lower sections of Berkeley and Oakland. Ironworkers, engineers, electricians, and plumbers went from building high rises in the Before to connecting solar panels to a geothermal system, building aqueducts, and creating other unique amenities in the After. The flooding had concentrated the broad expertise in the region into one of the slickest settlements Trader had ever seen.

One of those amenities was a consistent supply of fresh

water. In the Before, culverts had been built below the city at the intersection of four creeks. The creeks were always flowing, even in drought seasons, supplying a steady supply of water to the community with a low mosquito risk. Water was pumped from the surrounding creeks into multiple two-thousand-gallon rain barrels that sat in the parking structure on the east side. A network of aqueducts constructed of large plastic pipes connected the barrels to the buildings. The slight slope generated enough pressure that the community boasted running sinks and toilets.

Trader took the S. Main St. exit off the 680 and rolled into the town. He passed a few people on foot that he didn't know at the intersection of Newell and S. Main St. He raised a hand in greeting. They waved back before heading into the hospital on the corner. The last time he was here, they'd been trying to get the hospital back up and running. He wondered how far they'd gotten. Though this area had its fair share of abandoned buildings, Walnut Creek had a decidedly more lived-in feeling, and it was obvious that people were trying to keep the area looking tidy.

The trio turned right on Broadway Plaza Rd., stopping at the south parking garage. Beyond that, the road was blocked off to anything but foot traffic as it looped through the mall. This was where Trader, reluctantly, would have to part ways with Sasha, Boxer, and the wagon. The first few years on the circuit, he had parked the wagon across the street and slept there. After some coaxing, he started parking the wagon in the garage and sleeping in the guest quarters.

The bottom floor of the parking garage was used as a small stable and storage shed. On one side, there was space to park wagons, trailers, and other items to tow heavy loads. On the other side, five stalls had been built from wood. Walnut Creek had two resident horses. The other three stalls were for short-term housing, including any animals that pulled supplies back and forth from the surrounding small farms. They were also used for rare guests, like Boxer and Delilah. The parking levels above were used to store building supplies, like scavenged wood, metal, glass, and plastic piping.

Someone was always stationed at the garage to care for any animals in residence and manage the inventory of supplies moving in and out of the garage. It was a toss-up who he'd find there each year. Walnut Creek was big enough that he only knew a few people by name. Today, there was a woman he didn't recognize, probably in her teens, working with the resident horses. A large pile of dry native grass sat in a wooden bin. She was using a pitchfork to scoop piles out to eagerly awaiting horses. As soon as she registered the clopping of Boxer's hooves, she looked up and waved.

"Let me finish feeding these two and I will be right with you," she called out.

Boxer whinnied and started eagerly bobbing his head at the sight of the other horses, ears perked forward. The other horses softly whinnied back in greeting. Good old Boxer could make friends wherever he went.

Once the other horses were fed, the woman placed the pitchfork on a hanger on the wall, dusted her hands off on her pants, and walked over.

"Greetings," she said kindly. "Not sure I've met you before. Are you from one of the farms or just passing through?"

"Passing through. I'm Trader and this here's Boxer." He gestured to the antsy horse. "In the wagon there is Sasha. She's good and will stay out of your way."

Sasha sat primly in her cat bed, washing her face with her front paw.

"A cat! I can't believe she comes with you! I have never seen one travel with anybody before. I'm Jasmine." She reached out a hand and shook with Trader.

"Until I started working the stables, I never really got a good chance to get to know the passers-through," she continued. "We had someone come by to trade and left just this morning. Jesse was their name. Friendliest person ever. It was just them and their horse."

"I had the pleasure of breaking bread with Jesse on my way up actually," Trader said. "They're the best. I look forward to crossing paths with them every season. I always wish I could spend more time with them. But duty calls." He gestured to the wagon.

Boxer shifted his weight and whinnied softly again, drawing Trader's attention.

"Mind if I leave my wagon and put Boxer in one of your stalls?"

"Sure beans. Back your wagon into that spot there." She gestured over to an empty parking space next to a flatbed trailer. "You can put your horse in stall number three."

"Thank you," Trader said appreciatively. He knew that Boxer would be well taken care of, no trade required. Visitors were valued here, especially those bringing food. As such, they put effort into making guests comfortable.

Trader guided Boxer forward and backed the wagon into place. Once unhitched, he led him by the halter to the stall with a large "3" burned into the wood next to the door. Jasmine went about getting the small trough filled with water and put a pile of fresh grass out.

"I can brush him down for you if you like," she offered.

"Thank you. I'd appreciate it. Sorry about the gunk. We hit a mudslide."

"I got you. No worries."

Trader handed the lead rope over to her. Jasmine led Boxer first to sniff noses with the other two and then moved him into the stall. Though she was new to this duty post, Jasmine clearly knew her way around horses.

"For Sasha, I usually just let her do her own thing. Is that all right with you?"

"Absolutely," she answered as she released Boxer into the stall. "Cats are welcome around here. Helps keep the rats away."

Trader nodded in understanding. More cats meant fewer rats and less chance of Weeps, as well as various other infectious diseases. In a community this large, having a robust resident cat population was critical to disease control.

"She'll do her share to help you all out. She's an expert hunter. If you're lucky, she might even share," Trader teased.

"Blech!" Jasmine laughed. "No, thank you. Cats eat free. No trade required."

With Boxer and Sasha settled, Trader went back to the wagon. For now, he would pack enough to be comfortable in the guest quarters and collect enough trade items for dinner and breakfast. He planned on doing the serious trading tomorrow. He also grabbed *The Last Cuentista* and *The Gunslinger*. With the electric lighting here, he might have time to finish up Petra's story and get started on the next book. He loaded his pack, attached his bedroll, and hoisted it on his shoulder. He grabbed a jar of kimchi, a rarity at this settlement.

"This is for you," he said, handing the kimchi out to Jasmine. "Thanks for looking out for Boxer and Sasha."

"No trade required for you either," Jasmine said, putting her hands up, palms out. "Guests are welcome here."

"It's a gift or a tip or whatever. It's kimchi. If you haven't had it before, it's spicy and sour. The batch this year turned out really good." Trader held the jar up again.

Jasmine acquiesced and took the jar gratefully. "Thank you! That wasn't necessary but it's appreciated. I've had kimchi a couple of times, but it usually costs a lot in trades, so my parents didn't get it very often." Trader smiled and dipped his head before heading out, glad there was a way to do something nice for her.

147

***

Broadway Plaza Mall was an open-air shopping center, with storefronts hugging either side of the road. This had been a drivable street in the Before. Now the road was filled with raised garden beds and seating areas. On the opposite side of the stores to the right, there sat a parallel pedestrian pathway. This was also filled with raised gardens. Even the old fountain had been drained, being too risky to keep as originally intended, and replaced with an herb garden that spilled over the edges.

Trader walked north on Broadway Plaza Rd. The old Macy's store immediately to his right had been converted into a bazaar, which was where all of the trading happened. On the north side of the building, several small stores had been renovated into guest quarters for wanderers, farmers, scavengers, or anyone else who might stay a night or two before heading back out again.

This was the only settlement in Nor Cal with formal guest quarters, but, even here, the units weren't formally managed. It was first-come first-served, and the system worked well. The first two small stores were occupied, so Trader ended up claiming the old Aveda store and flipped the sign from "Open" to "Closed" as he entered. Thick curtains framed the front windows. There was a desk and a chair with a table lamp. Through a door in the back, the old storeroom had been converted into a mini bedroom. A small single bed, an adjacent end table, and a small chair filled up the space. Bathrooms were available in the adjacent Macy's store.

Trader unpacked his bedroll and laid it out on the bare mattress. The two books were placed on the end table. He was excited to have some time to relax and read. After the dust storm and the push through Livermore to Dublin, he was exhausted.

Back in the front room, he unpacked the trade items that would buy him a warm dinner and a shower before he hit the hay. Walnut Creek had a lot of mouths to feed and, despite all of the other amenities, keeping a steady supply of food was always a challenge. Food items were in high demand here. Trader could spare the preserves in exchange for a meal cooked by someone else.

Knowing how expensive things were in trade, he grabbed two jars of kimchi and a jar of nut butter hoping it would be enough. Immediately adjacent to the guest housing and connected to the north side of the Macy's was a cafeteria. People could choose to either make their meals at home, or they could trade for warm meals that someone else prepared.

Trader didn't recognize anyone he passed. There were so many people living in Walnut Creek that everyone was either friendly in an acquaintance type of way or politely ignored him. On occasion, someone could tell he was passing through to trade, but except for a few stall owners in the bizarre, not many people knew him by name.

The smell of spices, beans, and corn wafted over him when he stepped inside the cafeteria. It was late afternoon and the place was fairly quiet. An old man was eating at one of the many empty tables. Because of the time of day, there was no line, and Trader went right to the front. Three people were working and preparing food in the back. One server saw him and came to the counter.

"How can I help you? We have lentil soup, cornbread, and zucchini today. There's apple crumble for dessert if you want it."

"I'll take all of that. Sounds amazing." Trader placed his trades on the counter. "This enough?"

The server's eyes widened a little bit. "Too much actually," they said. They grabbed the two jars of kimchi. "This should do. Give me a bit to get it ready for you. Would you like water?"

"Yes, please," Trader said.

Trader grabbed the nut butter and moved down the counter to wait. The server brought him a tray with a huge bowl of soup, two generous slabs of cornbread, a small plate of sliced sauteed zucchini that smelled like thyme, a small bowl of apple cobbler, and a glass of water. Trader's stomach rumbled. He grabbed utensils from a cup on the counter and found a table.

The food was fabulous. The lentil soup was richly spiced. The cornbread had obviously been made with olive oil instead of butter, but was still tasty, especially when dunked in the soup. The zucchini was flavorful, seasoned with salt, likely sourced from the 49ers, and thyme from their own fountain garden. The apple cobbler was excellent, made from apple preserves, sweetened with honey, and topped with ground walnuts. The meal was quickly polished off, and Trader sat back, stuffed. It felt good to eat a warm meal again, even if he was sitting alone. After relaxing a while and watching a few people through the windows, he bussed his tray and dishes.

"Thank you. That was really good." He waved to the three behind the counter, and they waved back.

Trader stopped at the guest room to grab some clean clothes, a towel, a bar of lavender soap, and his sack of dirty clothes. With a full stomach, he just wanted to crash and take a nap. But he knew the dust and grime from the last few days would annoy him. With the nut butter still in hand to pay his way in, he headed into Macy's for a shower.

The first-floor bathrooms were still used for what they were originally intended, boasting both flushing water and electricity. The second-floor bathrooms had been converted to showers. The third level was now a washing area for clothes. After dropping his nut butter off with the person stationed at the entrance with a nod, he took a quick trip to the bathroom on the first level.

Going to the bathroom in a place that resembled the Before was an honest-to-god *experience*. Trader actually looked forward to dropping a deuce in Walnut Creek. They even had toilet paper! As with any plague, toilet paper supplies were the first to go, and stocks were never fully replenished once Weeps had hit. After over a year of wiping his ass with corn husks and leaves, the homemade tissue paper in the bathrooms was an outright luxury. He wished he had another shit to take just to use more of it.

With his restitution complete, he wove through the markets to the escalators. Electricity was not wasted on running the elevators or the escalators. Instead, the non-functional escalators served as a staircase between the floors. Because they were so narrow, they still kept the up and down directions for traffic.

On the second floor, Trader made his way to the communal showers. The originals had started off by getting the Macy's built just right. A ton of time and energy had been spent on converting the bathrooms on the second level into showers, leaving the original stall walls and doors to offer privacy.

Trader was the only one in the showers this time of day. The hot water prickled against his skin. He lathered up the soap, the scent of lavender filling the room. Thin streams of sand and dirt trailed through the water on the floor towards the drain. His hair was the worst, and he had to wash it a couple of times, digging his fingers deep into his scalp, to get all the grit out. His muscles relaxed under the warm water. After every bit of dirt had been scrubbed away and his skin was red from the effort, Trader dried off and put on a fresh set of clothes. It had been a rough couple of days, and he was grateful to have rinsed it all away.

After the shower, he headed to the third floor to wash his dirty clothes. It was a bit inconvenient to have the washing area that high up in the building, but it was a throwback to when the originals lived in Macy's. Back then, everyone had slept on the third floor, and having the washing facilities here made sense. Now that everyone had spread out into the surrounding stores, the third floor housed furniture, and the washing space was mainly used by people who were passing through.

The washing room was also empty of people. Trader cleaned his clothes using the wonderful smelling soap from the Nakamuras'. With a wet rag, he wiped away the caked mud on his boots. He wrung out his clothes and put them back in the freshly washed sack. Now that he was so clean, it was a shame that he had to sleep in a gritty bedroll. Back in the room, he used the clothesline from his pack to hang his clothes to dry. He hadn't done the best job wringing them out, and drops of water pattered on the floor below.

Feeling the tug of the animals, there was one more stop to make before heading to bed. Trader walked over to the garage, and Jasmine was still on duty. This time, she was leaning back in a chair with her legs kicked up on a table and a book in hand.

"What're you reading?"

Jasmine looked up and put her feet down. She turned the worn book around to look at the cover and then showed it to him, thumb keeping her place. "*The Galaxy and the Ground Within* by Becky Chambers."

"Any good?" Trader asked.

"Yeah, it's really good actually. There's like a couple of different alien species stuck on a planet. And it's about how they learn more about each other and help each other and stuff. It is kinda cool. Never read anything like it before."

"I haven't read that one," he said, interested. "I'll try to get a copy of it one of these days. I'm an avid reader myself. Sci-fi and fantasy mainly."

"I am just about done," she said, flashing the few pages she had left at the end of the book with her thumb. "If I'm done by the time you leave, I'll trade you for it?"

"Deal," said Trader, grinning. "How're the animals doing?"

"Your cat took off for a couple of hours and came back with a huge rat that she took back into your wagon," Jasmine replied. "Wasn't sure if that was okay. She seems to know what's what."

Trader laughed, nodding. "She does indeed."

"Your horse ate and was snoozing the last time I checked on him." She gestured over her shoulder toward the stalls.

THE BEFORE AND THE AFTER

"I'll just peek in, thanks," Trader replied. Jasmine waved him on with a smile and went back to reading.

Trader went to stall number three. Sure enough, Boxer was in the far corner, head down and back leg resting on the tip of his hoof. He looked content and was snoozing. Trader opted to leave him to rest without a goodnight scratch. It had been a rough couple of days, and he was sure the horse was tired.

At the wagon, he peeked through the canvas flaps to find Sasha curled up, sleeping. As usual, she had been tidy, and there was no evidence of the rodent evisceration. Waking slightly, she made a *merf* noise and started purring. He gave her some pets, and she started making air biscuits. Trader grabbed a few more bottles of kimchi for trading and headed back to the guest room with a last wave to Jasmine.

The solar-powered streetlights had kicked on, sparkling in the darkening sky. Light also streamed through the store windows as people returned home. Hopeful, he made a slight detour to the promenade. Sure enough, strings of lights tinkled in looping wires across the walkway, dancing in the air like stars. The lights here were always so pretty, and he took a moment to enjoy them.

At this time of day, more people were out and about, cooking in the central firepits or heading to the cafeteria for dinner. A small group of kids played tag around the raised beds. It felt really good to see kids, even just a few. They offered hope.

After taking in his fill of the lights and the crowd, he headed back. With his belly full and his body scrubbed clean, he was looking forward to nestling into bed with *The Last Cuentista* and getting a good night's rest, luxuriating in the amenities of Walnut Creek.

He turned the bedside lamp on and bundled himself in his bedroll, making quick work of the book. He took a moment after the last page, digesting the tale and connecting pieces of the story with his own life. Like Petra, the stories he collected on the circuit helped ease the loneliness.

The folklore of the After, he thought.

By sharing these stories, or 'gossip' per Jesse, he was doing his part to connect the settlements with more than just trade. He was surprised to find a book from the Before that seemed to understand the importance of preserving and sharing the collective experience.

He set *The Last Cuentista* on the table next to *The Gunslinger* and toyed with the idea of starting the next book. He usually liked to have a day or two to noodle over a story he'd just finished, letting it spin through his mind and settle over his shoulders. He was also tired. The last couple of days had been taxing, and the worry over Preacher kept chewing at him. But the idea of being able to read in a cozy bed by electric lighting was just too tantalizing, and he dove into *The Gunslinger*.

CHAPTER SEVENTEEN

Trader slept in the next morning and woke up refreshed. He'd stayed up late reading *The Gunslinger*. Roland's persistent and driving purpose in the book struck a chord with him. He had a hard time putting the book down and turning the lamp off before falling asleep. An afternoon read and a nap was definitely on the docket for today. There was no question that he would stay another night at this point.

Hungry, he grabbed two jars of kimchi and headed to the cafeteria. The place was much busier this time of day, but there still wasn't a line. The same server was at the counter as yesterday and swapped his two jars of kimchi for a plate of scrambled eggs, fried potatoes, cooked mushrooms, and two mandarin oranges. Trader found a table and started on the meal.

Staying true to form, the food was delightful. The eggs were perfectly salted. The fried potatoes were seasoned with thinly sliced onions, garlic, and oregano, crispy on the outside and soft on the inside. The cooked mushrooms had a hint of thyme. Sweet citrus flavor burst across his tongue when he ate the oranges.

As he devoured the meal, he watched patrons move in and

out of the building. It was weird being around so many people. They were polite and all, but there were just so many of them. Some of them knew each other and would greet one another with a wave or share a table. Chatter echoed through the place. It was more noise than he was used to. He suspected the settlement had grown yet again.

A quick stop at the garage was required before trading commenced. He grabbed his pack from the room and headed over. The garage was peaceful and quiet compared to the hustle of the cafeteria. Jasmine was scooping horse manure into a wheelbarrow when he walked up.

"Good morning," he said in greeting. Jasmine looked up, nodded with a smile, and went back to cleaning the stalls.

Boxer had his head out over the half door of the stall and whickered to him. Trader walked over and started scratching his mane. The horse let out a sigh of contentment and nosed his shirt gently. Even though it had been less than a day, Trader missed being around him all of the time.

"There're some apples by the desk if you want to give him a treat," Jasmine offered.

"Cool, thanks. May I give one to the other two as well?"

"Sure. They'd like that. They're so spoiled!" Jasmine laughed.

Fresh apples were rare this late in the season. Trader figured they must have a cold room set up somewhere to keep them over winter and into spring. Boxer would be jazzed to have a raw apple, as would Trader.

Trader found the apple sack near the desk and pulled three out. He walked by each stall, holding out one apple in the palm of his hand to each horse. They all happily snarfed the treat down, smacking their lips and swishing their tails.

"Your cat took off when I got here this morning," Jasmine called over. "Haven't seen her come back."

"Not surprised," he replied. "Thanks for the heads up."

Sure enough, Sasha wasn't in or around the wagon. He assumed she was off hunting breakfast and would be back when it suited her. Trader loaded up a large basket and his pack with kimchi, preserves, jerky, and jars of honey for trading.

The large settlement was always looking for food. In addition to the raised garden beds, the Apple store north of the west parking garage had been turned into a greenhouse, the large glass windows on the front of the store generating enough light to grow indoors without the need for supplemental lighting. A few farms had also been set up in the nearby parks. Chickens were kept in the west parking garage and were occasionally brought out to the surrounding farms in small groups to help build back the soil. Even with all of that, it still wasn't enough to feed the large community. People who moved between the settlements played an important role in closing that resource gap.

Trader left another jar of nut butter with the guy at the entrance to pay his way back into Macy's. The shops weren't very busy today. A few people wandered through with cloth bags full of trades. Trader made a beeline for the pharmacy.

Kuldeep had one of the biggest stalls in the market, taking up a quarter of the first floor. This was the one place in Northern California to reliably get pharmaceuticals. Kuldeep had excellent connections and, on very rare occasions, would even have Gen 3 Proxleep. Trader knew he could offload most of his items with Kuldeep before browsing around the rest of the market.

Kuldeep spotted him from afar and called out, "Trader! Here, here. Put that down." He tapped an empty spot on the table in front of him.

Kuldeep was in his late thirties and boasted an immaculately groomed mustache and beard. Gray strands speckled long black hair that was pulled back in a tight bun. He wore a tan kurta with embroidered cuffs, loose slacks, and woven flip-flops.

Folding tables were arranged in a curve around the trading space. Beautifully woven cloths covered the tables and must have cost a fortune in trade. A finished piece of wood was perched on one of the tables with "Kuldeep's Med Shop" burnt into it. Behind the tables, four-foot-tall library shelves were arranged in parallel lines. A wide variety of medicinals, both herbal and pharmaceutical, were organized neatly and alphabetically. Kuldeep had just about everything, from chamomile grown locally to fifty-year-old bottles of Tylenol from who knows where. Frankly, Trader didn't give two shits where Kuldeep found the stuff. People needed these meds to survive.

Trader dropped the basket and pack on the table and reached out to shake Kuldeep's hand. "Nice to see you, Kuldeep. Hope you've been well."

"Things have been pretty damn good actually. We had a small caravan come down from the north. They've been cooking some new stuff up there. You won't believe this, but I have some newly manufactured penicillin. They also brought some Gen 3 Proxleep that came from back east along the northerly trading route." Kuldeep grinned widely, the curls of his mustache turning up.

The news of penicillin shocked Trader. In the Before, most of the pharmaceutical manufacturing had been outsourced to countries in Asia. There were a few plants in the U.S., but most of them were on the east coast. Even with the existing plants, they often didn't have enough trained people, raw materials, or power to get everything up and running in the After.

If chemists could find a functional place to set up shop, they usually focused on making meds that would fight the Weeps. And even then, Proxleep manufacturing had been a hodgepodge affair over the last twenty years. Sure, stuff like antibiotics and painkillers would be helpful, and maybe prevent some deaths. But even after the pandemic made its initial sweep through the population, Weeps still picked off ten to twenty percent of the survivors' descendants each mosquito season. The fact that someone was making penicillin gave Trader hope

THE BEFORE AND THE AFTER

that human beings might see their way through this fucked up mess.

"Once they got a reliable power source, they set up growing vats in an old hospital," Kuldeep continued. "Rumor has it that they also set up a chem lab on one floor. They're trying to make propionic acid onsite and may have ibuprofen next year too. It sounds pretty slick. They're looking for anyone interested in helping out, or even trading on a circuit that goes that far north to the Portland area."

"That's a long trek, and the roads between here and there aren't that great. The trade would have to be pretty damn good," Trader mused.

"Yeah, they were talking about possibly using boats instead. But, with the weather and all...." Kuldeep shrugged.

The storms were unpredictable enough on land and even worse on the ocean. It was risky to trade by boat. That being said, it might be easier than weaving up the 5 through the mountains surrounding Shasta. Trader had heard that some of those roads were completely gone after a few nasty rockslides.

"I'll spread the word," Trader said. "Speaking of which, I know this isn't your line of business, but you know a lot of people. There's a group out in Modesto who are growing and weaving cotton. They are looking for apprentices. There's also a shoemaker out in Galt. I would recommend sending as much leather as possible in that direction and soon you'll start seeing more shoes passed around on the circuit. They'd make good trades with all of the pharmaceuticals you've got."

"Ohhh...It'll be nice to start seeing more new clothing and shoes. Modesto and Galt... let me write that down." Kuldeep grabbed some of the locally-made paper and jotted down the intel, nodding. With that done, he asked casually, "Okay, so what can I get for you today?"

"I'm looking for inhalers if you have them. I'll also take some antibiotics, painkillers, and Proxleep."

Kuldeep went weaving through the shelves, loading things into an old Albertson's hand-held grocery store basket. He spread out an assortment of bottles and small boxes onto the table. Trader started sorting through them, selecting the ones he wanted to trade for. He was asking for quite a bit, but Kuldeep didn't usually bring items forward he wasn't willing to part with.

"What'd you like for this?" Trader asked, hand circling over the items he had selected.

Kuldeep shifted through the basket and the pack Trader had brought. He pulled out four jars of honey, four jars of kimchi, a couple of large packages of beef jerky, and several other jars of assorted preserves. It was a ton of food, some of which was particularly valuable, but Trader knew the meds were worth it.

"Deal," Trader said, smiling, and they shook hands.

Trader shifted the remaining food in his basket to his pack, stacking the meds on top. The load was significantly lighter now. He had traded a lot away at this stall like he'd known he would, but it still felt like he had blown his wad. Kuldeep stacked the food at the back of the stall before coming back to chat some more.

"What else are folks needing here this year?" Trader asked.

"We always need food," Kuldeep answered quickly and then pursed his lips, trying to think of anything else. "Clothes and stuff too. Blankets, things like that."

Trader nodded. It was what he expected. They had a pretty good system for scavenging and storing stuff like nails, screws, and other metal works. They also had plenty of things like paper, which they made right here in the Nordstroms.

"How's the settlement doing?" Trader asked.

"Pretty good actually. No one died from Weeps this year, which was a shocker, frankly. We had enough food to make it through the winter. There were even a few births. A couple of groups passed through. Most stayed. Some left. With all the puts

THE BEFORE AND THE AFTER

and takes, the settlement still grew." Kuldeep leaned his hip on the table.

"Doc has also worked hard to get the hospital up and running. She trained a couple of nurses and hopes to train some to be doctors. They don't have reliable power yet, but the engineers are working on it. She's trying to convince me to move my booth over there into the old hospital pharmacy." Kuldeep shrugged. "I might once they get the power steady. I'll miss being here. If you come by next year and my stall is gone, check over in the hospital."

"Will do." Trader nodded slightly. "I only see you all once a year. But from where I sit, this place is doing pretty well. I see more and more people every year. Everyone looks healthy, too. Has to be the biggest settlement. On my circuit, at least."

"Yeah. I'm just hoping things don't get back to the way they were in the Before. It's nice trusting people not to steal your stuff and sleeping with doors unlocked. I keep seeing more and more people that I don't know. Once those personal connections go away, it's easier to do harm. I am hoping everyone will stay civil as the settlement grows," Kuldeep answered warily, a slight wrinkle marring his brow.

This brought Preacher to the forefront of Trader's mind.

"Did a preacher happen to pass through here at all?" Trader asked hesitantly, not wanting to ruin the friendly visit but also feeling like he had to know.

Kuldeep looked at Trader intently, slightly surprised. "As a matter of fact, yes. Very unusual character. He came and went fairly quickly. He preached on the promenade for a few days, recruited a couple of folks, and then the group left. Why do you ask? Do you know him?"

"Know *of* him more like," Trader answered. "I seem to be walking in his footsteps the whole circuit this year. What was he like?"

"I spend most of my time here, so I didn't see much of him.

Most of the information I have is from others. Some say he was mesmerizing, and others say he was just trying to brainwash everyone."

"But he didn't hurt anyone, right?" Trader pressed.

"He didn't physically hurt anyone that I'm aware of. He just made everybody nervous."

Kuldeep pressed his lips into a thin line. Trader had known Kuldeep for seven years, and it was unlike him to talk badly about anyone. Trader's shoulders tensed.

"I'm just glad he's gone. We've got a good thing going here, and he wanted to change that. I won't be sorry if I never see him again." Kuldeep waved his hand dismissively.

"I haven't heard of him hurting anybody either, but he puts everyone on edge who he crosses paths with. Do you know which direction they took out of town?"

"Nope, sorry," Kuldeep answered.

Trader sighed heavily and chewed his inner cheek, now raw from worry. Trader just couldn't shake Preacher, and it was nagging at him. He felt like he was being shepherded on a path behind Preacher, bearing witness to his destructive wake.

Kuldeep, sensing that Trader was upset, changed the subject. "Enough talk about this guy. How're the other settlements doing?"

Trader tried to shake off the ominous feeling and shared the happy news of Forty Two and the Nakamuras'. He purposefully left out the burned-down city of Lodi, trying to avoid as many topics related to Preacher as he could. He did share what happened at Live More. Losing the next-nearest settlement to Weeps was an important piece of information for the folks at Walnut Creek.

"You just never know," Kuldeep whistled softly, shaking his head sadly at the news of Live More. "Maybe some survived, and they're just trying to keep others safe."

"Yeah, hope so," Trader said. "I advised Jesse to steer clear just in case. We probably won't know how it all shook out until we head back through next year."

Trader rapped his knuckles on the table and slung his pack on. "Okay, I better get a move on. Thanks, as always, Kuldeep."

"Travel safe. Bring some shoes and clothes next year." Kuldeep shook his hand warmly.

"Will do," Trader replied. "Thanks again for everything. I appreciate you." Kuldeep grinned back and waved.

CHAPTER
EIGHTEEN

With the basket empty and the pack now lighter, he perused the other stalls casually. The stalls on the first floor offered mostly food, and he passed by, not expecting to buy anything. He saw the usual: dried fruit, eggs, nuts, sacks of ground corn meal, dried beans, and preserves. Though there were plenty of food stalls, he knew that there still wasn't enough to feed everyone in the settlement. He allowed himself one food item and traded for a small square of cornbread to snack on, carrying his basket one-handed.

On the second floor, there was an assortment of indoor items, such as utensils, knives, pots, pans, and other assorted goods. He meandered through, smiling and starting up idle conversations with some of the stall owners. He recognized some faces but couldn't remember any names. There was nothing he really needed or wanted here, but it was nice to socialize.

The third floor was packed with furniture. He breezed through the various chairs and tables to the back corner where there was a small electronics stall. CB radios, crank flashlights, and other assorted items were crammed on shelves, with wires dangling every which way. Trader couldn't afford anything this fancy and honestly didn't have reliable power to make most of it worthwhile anyway. He still liked to fantasize about what life was like surrounded by so many objects. The stall owner looked up from the circuit board he was working on and smiled before getting back to work.

At the linen stall, Trader treated himself to a new bedroll. It was a splurge, and he knew it. But he was sick of sleeping in gritty blankets. If the dust storms were moving north, it might come in handy in the next few years. The bedroll was an expensive trade, as most things were in Walnut Creek. It cost him two jars of honey, one jar of kimchi, and a package of jerky. On his way out, he traded more preserves for ten pounds of salt. Weighted down with the meds, new bedroll, and salt, he headed back to the wagon. It had been a solid day of trading.

Trader swapped his old bedroll for the new one before heading over to the garage. He stashed the old bedroll, salt, and meds safely away in his wagon. He repacked his pack with books to trade and filled the basket with more kimchi and nut butter to trade for meals. Sasha had since returned and was snoozing on the driver's seat. He gave her a scratch before heading back to the mall.

After leaving the basket of food for later, Trader took the books and headed towards the promenade. This time of year, the metal-framed raised beds in the promenade were full of leafy greens, such as Swiss chard, lettuce, and kale. There was also late-season broccoli. Bright climbing beans and peas wove in and out of lattices, speckled with white blossoms. They'd have snap peas in a few weeks. A couple of people were out working the beds, watering and weeding.

To ensure the gardens stayed plentiful, Walnut Creek had a slick composting system. Any food scraps were mixed with the animal feces and used bedding from the chickens and horses in the first bin. Someone always maintained the bins, collecting the finished compost in a large pile.

Trader often wondered why they didn't compost the human waste too, as a lot of nutrients were lost by not recycling. He figured it was likely tough to compost human waste in a dense population like this and still keep diseases from spreading. Weeps had already taken enough folks. The last thing they needed was cholera or some other fecal-borne infection nibbling away at their population.

Thin ropes arranged on pulleys stretched between the roofs of the opposing stores. Pinned to some of the lines were clothes in a wide variety of colors, shapes, textures, and sizes. They flapped high above the gardens like prayer flags in the faint breeze.

With the serious trading done, it was time to relax and pick through the books on offer. The Old Navy store had been converted into what now served as a bookstore-library hybrid for the community. It was the biggest collection of books that Trader had seen in his lifetime, and he always looked forward to making this stop.

Trader entered the Old Navy with the *ting* of an old-fashioned bell announcing his entry. Earl, the store owner, was sitting at what used to be the cashier counter with his nose in a book. Earl was in his eighties, with a bald head, dark skin, and reading glasses. A bow tie with cats on it topped off a well-worn dress shirt and sweater vest. He looked like a professor in one of the books from the Before.

An orange tabby tomcat trotted up to Trader with a deep friendly *meow* and started sniffing his legs. Trader bent down to give him a scratch. The cat started purring loudly, pressing his cheeks against his boots and rolling over on his back.

"Hello, Jonesy. Smell Sasha?" Trader said affectionately.

Jonesy responded with another deep, raspy *meow*. He scratched Jonesy's chin and belly a bit longer before heading over to the counter.

"Good morning, Trader. It is a pleasure to see you!" Earl

carefully placed a bookmark in the novel he was reading and rested it on the counter, each move made with intention and respect. The books in Earl's didn't dare be dog-eared.

"Nice to be back, Earl. Got lots of books this year." Trader placed the basket of books on the floor next to the counter.

"Do you have time for tea?" Earl asked, looking at Trader over his reading glasses, his fingers pressed on the top of the closed book.

"That would be wonderful," Trader answered warmly.

"Please have a seat. I'll bring it over in a moment." Earl went to the back of the store and plugged in an electric kettle. While the water boiled, he arranged cups on a small tray and added dried chamomile leaves.

The bookstore was a cozy retreat. Comfy sofas and chairs were arranged by the windows bordering the front of the store. Natural light streamed through the windows, making it the perfect place to settle down with a book. Verdant plants poured out of pots arranged throughout the seating area. The smell of books and that indescribable greenhouse scent filled the space.

Trader settled in one of the plush chairs that faced the promenade, inhaling deeply and feeling his shoulders relax. Jonesy hopped on his lap, purring and making biscuits. The affectionate tomcat closed his eyes in contentment. Trader smiled and kept petting him while he waited for the tea.

"Please be careful. It may be hot."

Earl set the tray on the table and handed a mug to Trader. Earl took the other mug and sat across from him. The mug warmed Trader's hand. He inhaled deeply, feeling the calming scent of the chamomile relax him further. He loved this place with every fiber of his being.

"Thank you, Earl," Trader said with a content sigh. "I needed this. How've things been this last year?"

"We have been fortunate," Earl said. "We did not have any

Weeps deaths this year. At the risk of sounding hyperbolic, it was an undeniable miracle."

"Kuldeep mentioned that. It's pleasant news."

"This is the first mosquito season that we have not had any Weeps mortalities. There were deaths from other causes, of course. Once the hospital is operational, I am hopeful that we can reduce the mortality rate further. True success will be when the death and birth rates are at least even again," Earl mused.

"Agreed," Trader said, nodding. "I've seen a few pregnant women on the circuit this year. I'm crossing my fingers for them. There're fewer people on the road, though. Not sure if that means they've settled or we're still losing people."

"As the settlements become more comfortable, I suspect that people will start to congregate in them," Earl said. "It is in our nature to gather in communities. Several more people joined Walnut Creek recently. More so than in previous years."

"The citizenship of Walnut Creek has changed significantly in the last decade. At times, I am nearly able to pretend it is still the Before." Earl paused to blow on his tea and closed his eyes. "But then, I remember that I am not in a library on a college campus. Instead, I am running a book exchange out of what used to be a clothing store," he added with a resigned sigh.

"Did you attend college in the Before?" Trader asked carefully.

Earl often avoided talking about the Before, though he was one of the few remaining who had been alive back then. For someone who bartered in stories, it always surprised Trader how reluctant Earl was to share his own. He could sense that Earl wanted to talk today and was grateful to hear his story.

"Yes. I attended UC Berkeley, where I majored in English with an emphasis on 17th-century literature. I continued my education there, completing both a master's and Ph.D. They had beautiful libraries on campus. I miss them dearly. It is such a shame they are all underwater now." He sipped his tea, staring out through the window.

"What did you do after that?" Trader gently probed, taking a sip of the tea himself.

"I was faculty at Stanford before they closed. In the beginning, the weather would force us to cancel classes occasionally, often due to the 101 or 280 being flooded. When we entered the great recession about fifty years ago, the university cut the entire English department, to my utter dismay. They invested all remaining resources in the hard sciences. The university did not stay open for much longer after that and eventually flooded several years later. I had already moved inland by that point."

Earl looked down and fiddled with a piece of lint on his sweater vest.

"After Stanford, I lived with my parents in Concord and was fortunate to find employment at the local library. When it first came through, Weeps took both of my parents within weeks of each other. Then, everyone started dying." Earl's voice caught. He coughed lightly and took a sip of tea.

Trader could see the weight of survivor's guilt on his shoulders. He let the silence sit between them, giving Earl space to gather his thoughts.

"I remember watching the news. I had never seen anything like it before. It was reminiscent of the accounts in some of the primary sources about the plague. Whole blocks of people dying, mass graves, and empty home after empty home. I doubt that medical professionals and politicians thought what happened was possible on such a massive scale in the modern world. I suspect, but have no way to prove, that climate change negatively impacted our ability to fight the disease. Supply chain issues combined with frequent natural disasters made it virtually impossible for any significant research to be conducted. Frankly, we are fortunate to even have Proxleep."

Trader continued to sip his tea, encouraging Earl to share his story with his silence. Jonesy, sensing Earl's distress, switched seats and jumped into Earl's lap. Earl stroked him absentmindedly, lost in thoughts of the past. After a few minutes, he continued with his story.

"I lived a few years on my own. Thankfully, I have a green thumb and was able to grow enough food in the backyard. The lack of clean water was a constant pressure." He paused to take another sip.

"The loneliness was unbearable. There were a handful of people around Concord. Of course, everyone was amicable. I would often go to the library and just hope that others would be there as well."

"Rumors about what they were building at Walnut Creek started circulating. I moved here after the power grid went down twenty years ago; it was still fairly early in the settlement's inception. The founders were gracious and accommodated an old man's whimsy, letting me set up this place." Earl gestured to the store, his face softening.

"Books are important. Our stories are important," Trader finally spoke up. "They're just as important to the community as clothes or tools."

"Yes, yes." Earl nodded. "Nonetheless, I am grateful that they let me run this place. It may not be the Bancroft. However, I do enjoy my time in this space with Jonesy and the patrons of this establishment. It is also nice to be part of a community. It is so dreadfully lonely out there. I am not quite sure how you do it."

Earl looked up, hoping that Trader wasn't offended. Trader smiled, reassuring him that no offense was taken.

"Enough of an old man's musings. What are the stories from the road, my good friend?" Earl asked.

Trader dove in, passing along the tales from the circuit, refreshing their cups in between stories.

At the mention of Preacher, Earl chimed in. "Yes, I

remember the gentleman. He came in off the highway with two others, bedraggled and road-worn. They were malnourished and penniless in the trade sense.

"They stayed in the guest space. Many members of the community took pity on them and shared their food. Preacher came into my store only once and without his followers. I offered tea, as I normally do, and we sat just over there," Earl said, pointing across the seating area, looking pensive.

"What did you think of him?" Trader asked.

"I am old enough to have seen videos of great orators and influencers." Earl pursed his lips thoughtfully. "Preacher has a dangerous mix of charisma and fanaticism. He is subsumed by his own fervent beliefs.

"My concern with the gentleman is his firm assertion that his method is the only manner of living. When people disagree, even politely, he becomes aggressive and angry. Even after gifting him the Bible he asked for, he left quite agitated. Please be careful, Trader. He was headed north, and I suspect that you will cross paths with him at some point."

Trader's stomach clenched. "I've heard similar warnings from others. Did he ever hurt anybody?"

"No. Not that I am aware of. However, violent behavior is an inherent aspect of the human condition, especially if underscored by a deep-seated belief. Charismatic leaders, like Preacher, have a higher probability of enacting more widespread damage. Their ability to bring forth pain and suffering is amplified by their ability to compel others into believing that doing harm is justified." Earl paused, and Trader let the silence sit once again between them.

"While he was here, he spent the majority of his time standing on one of the stone benches proselytizing to the passersby. Even if the promenade was relatively empty, he would still deliver sermons to his mesmerized followers. Over the short period he was here, he convinced a few others to join. I do not know precisely why Preacher and his followers eventually left. I suspect it was because he found it difficult to convert a community this large. Be wary. His power base is growing, and his ego is likely growing along with it. At the risk of sounding cliché, history tends to repeat itself," Earl warned again.

"How does he convince people to join him?" Trader asked.

Trader was honestly curious as to why people choose to follow a relatively unknown person out into the middle of nowhere with no provisions. Regardless of the rumors, he still couldn't believe people would believe in such an insubstantial message.

"An interesting question. I have been pontificating on that myself. As a species, we have experienced several significant events that have dramatically impacted our way of life and social structure within a short period. It happened so quickly that we have not had time to fully adapt. We are social creatures and seek stability. The world is very lonely compared to what it was fifty years ago. When you add food insecurity and the constant threat of death from infection, it becomes overwhelming. People seek answers during times like these.

"I think Preacher knows their fears and offers his version of the truth, carefully branded and packaged," Earl continued. "He even has a symbol, which is a powerful tool to manipulate people. It is comparable to the swastika or the hammer and sickle. It is an instantly recognizable symbol that represents an entire belief system. I think people decided to follow Preacher because the emptiness of the After was too much for them to cope with. They are looking for purpose and reassurance, and Preacher has handed it to them, neatly wrapped with a bow."

It was difficult for Trader to see the appeal of what Preacher had to offer. In his opinion, Preacher was selling false hope, preying on those who had already suffered the most. Bryson was healthy and part of a tight-knit community at the Silvas'. Trader didn't understand why he would leave all of that behind to wander between settlements with no supplies.

"What do you think will happen once they realize he's full of shit?"

Earl burst out with a low, throaty laugh. "Ahhh...that is the crux of it, is it not? He may be successful in creating a community that offers a sense of belonging. I suspect, as his power base grows, his narcissism will begin to taint the experience. The pattern repeats itself. We have seen the likes of him before in people like Jim Jones and Yahweh ben Yahweh."

"Who were they?" Trader asked.

"Both men established cults and drew in a large base of followers, similar to what Preacher is trying to do. They came to power during a time when Americans were exploring a different way of living. The U.S. was emerging from the cookie-cutter confines of the 1950s. The Civil Rights Movement and Vietnam War dramatically impacted American culture. Many people were looking for a new way to belong and exploring alternative lifestyles. The U.S. was ripe for emerging cult leaders.

"Jim Jones began as a humble preacher in Indiana, advocating for unity and acceptance. This message brought people hope, a sense of purpose, and connectivity in a period of uncertainty. He was successful in building a congregation of over three thousand people. In the beginning, I think his intentions were good. However, as his power grew, the neglect became evident in the malnourishment and abuse of followers. Sadly, in the end, he convinced over nine hundred church members to commit ritual suicide by drinking cyanide. Similar to Jones, Preacher puts the gospel first, oftentimes to the detriment of the basic needs of his followers."

Trader raised his eyebrows in disbelief and shook his head slowly.

"Yahweh ben Yahweh began as a faith healer. In the beginning, he brought hope to his congregation, offering a safe haven and a sense of empowerment. Again, at the start, I think his intentions were good. He was a prominent community leader, and his congregation cleaned up several rough neighborhoods in Miami. However, absolute power corrupts absolutely. As his influence grew, he started leading by fear and meticulously controlling the members of the Nation. They turned to extreme violence to punish dissenters. High-ranking members and enforcers were recognizable by their all-white attire."

"Like Preacher. How creepy is that...," Trader said quietly.

"Indeed. Wearing white is a symbol of purity, peace of mind, and spiritual clarity. Several cult leaders have made their followers wear white, like Brother Julius and Shoko Asahara. In addition to having powerful symbolism, forcing cult members to wear white also removes their individuality. The members lose their sense of self-identity and take on the identity of the cult, making them easier to control."

Earl paused and then said ominously, "Interestingly, white is also the color of mourning in some cultures." He took a deep, thoughtful sigh before continuing.

"Unfortunately, there are numerous examples of cult leaders throughout history. David Koresh and roughly eighty of his followers died in a standoff with the U.S. government in Texas. Charles Manson's followers were fewer in number. Still, they committed extremely violent crimes in a short period which resulted in their imprisonment before he could expand his sphere of influence further.

"Preacher may only reach the levels of Manson, collecting a few followers and then coming to a quick, violent end. Alternatively, Preacher may be successful in collecting a large group around him like Jones or Koresh. I suspect he is looking for a place to build his Eden, one where he can isolate and control people. The neglect of his congregation may be benign in nature rather than a mechanism of control. I hope that this is one instance where history fails to repeat itself. Time will tell with

Preacher. The world is different now. There are so few people, but the people left also have little hope."

Earl set his teacup down. "If you are interested, I think I may have a book on at least one of them."

Trader laughed nervously and held up his hands. "That's okay, thanks. There's enough heavy stuff out in the real world. I prefer to get lost in sci-fi and fantasy, but I'll for sure take your advice and be careful. I'll warn others along the way as well."

Earl patted the armrests with both hands. "Well now, enough of that talk. I am famished," he said, signaling the end of their chat. "Let's see what delights you have in your basket of treasures. After our exchange is complete, perhaps I can convince you to join me for lunch?"

"Sounds great, thank you," Trader said.

Trader loved listening to Earl and wished he'd continue. He also knew when to take a hint.

Earl gently put Jonesy on the floor and stood up to bus the dishes into the back. Trader headed over to the counter and set the books out for Earl to look through. Earl put his reading glasses on and began carefully sorting the books into small stacks.

"Please feel free to browse the wares as I log all of these." He pulled out a thick book and started making small, tidy entries into his ledger.

Though Trader wanted to browse for books he would enjoy, he also knew that this was the best place to find books to trade along the circuit. Children's books that had survived from the Before were difficult to find. He started in that section, which was also the smallest one. He grabbed two well-worn board books, *Goodnight Moon* and *The Big Red Barn*, thinking of the two babies that he hoped would be alive and well in Forty Two next year. *Go Dog. Go!* and *Big Shark, Little Shark* were added to the pile, thinking of Izumi. He selected some books for older kids, always hopeful, including a *Henry and Mudge* book. Luck also landed a copy of *The Lightning Thief* into his stack. After dropping the children's books off with Earl, he dove back into the aisles, taking a deep breath of the woody book smell.

Careful selections were made as Trader moved through the shelves, and he thoughtfully considered what each of the settlements along the circuit might be interested in. He wasn't able to find any books on homesteading or wheat processing for the Machados, as he suspected. Instead, he selected a military history book that he was sure Manuel would be excited to read. He discovered the fifth book in the *Dark Tower* series and grabbed it, certain that he'd make it quickly through the first four books that Gilberto had lent him before next year. An old beat-up paperback copy of *Dragon Wing* by Margaret Weiss and Tracy Hickman topped the pile. The book summary described a lone wanderer who had escaped a labyrinth through Death's Gate to a world fractured into elemental realms. This was a pick for himself.

Trader never much minded if Earl got more out of the trade or not. Earl was the same way. It was about making stories available to those who enjoyed them. He knew that Earl would take all of the ones that he brought in just as he knew that Earl would let him walk out with the stack he gathered. All of the ins and outs were carefully annotated. Content, Earl closed the ledger and took his glasses off.

"Ready to eat?" Earl asked.

Meow, answered Jonesy.

"It is not your dinner time yet. You know that," Earl said affectionately, bending over to pet him.

"Yep. I'm ready," Trader said, rubbing his stomach. He grabbed the basket. "Goodbye, Jonesy," he added with a smile down at the affectionate cat.

Trader turned to look at Earl over his shoulder. "Let me drop this off, and I'll meet you by the cafeteria?"

Earl nodded, following Trader out, leaving the store

unlocked. Even though this was a large settlement, the unspoken rules regarding thievery were still followed. Everyone trusted that things would be safe.

Disappointed at the lack of food, Jonesy jumped into a large, sun-soaked chair facing the promenade, huffed, and curled up for a nap. Trader watched him through the window longingly, wishing he could stay a bit longer in those comfy chairs.

CHAPTER
NINETEEN

Back at his guest room, Trader swapped the basket of books for jars of kimchi. He met Earl at the front of the cafeteria. Holding the jars up for Earl to see, he said, "My treat." Earl smiled and nodded his thanks.

Since it was a bit after lunch, the cafeteria was fairly empty. The jars of kimchi were traded for two plates of ratatouille and cornbread with cool mint tea sweetened with honey. Earl and Trader tucked in across from each other at a small table near the windows. Earl had been uncharacteristically open today. Trader tried his luck and pressed for more stories.

"What was it like eating at a place like this in the Before?" he asked.

Earl thoughtfully chewed a bite of cornbread. "There was a constant plethora of options at one's fingertips. I would patronize a restaurant such as this and be able to order a Reuben on rye bread with a side of chips. Oh, how I miss fresh sandwich bread." He sighed, closing his eyes as if savoring the imaginary sandwich. "Then, I might decide to walk to the other side of the mall and order a mint chocolate chip ice cream on a waffle cone.

I miss ice cream dearly. We took so much for granted." He shook his head sadly.

Trader had never had ice cream but had read about it in books. He couldn't imagine wanting to eat something frozen. Per the old-timers, it was just as delicious as a cobbler or other dessert.

"In this part of California, you could buy almost anything you wanted at any time of the year," Earl continued, surprising Trader with his talkativeness. "At least, that was before the supply chains crumbled. Now, no one dares to transport a plantain through the valley from Mexico, and we no longer receive mangoes shipped from India. We enjoy what we can grow locally. In a sense, I think that is all for the best. Having been on both sides of the Before and the After, I think it is better for us and the living beings that we share this planet with that we live within our local means."

"I can't imagine wanting a piece of fruit so bad that someone would ship it halfway across the world." Trader shook his head.

"You have never tried mangoes," Earl teased and laughed softly. "In all seriousness, we had so many choices at every second of every day. It was a miracle we did not suffocate from the pressure of all of the small decisions piling up over us." He took a bite of the ratatouille. "I suppose in a way we did suffocate from them at the end of it all. We buried ourselves in our phones, ate our mangoes from India, and kept our homes at an even seventy-five degrees in the summer. In doing so, we let the world die around us without bothering to even look up.

"Sometimes, I find myself desperately missing the Before," Earl reflected. "Other times, I appreciate the balance that nature has brought. I am not saying our lives are easier. Conversely, our lives are probably more complicated as we struggle to adapt. However, that oppressive feeling of being buried in choices and hurrying to and fro in the Before...I am grateful that we are out from under that."

Taking a sip of the tea, Earl looked at Trader. "I do wonder how you, Jesse, and others manage on your own. I get lonely here, and this is the biggest settlement in Northern California." He looked out the window. "The store grounds me and gives me purpose. I think purpose helps us stay on our true path."

They sat in companionable silence as they ate. Trader mulled over what Earl had said. The importance of connection resonated with him. For him, connecting all of the settlements, bringing them useful items, and collecting their stories helped him stay hopeful and kept him going. The more he thought about it, the more he realized how everyone's idea of community, connection, and purpose differed. What made one person content may not satisfy another.

Earl suddenly perked up, stirred by something he remembered. "Have you been to the north end of the mall yet?" he asked avidly, one eyebrow arched.

Trader was pulled out of his thoughts. "No, I thought I would take a spin after lunch. Why?"

"The See's Candy has been turned into a music store!" Earl said excitedly.

"What?" Trader swallowed the half-chewed bite and looked up at Earl, confused.

"A music store!" Earl continued. "Bess is an audiophile. She has amassed an array of musical instruments, devices, and electronics. There are records and CDs. She also has several devices with music from Before on them. Because devices are so rare, patrons have to listen to them in the store. It is still worth your time to stop there. Bess' appreciation and desire to share music are comparable to my fondness for books. Make sure to visit before you leave."

"Huh," Trader said, surprised. Walnut Creek was the most advanced settlement on the circuit. Of course, Walnut Creek would have the first of any kind of store in Nor Cal in the After.

It was just hard for him to wrap his mind around the concept of a store just for music.

"She has a variety of music. My preferred genre of music was Lofi, which I guess some would call silly for a Stanford English professor," Earl said nostalgically. "I had a carefully curated playlist on YouTube. That would be almost sixty or seventy years ago now."

Trader had no clue what Lofi was but made a mental note to see if Bess had any. He also had a high-level awareness of what YouTube was from the books from the Before. But he couldn't fully comprehend the idea that he could watch a video or hear music from anywhere in the world at any time without even leaving home. He could empathize with Earl's musings about feeling overwhelmed by choices.

"I'll make sure to check it out," Trader answered.

Earl nodded, happy to have directed a friend to a unique experience. Beneath that, Trader sensed a deep sadness. He wondered what was driving Earl's openness this season. Earl was extremely old for someone in the After, and Trader could see the eighty-plus years weighing on him. He couldn't imagine what Earl had seen. What he had lost.

Thinking about all that Earl had been through, Trader asked, "Have you ever thought about writing your stories down?"

"I prefer to read books rather than write them," he answered quickly.

"I get it. I really do. But you're one of the few people who remembers the Before and can capture it through the lens of someone who has also seen the After. The books we have…they feel like another universe really, even the non-fiction. Now that we're starting to get our feet underneath us, I think it's important for people to hear your stories, even if they're hard to write down. It helps us see that bridge between then and now."

Earl picked at the food on his plate thoughtfully. Trader knew he didn't like talking about himself or anything from the Before and felt a twinge of guilt for pressing his friend.

"I might be able to find you a typewriter. Surely you guys can figure out the ink part of it. Or you could just write it down. And you make your paper right here." He tried to catch Earl's eye. "I would genuinely like to read your stories."

Earl put his fork down, placed his hands in his lap, and looked at Trader. "I suppose I should consider it. I honestly never thought that I would be someone creating a history that others would read years from now. There is something sentimental about that."

"Just consider it. For me?" Trader nudged.

"I will. I will," Earl responded, laughing lightly. He still looked sad. Trader hoped he would find peace in writing his own story, knowing that Trader and Jesse would pass the tales along the circuit.

The two friends resumed their idle conversation about good books they'd read. Earl listed a few that he was looking for, and Trader made a mental note. After their plates were practically licked clean, they cleared the table and headed out.

"It was lovely seeing you again, Trader. I always enjoy our conversations and look forward to your visits. When will you be leaving us?"

"I'm going to stay one more night and head out in the morning," Trader answered. "I lost some time on the circuit already and need to keep moving if I am gonna hit the foothill settlements this year."

Earl put out a hand. "I wish you safe travels, my friend. I will part ways with you here. My old man bladder is calling."

Trader shook his hand. "It was great seeing you, Earl. I'll keep an eye out for those books for you. And I am looking forward to reading the first few chapters of your book next year!"

***

Trader meandered down the promenade, peeking in stores as he walked by. Some, like Earl's bookstore, were used for production or trading. Others were used as residences. The latter often had curtains over the windows. If the curtains were pulled to the side, homey interiors suggested comfortable living spaces.

At the north end of the promenade, the smell of the paper factory in the Nordstroms filled the air. The sound of chatter as people worked spilled out from the open doors. He turned left towards S. Main St. The greenhouse in the Apple store was doing well. Tall shelves overflowing with lush plants filled the windows.

He turned south on Broadway Plaza Rd. where more workshops filled the buildings. A small store without a sign appeared to be an electronic repair shop. Wires hung in loops on the walls and baskets of electronic parts were neatly sorted on shelves and tables. The Banana Republic had been converted to a woodworking shop for furniture repairs. The sound of hammering could be heard through the open doors. Zara's had been replaced by a large sewing shop, where they repaired and made clothes. Piles of repurposed fabrics were arranged by color on the shelves. A few people sat at tables, either stitching by hand or using ancient sewing machines.

Trader was impressed by how organized the settlement was compared to last year. Walnut Creek had grown and matured significantly. He had half a mind to check out the hospital but decided against it; it was already late in the afternoon. The music store was a must-see, and he still needed to rest and pack up for tomorrow. He looped back to the See's Candy.

The small candy shop was overflowing with musical items. Trader was surprised they hadn't moved to a better location with more space. Music posters plastered the walls and ceiling. A thin path ran down the center of the store. One side had records and

THE BEFORE AND THE AFTER

CDs in crates piled on tables with old radios stacked haphazardly underneath. The other side had an assortment of instruments hanging on the wall, on stands, and piled on top of each other. All of the clutter was overwhelming.

A young woman with straight jet-black hair arranged in two buns on the top of her head hollered from the back. "Come on in!"

She was thin and wore a loose, hand-knit sweater that went down to her mid-thighs. Baggy pants and well-worn clunky military-style boots finished off her outfit. A pair of bulky headphones rested on her collarbones like a necklace.

"Hello, I'm Trader. I don't think we've met. I pass through once a year. Earl said I should check this place out." He reached out to shake her hand.

"Oh, I positively adore Earl. He's my fave. Yeah, yeah, come on in." She stepped around the counter to take his hand in hers.

"Have a look around, make yourself at home, whatever," she said warmly. "Oh, I'm Bess by the way."

"Nice to meet you." He looked around the store. "You have a lot of stuff here. I don't even know what a lot of these instruments are. Where'd you get them all?" He tapped a rhythm out on a drum with his fingers.

"Most of it I scavenged out of an old high school," Bess answered. "Lucked out that the stuff was just left there. Still trying to figure out how to get the piano out. Not a priority item for the work teams."

"The best stuff is the old electronics though," she continued. "I scavenged most of it, and Sarika helped me get it up and running. Have you been to her electronics shop yet? It's pretty slick. Most of her time is spent making sure the power stays on. But she also tinkers with stuff, repairing radios and old walkie-talkies in her spare time."

"I think I saw her shop when I was walking around. Is it by the woodworkers?" Trader asked.

"Yep, that's it. She's a rockstar. She found me an iPod cable from who knows where. I am trying to get the digital music up and running; it's just harder." She noticed Trader fiddling with a guitar.

"Here," she said as she picked it up and played a short tune. "Know anyone who plays?"

"I don't, sadly." Trader didn't know anyone who played *any* kind of musical instrument. Life was focused on surviving. It was only in the last couple of years that he had seen solid attempts at production for trade, such as the Silvas weaving fabric and the shoemaker at Forty Two. Sure, people sang songs and would maybe beat out a rhythm on a table. But he hadn't actually seen anyone play an instrument.

"Where'd you learn to play?" Trader asked.

"My dad taught me," Bess replied. "He played the guitar, acoustic and electric. He also played the taiko drums."

Bess put the guitar back in its place and waved him to the back. "Check this out. It's gonna blow your mind," she said with a huge grin.

Trader followed her to the back, where she pulled the headphones from around her neck and placed them over his ears; the pealing plastic of the earpads scratching lightly. All sound was instantly muffled. She fiddled with the iPod, and suddenly, music filled his head. He felt a wash of emotion and electricity race through his body. He'd never heard anything like this.

Bess must have seen his face. "I know, right?"

He saw her lips forming the words, but he couldn't hear her over the song. The song had an incredibly fast beat. It was amazing and overwhelming all at once.

When the song was over, he took the headphones off, grinning. "Wow…" was all he could say.

"That's 'Pump It' by the Black Eyed Peas. We're kinda limited with the iPod. Whatever is on it is what we get. Earl said that

THE BEFORE AND THE AFTER

people used to be able to program the music they wanted on these. There's even a way to get them off the CDs and onto the iPod. But Earl said I need a computer." She shrugged. "Maybe we can find one with a CD ROM. Sarika is keeping an eye out for me."

"I know a great scavenger outside of Sac," Trader said. "I'll ask him and bring one back by next year if he has it."

"That would be rad, thanks. I can play CDs on an old stereo Sarika got up and running for me. With an iPod, you can create playlists and stuff. If your friend has any iPods or other musical stuff, save it for me, please?"

"Will do," Trader replied. "Do you have any Lofi?"

Bess laughed in a friendly way. "No. Lofi came after the music switched over. Earl said people started streaming everything when iPods were replaced by cell phones. We pretty much lost any music made after that 'cause of the servers and all." She shrugged. "Earl said Lofi is like an evolution of electronic music, like the great, great grandbaby of the Eurythmics. He said that is the only CD I have that is even kinda close."

Trader had no clue who the Eurythmics were but didn't interrupt.

"I found a beat-up old synthesizer and a trap box. I am in line with Sarika to get them up and running again. It's super low priority. I am gonna play around with it a bit once they're working and see what music I can make."

"Can I listen to another song?" Trader asked.

"Sure, did you like the last song? Whoever loaded this iPod had a distinct taste. I might be able to dig something slightly different up," she offered.

"Honestly, I haven't heard any music like this before. Consider me open to all options."

"I got a great one. 'Good Feeling' by Flo Rida," she said, grinning in anticipation. "This one will blow your mind if you liked the Black Eyed Peas."

187

She picked up the iPod and started scrolling through the songs. Finding the one she wanted, she hit play.

Trader put the headphones back on. The music once again swirled in his ears. A tingling shiver went up and down his body. The deep, booming bass thudded along with his heart. He felt his head start to bob, and he started tapping his foot. He was surprised at how much power music had over his body. The feeling was indescribable. He hadn't ever experienced anything like that in his life. Bess' grin grew bigger as she saw the music affect him.

When the song finished, he was speechless. "I...wow...," he stumbled.

"I know, I know," Bess said, nodding. "It's incredible. Hearing music live is one thing. There is a certain power to hearing someone play music in-person, especially the taiko drums. You can feel the beat echo in your chest with those. But there is something special about listening to electronic music through headphones...it's an entirely different, very personal experience."

Trader agreed wholeheartedly. Singing around a campfire brought everyone together and was powerful in its own way. Listening to headphones was a whole other bag of beans. It felt like the music was actually in his head and all other sounds were cut out. With eyes closed and headphones on, he could see escaping fully and completely into the music. It was a uniquely isolating experience. He took the headphones off from around his neck and reverently set them on the counter.

"Do you want to listen to more?" she asked hopefully, eager to share.

"I...um." He cleared his throat. "That's a lot."

"Yeah. Yeah. I totally get it." She grinned again. "If you want another hit before you skedaddle onto your next stop, just come on by."

THE BEFORE AND THE AFTER

"I will. Thank you. I enjoyed it, I truly did. But...," he stammered.

"I get it. I love music, and the first time I heard it I just about shit myself," Bess tried to reassure him. "Now, I can't stop listening. I have all of the songs memorized. I know you don't know anyone who plays. But I got an extra guitar and an intro playing book if you are interested in trading for it. Wanna spread the love and all, you know? You'll probably want some extra strings too. They're *super* hard to find and will occasionally break."

"I will take you up on that," Trader said, relieved she had changed the subject. He was still trying to recover from listening to the iPod. It was a lot to process and exposed a raw nerve for him.

"I hadn't planned on trading anymore today. But I got lots of stuff back in my wagon. What are you looking for?" Trader asked.

Bess folded her lips in, thinking. "Food is always good. Anything electronic if you got it, like wires and stuff. What do you have?"

"I have plenty of food to trade. I have jerky, honey, kimchi, and a ton of other preserves, including nuts and nut butter. The rest of the trades you have plenty of here: meds, tools, books, building supplies, charcoal, and stuff like that. I don't have anything electronic. Hasn't been much need for it since I started on the circuit. Promise I'll bring some next year, though. I'm sure Rat has a ton."

"I'll take some nuts, some nut butter, and honey. Plus, if you have any, dried or preserved fruit." Bess didn't say exactly how much of each item she wanted. Trader, being experienced at this sort of thing, would make sure that he did right by her.

"I got just the right stuff. Let me run to my wagon."

"Here, let me grab the stuff for you now so you only have to make one trip." Bess selected one of the acoustic guitars from the wall, quickly tuned it, and passed it to Trader. She then went in the back and returned with a beat-up *Guitar for Dummies* book and a small roll of what looked like stiff wire of various diameters.

"It's all tuned up. It takes a good ear to tell. Pack it carefully in your wagon. Whomever you trade it to, have them play the strings to hear how they sound before they go hard at it. The book will show them how to tune it, restring it, and stuff. Replacement strings are super hard to find. So, I don't have all of the sizes. But it's a start." Bess handed everything over.

"I'm sure it will be fine," Trader said appreciatively. "I'll make sure it finds a good home and will fill you in next year. I'll be right back."

Trader took care of the swap with Earl's stories and the memory of Bess' music swimming through his head. It had been a long and slightly overwhelming day. He decided to spend the last few hours of daylight reading *The Gunslinger*, falling into the solitude of the book.

CHAPTER
TWENTY

Trader woke up at dusk, having fallen asleep reading, and the book now lay on the floor. He flipped through the pages, trying to find where he left off, marking it before setting it on the end table.

Damn, he said to himself.

His head was still swimming with all of the input from the day. Though he enjoyed the amenities of Walnut Creek, it was just *busy*. He didn't know how else to describe it. There were a lot of people, many of whom he didn't know. Information came at him in constant waves. And all of the choices before him were overwhelming. His feet were urging him to move on. A day or two here was just right. He'd had his fill, and it was time to move on.

He took his dried clothes down from the line and packed them, along with the other items scattered around. He briefly contemplated another shower seeing as it might be a while before he could have one as luxurious as he could get here and decided against it. Instead, he chose to grab a hot meal from the cafeteria and tuck in early for the night.

The cafeteria was busy when he walked in, and there was an

actual line. Dinner was a thick slab of tajine, which Trader later learned was a heavily spiced egg-based dish with baked-in layers of potatoes and spinach. The flavors were powerful, and unlike anything Trader had tried before. This was served with a mixed lettuce salad. Cookies were offered for dessert.

He grabbed one of the few empty tables. It was noisy at this hour, and the place was packed. Tajine night appeared to be popular. Trader wondered if this is what it was like in the Before. He tried to imagine coming in here with his own group, picking what he wanted to eat, and enjoying a meal with all of the hustle and bustle flowing around him like waves.

His meal finished, he picked up the last bit of the cookie crumbs with a finger and bussed his tray. After winding his way back through the queue, he grabbed some cookies to bring with him on the road. They were particularly tasty and not something he often had.

After dinner, he collected everything but his bedroll, book, and some food to trade for breakfast and made one last trip to the wagon for the day. By this time, the sun had fully set. Electric lights once again twinkled around the settlement.

Jasmine was gone when he visited the garage, likely done for the day. He was pleased to see Sasha taking a bath on the driver's seat. He'd started to miss her snuggles. She made a *merf* noise when she saw him, hopping down from the wagon to rub against his legs.

"Give me a sec," he told her affectionately, trying not to trip as he dropped off his load into the wagon.

Once his hands were free, he picked her up, cradling her. A deep throaty purr rattled as she pushed her face into his free hand. He scratched her under the chin. It was nice to be back with his buddy. Right here in this moment, Sasha and Boxer were all he needed.

Reluctantly, Trader gently placed Sasha in the back of the wagon. He petted her until she settled, content enough to sleep.

When he tried to leave, she batted at his hand. He laughed affectionately.

He grabbed a fresh carrot from the back of the wagon and went over to stall three. Boxer had been watching him and whickered excitedly at the sight of the carrot. The other horses, noticing the treat, whickered as well. Trader felt a twinge of guilt for only bringing enough for one. He decided to break the carrot into three pieces, laying a piece in his open palm, one for each horse. After scratching Boxer's mane and fiddling with his nose, Trader left to crash for the night.

* * *

The next morning, he woke early, with the dawn sunlight streaming in the windows at the front of the store and through to the back alcove. He was one of the first ones in the cafeteria, quickly eating his meal of eggs, orange slices, and potatoes. He was antsy to get back on the road. It was too early to say any last goodbyes to Kuldeep, Earl, and Bess. He knew they would understand. He grabbed his last few items, made sure the room was tidy, and switched the "Closed" sign back to "Open". With mixed feelings, he gave the room one last look and closed the door behind him.

Jasmine was already on duty at the garage feeding the horses when Trader came in. When she caught sight of him, she waved and leaned the pitchfork against the stalls.

"Leaving so soon?" she said casually.

"Yep. It's been a pleasure, but I've got a lot of miles to go before it gets too hot," he replied.

"Make good trades at least?"

"I did. I also had a chance to visit the music store. That was pretty incredible."

"Oh! Bess' place is great," Jasmine said enthusiastically. "I go in there just to listen to the iPod sometimes. She's super nice. Before you go, I finished up the book. You should check it out."

She walked over to the table at the front and rummaged around her pack, pulling out the beat-up copy of *The Galaxy and the Ground Within*. "If you come across any more books by Becky Chambers, please grab them for me. She's real good."

"Thank you, Jasmine. Much appreciated. Let me put this down. I'll be right back." He gestured with the large bedroll.

After storing the bedroll in the wagon, he fished out a jar of honey and some jerky as a gesture of thanks. Jasmine had taken good care of Boxer and Sasha. When he returned, he noticed a small canvas bag filled with apples next to the book.

"Boxer has been a great guest. I thought I'd send you off with some apples, too. He likes them. You can eat them too, if Boxer will share. They're tasty."

"Thanks for thinking of him." Trader laid down the honey and jerky. "This is for you."

"No need to trade for the book and the apples. Truly. My treat. It was a pleasure looking after Boxer. Even Sasha started warming up to me yesterday. She's sweet."

"Take them, please," he said. With a nod, she acquiesced.

He took the book and sack of apples to the wagon, checking to make sure everything was secure. Sasha was already sitting in her bed on the driver's seat, ready to go. Jasmine led Boxer over by the lead rope and helped Trader hitch him up.

"I brushed him last night and checked his hooves. He should be good to go," Jasmine said.

"Take care and see you next year. I'll keep an eye out for more books for you. I didn't have a chance to say goodbye to Bess, Earl, or Kuldeep. If you see them, please tell them I said goodbye?"

"Will do. Safe travels, Trader."

With Boxer fully hitched, Jasmine stepped back. Trader made a clicking sound and lightly flapped the reins. The wagon lurched forward as they headed out of the garage and back on the road. Trader raised his hand one more time, and Jasmine waved back.

He left Walnut Creek with a mixture of feelings. On the one hand, he'd enjoyed his time there, especially hearing Earl's stories and listening to the music. *The music!* He was already eager to listen again when he came back through next year. It was nice to feel like a part of something bigger, even just for a moment, and have all of the luxuries of a large community. But Walnut Creek was just that — a large community. All those people were too much for him.

The wagon turned north on the 680. The goal today was to get over the Carquinez Strait to the north side of the bay. The trio had started fairly early, but he wasn't sure he would make it all the way to the Machados' today. He might need to sleep in the wagon, which didn't sound half bad after the hustle and bustle of Walnut Creek.

Sitting in the driver's seat was like putting on a favorite pair of shoes. The rhythmic clopping of Boxer's hooves and the swaying of the wagon was soothing. It was also comforting to have Sasha curled up next to him, eyes open, watching the miles slowly roll by. It had only been two days, but he missed being around the two of them.

The 680 was in fairly good shape as he passed through what used to be Pleasant Hill and on through Concord. This area had been heavily populated in the Before. Now, empty buildings sat vacant in a large sprawl on either side of the highway. Trees, bushes, and other plants were starting to push their way in. Soon, the greenery would completely engulf the buildings, like the ancient temples of the Mayan and Incan empires. He imagined someone traveling the highway twenty or thirty years from now, finding ruins from the Before peeking out through a sea of trees.

After the hustle and bustle of Walnut Creek, the highway seemed eerily deserted. Around midday, the Benicia-Martinez

Bridge crept into view. The rising sea levels had pushed the borders of the bay south, covering the land in patches up to the intersection of the 680 and the 4. They navigated a small, flooded portion of the road before it sloped up to the bridge.

In the Before, there had been a sweep of wetland marsh that stretched eastward, providing a sanctuary for waterbirds. The preserve was now underwater, with the edges of the bay lapping at the cement border of the highway. Common Gallinule bobbed in the gentle waves. In the After, flooding had pushed silt across the freeway and into the space on the west side of the road. The marsh grasses had followed. A black-crowned night heron and several egrets were slowly wading through the water.

The trio broke for lunch just before the toll plaza, giving Boxer a short rest before taking the wagon over the tall arching bridge. Trader set up water for the animals but left Boxer hitched. He sat on the back of the wagon, munching on dried fruit and nuts, and bird-watched.

It was peaceful, with the occasional birdcall breaking the silence. He was grateful to see wildlife thriving here. With the oil refineries from the Before having flooded a couple of times, he often wondered how much had leached out into the surrounding water table and bay. It seemed like nature always found a way to bounce back despite the black blood of human greed seeping into the environment.

After their quick rest, Trader led Boxer and the wagon over the bridge, opting to walk and spare Boxer the extra weight. The Benicia-Martinez Bridge was the tallest one that Trader had ever been on, stretching high over the strait. They walked up the steep incline slowly and paused to catch their breath at the top.

The bridge had stood up well over time and offered jaw-dropping views of the bay. The sun sparkled on the water, contrasting brightly with the surrounding hills, which were still bright green and lush from the winter rain. A spray of orange California poppies spread across the northern hills. The views would change when the lush winter grasses turned amber in the summer sun, still beautiful in their own way. He could see the old rail bridge to the right. Far off in the distance, retired battleships were stacked along on the northern edge of the bay, like coffins arranged in a cemetery. An osprey coasted on currents above the water.

The downslope of the bridge was a piece of cake. His only worry was making sure the wagon didn't gain too much momentum on the descent. The highway forked at the base of the bridge. The trio took the eastern fork, staying on the 680.

Trader didn't know what to expect on this stretch of the road. Last year, several sections had been flooded, and a mudslide had partially blocked one segment. They could still wade through or go around. But, if the water hadn't receded, he expected there to be significant damage to the asphalt. He may even have to backtrack and take the wagon over the country roads that wove back and forth next to the highway.

They made their way across the overpass that crossed a dilapidated industrial area. The battleships were closer now. Though they had been near the water's edge in the Before, the ships were now so far from the shore that it would take a lot of rowing to get out there to scavenge. He idly wondered if anyone had converted one of the ships into a living space, but decided it was unlikely given the brackish water and limited access to farmable land. An isolated stronghold like that might be useful in a zombie apocalypse but wasn't very practical given the current state of affairs.

As they rounded the bend in the highway, Trader's heart sank. Water covered several stretches of the road. From this far away, he couldn't tell if they could safely wade through. He decided to exit and take Lopes Rd., which ran parallel to the highway on the side opposite the bay. Lopes Rd. was narrow and more pocketed, but it was less likely to be deeply flooded because the highway barrier formed what was essentially a two-foot breaker.

It turned out to be the right choice. Though the road was also flooded in some areas, it was shallow, not going above the tops of Boxer's hooves. By the irritated swishing of his tail and the bobbing of his head, he knew Boxer wasn't pleased to be wading in the water. He would have to give him extra treats tonight, perhaps one of Jasmine's apples.

Trader decided to press on and get further up the 80 before stopping. Most of Cordelia was underwater, and it would make an unpleasant night on the 680 between there and Benicia. He wanted to make sure Boxer had a nice place to graze.

As he turned east on the 80, the edges of the bay retreated. Off to his right sat an old shopping center, fast food restaurants, and Scandia. His first time around the circuit, Trader had nosed around the old minigolf and go-kart amusement park. He'd read about places like these, but couldn't imagine paying money to hit a small ball into a miniature castle or a tiny windmill. He took great pleasure in simple things, like eating a nice meal with friends or watching the waterbirds from the base of the bridge. The idea of being so busy that the people of the Before had to do *even more* just to relax always confused him.

Lush pastureland sat on the other side of a small hill from Scandia, and Trader decided to pull over there for the night. Sasha immediately jumped off the wagon and disappeared into the tall grasses. He unhitched Boxer, brushed him down, and checked his feet before setting him loose to graze a bit before sundown. Eventually, he would need to tie Boxer's lead rope to the wagon and make sure Sasha was safely tucked in. There were mountain lions around here.

A meal of nut butter, carrots, and the cookies from Walnut Creek was assembled. He settled on the front of the wagon, feet dangling over the edge, to eat. The soft rustling of Boxer wading through the grasses broke the vast silence. Water pressed in close to the eastern side of the hill, sparing only a small strip of tall grasses. Water birds coasted off in the distance. The heavyset profile of a red-tailed hawk was perched on a tall skeleton of an electrical tower. Across the highway to his left, a female northern harrier coasted low over the tall grasses, listening for prey.

After he finished his meal, he still had a bit of daylight left. He nestled into his new, clean bedroll, deciding to read a few chapters of *The Gunslinger* before getting the animals put up for the night.

CHAPTER
TWENTY-ONE

Trader jerked awake to the sound of Sasha's low growling. She was tucked in close to him, hair raised. The eerie sounds of coyotes yipping in the distance sent a chill down his back.

"Fuck!" Trader said frantically, realizing that the sun had fully set.

With his mind still foggy, he painfully half-fell out of the wagon. He squinted through the darkness, trying to find Boxer. The moon was just a sliver in the sky, but the stars sparkled brightly. Boxer's shadow was right next to the wagon. Hearing him, the horse let out a soft nervous whicker.

The coyotes were yipping again, the sounds closer than before. Trader cursed himself for falling asleep. As Trader's heart slowed, he quickly took stock of the situation. He felt his way around the wagon towards Boxer. He cursed himself again as he realized he had forgotten the lead rope. He looped an arm over his withers as Boxer brushed him with an irritated tail.

"Come on, boy," Trader whispered.

Trader nudged Boxer softly behind his front leg and made a muffled clicking sound. He led him to the front of the wagon and fumbled around for the lead rope. He put the halter on and tied him securely to the wagon.

The coyotes sang to each other, urging Trader to move faster. Trader quickly closed the canvas flaps in the front, lacing them up tightly. He moved to the back and patted around the inside of the wagon for Sasha. She let out a startled hiss when he touched her. Reassured that she was still in the wagon, he climbed in and secured the back flaps, lacing them both in.

"Stay here tonight," he whispered to her, pulling her close and petting her poofy hair.

She let out another low growl.

"Shush now."

She quieted down, but her tail swished back and forth, and her body was tense.

Boxer's hooves clicked on the pavement as he shifted around outside. Trader hoped the smell of the wagon and the threat of a swift kick to the head by one of Boxer's large hooves would keep the coyotes back.

Trader tried to go back to sleep, but every small sound woke him. A great-horned owl hooted several times, waking him up the first time. A medium-sized critter, like a raccoon or an opossum, padded through the grass, starling him awake yet again. He lay in his bedroll, heart thundering, listening intently. Sasha was like glue next to him, also alert.

Right before sunrise, he was frightened awake again, this time to the sound of multiple large animals moving around the wagon. Boxer's hooves danced nervously along the pavement, followed by a low aggressive whinny. Based on the rustling, he suspected it was the pack of coyotes, brave enough to come sniffing around the wagon. Trader grabbed hold of Sasha tightly.

"Get the fuck out of here!"

He started slapping on the canvas side of the wagon. The skittering of surprised toenails clicked on the asphalt. Sasha tensed but didn't try to claw her way free. Trader continued shouting and making noise until he couldn't hear the animals rustling anymore. Eventually, he heard yipping off in the distance. By the sounds of it, Boxer seemed to have settled, and Trader suspected that the coyotes had decided to buzz off.

After the adrenaline dump, there was no going back to sleep. With his eyes dry and sandy from a poor night's rest, he sat in the dark of the wagon, cradling Sasha, until the dim light of the sun started streaming in through the crack between the canvas flaps. As soon as it was light enough, Trader unlaced the flaps and peaked outside.

"Stay there," he said sternly to her.

No way in hell I was going out there anyway, stupid. She glared back at him, tense.

Once outside the wagon, he checked on Boxer and did a quick circuit. The horse looked tired, but otherwise unharmed. Trader was grateful that they only had a short distance to travel to get to the Machados' today. Trader untied the lead rope to let Boxer graze a bit. The tilt of Boxer's ears and swishing of his tail spoke volumes about how irritated and miserable he was.

"Okay, okay. I get it."

Trader scratched the horse's mane and fed him one of Jasmine's apples. He hitched Boxer up and grabbed jerky to munch on for breakfast. As soon as they started moving and the smell of jerky wafted back, Sasha tentatively joined him up in the driver's seat.

"Knew you wouldn't be able to resist. Sorry last night was so terrible."

Trader offered her some jerky. She ate it daintily in her cat bed in the driver's seat. Despite the sun still not being fully up, the trio was glad to be back on the road and away from the deserted city.

* * *

The 80 took them east and then arched north through the city of Fairfield. The city was in fairly good shape, spared from fires and flooding. When there'd still been enough water piped in from surrounding areas to create breeding pools for the mosquitoes, Weeps had hit the city pretty hard. Once the power grid went down, the water was shut off, and the drought suffocated the city. There simply wasn't enough water to support a large settlement in Fairfield without the power to pump it in, even with rain barrels helping them out.

In previous years, Trader had connected with a few holdouts in town, swapping items more out of charity than a truly fair trade. The few people who'd stayed behind had struggled fairly hard. Last year, the handful of people that he knew about had abandoned their place and moved north to join the Machados. Trader guessed there still might be folks eking out an existence in the dry city, but they'd never made themselves known to him.

Fairfield reminded Trader of Pleasant Hill and Concord. The buildings of the city sprawled out in either direction, straddling the highway. Drought-tolerant trees and other plant life were slowly moving in, quickly sucking up the little bit of water that fell and replacing the water-greedy plants typically used in landscaping in the Before. Sprouts of stubborn, scraggly grass poked through broken concrete. Sycamore, oak, and acorn trees had moved in, providing more shade and organic material to support some of the less hardy plants. The north end of Fairfield abruptly transitioned to broad stretches of grassland that folded into low, rolling hills spotted with trees separated by bright swaths of purple lupine. The Machados' was just a tad north of the city. Rather than break for lunch, they pressed on to the settlement, having started on the road so early that it wasn't worth stopping.

The Machados' was uniquely positioned in a small hollow next to the Lagoon Valley Reservoir. It was close to Fairfield and Vacaville for easy scavenging, but surrounded by enough land that they could easily farm and raise livestock. They had

THE BEFORE AND THE AFTER

converted the preserve into extensive farmland and even started building trellises up the sloping hills.

The reservoir was the lifeline of the community. The hills bordering the eastern side of the reservoir served as a sort of rain catch, collecting the low clouds blowing in from the ocean and forcing them to release their moisture before passing into the Sacramento Valley. The reservoir was heavily stocked with catfish to keep the mosquitoes down. It lowered the risk of Weeps, but it wasn't perfect. Living next to standing water, there was always a risk of crying the bloody tears.

Because there were no rivers or creeks in the immediate area, the reservoir levels would sometimes drop to a nail-biting level. Rain barrels were attached to most homes as a backup. They also had the Alamo River on the other side of the low hills from which they could fetch water in difficult years. It was a long trek though.

The reservoir was small enough that it was easy to walk around. If not properly managed, it had the potential to flood the small homes that hugged its edge. Nari had set up an extensive irrigation system from the lake to the surrounding farmland. Their primary function was, of course, to water the crops. But the system also acted as a spillway and allowed the community to control the water levels in the small reservoir in times of heavy rain.

The biggest downside to the Machados' was the fire risk. The dried native grasses on the surrounding hills were a tinderbox. All it would take was one dry lightning storm, and the entire farm would be wiped out. They'd been spared this catastrophic possibility to date, but they did worry about it. Large fire breaks were built around the community and in between farm plots. They also had a solid exit strategy to get everyone out should a fire come sweeping through.

Trader turned the wagon east on Lagoon Valley Rd. On his right, there were plowed fields with furrows and mounds. Two figures were off in the distance working with irrigation pipes. He raised a hand, and one of them waved back. Freshly sprouted wheat peeked out from the rich soil. Trader's stomach rumbled, remembering the bread Jesse had shared.

To his left, there was a herd of several dozen Nubian goats grazing on a native grass pasture. A donkey was with them, serving as a sentry. This particular donkey was a nasty little shit. No one could get close to him to brush him down or check his hooves. But the salty old bastard was tough enough to scare off any mountain lion that might be passing by and thinking about having a goat as a snack. The donkey also kept coyotes away from the goats when they were kidding. Nature had found a nice balance in the After, and the idea of a tasty goat simply wasn't worth the risk of getting one's head bashed in by a pissed-off ass.

Trader guided the wagon north on La Costa Dr. The reservoir and the surrounding homes soon became visible off to the right. The area had once been a nature preserve where people could walk the paved path and picnic around the reservoir. Because of that, there was pre-existing architecture that had been built out in the After.

The last time he was here, the settlement had boasted about thirty or forty people. Guessing from the number of residents milling about and considering how many were likely out in the fields, that number still seemed about right. A cluster of homes hugged pre-existing fire pits and picnic tables from the Before. A few people were out cooking or eating lunch. He was relieved to see that no one was dressed in all white.

As he neared the community space, two children got up from what appeared to be an outdoor school session and ran to the wagon. A few people looked up and some waved. He was familiar here, and the folks were friendly.

"Hey, kiddos," Trader said, smiling down at them and pulling the wagon to a stop. He remembered their faces but not their names. He was happy to see them alive and kicking.

THE BEFORE AND THE AFTER

The children started petting Boxer, who whickered low and appreciatively. They both giggled. The teacher called for them to come back, and they dashed to the picnic table in a flash.

Brianna left her spot by a fire pit and walked over, smiling at the children as they ran past. She was in her late thirties and slim. She had dark skin and hair woven into long, thin braids. She wore a pair of heavily patched jeans and a loose, hand-embroidered shirt. Her thumbs were slung in her pockets.

"Well, look what the cat dragged in. Nice to see you, Trader. Jesse passed through less than a week ago, so I figured you'd be along soon, too." She reached out to scratch Sasha under the chin.

"Nice to see you and yours are doing well, Brianna."

Brianna was one of three on the small community council, along with Manuel and Nari. Though the community didn't have a hierarchical leadership, the council helped allocate resources, assign tasks, and settle any small disputes. It was an effective type of governing for a settlement this size.

"Go ahead and park your wagon down there," she said, pointing to an empty picnic area with an adjacent parking spot. "I'll ask Carlos to run some grass over for Boxer. Come on over to the fire pit once you're settled. Manuel is out in the wheat field with Nari, working on an irrigation issue. They will be back later, though."

"Sounds good," he replied.

Trader led the wagon past the small cluster of houses and backed it into the slot. He set out water and unhitched Boxer with practiced ease. He decided to leave him haltered, with his lead rope loosely tied to the wagon. There were just enough places for Boxer to wander and cause accidental damage that he thought tying him up was best.

Just as Trader finished brushing him down and checking his hooves, Carlos came over with a large armload of dried native grass. Boxer neighed softly, excitedly shifting his feet. Carlos

207

laid the grass out within reach of the lead rope. Sasha had already scampered off to find her meal. The animals had quickly shed the stress from the escapades the night before and were instantly comfortable at the Machados'.

"Thank you, kindly," Trader said.

Carlos tipped his hat and went back to the main part of the camp.

Trader decided to eat a late lunch before heading over to socialize. Dining on dried fruit and nuts, he sat on the back of the wagon, looking out over the water. Several ducks and geese bobbed on the surface and walked along the shores. A red-shouldered hawk perched in a cluster of trees on the far side. Every once in a while, the still water of the reservoir would bubble as a fish reached up to catch an insect hovering close to the surface.

With his hunger sated, Trader headed over to the cluster of homes. Repurposed wood had been used to build studio and one-bedroom structures. These homes typically sat in a space next to individual picnic areas and often boasted fire pits. There was also a larger building used as a community space where they could work indoors when the weather was bad. The community space and most of the homes were clustered together, close enough to the bathrooms to be convenient. Several other homes were dotted individually around the reservoir. These homes boasted more privacy but had a longer walk to the commode.

Trader was surprised to find that several of the buildings had been painted with large murals since the last time he had been there. The first mural was small, covering about a third of the outer wall of a small studio place. There was a detailed, grayscale profile of a young girl from the shoulders up. In her hand, she held a dandelion that she was blowing. The dandelion was in color, popping out from the wall. The stem of the dandelion was the usual green. But each seed head exploding from the flower dazzled in various colors of the rainbow, sparkling away from the girl. The most striking feature of the art piece was a bright red tear streaking down the girl's cheek. It was such a vivid contrast that Trader paused to take it in.

The next mural covered the entire length of one side of a large dwelling. Broad diagonal lines created a rainbow. Each color artfully blended into the next such that it was difficult to draw a line between two distinct colors. It reminded him of real rainbows when the sun peered through a rain cloud. Further on, he saw an artist he didn't recognize at work on a third mural. Vibrant pops of red were visible even from afar.

Trader was reminded of the Before murals scattered throughout Sacramento. He had a few by his house, but his favorites were downtown. Most adorned the sides of flooded buildings, and some were partially covered. He would take a kayak out to see them sometimes. It was peaceful out on the water, with the slow rocking of the waves and the beautiful art rising from the watery depths of the Sacramento Bay.

Trader was fascinated to see mural art reemerge in the After. He wondered whether the artist had found paint that somehow hadn't dried to a block or if they made their own. Curious, he walked over to introduce himself.

"Hey. How's it going? Did you do those other paintings? They're beautiful." He gestured to the girl blowing on the dandelion.

The man paused and rested his brush on a small piece of scrap wood. He looked up at Trader and quickly broke eye contact, looking down at the paints.

"Yeah," he said uncomfortably.

"I'm Trader. I don't think we've met." Trader would normally have offered his hand but decided not to this time. The man had put his hands in his pockets, hunched his shoulders, and kept glancing at Trader's face without really looking at him. He could sense that social situations were difficult for the man.

"Malikai," he answered, fidgeting.

Malikai was young, probably in his late teens, with a shadow of a beard coming in. He had thick, dark, wavy hair and light brown skin. He wore what appeared to be hand-sewn, cotton pants and a woven shirt. Paint was splattered over his clothes, and his hands were stained in colored splotches.

Trader took in the developing mural. There was a faint outline of what appeared to be an ancient Mesoamerican man. Thick necklaces hung around his neck and broad bracelets encircled his arms. A large headdress of long feathers sat on his head and tipped over his back. He carried a spear. In the background were Mayan pyramids, blocky animals, and flowers. Malikai had been working on one of the bright red flowers.

"That's really cool," Trader said with genuine appreciation. "How do you make the paint?"

Malikai picked up one of the small pots on the ground and tilted it to him, still not making eye contact. The crimson paint appeared pasty and slightly granular.

More comfortable talking about his art, he said, "I had to try a couple of things and it still doesn't work perfect and it can be clumpy. Limestone and beet juice make this color. I have to play with different plants and stuff to find the colors I want. Like onion skins for yellow and spinach for green and black beans for blue. Sometimes it doesn't work for some reason, it doesn't stick to the wall, the paint washes off. Finally got it down with my first one. That rainbow over there." He pointed to the second mural.

"Who taught you to paint like that?" Trader asked.

Malikai shrugged, uncomfortable again. "No one. I drew on the walls when I was a kid. As long as I get my chores done, they let me make art."

"Seriously though, dude. This is really cool. Where do you get your ideas from?"

Malikai shrugged again, bashful. "Most of it's in my head. This one here…They let me go on a run with them to Fairfield to the library there. I grabbed a couple of art books and liked the Mayan style."

"I haven't seen anyone do anything like this in the After. You're incredibly talented."

As soon as the words left his mouth, Trader wished he could pull them back in. Trader could tell Malikai was getting increasingly embarrassed and was uncomfortable accepting compliments. Trader sensed him closing off a bit.

Changing the subject, he asked "Any other books you're looking for? I can keep an eye out."

Malikai shrugged, looking at the ground. "I just like seeing what others have done. Gives me ideas."

"I'll grab some from Walnut Creek and bring them by next year. You ever been to Sac?" Trader asked.

"No," he said, digging at the ground with the toe of his worn shoes.

"If you ever get a chance to come up that way, it'll be worth it. There're murals all over the city from the Before."

"Isn't Sac flooded?" Malikai asked, interest piqued but still looking at the ground.

"Yeah, most of it is," Trader admitted. "The murals are really big though, and are on buildings that are hella tall. So, you can still see them…or most of them at least."

Malikai's only response was to fidget with the edge of his shirt. His eyes shifted between the mural and his paints on the ground.

"Well, thanks for letting me interrupt and pick your brain. Again, it looks great. I'm looking forward to seeing the finished product when I come back by next year. Think about heading up to Sac sometime. I can even give you a ride when I pass through again."

Malikai smiled and nodded slightly, still looking down, and picked up his brush to get back to the painting.

It filled Trader with hope to see him creating art for the

simple pleasure of making the world more beautiful. When people were just trying to survive, it was hard to find the time to make stuff that didn't have a functional purpose. Sure, folks like Hiroshi might whittle by the fire, but the murals were something else altogether; they took a lot of time and energy. It was nice to see a community secure enough in the future that they could dedicate resources to the simple act of bringing joy to others.

CHAPTER TWENTY-TWO

Trader joined Brianna by the fire pit where she and two others he didn't recognize were weaving baskets and idly chatting. Trader grabbed the empty seat closest to Brianna.

"Hello," Trader said to the group, nodding to the two others. "The murals over there are beautiful. Reminds me of some of the ones from the Before in Sac."

"Malikai does excellent work. It's nice to see creativity beyond necessity." An older man said, looking down at the large basket he was working on with knobby, arthritic hands.

"Reminds me of pictures in some of the books you bring, Trader. You say people drew on the walls in the Before?" Brianna asked.

Brianna was in her early thirties, having been born right before Weeps hit. She'd shared on a previous visit that she was from Fairfield, but the lack of water had driven her group north to the Machados'. She'd never been anywhere else.

"Yeah, murals are stashed all over the city, like little treasures to be found," Trader answered. "I feel like I find a new one every time I wander around. The best pictures are on the sides of buildings that are now part of the bay. They're still worth a trip on a boat to check them out though. There's one just north of the river. It's small and looks like the area flooded at one point, but the bay doesn't reach there yet. Anyway, it's of a lovely woman wearing a see-through surgical mask. Makes me wonder if it was a COVID-related painting."

"I've read a bit about that plague," said a young woman sitting across from Trader. "I've always wondered why the influenza and COVID outbreaks were just bumps in the road and then things like smallpox, the bubonic plague, and Weeps took out entire regions or civilizations. From what I understand, it took Europe a long time to bounce back after the Black Death. I wonder how long it'll take us."

"It was more than just Weeps that hit us," the old man mused. "The problem was all the stuff that knocked us down before that. If it'd just been Weeps, we would've been able to keep up with creating and distributing treatments. We may have even gotten a vaccine. We were just taking too much, and then we got put in our place.

"Sacramento used to be the heart of this region," the old man said, shifting the conversation. "The capital survived a bit longer than other places. When I was little, they still had Kings games at DOCO. Man, I loved watching basketball and chanting, 'Light the beam'. My dad would always take me for a treat at a little French patisserie right there. Some of the other places were already closed. But Starbucks and that little place stayed open until the end. My favorite was the macarons. I miss those." The old man sucked on his lips, thoughtfully.

Brianna and the other woman continued weaving, listening to the story. Trader recognized the man from previous seasons but didn't know his name and had never heard his stories before. He leaned in, elbows perched on his knees.

"I remember those murals in town," the old man continued. "Tucked behind that patisserie was a painting of two snakes entwined around each other. It was just some random alley with dumpsters and stuff. Those damn snakes were made to look like they were coming right out of the wall; they were done so well. I remember always asking my dad to go look at them when we went to games."

Trader knew exactly where the old basketball stadium was. He didn't have the heart to tell the old man that all the little stores were underwater now. Being familiar with most of the murals in the area, he was pretty sure the snake painting was in a watery grave too. He kept his lips sealed. The old timers had already lost too much.

"I can't remember if the Kings stopped playing or if the place flooded first. We just stopped going. And then my parents didn't have work anymore, and that was that." The old man's voice caught.

"Seeing Malikai paint…." The old man paused, gathering his thoughts, his face a mixture of both sadness and hope. "I'm just grateful to see a little bit of that come back before my time is up."

Brianna stopped her weaving to look at the old man. She reached over and rested her hand on his gnarled one.

"We are on our way, 'Betto," Brianna said. The old man looked up at her and smiled sadly.

"Yes, we're definitely on our way," Trader reassured them. "This year on the circuit, communities have started to branch out. They have a shoemaker at Forty Two." Trader showed off his boots. "The Silvas are working on training people to weave cotton so they can grow and weave their own. And, no joke, there is a music store in Walnut Creek now. We'll get there."

"I'd love to work on better access to medical care and treatments," the young woman said. "We only get medicine that is expired or only works sometimes."

"I hear you there," Trader said. "I traded for some brand-new penicillin from Kuldeep in Walnut Creek. He said it came down from up north around Portland. Kuldeep thinks they'll have fresh ibuprofen next year."

Intrigued, the young woman looked up from her weaving. "Really? That's hella cool!"

"You know, if you're interested in medical training, you may want to head to Walnut Creek," Trader continued. "They have the hospital up and running and are training staff there. You could always do a stint up in Portland to learn how they make meds and bring the process back to Walnut Creek if you want to keep it local."

"That would be wonderful!" the young woman exclaimed. "I've always wanted to learn to be a nurse or a doctor. Maybe even make medicines one day. I've never been to Walnut Creek. How does it work there? I've heard it's huge."

Trader went on to explain the settlement, how it had come together, and how best to travel there should she decide to. Brianna chimed in at one point, encouraging her to go, even suggesting she bring another of the settlement's residents along on the journey. He suspected Brianna was thinking that, strategically, it would be pretty nice to have well-trained medical professionals onsite. Even if the young woman decided not to come back, it was a good skill to send out into the wider world.

Brianna put her basket down and rubbed the muscle between her thumb and pointer finger. "Well, Trader, if you're about ready, I'll go make the rounds and let everyone know that you'll be open for business right before supper. That'll give you some time to relax before the locusts descend."

"Sounds good. I'm gonna go for a loop around the reservoir and then check in on Claire."

"Make yourself at home. I assume you're planning on staying tonight at least?"

"Yes, ma'am," Trader answered. "Will head out in the morning, though. I'm a little bit behind this year and want to make it up into the mountains before the heat sets in."

THE BEFORE AND THE AFTER

"If you don't have any plans, we'd love to have you for dinner tonight," Brianna offered. "I'll ask Nari and Manuel to join us if you are up for it."

"That sounds great, thanks," Trader replied. He appreciated how friendly and welcoming they always were to him.

They both rose and nodded to the young woman and old man who continued their weaving. Brianna started walking around the different working groups, filling them in on the trading plan. Trader headed in the opposite direction, away from the cluster of homes, along the footpath around the reservoir.

* * *

The walk around the small reservoir was a pleasant one. The sky was bright blue, with small cotton ball puffs of clouds floating merrily along. A flock of goldfinches chittered away in the trees. A hummingbird sipped from the delicate purple flowers of a desert lilac. Trader startled a jackrabbit, who skittered across the path and into the shelter of a cluster of cacti.

On the opposite side of the reservoir, there was a small house set back from the water, alone. Clustered around it were a dozen or so fruit trees. Three of the closest trees were citrus of some kind and were lush with sweet-smelling, white flowers. He took a deep breath, feeling himself relax.

The small home was truly beautiful. The front had been outfitted with trellises that boasted a spray of bougainvillea, the bright pink flowers making the place look warm and welcoming. The front garden was a flower paradise, overflowing with California poppies, island alumroot, lavender, manzanita, and hummingbird sage. Further from the home, there was a small cactus garden, complete with a sandy walking path and a palo verde tree.

The garden was busy with wildlife. There were two types of bees, including the traditional type that the Nakamuras kept as well as the large, fluffy, native black bees the size of the end of his thumb. Painted lady butterflies and hummingbirds fluttered about the yard. Squirrels chased each other up, down, and around the trees.

This was his favorite dwelling on the entire circuit. He envied the old woman who lived there and her amazing green thumb. He had often thought of coming out to the Machados' and setting up his own spot; close enough to the community to be around people but far enough away that he could enjoy personal time. But his heart was in Sacramento. Though he toyed with the idea of settling somewhere else, he knew that, ultimately, he would miss his house, Carla, and the skeleton of the Before that surrounded his home there. He took a deep breath, savoring the moment and enjoying the peaceful abundance of the little garden before moving on down the path.

He circled back to the edge of the reservoir where he had entered the settlement and crossed out into the pasture. From previous visits, he knew that there was a small structure near the goats that was used for milking and making feta cheese. This was the only building that boasted 24/7 power. Solar panels had been connected to several house batteries that kept the antique refrigeration units running. He was hoping to check in on Claire and the goats before heading back to his wagon.

The building was broken into sections. The first was a three-sided barn that served as the milking parlor. This was connected to a second room, where the milk was cultured and pressed. Next to that was the cold room where battered, sixty to seventy-year-old fridges of various shapes and sizes were chugging away, hanging on by a wish and a prayer.

To help reduce the stress on the units, other systems had been put into place to keep the room cool in the blasting heat of the summer. The building itself was strategically located under the shade of several large trees, including an ancient sycamore and a handful of old oaks. Small shrubs were also pushed up against the walls, offering a buffer and creating a small microclimate. The cool shade also served to shelter the adjacent chicken coop.

The fridges themselves produced a lot of heat. During the summer, small rectangular windows at the top of the structure were opened and small fans circulated the hot air out of the building. Sometimes it still wasn't enough, especially when summer temps peaked over 115 degrees Fahrenheit. Then, they'd have a feta feast, eat everything, and shut the fridges down for the summer. Electricity was redirected to misters in the milking parlor to keep the goats comfortable.

The goats were milked by hand into large metal pails in the early morning. By the time Trader finally made his way over, milking had long since finished. All of the goats were out in the field, munching away. He loved watching the clever creatures. Even the mean, old donkey that stood guard made him smile, despite being an ornery little turd.

Trader could hear soft clanging in the second room and announced himself with a light knock on the wall. Claire walked into the milking parlor, wiping her hands on an apron.

"Trader! Glad to see you!" She gave him a big hug.

Claire was tall and curvy, her arms thick with muscle from working the goats and the cheese. She was about Trader's age, with straight dark hair and almond skin. She had an old tank top on with a loose, long skirt. She wore battered work boots from the Before, leather popping open at the seams.

"Nice to see you too. How're the goats doing?" Trader followed her back into the prep room.

"Quite well. The goats keep making babies and making milk. We're lucky."

On the far wall was an old electric stove that she used to heat the milk to separate the curd. She must have done that earlier, because now she was working with the curd, cutting it away carefully from the top of the pot and separating it into layers of cheesecloth. Each bundle of curd was spun tight and hung on an old laundry rack, where it would drip into a pan below. Each bundle would sit for about half a day. After dinner, Claire would come back out and place each chunk in brine overnight. The next morning after milking, she would pull the chunks out of the brine to sit at room temperature for a day or two until they would be packed to store in the fridges.

"Hope you brought lots of salt this year. The amount of milk is outpacing the salt and the vinegar. I was thinking we probably need to start making vinegar soon. Apple Hill is a long way to go for something we should be able to make here."

"Apple Hill *is* a long way." Trader's eyebrows creased. "I don't recall seeing any apple trees here though. How are you planning on making your own vinegar?"

"We don't have any full-grown trees here. I do have a few seedlings about yay high, though." She held her hand up to her knee. "If any of them make it, we're looking at a good eight to ten more years before we can produce a solid crop."

Trader whistled. "Dang…I do have salt for you, but I'm not sure if I have as much as you want. I stocked up at Walnut Creek. I pretty much guessed based on what you said you needed last year. Did Jesse bring you vinegar?"

"They did," Claire said, beaming. "Lots of it. Not sure how they fit it all in their little camper thingy. As an upside, getting all that out of the trailer made space for all the bread they traded for." She laughed.

"Oh my god, that bread," Trader said, salivating. "I ran into Jesse south of Walnut Creek. They shared some with me. I haven't ever eaten anything like that."

"Manuel has done an amazing job getting the wheat pasture up and running." Claire nodded in agreement. "We should have more bread next year to trade. The hard part is the damn irrigation. Nari has been dinking around with it for almost a year, and it still isn't right."

With the last bit of curd set out to drain, she wiped her hands off.

"Here. Come have a bit of cheese."

Trader followed her into the cold room, where she rustled around in a fridge. She had a system for storing the cheese, rotating them between fridges and shelves to help keep track of what was ready and what could do with more time. She brought out a metal pan and set it on a table. Blocks of cheese rested in yellow-tinged, slightly cloudy water. The sharp smell of the cheese filled Trader's nose. Fermentation was happily chugging away.

She broke off a piece of one of the squares and handed it to him. She then broke off another piece for herself. Trader nibbled at the tangy cheese, the sharp flavor exploding on his tongue. He savored it, pressing it to the roof of his mouth. He loved feta, and always looked forward to getting his annual fill at the Machados'. He wished he had a side of dried fruit or salad to crumble it on. It was too early for basil, but he knew that the feta would also be tasty layered with the strong herb and tomatoes.

"Mmmm," he murmured appreciatively.

"Mmmm, indeed. It's a good batch this year," she bragged in a friendly way. "We're getting so much milk. I'm thinking about making soap too. Alina grows all sorts of scented flowers, so I'm thinking I might even be able to make it smell good."

"It'd make a good trade. Just about everyone wants some of the Nakamuras' lavender soap. Not sure how they make it though. Do you?"

"Nope. Figured I'd just trial and error it." She shrugged as she leaned back on the table, nibbling a second piece of cheese.

Noticing Trader had finished his, she passed him another small piece.

"I'll ask the Nakamuras when I pass through next year. I'll also keep my eye out for any books about it. Unfortunately, homesteading books are few and far between."

"I bet. They're like gold nowadays." Claire shook her head slightly.

"Nice to see the settlement doing so well," he said. "I saw Malikai's murals. I haven't seen anyone make anything like that in the After. Feels like we're on a tipping point."

"Mm-hmm." She slowly nodded.

She gestured to him with another piece of cheese, and he shook his head.

"No thanks," he said not unkindly. "I'll grab some in the morning for breakfast. That's one trade I can't take with me that I wish I could."

She smiled, putting the tray back in the fridge and closing the door with her hip. "Want to go out and see the goats? I can clean up later."

"I'd love to," he answered genuinely.

Claire kept things fairly close to her chest and often didn't share stories, instead preferring to talk about the goats, milk, or cheese. Trader didn't mind. He just enjoyed her relaxed company and unwavering care for her animals.

After hanging up her apron, she donned a light long-sleeved shirt and a broad woven hat. He followed her out into the pasture. Once the herd noticed Claire, they wandered over. The donkey followed, reluctantly letting the humans get close to his charges.

A couple of goats stood on the wire fence, the splits of their front hooves stretching over the wire. They snuffled around Trader and Claire, looking for treats, prehensile upper lips twitching back and forth. Trader laughed, scratching a brown and black goat that was nibbling gently on the collar of his shirt.

"I thought about keeping goats at one point," Trader reflected. "But I couldn't have just one. That isn't right. And I don't have the space to keep a small herd."

"They're nifty creatures. So intelligent." Claire scratched one of the goats behind the ears. "But you're right. You'd need a couple, and you'd need to rotate them around areas to eat."

"Yeah, we just don't have that in Sac. It wouldn't be fair to them, I think. I'll just have to come here for my feta fix and goat snuggles." He smiled warmly.

"You'd always be welcome here. You know that," Claire said, color rising to her cheeks and avoiding his gaze. "You could get a daily dose of goat nibbles."

"That's nice of you," Trader said, also a bit embarrassed.

Silence stretched between them as they pet the goats. One of the goats managed to reach Claire's hat and made a grab for it, tugging it askew on Claire's head. Claire caught it, straightened it on her head, and backed away a step.

"Marietta, you little shit." She laughed. Trader laughed with her.

"I better get back to the wagon. I think people will want to start trading soon so that they can get home for dinner. I know Brianna was passing the word."

"I'll join you on the way," she said warmly. "I need to grab some things from my place to trade for the salt." They walked back to the cluster of homes, in a natural, companionable silence.

Trader gazed out at the small community, giving himself a quiet moment to fully ponder the idea of setting down roots here. He glanced over to Claire. She was watching him as they walked. As if reading his mind, she smiled sadly. They each knew they had roles to play, and his was on the open road. She reached over, grabbing his hand for a quick squeeze.

CHAPTER TWENTY-THREE

Back at the wagon, Boxer was taking a standing snooze, back leg bent and head drooping. When Trader approached, the horse greeted him with a soft whicker, shifted legs, and snuffled at the ground. Trader gave his withers a scratch before checking his water.

Sasha had also returned from her adventures and was now splayed out in the sun on the picnic table. With a *merf,* she acknowledged his presence and started purring. He stroked her hair, feeling the warmth of the sun.

"I'm gonna have to move you, girl. Trading is going to start soon."

He gently picked her up, and she butted her head against his face, her purr turning deep. He placed her on his bedroll in the back of the wagon, petting her until she settled in a meatloaf position, returning to her nap.

Trader set his wares out on the picnic table. Even though they were pretty well fed here at the Machados', he laid out a couple of jars of honey and kimchi, thinking them to be unique enough that some might be interested. He added some of the Nakamuras' leather and lavender soap. He set out about a quarter of the salt, saving some for himself and making sure there would be enough for Claire as well. He also laid out what he thought would be the most popular items: the medicines from Kuldeep. On the benches, he placed fiction and non-fiction books for various ages. On the ground, he spread out some of the metal tools, knives, wire, screws, and nails.

He grabbed *The Gunslinger*, now almost finished, and took a seat on the back of the wagon, waiting for people to come and trade. When he first started reading, he felt a kinship with the main character of the story. Roland was laser-focused on a single destination, crossing paths with others, but seemingly always alone. The way Roland traced the path of the wizard, just one step behind him, mirrored Trader's own experience with Preacher. But, after reading the part about where he let the kid die, he wasn't sure how to feel about Roland anymore. There was a moment when he almost stopped reading it. Who would be so driven by a singular purpose that they would destroy anyone in their path? He kept at it anyway though, trusting Gilberto's recommendation.

Before he managed to finish the book, his first trade came up. After that, there was a steady stream of people to keep him occupied. He traded just about everything he had out. In exchange, he got several sacks of flour and just enough loaves of bread that he was sure he could eat them all before they started to mold. They also had fresh prickly pears, which he had never tried before and was intrigued enough to accept after a quick tutorial on prep.

Trader also selected several of Malikai's smaller, portable paintings. His favorite was a human skull surrounded by vibrant carnations. The skull was intricately decorated with tiny hearts, flowers, and swirls. He liked it so much that he thought he might end up keeping the painting for himself.

Claire traded some goat jerky for the salt. The jerky had been made from last year's males before their adult musk could settle in the meat. The meat provided a slow trickle of nutrition to the community through the winter months. Claire also brought a jar of fresh, cool milk, which they shared over the last of the cookies from Walnut Creek, legs dangling from the back of the wagon. After the sun had fully tipped over the western hills, Trader gave Claire a long hug goodbye.

"When are you leaving?" she asked softly.

"I'm going to head out in the morning."

A sad smile crossed her face.

"I'll try to catch you before you go," she said as she squeezed his hand.

Trader's heart tugged as he watched her head back to her home, a shadow in the darkening light.

* * *

When he arrived at Brianna's house for dinner, he could hear laughing from outside. Manuel and Nari had both beaten him there. They were both seated comfortably at the table, chatting, as Brianna bussed food from the prep area to serve. When they spotted Trader, they all came over to shake hands and give half hugs, everyone smiling and happy to see him. He always felt relaxed and like part of the family with the three of them.

Trader passed out the host gifts and received appreciative smiles. Manuel was particularly pleased with the military book. He made a side comment that he might have to ask Jorge to read to him because of his "old eyes". Trader made a mental note to try to find him a pair of reading glasses along the circuit somewhere. Though prescriptions might not always match up, if he collected a bunch, he could have people try them. He wondered if the hospital in Walnut Creek might have some to trade.

The group sat down at the table and started passing around bowls and plates. Brianna had outdone herself. Ravioli filled with soft goat cheese was covered in sweet tomato sauce seasoned with basil, garlic, and oregano. Thick, crunchy bread sat on the table along with soft, goat's-milk butter. There was a fresh salad with sun-dried tomatoes, olives, and feta, sprinkled with olive oil and dried oregano.

"Wow, Brianna. This is incredible. Did you make the pasta?" Trader asked around a mouthful.

Brianna nodded, smiling. "It's a total pain and takes a long time. But a special guest deserves a special treat."

"I thought you all only made feta? What kind of cheese is inside these?" Trader sliced one in half and peeked inside.

"If we ask, Claire will hold some of the curds to the side before adding it to the brine. It makes a nice soft cheese. You have to use it fast or it molds," Nari answered. "We make butter from the cream as needed. We have to plan on eating everything we make because it doesn't last."

"I don't remember you having this last year."

"Claire did a lot of experimenting in the fall. The goats are making quite a bit of milk. It allows us to make on-demand products that have a shorter shelf-life."

"Oh, good lord… and this bread." Trader sighed, leaning back in his chair and closing his eyes. "This alone would make anyone stay here."

The group around the table laughed.

"It's tasty," Nari agreed.

"This place seems to have reached a kind of normal operating tempo. Gives you guys a chance to start trying new things," Trader complimented.

"It's been a lot of hard work," Manuel said. "We've certainly had bumps in the road. Not having any cases of Weeps this year helped."

"All it'd take is one big fire, though. I'm always worried about that." Nari's eyebrows pinched.

"Me too." Manuel nodded. "The fire breaks should help a

little bit. But it's a matter of *when*, not *if*. We just have to hope what we've put in place is enough."

Nari, the water expert, nodded. "Now that we have the wheat field irrigation almost fixed, we may want to start thinking about setting up an emergency fire system, almost like sprinklers or something, that we can use to wet down the area around our homes. We need something out by the goats and chickens, too."

"I just wish we could figure out how to build with something other than wood. It's like, do we worry about clay and stone homes collapsing in earthquakes or everything burning down?" Brianna shook her head. "I want everyone to feel safe and stable, especially now that kiddos are starting to be born again. Our community is only going to grow."

"Walnut Creek's population grew too. Some kids, but mostly migrants. Are you picking up any migrants too?" Trader asked.

Everyone at the table paused, and Manuel stiffened. Trader's shoulders tensed as he realized what topic he had accidentally stumbled onto. He knew what they were going to say before they even said it.

"We had a couple join us at the end of summer. They were from up by Winters. Used to trade with us sometimes. A pretty brutal fire wiped out their farm." Manuel danced around the subject before diving right in. "We recently had another group pass through. It was the one time I can confidently and without guilt say that I'm glad that they decided to move on." He knocked his knuckles on the table for emphasis.

Trader sat through the silence, before deciding to just outright ask it. "Was it a preacher and his followers? Has a symbol like this?"

Trader traced out the Preacher's symbol on the table. They all nodded and looked up at him, waiting for him to continue.

"I've been following in his steps since Lodi," Trader said, frowning. "What was he like? What did he do when he was here?"

"The group came up along the 80, like you, but on foot," Manuel began. "There were seven of them, I think? All adults. They must have seen us working out in the fields and decided to stop."

"I went out to greet them," Brianna filled in. "Something felt wrong from the start. They just felt…I don't know…cliquey? Like they didn't trust anyone? They didn't filter out and try to meet others. They just stuck together. We only had one empty place at the time. We offered to put them up in our homes, but they chose to all pile into one studio."

"And painted that symbol on their door in blood and ash," Nari huffed. "Who does that? It creeped the kids out."

"Preacher immediately started preaching every day, *all day*," Brianna added. "He was very firm on the point that only God's light could make the loneliness go away and provide purpose."

"I'm sure that didn't land well. You're a pretty tight community, probably one of the most connected settlements I visit on the circuit. The Machados' is an oasis."

The three council members smiled at the compliment.

"It is beautiful here," Manuel said. "We try to welcome everyone. But his group and what they offered… none of it fit. It started making people uncomfortable. People were afraid to leave the kids alone. It sounds mean, but it just felt like they poisoned the well."

"They passed through Walnut Creek too," Trader said. "Earl said Preacher felt like a cult leader, like Jim Jones."

"That's *exactly* it," Manuel agreed. "Something about him didn't feel right. There are so few people left now… it's hard to exclude anyone or make them feel unwelcome. About a week in, people started complaining to us. He was cornering people, trying to convince them to join him. Some people were even scared."

"The council met and decided to talk to him," Nari added. "We tried to explain how he was making people feel. We even offered to build him a place to worship so his preaching wasn't disrupting school or groups who were out working by the fire pits. We sincerely tried to work with him and his followers."

"When we tried to negotiate with him, he got really angry and started shouting at us," Brianna said. "He was adamant that everyone joined his congregation. I felt nervous he was going to hurt us."

"Me too," said Manuel. "We politely asked him to leave if he couldn't change his behavior. We told him that his followers were welcome to stay if they wanted to. That was probably the wrong thing to say because he only got angrier. He left with his entire group the next morning."

"He was pissed," Nari added, shaking her head. "I'm glad he's gone." She crossed her arms.

"What about the people following him? What were they like?" Trader asked, leaning forward intently.

"They stuck to themselves. I was never able to get to know them all that well. Did either of you?" Manuel looked at Brianna and Nari. They shook their heads.

"They seemed captivated by Preacher," Manuel continued. "Worshiped him. They didn't appear hurt or afraid. Perhaps he gave them something they needed? A different way of living?"

"Who knows," Nari said gruffly. "I think if any of them had looked scared or turned up with bruises at all, the council meeting likely would have gone very differently." The other two nodded in agreement.

"I feel bad for his followers," Brianna said sadly. "They didn't take anything with them when they left. I'm not sure how they'll survive without water, food, and other supplies."

"You do you, I guess." Nari shrugged. "It's their choice. Let's not talk about him anymore. It's depressing."

Trader decided to let the matter pass without sharing the gossip from the rest of the circuit. He got the impression that

Preacher was like a bad taste in their mouths. They just wanted it to pass and forget about it.

Brianna tactfully changed the subject. "Where are you headed after this?"

"I'll stop off at Les and Rodger's, probably stay the night, and then maybe stop at home before heading to the foothill circuit. Trying to get back to Sac before the heat settles in. I think I can make it in time. I spent longer than I'd planned at the Silvas'." Trader omitted the reason *why* he was delayed.

"Say hi to Les and Rodger for us," Brianna said. "They come by every so often. Even with the bikes, it's still an all-day trek for them."

"I will. They're nice guys. I always enjoy my time there."

"Did you have a chance to see the wheat processing yet?" Manuel asked.

"Nope, not yet. Would love to, though."

"Come by my place in the morning," Manuel offered. "I'll make you breakfast and take you out there before you head out."

"Sounds great, thank you," Trader said, smiling appreciatively.

Brianna brought out a bowl of fresh strawberries for dessert. They talked late into the night, mostly about fluff and a little about military history; Manuel couldn't help himself. A deep darkness had settled over the settlement when Trader finally crawled into the wagon, snuggling up to the purring Sasha.

CHAPTER TWENTY-FOUR

When Trader woke up the next morning, a chill nipped his nose. The pressure had changed and the air hung heavy and damp. Thick waves of fog poured over the western hills and into the reservoir basin.

After a quick check on Sasha and Boxer, he bundled up, grabbed peach preserves to share, and headed over to Manuel's house. Manuel was outside cooking over the fire pit, his breath visible in faint puffs. The smell of cooking potatoes wafted through the air.

"Morning," Trader said.

He placed the preserves on the picnic table next to a large bowl of strawberries, a bowl of eggs, and scattered fixings. Grabbing a seat next to the fire, he leaned in and put his hands up to get warm.

"Sleep well?" Manuel asked.

"Yes, I did, thanks. Pretty quiet this morning," he mused.

Trader saw two people outside cooking. Otherwise, everyone seemed to be hunkered indoors, enjoying the warmth of their beds for just a tad longer as the cold foggy air pressed in.

"The early risers are already out working the animals and the fields. The rest of us are just waking up and starting the day. Here. Watch the potatoes. I'll start on the omelets." Manuel handed Trader the spatula to keep the fried potatoes from burning.

As they cooked, they chatted about the weather and made bets on how hot it was going to get this coming summer. Then, they enjoyed feta and tomato omelets with fried potatoes, strawberries, and peach preserves. Manuel served rose hip tea. The meal helped warm them and shook off the penetrating damp air.

"Would you still like to see the wheat processing?" Manuel asked as they ate.

"Yep. If you've got time," Trader answered. "It's a good thing to pass along the circuit."

The conversation drifted to the other new goods that were popping up on the route, and they tossed around ideas for spreading the knowledge and skills along the circuit. After they finished, they tidied up and headed out to the wheat field.

Manuel explained how they'd started a test crop the previous year, and it had been successful. With Nari's efforts building the irrigation, they doubled the field size for this growing season and hoped to have more flour to trade next year.

Next to the field was a simple, open, pole barn that Trader had missed on his way in. Manuel described how they separated the wheat from the chaff, and that it had caused quite a few chapped hands last year. The wheat was ground by hand with large mortars and pestles. They were working on an easier way to do it for the next harvest.

"The whole process takes a ton of time. If you come across any small hand-crank mills, we're looking for those." Manuel mimed the size and shape of what he was looking for. "We're also looking for any diagrams you may come across for building bigger ones."

"Jesse mentioned that. I didn't see any relevant books at Earl's this season. I'll keep an eye out and also ask Rat about the hand-crank mills," Trader said, adding to his ever-growing mental list of settlement requests. He was pretty good at remembering stuff, but the list was getting mighty long this year.

"Speaking of new crops, are you interested in growing cotton? The Silvas in Modesto are taking apprentices. I know that's pretty far away. I can bring seeds next year if you want to have a go at it. I can show you what the spindles look like and how to use them. I also have diagrams of the looms in case you ever want to copy them."

"I'll take you up on that," Manuel said appreciatively.

They meandered back to the little cluster of domiciles, enjoying each other's company. They caught Claire and Brianna on the way back, giving Trader the chance to say goodbye before he headed out. Claire passed him a small chunk of fresh feta for the road. They shared another long hug.

Back at his wagon, Manuel copied the loom diagrams. Once he was done, he shook Trader's hand and patted him on the back.

"The door's always open, Trader. If you ever want to stay, you have a place here."

"Thanks for the invite. Truly. But I gotta keep stuff moving between the settlements."

What Trader left unsaid was that he also enjoyed being alone with Sasha and Boxer. The spaces between stops were just important to him as the stops themselves. He didn't want to risk hurting Manuel's feelings by saying this though.

"Well, we could always be your home base." Manuel nudged a bit more.

"I know, I know," Trader said, laughing lightly and smiling to let Manuel know that he appreciated his offer.

Manuel stuck around to help Trader get Boxer hitched up. Trader promised to see him next year, hopefully with another military book, a pair of reading glasses, and some cotton seeds. Manuel wished him a safe journey. They parted with a wave as Trader pulled out of the settlement and headed back out on the road. It stung a bit as he left. This had always been the hardest place for him to let go of each year.

* * *

Trader headed back on the 80 towards Sacramento. The next stop was a commercial greenhouse just outside of Davis, where Les and Rodger had set up shop. It would take most of the day to reach them, but the trio was well-rested and the road was a flat, clear shot.

As expected, the highway was in pretty good shape as it arched over Vacaville. A few creeks intersected in this area, leaving behind pools of brackish, oily water following the seasonal floods. Weeps was too high of a risk to live anywhere near here. The folks from the Machados' would occasionally scavenge what they could from the skeleton of the city, but they'd only risk it during the dry season. Jesse had said they lived somewhere in the area, but Trader didn't know exactly where since the city was so inhospitable. He suspected it was on the far east of town, where it stayed dry.

Between Vacaville and Dixon, he saw a lone man walking in the opposite direction on the highway. He carried a large pack and led a horse loaded down with more supplies. Trader didn't recognize him but lifted a hand in greeting. They both stopped to have a quick chat over the center divider with Trader still seated in the wagon.

The man was tall and lanky. He was dressed in well-worn clothes and a wide brim hat to protect his pale skin. He had a thick, well-groomed, brown beard and long, brown hair braided down his back. The divide was too wide for handshaking, but the man tipped his hat and Trader nodded in greeting.

"Well met. I'm Daniel. This here's Tank." The man gestured to the loaded-down horse. The dainty Arabian was about as far from a tank as a horse could get. Trader smirked slightly at the cheeky name.

"I'm Trader. That's Boxer pulling the wagon and Sasha here in the driver's seat. We just came from the Machados', following the circuit, but Sac is home for us. Haven't seen you before. Where's home for you?"

"We're not from around here. Tank and I are wanderers. Trade when we can, work when we can, but we like to keep movin'. What's the circuit you run?"

Trying to hide his surprise at meeting one of the rare wanders, Trader answered, "From Sac, I head down south on the 99 and then back up north on the 680 to the 80, with a loop at the end into the foothills. I try to call it quits and get back home before the weather starts to get too hot down in the valley."

"Yeah, I hear you. The asphalt is scorching in the summer." Daniel nodded.

"Are you headed all the way to the ocean, turning north, or headed south?" Trader asked.

"Never seen the Pacific before. Was hoping to go there but wasn't sure what the roads looked like. Have any intel?"

"Been a while since I've gone out that way," Trader answered. "Most people have moved inland. Unless you have a burning desire to see what's left of SF, I would recommend taking the 12 through Napa. The 101 is pretty shit and is flooded in multiple spots. And it's pretty sketch taking the roads around Mount Tamalpais. If you don't care about seeing the Golden Gate—it's not that cool anyway—I'd recommend going through Petaluma and catching the ocean at Tomales Bay.

"There used to be a few people living in Napa and Petaluma. But I'd make sure you have enough food to last without having to trade. The fires hit that stretch fairly often, and I'm not sure they're still holding out there. It gets pretty damn cold by the ocean, and the fog just bites right through you. So bring layers if you don't have them."

Daniel nodded, considering. "Thanks for the advice, dude. I'm all set with cold-weather gear but may need to top up on provisions before I head out there just in case. Hunting and fishing any good?"

Trader shrugged. "Don't do much of either, I'm afraid. But see plenty of jackrabbits. Watch some of the creeks, though. If they are anything like Putah Creek back the way you came, the mercury is too high to eat more than one in your entire life. The Machados will top you up. They're good people. Take the La Costa Dr. exit. You should see them from the 80."

"Thanks, dude," Daniel said, tipping his hat again.

"Out of curiosity, see anybody heading east on the 80?" Trader asked, fishing for sightings of Preacher.

"Not a soul, dude. I stayed with Les and Rodger last night but haven't seen anyone on the highway for several days now. Why you ask?"

"No reason." Trader shrugged, not wanting to worry the guy and figuring Daniel's chances of running into Preacher oceanside were close to nil. "Just noticed less people on the road this year and suspect more are starting to settle."

"Yeah, I've noticed that too. The settlements are getting bigger and the smaller ones are pulling up their stakes and joining the bigger ones." Daniel pulled his hat off to swipe his forehead and then put it back on.

"Anyway, I better get a move on. I'd love to swap stories and maybe trade a little but it looks like a nasty storm is coming." Daniel gestured to the west.

Trader peered around the wagon behind him and froze. Sure enough, a large wall of angry clouds loomed in the distance. They had a fuzzy, blurred look to them with an ominous brown-green tinge. When the blue sky abutted a thick wall of clouds like that, it was never good. Best case scenario it'd be heavy rain with maybe a bit of hail. Lightning was also possible. In the worst-case scenario, a storm like that might throw down a tornado. It wouldn't be the first time in this area.

"Shit!" Trader said, eyes wide. "That snuck right up on us. You oughta hustle. You're heading right into it. The Machados' is just on the other side of Vacaville. You might make it."

"Hope so," Daniel said with little optimism.

"Stay safe and nice meeting you," Trader said as he lightly slapped the reins and waved.

Daniel dipped his head and trudged off in the direction of the looming storm.

CHAPTER
TWENTY-FIVE

With the wall cloud chasing them down the 80, Trader pushed Boxer fairly hard. The horse, sensing the weather change, was already putting a hustle into his step. The dark clouds pursued them, edging closer with each mile, the wind pushing them faster than Boxer could pull the wagon. Lightning was now visible, often arcing from the sky, the booms following closer and closer after the flash of light.

On the north side of Dixon, Trader felt the deep pressure of wet, heavy air settle around them as the edge of the wall cloud pressed in. He glanced anxiously around the side of the wagon and saw that the storm would reach them at any second. Endless grassland stretched in either direction, with no shelter in sight. At this point, their best and only option was to press on to Les and Rodger's.

A sense of panic slowly crept over the three of them, and Boxer quickened his pace. Sasha jumped into the back, curling her feet and tail beneath her, ears pressed back. Leaving the reins loose across the driver's seat, Trader climbed into the back of the wagon, tightening up the flaps, and hoping the rain wouldn't be heavy enough to soak his precious books. Wrapping himself in a water-repellant canvas, he tugged his hat on and dropped to the ground. He grabbed one rein close to the halter, jogging next to Boxer, and urged him to speed up.

The sky went instantly dark, with a thick press of small hail pelleting down. As the clouds moved over them, the wind blew in strong gales, pushing the hail down at a forty-five-degree angle. Trader placed one hand on his hat to keep it from blowing away, the broad sides flapping against his hand. Boxer's ears flipped back, and he started a slow trot. Trader hustled to try to keep pace.

This storm's gonna throw down a tornado, Trader thought with despair.

The hail was quickly followed by lashing rain, which hounded them all the way to the Kidwell Rd. exit. They made an immediate right on Olmo Rd. The rain was pouring in thick sheets, making it hard to see. Frantic, Trader searched for the outline of the greenhouse that he knew was tucked back down the road. Finally, a beacon of hope appeared as a shaded block in the distance. The old building where Les and Rodger set up camp was within sight. Poor, soaking Boxer whickered in anticipation, recognizing the place.

As soon as they entered the parking lot, Trader jogged ahead and banged on the loading bay doors. Strong gusts of wind whipped the surrounding trees and threatened to push him over. Within a minute or two, Les opened the large, rolling door, the normal rattle of the metal muffled by the ferocity of the storm.

"Come in, come in! It's awful out there!" Les shouted over the storm. Relief washed over Trader, and the group piled into the giant building, wagon and all. Les pulled the door closed behind them with a loud *bang*.

The storm continued to rage outside, rain pelting the sides of the building. A tornado could still drop at any moment, and the greenhouse wouldn't protect them at all. But being inside sheltered them from the stinging rain and the threat of being tagged by lightning. It was pretty miserable outside. He hoped Daniel and Tank had beat the storm to the Machados', but that was unlikely.

Trader took off his hat and shrugged off the canvas, dropping it in a wet pile on the ground. He was soaked, despite the shroud. The strong wind had ensured that the cold rain found its way into every nook and cranny. Boxer was irritably shaking the water from his mane and swishing his tail. Worried about the steadfast horse, Trader went about making him comfortable.

"Damn," Trader exclaimed, winded and shaking. "Glad you were close by to get the door, Les. That's one hell of a storm."

"Here, let me help. You poor things. Look at Boxer!"

Les fussed, assisting Trader as he unhitched Boxer and toweled the horse dry as best as they could. Bright flashes of light sparked through the glass ceiling and were almost immediately followed by loud booms that rattled the windows. Boxer whickered nervously.

"You're a trooper, Boxer," Les cooed to the horse, squeezing the water out of his mane with a towel. "You look a mess too, Trader. Go now, get yourself out of those wet clothes. You must be freezing."

"Thanks for the help, Les. I'll be just a sec." Trader's voice stuttered a bit with the cold.

"Take your time, geez!" Les exclaimed. "You guys just got spanked by that storm. We'll meet you in the kitchen when you're done."

Trader opened up the wagon. Sasha was crouched in the back with her ears flat. She hated thunderstorms, and he knew it would take her time to chill out. Thankfully, the inside of the wagon had stayed pretty dry, with only the edges near the flaps looking damp.

Shivering, he peeled off his wet clothes and shoes, leaving them in a pile on the ground. He tried to dry himself off as much as possible before putting on a fresh set of dry clothes. His boots now soaked, he opted for a set of woven flip-flops for the evening. The chill of the rain still ran through his bones. He gave himself a moment to try to relax and get his mental shit together before greeting his hosts. That was one heck of a jog through that storm. The muscles in his legs were burning and shaky. As the stress eased, the exhaustion started to settle in. He took a deep breath before heading toward the kitchen with a jar of honey, a loaf of bread, and a couple of jars of fruit preserves as a gesture of thanks.

Les and Rodger lived in an industrial-sized greenhouse. The building had light opaque siding and clear glass ceilings that could be shaded in the extreme heat. Thankfully, the floor was concrete, and Trader didn't feel bad about bringing a flood of water in with him and the wagon.

Ever since Trader had been working the circuit, Les and Rodger had been at the old greenhouse. Both of them had started in the Davis area and had been slowly pushed out by the encroaching Sacramento Bay. They had taken over the abandoned structure, rebuilding the water catch system. They'd scavenged solar panels from the university and connected them to several house batteries. The system had just enough juice to run a few small lights and an electric stove, the latter of which was on its last legs but still functioned.

Trader could hear the rain pounding on the roof and rushing through the gutter system. The gutters skirting the roof fed into large pipes that were routed back inside the greenhouse, feeding a series of two-thousand-gallon rain barrels along the back wall. The water in the barrels would be used to irrigate the broad expanse of raised beds that filled up the bulk of the building. The rain barrels were also used for drinking. Given the unpredictability of rain in this area, Les and Rodger couldn't always count on the barrels being full year-round. They typically went out to Putah Creek to do the less critical tasks, like washing clothes or bathing.

Les and Rodger had retrofitted and planted the raised beds, which took up most of the place. Dwarf fruit trees in pots were arranged on the left wall. The building had a pleasant earthy smell, rich with oxygen. Trader inhaled deeply, relaxing further. He hadn't realized how much the storm had freaked him out.

The right side of the building had been converted into a living area. They had a bed, a couch, a table and chairs, and a true kitchen area. They'd built a counter and cabinets off of a pre-existing sink. The only thing the cozy setup lacked was a full bathroom with running water. Instead, they had a composting toilet in the far corner which worked well enough.

They'd tried to keep chickens at one point. But one visit from a predator had decimated the population, leaving them both in tears. They'd talked about trying to get chickens from another settlement and setting them up in the greenhouse but had decided against it. For protein, they had almond and walnut groves in a small orchard next to the greenhouse that was irrigated as needed by creek water. They also grew several varieties of beans and lentils in the greenhouse.

Les and Rodger were bustling around the kitchen when Trader made his way over. They were both tall and lean. Les had thinning red hair with a short beard and pale skin speckled with freckles. Rodger had light brown skin and long black hair that was beautifully arranged in thin, tidy dreadlocks tied back with a piece of twine. They both wore threadbare cutoff shorts and graphic design t-shirts that were so old they were practically see-through. They both went barefoot.

Les had started a pot of water to boil and was making some herbal tea with lemon for them to share. Rodger was cooking at the stove, stirring something in a large metal pot. Trader set the items on the table and had a seat.

"It's pretty wild out there. Wouldn't be surprised if that storm dropped a tornado or two along the way. I'm very grateful you heard me pounding on the door. It would've been a rough go trying to get all the way back home." Trader leaned back in his chair, stretching his sore legs.

"Where did you come from? The Machados'?" Les asked, pouring hot tea into three cups at the table. Trader offered him the honey, which Les stirred into his cup.

"Yep, left about mid-morning. It was only foggy earlier; the storm came in really fast. It wasn't there when we left, and caught us out after Dixon. Only option was to press on."

"Glad you made it safe," Rodger said, dropping chopped fresh herbs into the pot.

"I hope that nice young man who came through found shelter," Les added

"Was it Daniel? Guy on his own with a horse?" Trader asked. They both nodded.

"Not sure if he made it in time, but I told him about the Machados' and advised him to stop there. I think that guy has seen some miles. Pretty sure he's okay even if the storm caught him.

"Oh! By the way…." Trader unwrapped the bread, smiling. "Sure you've been out that way and had some already. But this bread from the Machados' is pretty amazing, and I thought you might like some."

"Yessss!" Les said. "Thank you so much! Their bread is to die for. Sometimes I want to just ride out there to trade for some. Here, honey." He broke off a piece of the bread, split it in half, and shared some with Rodger.

Trader wrapped his hands around the mug, trying to shake the remaining chill away. "Thanks again for getting us in so fast and helping me get Boxer unhitched. I feel bad for the guy. Hasn't been the easiest of runs this year."

"Ohhh, you have to tell us about what's going on. Same route this year? How's everyone doing? Any new babies?" Les threw questions at Trader, eager for the gossip.

Trader filled them in, starting at Forty Two and working his way around to the trades he made at the Machados'. As he was telling his story, Rodger served up tomato soup. Between the tea and the soup, Trader had finally stopped shivering.

"Wow!" Les exclaimed at the mention of Malikai's work. "When we were there last, he'd only completed one mural. He didn't have any art to actually trade. You totally have to show us some of those paintings you picked up. We might snag one from you. I always felt like this place needed a bit more pizazz."

Rodger harrumphed.

"What?" Les said, shrugging between slurps of soup. "For years, it's been about making sure there's enough food and scavenging everything else. It's about time we snazzied things up." He looked over to Trader. "I *for sure* want to check out the paintings. We have a ton of food this year to trade, but not much else. We haven't had a lot of time to scavenge. It takes the two of us just to keep this place up and running."

"Bigger communities have economy of scale," Rodger said gruffly. "Can't compete with that."

"I like it just fine here, honey," Les said, leaning over to give Rodger a half-hug. "It's nice to see Nari and all of them every once in a while. But it's also nice having our own space."

"That's what trading is for," Trader said, smiling as he dunked some bread in his soup. "Jesse and I can bring the cool shit to you guys so that you can enjoy your space and still have the luxuries from the bigger communities. Next year, I hope to have more fabric and shoes."

They continued idly chatting about the harvest, how the worms in the walnuts were particularly bad this year, and how they were lucky that Putah Creek stayed full year-round for the first time in forever. The soup bowls were wiped clean with the last of the bread, and they cracked open the fruit preserves for dessert. Though the storm continued to rage outside, Trader was finally warm and comfortable.

CHAPTER
TWENTY-SIX

After their meal, Rodger took Trader on a tour of the greenhouse, plucking snap peas right off the vine to snack on as they weaved through the raised beds. Trader was amazed at how much they were able to grow through the winter. Even the serrano plants were still producing, and they were covered in dozens of thin, small peppers. Rodger had also started growing apple and apricot trees in large plastic drums. Trader wasn't sure they'd make it but admired his gumption.

The rain had petered off to a light drizzle, and small rays of late sunshine started to peek through the glass roof. When they circled back to where the wagon was parked inside, Trader realized Boxer had let one drop inside the greenhouse. Trader scooped it up and, to Rodger's gardening delight, added it to their compost bins.

"Now that the storm has died down a bit, I'm gonna take Boxer out to graze," Trader excused himself.

Rodger nodded in reply and headed back deep into his garden.

Trader led Boxer outside to a grassy stretch between the road and the highway. The ground was soaked, and the native grasses were limp with rain. But the sky was clear to the west, with a gentle breeze. Boxer, hungry from the hustle through the storm, whickered appreciatively and started grazing, tail swishing.

Trader sat on a cement ledge in front of the greenhouse, watching the sunset. There was a rich smell of earth after the rain. Other animals were also coming out of their shelters following the torrential storm. Just as the sun tipped over the far hills, he saw the white flash of a barn owl leaving the orchard and heading out over the fields to hunt. Crickets buzzed in the grass.

After letting Boxer graze for a while, Trader led him back in. Boxer might have been okay outside by himself overnight. But Trader just didn't feel right leaving him out there. This season had already dumped a few surprises in their laps, the biggest of which was the dread building in his gut over Preacher.

Trader wasn't sure why the guy made him so nervous. Everyone just said he was *off*. Nobody said anything about him stealing or hurting anybody. Yet, everyone Trader trusted was a little apprehensive about Preacher, and Trader felt he'd be stupid not to be wary too.

Never hurts to be a tad careful, he thought.

With a full belly, Boxer looked tired and willingly followed him back inside. Trader tied the lead rope loosely to the wagon to make sure Boxer didn't decide to sample the greenhouse gardens. The last thing Trader wanted to do was to put a dent in Les and Rodger's food supply. Les was by the wagon, bending over and petting the purring Sasha, who was weaving in and out of his legs.

"Wish we had a cat," Les said longingly. "We've tried to catch a couple of the feral ones, even just to lock one up in here to keep the mice down. We haven't had any luck yet. There's probably a reason that the ones who're around have made it this long, I guess."

"You could probably build a live trap," Trader suggested. "I

THE BEFORE AND THE AFTER

can jot down a design of one I've seen out at Rat's. I've got some dried meat you could use as bait. I bet that'd attract them."

"I'll take you up on that. Don't tell Rodger, though." Les smiled mischievously. "He always says we're just fine and don't need anything else to worry about, but the mice are annoying. I hate finding mouse shit on our utensils."

Trader reached into the wagon, grabbing some paper and charcoal. He drew a quick no-kill box trap, explaining how the latches worked. "Metal works better if you have it."

"I'm sure we can scavenge what we need from around town. There's lots of that kind of scrap lying around."

With the knowledge transfer complete, they discussed trades. Trader gave Les free rein of the wagon, bringing items out that he thought the two of them might want. Les grabbed a quilt, soap, dried meat, honey, a sack of flour, and a box of Gen 2 Proxleep. He also selected one of Malikai's paintings of a monarch butterfly perched on a flowering cactus.

Les saw the bolt of cotton fabric tucked away. "Ohhh. Is that up for grabs?"

"Sorry, that's my last one, and I need it. But I promise to get all that's available at the Silvas' next year and save some for you. They're looking for apprentices. If they get any, they should have way more next year. They even gave me some cotton seeds to try. I have a copy of the loom blueprints and am gonna give it a go myself if I can get enough of a harvest."

"I bet I can dye this fabric," Les said, running his hand over the soft cotton. "Rodger found an old, pedal sewing machine for me and got it working again. I bet I can start sewing clothes. Please, please, please bring me some next year. I'd love to try it."

"Tell you what, why don't you cut the bolt in half. We can share," Trader offered. He couldn't resist when he saw someone who wanted something so bad.

"Really?" Les said, flabbergasted. "Thank you so much!"

Les grinned ear to ear and grabbed the bolt to his chest and

251

headed towards the living area. Trader grabbed the items they had pulled from the wagon and followed behind him.

With the items on the table and the remainder of the bolt returned, Les asked, "What can we get for you?"

"I'll take some of your dried peppers; they make the best kimchi. And several pounds of dried nuts. Both kinds if the walnut crop wasn't entirely ruined."

Trader loved the walnuts that Rodger grew. Most of the walnut trees that Trader came across were the black walnut variety, which always stained his hands and had a bitter taste to them. Rodger grew walnuts that were sweet and fleshy, never bitter or shriveled. The nuts were already shelled, picking the best ones and relegating any with the dusty webbing of worms to the compost bin.

Les went back to the shelves, grabbing what Trader had asked for. He also brought fresh limes, lemons, mandarin oranges, and grapefruit. Next to that, he placed several jars of preserved green beans with slivers of pepper and dried tomatoes.

"I know you didn't ask for these, but I tried a new recipe for the green beans. They're delectable. Try them."

"I will, thank you," Trader replied.

"Will that be enough? I always feel like you give more than you take. We appreciate you. I don't ever want you to feel like we're short-changing you, sweety." Les gave him a big side-hug.

"Not in a million years," Trader said, hugging him back. "I appreciate you, too. You should come to Sac more often. I'd love to have you in the winter if the causeway is passable."

"You know how Rodger is." Les shrugged. "I can try to get him out. But he kinda likes to do his own thing."

Trader understood. Even now, Rodger was back off with his plants. He preferred to socialize very briefly, and then enough was enough.

"Door is always open," Trader said.

Les helped him load everything in his wagon. By that time,

the sun had fully set. The greenhouse was lit by a small string of lights, powered by the battery, like a beacon in the vast darkness.

"I'm gonna hit the hay. Say goodnight to Rodger for me. See you in the morning?"

"Will do. Sleep well," Les said, giving Sasha a scratch before heading back over to the living area.

It had been a rough day. The storm had sucked the last ounce of everyone's energy away. Now that they were safe and fed, the exhaustion settled in. Boxer was already snoozing. Sasha was curled up on the bedroll. Trader followed close behind her and fell asleep as soon as his head hit the pillow.

* * *

Trader woke to the thin sunlight of dawn. Sasha was M.I.A., and he assumed she was off helping Les and Rodger with the mouse problem. The greenhouse was peacefully quiet. Les and Rodger were late risers and probably still in bed. He quietly got dressed, grabbed *The Gunslinger*, and snuck Boxer outside to eat.

He sat on the ground next to the greenhouse, legs bent, and back leaning against the wall. The sunshine finally crested the Sierras and warmed the side of his face. The crows that had perched in the orchard overnight were starting to wake. It was a large murder, and the rustling of their wings and loud caws could be heard from where he sat. A Swainson's hawk coasted on the updrafts in the distance, and its negative wing pattern flashed as it turned. With his arms resting on his knees, he opened *The Gunslinger*.

The sun passed slowly across the sky as Trader finished the book. After flipping the last page, he rested it on the ground, letting the ending settle around him. His head was spinning after reading Walter's perspective of the universe during the final confrontation with Roland. The ending was a cliffhanger, leaving him eager to read the next book, but with a bitter, nasty taste in his mouth. The contradictory feelings puzzled him. *The Gunslinger* was a heavy read with layers to unpack, and he needed to noodle over it before tucking into the next novel in the series. A spacer-story was in order.

Trader heard some movement in the greenhouse and figured the guys were up. He left Boxer out to munch a bit longer, feeling safe leaving him alone with the door open and everyone awake. Sasha was back in the wagon, taking a bath, looking content. Trader dropped off the book and grabbed some almond butter and another loaf of bread. He knew Rodger grew raspberries, and Les made a mean jelly.

Les was boiling water for tea, and Rodger was already moving about the greenhouse near the kitchen. "What would you like for breakfast?" Les asked.

"Unless you have something else planned, I was thinking we could have peanut butter and jelly sandwiches?" Trader offered, holding the goods up.

"Oh, my lord, that sounds absolutely fabulous," Les said. "I haven't had a PB&J since I was a little kid."

With the food spread out and the tea poured, Rodger joined them for breakfast. They talked about the weather, how the air smelled so fresh and crisp after the rain, and how the sun would be particularly rough today. After they finished eating and washing up, Trader said a quick goodbye to Rodger, who peeled off to the back of the greenhouse. Les helped Trader collect Boxer from outside and hitch him up.

"Les, I forgot to bring it up earlier. Have any groups come through here?" Trader asked apprehensively.

"No one has stopped in, other than Daniel, if that's what you mean," Les answered as he fussed with Boxer's mane, pulling the hair around the halter. "But we don't advertise ourselves. And, unless someone knows we're here, they don't usually stop. The only real chance for us to see people on the highway is when we're outside, which isn't very often. I only ran into Daniel because I happened to be bringing the wash up from the creek."

"That's good news," Trader said, relieved. "I've just been hearing some rumors about a group led by a shady preacher. I've been inadvertently trailing him since Lodi and suspected he passed this way. Just...be careful, okay?"

"Oh Trader," Les said kindly, giving him a big hug. "We'll be fine. Don't you worry about us. If I can get Rodger to step away from his babies for a minute, we'll see you in Sac sometime over the winter. Otherwise, see you next year when you come by?"

"Yep, looking forward to it." Trader climbed into the driver's seat just as Sasha hopped into her cat bed to join him. With a click, Boxer pulled the wagon in a tight U-turn and out of the greenhouse. Les waited at the wide door until they were about a block away. When Trader peered back over his shoulder, Les waved before shutting the rolling door, locking them both in from the outside world.

CHAPTER
TWENTY-SEVEN

From the 80, Trader turned the wagon north on the 113 to avoid the pockets of flooding that were peppered around Davis. The small ponds and standing water were a hotbed for mosquitos. On top of that, the 80 dipped down as it passed through the abandoned college town. It was best to make a circle north, taking Covell Blvd. as it ran east, and then loop back down to meet the 80 in a curving arc. Trader would get back on the 80 right before the causeway and cross his fingers that the flooding wasn't too bad.

The causeway had been a land bridge that spanned a watershed in the Before. Every year, the watershed would flood, forming a broad seasonal lake that spanned more than a mile. Old timers said that the land in the depression was used to grow water-loving rice in the wet season and then to raise cattle in the warm season. In the After, the area was flooded year-round, forming the northern edge of the Sacramento Bay. The water softly lapped against the bottom of the causeway. Ducks, geese, and other waterfowl bobbed across the water.

As the highway dipped into West Sacramento, the road was flooded a couple of inches. Trader and a few others had tried to dissuade the edge of the Sacramento Bay from creeping this way with sandbags stacked against the concrete barriers, but there were always leaks that left a low level of standing water through the winter and spring. In the summer, it got hot enough that most of it evaporated away.

The highway rose again as it arched over what was once the Sacramento River. At the crest, the 5 dipped to the north and south, and was now covered by water. Trader loved this view. To the left, the golden tips of the Tower Bridge pierced through the water. The tops of the capitol building, DOCO, and other high-rises also reached out to touch the sky; their lower levels sunk beneath the bay. In the Before, a lush canopy covered most of downtown. The bay had since killed off any trees, but Trader could imagine what it looked like based on the canopy in the eastern part that wasn't flooded. The highway stood tall over the city for the length of the overpass, lasting a mile or so, with the waters darkly rippling below.

Right after the 5th St. exit, he drew the wagon to a quick stop. In the middle of the fast lane, there was a small ash pile, dark and smeared from the recent rain. On the adjacent cement divider, Preacher's symbol had been drawn in blood and ash. The drawing looked slightly melted from the recent downpour, but the curve of the divider had sheltered the graffiti enough that the symbol was still discernible. Trader's chest went tight.

The fucker had been *here*. In *his* hometown. And Trader had no idea if Preacher and his followers had continued through or stopped in the east part of Sacramento.

Early this morning, he had debated whether to go home and call the trading season done or blast right through Sacramento to the foothills. Between the storms and the anxiety over Preacher, he felt exhausted. But he also felt obligated to continue the circuit into the foothills. The people up there needed the goods he had to offer, and he didn't want to let them down.

Seeing Preacher's symbol on the highway flipped the table

on his plans. He decided to stop over for at least one night to check on Carla, confirm his place was as he left it, and make sure Preacher wasn't on his turf. After he assessed the situation in Sacramento, he would decide what his next steps would be.

Trader guided the wagon south on the 99. As soon as he took the Martin Luther King Blvd. exit, Boxer picked up his step. The horse knew that home was close and was excited about it. Trader kept an eye out for more of Preacher's marks but hadn't seen any since the highway.

Trader halted the wagon out front, surveying his home. From the outside, everything appeared as he had left it. The only sounds were the birds chirping in the trees. The place felt empty.

Boxer shifted anxiously, eager to park the wagon and shrug off the harness. Trader backed the wagon into his driveway and quickly unhitched him. The horse bullied his way to the backyard to graze. Sasha had also already disappeared into her usual hunts.

If he'd been asked before he went out on the circuit this year, Trader would've said that no one needed locks anymore. But Preacher had changed everything. Trader wasn't sure what he would find inside, and he cautiously let himself in.

The house was exactly as he had left it, furniture covered to keep the dust off and everything put away in its place. It also had the musty smell of a home that had been shuttered for a few weeks. If Preacher had come this way, he'd left Trader's place alone. Trader relaxed slightly.

Before he unpacked the wagon, he had to check on Carla to make sure all was in order over there too. He decided to patrol the neighborhood first, looking for any signs of Preacher, and then he would check on her place. Not wanting to alarm her, he grabbed a loaf of bread as a cover for stopping by. He slipped his knife into his waistband.

The neighborhood was quiet and looked untouched. The houses sat silent, almost judgmental. The caws of a crow echoed through the streets. A tabby cat streaked across the road between empty homes. There was no sign that anyone else had been here while he was away.

Carla's place was relatively close. She lived in a small, two-bedroom house that had sat next to an empty lot in the Before. With her verdant thumb, the lot had been converted into a cornucopia with every inch dedicated to growing ground crops. She had a few fruit trees as well. Chickens rounded out the homey setting, giving her just enough food to fend for herself. She was usually home, and Trader was hoping that was the case today.

"Howdy Carla, you home?" He called out from the front, not wanting to startle her. He circled around the back. She was working the garden, kneeling on an old chair pad. She stood up, surprised, and dusted her hands off on her dress.

"Trader!" She gave him a hug. "You're back early. Decide to skip some stops?"

Carla was in her sixties, short, and plump with light brown skin. Her once-dark hair was now almost entirely gray and pulled into a bun at the base of her head. She wore a brightly-colored, patched muumuu and was barefoot. A broad hat to shade the sun topped it all off. She had been a middle school art teacher in the Before and had a favorite-grandma feel about her. He was always grateful that they lived so close to each other. He was relieved to see her standing there happy, and apparently unaffected by Preacher.

"Just stopping overnight." He held out the wrapped loaf. "I brought you this."

She pulled the fabric back, and her eyes went wide.

"Lordy! Where on earth did you get this!" She took a deep breath of the bread, closing her eyes. "I haven't had bread in ages. What a treat." She took a bite right out of the loaf, savoring it.

Trader laughed kindly. "The Machados are growing wheat

now and making bread. I snagged a sack of flour for you, too. I'll bring you everything later. I just wanted to check in on you."

"Well, aren't you sweet, honey. I'm fine. Not much happening here. Just taking care of the girls and tending the garden." She gestured to the chickens who were scratching away and clucking quietly to each other.

"No one pass through?" he asked.

"Not down here. Just me and the ladies." She paused, studying him. "That's an odd question."

"I'm glad it's been quiet," Trader said. He was surprised to feel his shoulders relax; he hadn't realized how tense he'd been.

Carla took another bite of bread, chewing slowly, and watched him expectantly. Trader shifted uncomfortably under her gaze. He hadn't wanted to worry her. But he now realized that asking that question had been enough to tip her off.

"See, there's this cult leader with a small group that's been walking the circuit. Saw his symbol on the highway, and I was worried he might have set up shop here."

Carla's eyebrows went up, and she stopped chewing.

"I'm happy to see that you're okay…," he trailed off, catching her piercing stare.

"I can tell there's much more to that story, young man. Come by for dinner and fill me in?"

"I'd love to," he said genuinely. "I'm gonna go get cleaned up. How about I come back around sunset and bring some stuff? Sound good?"

"It's a date." She grinned.

She carefully wrapped the rest of the loaf, placed it on the table, and returned to work in the garden. Trader was surprised how the news of Preacher just seemed to roll off her back. He was sure she'd seen a lot, and much of it unpleasant as the Before had slowly bled into the After. There was a reason she'd survived all alone for so long.

I just can't let her get complacent, he thought, protective of her.

If he was honest with himself, Preacher terrified him, and he certainly didn't want to underestimate the man's ability to bring a new, dark order to the world he had grown to love.

* * *

Back at home, the lackadaisical behavior of the animals contrasted sharply with Trader's worry. Boxer had already mowed down a large stretch of the overgrown backyard grass. He lazily grazed, tail swishing. Sasha had done her hunting and was sleeping in the sun by the back door.

For the next few hours, Trader busied himself with small tasks, trying to shake the foreboding feeling and relax into the routine. He grabbed the nastiest of his two bedrolls, still gritty from the dust storm down south along with his dirty clothes. He washed everything in an old metal tub using water from the rain barrels and hung it out on the clothesline to dry in the bright warm sun. Despite the storm last night, the air was dry enough that the slight breeze would ensure everything was dry by tomorrow morning.

With the clothes waving gently in the breeze, Trader set to work organizing his wagon. He unloaded all of the leather, the last half-bolt of cloth, and several of the books that he planned to read. He gently carried the guitar into the house, deciding to bring it to Forty Two next year, thinking of the group who had been singing by the fire. He kept *The Galaxy and the Ground Within* to the side, stacking the rest of the books he planned to read on his bookshelves.

Next, he sorted through all of the food items, transferring one of the sacks of flour to a sealable plastic bin for himself. He stacked the flour bin, a few jars of honey, nuts, dried hot peppers, the spicy preserved green beans, and a bag of salt into his pantry. The lavender soap was left by the kitchen sink.

Trader didn't have running water set up, but the kitchen sink was a nice place to stash stuff for washing up, which he normally did outside next to the water barrels. He took some time to hang his favorite picture from Malikai above his kitchen table. He was looking forward to picking up more art next year. It cheered the place up and made him feel less alone, reminding him of Malikai and all of the other people along the circuit.

After taking a quick washcloth bath and changing into fresh clothes, he sat out in the bright sun of his backyard to read, his straw hat on his head. Sasha assumed the meatloaf position, eyes lazily closed. Bees and hummingbirds buzzed around the flowering bushes that clustered around his rain barrels. Squirrels ran up and down the large sycamore, chirping at each other.

Trader noticed that Carla must have snuck over to guerilla-garden. She did that every year, making sure that he always had something in the ground and ready to harvest when he returned from running the circuit. Two of his five raised beds had well-tended tomato, bell pepper, and cucumber plants growing. He expected she'd probably add okra in the third bed by the time he got back. Carla always looked out for him, and he gave back in his own way, checking in on her and making sure she had the trade items she needed.

Trader took a deep breath, relaxing in his chair, enjoying the sun, and started in on *The Galaxy and the Ground Within*. The title was a mouthful and the cover art was a bit *meh*. But the story immediately drew him in. The characters felt real, almost like they were sitting across from him at a settlement fire and sharing their stories. Each species had their own unique, vibrant culture. Who would have thought to make a sentient crustacean a main character in a novel? The story was brilliant.

He devoured about half of the book before the sun started to set. Sasha had since made her way inside and was napping on the couch. Boxer, having eaten his fill, was also snoozing. Trader grabbed an old metal granny-cart and loaded it with a sack of flour, a sack of salt, some of the meat jerky, a jar of nuts, a box of Proxleep, and one of Malikai's pictures that he thought Carla would like.

When he arrived at Carla's, he could see her shadow moving around the dimly-lit house through the open windows. She was humming a tune and the clanging of cooking rang out. The chickens, having been cooped for the night, were quiet. Trader called out softly, announcing his arrival.

Carla wiped her hands on her apron and came out to give him a hug. "Look at all of this! You've been busy. And salt too!"

"Thought you might like this." He handed her the painting. "There's a guy, Malikai, who paints at the Machados'. He mainly does murals like around here. But he paints these to trade. This one reminded me of you."

The painting was of an older woman in a loose embroidered dress and a hat tipped so her face wasn't visible. She was tossing feed out to chickens from her apron. She was surrounded by flowers, climbing vines, and herbs. A pueblo-style home sat in the background.

"This is beautiful," Carla said, holding the painting out towards the last of the light to take it all in. "He's very talented. Where does he get the paint? I haven't seen anything like this since the Before."

"He actually makes it himself. Pretty clever technique. Maybe one of these days I can convince you to take a trip out to the Machados' with me?"

"Oh, I'm too old for that." She waved his words away, smiling. "And I have to take care of my ladies here. You just keep bringing back these little bits of joy for me. I'm going to put this up in my front room. Come on in."

Trader unloaded the rest of the stuff in the cart and joined her in the kitchen. Carla served him a slice of a nut-crust quiche she had made in a cast iron pan on the barbeque. On the side, she'd added a salad made of jicama, oranges, and grapefruit with small flecks of fresh mint. Apple slices drizzled with honey were served for dessert. She'd gone all out to welcome him back.

Over dinner, Trader shared tales from the road, passing on all of the stories he had collected, like Petra from *The Last Cuentista*. Carla listened avidly, asking questions to dig out more details.

"It sounds like this year has been quite the adventure already. You should consider writing your stories down. Have you ever thought about it?"

Trader pursed his lips. "Not really." He shrugged. "Those are other people's stories. Not mine."

"But they *are* yours, honey." She placed a hand on his. "You connect them all together. This world is very different compared to the Before. We need people like you to bring everyone together with their stories, weaving them into a single tale."

Trader shrugged again, uncomfortable.

"I'm very serious," she said. "You're important to all of these people. Your visits mean something to them, and it isn't just the stuff you bring."

Trader thought of his time with the various people along the circuit, like Earl or Liluye and Gilberto. In his heart, he knew that visits from Jesse and him brought joy to the settlements. And Carla was right; it was more than just bringing supplies to trade. Part of what made the visits important was the feeling of connectivity to the larger world that they brought with them as they passed through.

"You're going to the hills next, right?" Carla asked

"Yes. I debated just finishing up for the year given how rough the circuit has been. But I thought I'd do a short run up into the hills to make sure the settlements have what they need to make it through the winter. Probably not as far as Tahoe. I'm thinking of just hitting Gold Bug, cutting over to Wild Bluff, and then taking the 80 back home before it gets too hot."

"I am glad you'll make a few more stops," Carla said. "Being out on the road does wonders for you. You always come back happy. Seeing you happy makes me happy." She patted him on the leg.

"Now you owe me one more story before you go. Tell me about this cult leader." She leaned back in her chair, expectantly.

Trader's palms began to sweat just thinking about it, and he shifted uncomfortably in his chair. He could feel the shape of the knife pressed against his back, hidden beneath his shirt in his waistband.

He started at the beginning, explaining the devastation he stumbled on in Lodi. He wove together all of the signs and tales from people along the circuit, ending with Preacher's symbol on the highway just a couple miles or so away. Once he had it all laid out, his heart sank. Even though he'd found Carla and his home untouched, his gut told him that he hadn't seen the last of Preacher.

Carla sat still, her face thoughtful, as he finished the story.

"I didn't think I'd live long enough to see something like this again. History tends to repeat itself."

"That's exactly what Earl said." Trader sighed, chewing at his cheek.

"Did you know there used to be a cult right here in Sac in the Before? They had a house on X St. My parents used to point it out to me as a warning."

"Really?" Trader said, surprised.

"Yes...I can't remember what they were called." She tapped her fingers on the table, thinking. "Aggressive Missionary something-or-other. The cult moved to another state well before the area flooded."

"Were cults really that common?"

"I'm not an expert in cults, but I know enough to be nervous when one is around. They rarely end well. Be careful."

Trader looked down at his hands. "I feel like the man is pulling me behind him. I don't want to meet him. In fact, I'd be fine if Preacher just disappeared. But I feel like no matter what I do, I'm going to have to come face-to-face with him."

Carla reached over and gave his hand a long, soft squeeze. "You're a good person, Trader. An old soul. If this is your path, then you must walk it. But do so with your eyes wide open."

He looked up at her, and she squeezed his hand again.

"You be safe out there and come back home. I'm not going to watch your garden all summer, young man."

Trader huffed with a smile, catching her hand to squeeze it back.

Carla pulled the conversation back to lighter things, talking about the weather, the expected harvest, and the chicken shenanigans. After dinner, Trader helped her clean up, enjoying their quiet time together. When it was time to say goodbye, she folded him into a big hug.

"Take care of yourself, honey."

"I will, Carla. You too. I'm going to be upset if I don't have any okra to eat when I get back," he teased.

"Don't you worry about me or your okra," she said with a mischievous grin. "I can take care of myself," she added, understanding the meaning behind what he had said.

Trader knew she'd be okay and tried not to worry. He'd seen her lay the beat down on a rabid raccoon a couple of years ago with her walking stick. Carla looked like a cuddly grandma, but there was a reason she'd survived on her own for so long. Any cultist would rue the day they crossed paths with her; she was a tough cookie.

With one last hug goodbye, he headed home. He walked through the cool night air, empty metal cart rattling along the sidewalk and echoing through the vacant neighborhood. Back at home, he settled into his bed with Sasha curled at his side, purring and making biscuits in the quilt. Within a few minutes, he was fast asleep.

CHAPTER
TWENTY-EIGHT

Trader woke at sunrise and shuffled into the kitchen where Sasha was patiently waiting by the back door.

You're late, her look said. *Let me out already.*

As soon as the door cracked open, she dashed out.

"Don't take too long! We're leaving soon!" he called after her.

His clothes and bedroll had fully dried overnight, and he took everything down to pack in the wagon. He toyed with the idea of making a hot meal in the fire pit and decided against it. He didn't want to leave the coals unattended when they headed back out on the road. Instead, he enjoyed some bread slathered with nut butter and honey.

Sasha reappeared as Trader was hitching Boxer. She hopped in the driver's seat and curled up with a *merf* of greeting. Just as he was about to leave, he realized that he had forgotten the book. He jogged back in and grabbed it before heading out. *The Galaxy and the Ground Within* was really good, and he'd have kicked himself if he had to wait another week or so to read it again. He stashed it next to the sack of apples in the wagon, grabbing one for himself to eat on the road. With the house all closed up, the trio headed out for the last leg of the journey.

The wagon headed down Broadway to Stockton Blvd., passing by the large empty hospitals that bordered the freeway onramp. By the time Trader was born, hospitals weren't really a thing in Sacramento anymore, just empty buildings with broken windows and graffiti. Trader had gone into Shiner's once, just to see what it was like. It had been dark, empty, and his footsteps had clanged eerily through the building. Dust coated everything, dimming the artwork that had once helped kids feel more comfortable in the big, scary place. He was surprised to see so much medical equipment left behind and then chided himself for even thinking that. What use was most of the stuff without power and doctors who knew how to use it? When passing by this year, he made a note to see what was still left when he finished up the circuit. If Walnut Creek got their hospital up and running, some of this stuff might be of value to them.

The trio took the onramp to the 50, heading east. The plan was to break for an early lunch at Rat's and do a bit of trading. After that, they'd try to make it as far as El Dorado Hills. They would camp there overnight before heading up to Gold Bug.

Rat's place was off Folsom Blvd. and had been a recycling center in the Before. Rat had gutted the small office, using it to live in. The rest of the yard was used for sorting his treasures; he would scavenge from the surrounding junk yards, fix stuff up, and bin it here. He was a tinkerer, often using various pieces of scrap to get things up and running again.

Rat had built a windmill from repurposed metal which, combined with the solar panels and a rack of house batteries, kept the place fully powered. For water, he had a few rain barrels set up. But he also had the advantage of being relatively close to the Folsom South Canal which, by some miracle, never ran dry and never flooded. It also had a steady enough flow that mosquitoes didn't have much luck trying to breed there.

THE BEFORE AND THE AFTER

As good as Rat was at finding and fixing shit, he downright sucked at growing and preparing food for storage. He was also a cantankerous little turd and preferred to live alone. He relied heavily on Trader, Jesse, and other folks to trade for food. If people wanted any of his stuff, they definitely had to come to him. Trader had once offered to hook him up with six months of food to install solar panels and a battery at his place. Rat had outright refused, grumbling a "hell no". Rat would only leave his place on a rare scavenging excursion, and even then, he would only go alone.

Trader pulled into the parking lot and hollered loudly, letting him know he had arrived. Rat probably already knew anyway. He'd somehow rigged a security camera system to an ancient monitor in his workshop out back. It allowed him to keep an eye on his roost, not that anyone in the After had ever been a real threat. Rat was just anxious and protective by nature.

Maybe being extra cautious will become the norm with Preacher roaming the roads, Trader thought glumly.

Trader hopped out of the wagon, unhitching Boxer and waiting for Rat to come out front. Rat was very protective over his stuff. And twitchy. Trader had to give him space and time to come out front to officially let him in.

Rat finally marched around the corner, tense but as welcoming as he could be. It was always a good sign if he appeared without his large Bowie knife in hand. He was about Trader's age, thin with tanned to almost burned skin, and wispy, chin-length blond hair that fluttered around in the breeze. He wore a threadbare, white tank top and cut-off military pants. He had a metal prosthetic leg on his right side.

"You're late this year," Rat grumped.

Trader rolled with it, knowing this was just about as friendly a greeting as anyone could get from him. "Yep, got held up in Manteca. How have things been?"

Rat harrumphed.

"Come on back when you are done getting them set up." He gestured absently to Boxer and Sasha.

Trader let the horse loose to wander over to a patch of tall grass in the lot next to the scrapyard. He grabbed some lunch provisions, including his last loaf of bread, and headed back to the workshop. Rat was sitting at a large table in a three-sided garage. He was focused on a bunch of wires and equipment parts arranged around him.

"Brought lunch. Hungry?" Trader asked.

Rat looked up and cleared a small spot on the table with his thick, calloused hands. Trader laid the loaf of bread, a jar of honey, apricot preserves, and some nut butter down.

"What the actual fuck is that?" Rat looked doubtful at the loaf of bread.

"It's bread, dude."

Trader tore off a piece, slathered some nut butter and preserves on it, and passed it to Rat. Rat leaned back on his stool and accepted the food. He took a bite. Normally, Rat was pretty good at hiding any emotion but "irritated". For the briefest of moments, however, Trader saw joy flit across Rat's face as he tasted the food. Rat chewed and harrumphed again, this time with a slight upward inflection in tone.

"That for me?" Rat asked with his mouth full, gesturing towards the rest of the loaf.

"Take it all." Trader nudged it towards him. "That's my last loaf of bread. But I've got plenty of other types of food for you if you need it."

Rat took out his Bowie knife, cutting the bread in thick slices. He handed one to Trader, and then slathered his own slice in more butter and preserves. Trader accepted the slice, savoring it, knowing it would be the last bit of bread until he tried his hand at making his own with the sack of flour back at home.

"What're you working on?" Trader asked.

"Trying to get this radio operational. Not that I want to

THE BEFORE AND THE AFTER

fucking talk to anybody. But some of those fluffies out there...." He flitted his fingers. "I figured they might want to talk between settlements. If you come by again before you head out next year, I think I may have two or three working for you. They have to have power, though. I thought about a hand crank...but that'll take more time."

Even though Rat acted gruff and didn't like being around people, he still cared about them in his own way.

"Sounds good." Trader smiled to himself. "I may swing by before that in the fall too. See what you got." He mainly wanted to check on Rat and make sure he had enough food for the winter. Trading was always a nice cover.

Rat grunted in reply, seeing straight through Trader.

"Anyone else come by since I was last here?" he fished.

"Just Jesse," Rat answered around a mouthful.

Trader relaxed a bit. The scrapyard was a bit off the road and only a few people knew where to find it. But Rat also had a sixth sense about things. He would've caught anything that was out of place, like an ash pile on the damn highway.

"I have a long list of items the settlements need," Trader said, changing the subject, not wanting to make Rat any more anxious and flightier than he already was, if that was even possible.

"Can you keep an eye out for me?" Trader continued. He listed the items that had been requested along the circuit so far this year. "Also, a woman named Natalia may stop by. She's using a bike to trade between settlements and is looking for spare parts."

Rat pursed his lips, listening intently to the long list. "I'll see what I can do."

"Anything you want me to take up to the hills?" Trader asked.

"I got several crates of jars and bottles for you to take up to Gold Bug."

He got up and started sorting through the crates in the back of his workshop. The place perfectly encapsulated the term "ordered chaos". There was stuff crammed everywhere, and yet each item had its specific place.

Trader knew this was his cue that their limited social time was over. He went to help Rat pack up. The two of them loaded four crates of glassware into Trader's wagon. Trader stuffed some clothes and quilts between the bottles so they wouldn't rattle the next two days.

Trader pulled a couple of baskets out of the wagon. "How's the pantry looking?"

Rat listed off the things he wanted, mostly jerky, nuts, preserves, and some fresh carrots. Trader loaded the items into the baskets. Because he knew Rat didn't cook, he didn't even bother to offer any of the potatoes or salt. The two took the baskets into the small home.

"Need any meds or anything else?" Trader offered, though he knew Rat would say no.

"Nah, man." Rat shook his head.

"Thanks, Rat. I'll probably see you after the summer heat lets up."

Trader took a slight risk and held his hand out. He was pleasantly surprised when Rat briefly clasped his hand and shook it firmly. Rat grunted, which was as close to a goodbye as he would get, and went back to his workshop.

* * *

Trader led Boxer back to the wagon. The horse was a tad miffed to cut his lunch short and flicked his ears in irritation. Sasha hadn't bothered to leave her bed on the driver's seat and was curled up, asleep. Trader hopped in the wagon, and guided it back on the 50, heading north to Placerville. He wouldn't be able to make it there today, and they'd have to stop overnight along the way. But Trader wanted to make sure he had enough time to find a safe spot to get them set up for the night. The foothills weren't safe after sundown.

The 50 sloped gently east, towards the purple silhouette of the Sierra Nevada. As the suburbs hugging the city of Sacramento petered off, the rolling fields of native grass spread out in either direction. The air started to become crisper and cleaner as the road wound upwards out of the dust that lay heavy in the bowl of the valley. A group of turkey vultures circled off in the distance. The journey was relatively quiet, with just the clop of Boxer's hooves, the creak of the wagon, and the subtle rattle of the bottles that apparently hadn't been padded well enough.

They made good time, and the city of Folsom soon spread out across the hills on the north side of the highway. Trader had explored this area a few years back, and there were plenty of places to hole up for the night in the large, open-air shopping centers. However, the mosquitoes loved making their babies in the numerous man-made ponds, fountains with stagnant grimy brown water, and pools of water in the cracked and pitted asphalt of the sprawling parking lots. The risk of catching Weeps was too high to stop there.

Trader decided to press on to the Silva Valley Pkwy. exit. There was a church on Tong Rd. that had a large rolldown door that he could drive the wagon through. Bears had been known to venture down this far, and they'd make short work of his wagon in their search for food. Between the bears and the mountain lions, it was too risky to leave his wagon or Boxer outside overnight.

They arrived at the church, and Trader got the animals set up inside well before the sun tipped over the horizon. Off in the distance, a family of burrowing owls peered out from their underground burrows, watching him. He had enough daylight left to make a small fire in the parking lot outside. He cooked fried potatoes and fresh eggs from Carla's chickens. On the side, he had some pickled bell peppers and okra. He relaxed, enjoying his meal, and held his book open with his free hand to read while he ate.

In the fading light, Trader was once again drawn into *The Galaxy and the Ground Within*. The five main characters were all unique; their physical differences echoed their contrasting cultures. Oolo and Tupo brought the waylaid, hodge-podge band of aliens together with their warm, welcoming demeanors, creating a safe space that allowed everyone's individual light to shine through. Despite their dramatic differences, the characters were slowly able to break down barriers, bringing their unique perspectives and accepting each other for who they were.

There was a strong live-and-let-live tone to the book that Trader appreciated. He'd met many people on his yearly journeys, each bringing a fresh perspective and coming with their own baggage. Each person's story was unique, and each person had their own way of finding purpose and meaning in their life. And, in the book at least, each character came from a good place with a desire to belong and be accepted for who they were.

Trader read until the last possible bit of light fled the sky and then tucked in for the night, thoughts of the story circling in his mind.

CHAPTER
TWENTY-NINE

Trader woke up before dawn, with the morning chill of the cooler foothills biting at his nose and fogging his breath. After getting dressed and grabbing a handful of dried fruit, he led Boxer out on a lead rope. The church was surrounded by tall grasses, scrub brush, and scattered acorn trees, making it perfect for the horse to grab a morning snack before the long trek up to Placerville. The sun was just starting to peek over the mountains as they stepped out of the church. The burrowing owl family was already up, intently watching the horse shuffle through the tall grass.

By the time Trader had finished eating, the sun had fully risen over the mountains. A chill still pricked the air. A light fog had settled in the low spots, forming a crisp blanket over the meadows and ditches. Dew glistened on the grasses poking through the asphalt, and the wet air penetrated through his clothes, making him shiver.

Trader led Boxer back into the church, checked his feet, and hitched him up. With a low whistle, Sasha came trotting out of a dark corner in the back of the church and hopped into the wagon.

Trader grabbed some jerky to snack on while they traveled, sneaking Sasha a small scrap.

It was a steep climb up the deserted highway and into the mountains for their next stop. Last year, the road had been in good shape, and he suspected he would find it just about the same. They headed back to the 50 and turned east, Trader walking next to the wagon and keeping pace as the road inclined.

The road was empty, and he didn't see any other travelers. He wasn't too surprised as folks tended not to head in this direction. There were only two settlements off the 50 that he knew about this high up in the hills. Gold Bug, just off the highway in Placerville, was one. There was also a fairly large group up at the Washoe settlement by Lake Tahoe. Singletons roamed the mountains too but tended to keep to themselves and often stayed hidden unless they needed to trade. Despite all of that, a part of him still expected to see some sign of Preacher along the 50. He hoped their paths had diverged, but his gut told him they hadn't.

It was rough living this far up in the Sierra Nevadas. Snows were often very heavy, blocking access for most of the winter and limiting how much food could be grown. The Washoe settlement lived with the high risk of forest fires in the dry season and the looming threat of starvation in the winter. Some years, Trader would venture up to Lake Tahoe just to check in with them. He couldn't this year; he was already running late, and he'd bake on the hot asphalt on the way home if he didn't get a move on.

Jesse had told him that the roads leading up to and through Donner's Pass were now covered in landslides or had crumbled away. Even if someone could get over the pass, Nevada was supposed to be a high-desert wasteland, with the oppressive drought pulverizing most of the state. Rumor had it that it wasn't even worth bothering to explore in that direction, and Trader had no burning desire to try.

Around midday, Trader stopped for lunch. He unhitched Boxer so that the horse could relax, drink, and graze if he wanted to. Sasha hopped off to prance around in the tall grasses adjacent to the highway. Trader had a quick lunch of carrot sticks and nut butter, making sure to drink lots of water. Twenty miles was a long way to go, and he reckoned they were only about halfway.

As they reached the higher elevations, oak and acorn trees were slowly replaced with tall pines that had trunks so wide that Trader could barely put his arms all the way around them. There were a few redwoods scattered around Sacramento, and he loved to run his hands over the pebbly rust-colored bark. But it wasn't until he was deep into the forest up here that the rich pine smell would kick in. He inhaled slowly and deeply, enjoying the moment.

He loved the smell of redwoods. He'd heard stories from the Before about how people would try to package that smell and bring it back into their cars or their houses. On some holidays, they'd even chop a pine tree down just to stick it in their living room for a couple of weeks as it slowly died. He didn't understand why they didn't just come to the forest, take in the rich smells, run their hands along the trunks of the ancient trees, and hear the gentle creaking in the breeze.

It was late in the afternoon when the trio reached the town of Placerville. The sound of the wagon startled a herd of deer, who bounded across the road. Trader spied a red-shouldered hawk perched in the pines across the creek that ran next to the highway. The sound of the rushing water called to him, and Trader had half a mind to go down to see if he could catch some rainbow trout. With only a few more hours of light left, he decided to press on. The trio took the 49 exit, curving north and deeper into the forest where the Gold Bug settlement was nestled.

Gold Bug was named after an honest-to-goodness gold mine from the late 1800s. The mine had eventually run dry, and the area had then been designated a historical site with a museum to follow. The recreational area at the old mine was perfect for a settlement.

There were three pre-existing structures that had been slowly renovated and expanded. The structures were connected by paved walking trails, making it easy to move about. The settlement also boasted two wells, and Big Canyon Creek ran right through it all.

The mine offered year-round cold storage for meat, which was their main source of food. The families that lived at Gold Bug were mainly hunters and fishers, living off a variety of game. They farmed some, but the heavy winter snows limited their growing period.

Early on, they'd started cultivating apples and olives, and the settlement boasted two small orchards. In addition to creating preserves with the harvests, they also pressed olive oil, made apple cider, and fermented vinegar. They had their own mini-trading circuit for the oil and the vinegar, riding horses on deer trails to connect with the mountain folk and Singletons who hadn't given up living rural.

The de facto leader of Gold Bug was Orko. His family had been one of the few groups of survivors when Weeps first broke out. They'd been homesteading further up in the mountains in Foresthill when a pretty nasty fire burned through, and they'd barely made it out alive. The fire pushed them out of the rural mountain areas to settle closer to the main highway and its many exit routes. Over time, two other mountain families had joined them.

Trader liked visiting the settlement. It had a rustic ambiance, and he always felt like he was back with the miners and panners in the 1800s. The people were brisk and no-nonsense, but also fair. And, he'd seen them be exceptionally generous even during hard times. They looked after each other, making sure everyone survived. Orko, having been there almost thirty years now, led by example.

The road leading to the settlement was marked with a faded American flag on a tall metal pole. Trader turned onto Gold Bug

Ln. and pulled the wagon into the second parking lot near the first log cabin. As he hopped out of the wagon, a startled jackrabbit scurried into the scrub brush.

Orko was outside, splitting logs from a giant pile and stacking them neatly. It could take as many as six or seven cords per winter to keep a home warm this far up above the snow line. The residents of Gold Bug would spend most of the spring and fall cutting down trees and getting ready for winter.

Orko raised a hand in greeting and slammed the ax into the chopping block before heading over. He was tall and burly with light brown skin, a thick beard, and soft, brown hair that fell to his shoulders in loose curls. He wore a loose cotton shirt dark with sweat, deerskin pants, and beat-up boots.

"Well look who's here," Orko said in a friendly way. "Getting kinda late in the season. We wondered if you were gonna come at all."

"To be honest, I wondered the same myself," Trader said, shaking Orko's hand. "I stayed for about a week to help some folks south of Sac, and that put me back a bit. I figured I'd make a quick loop up to the mountains and get some of the fresh air before making my way home."

"You going straight back home after this?" Orko asked.

"I'll stay just one night here, circle to Wild Bluff, and then take the 80 home," Trader answered.

A guarded look passed over Orko's face, and the big man tensed.

Watching him closely, Trader continued, "I thought about going up to the Washoe, but it's just too late this year. I don't want Boxer's hooves melting in the summer heat on my way home."

Orko shifted his gaze away, still cagey. An ominous feeling settled on Trader's shoulders.

"Come on in," Orko said before he could ask any questions.

"Helga's out cleaning a deer. I'll ask her to let everyone know you're here if they don't already know."

He clapped Trader on the back. Trader, still a tad anxious, decided to roll with it. Stories had a way of being told if he waited long enough for them.

Trader followed him into the house, where Orko poured them both tall glasses of cool apple cider. They sat at an old log table, polished smooth with years of use. Orko grabbed some dried salmon jerky, dried apples, and cracked a jar of olives, setting them out to snack on.

"How's it been?" Trader probed gently.

Trader took a sip of the cider. The drink was slightly sour and puckered his mouth but was refreshing after the long hike up the hills.

Orko sighed. "We lost two last fall. After that hot summer, the creek dried down to puddles, and the skeeters were real bad. Lost one to Weeps. Managed to still save Dedra and Steve with the Proxleep you brought last time. Gonna take more of that off you if you've got it."

Trader nodded to indicate that he did indeed have some up for grabs.

"Lacey got bit by a rattler and died," Orko continued. "Surprised us all. Usually, rattlers just mind their own and slither away when they hear you coming. But they were swarming this year after the thaw." He looked resigned.

"Otherwise though, not too bad. The hunting and fishing have been good. Katrina had a baby. We just keep chugging along."

Trader nodded in understanding. It felt like rinse and repeat between the settlements. Every year one or two died, and every year they were lucky if one or two were born. Each settlement had its own tales of gains and losses. This year was a bit different, though. It was the first year he'd seen the scales tipping just a bit to favor the wins, like Bess' music store in Walnut Creek and Malikai's murals at the Machados'.

"How's the trip been this year?" Orko asked.

"Mixed bag myself," he answered between bites. "A few rough spots. But the settlements as a whole are really doing good. Forty Two has a shoemaker now. I'll try to bring boots by next year. The Silvas are making enough cotton now that they can trade the extra bolts. I don't have any left to trade, but should have some next year. Walnut Creek has the hospital up and running. And, get this, the Machados are growing wheat and making bread. Kinda cool to see things building back up."

"That's good to hear," Orko said, nodding slightly to himself.

Trader continued sharing stories from the road, even the one about the dust storm that was now far enough away that he could inject some humor into it. Orko boomed with laughter, knowing all too well the pain of having grit in one's taint. They traded in tales casually and companionably as they finished their snack. After a bit, Helga came in to let them know that everyone was ready to trade, and they all headed outside, more relaxed than he was when he first arrived. Trader knew there was still one tale left untold but was hoping he could draw it out of Orko before he moved on.

CHAPTER
THIRTY

When Orko and Trader headed back out, there was already a small group waiting by the wagon to trade. The people of Gold Bug grabbed all of Rat's empty bottles and jars. They also took some of the comfort items, like quilts, a few tools, and books. They refreshed their stock of medication, having used the last of their Proxleep. In return, Trader was able to grab a crate of apple cider vinegar, several bottles of olive oil, and a few pelts.

After trading was done, everyone but Orko went their separate ways. Most of the people at Gold Bug kept to themselves, and Trader still didn't know many of them by name. They lived close enough together to survive but otherwise liked their space. Trader respected their way of living. In a way, it was very similar to Carla back home in Sacramento.

"Thanks for stopping by," Orko said. "Interested in joining Helga and me for dinner?"

"I'd love to," Trader answered as he packed the last few items away in his wagon. "Thanks for the invite."

"I reckon we've got about an hour of daylight left. Helga's gotta finish up that deer, and I have a never-ending pile of wood calling me. How about you come on over after the sun fully sets?"

Trader dipped his head. "Sounds good."

Trader briefly thought about offering to help but, having been here several years in a row, he knew that Orko would kindly decline. They were fiercely independent. And the way Orko worded the invite, he wasn't looking for company when he finished up the chores either.

Taking advantage of the remaining bit of sun, he settled in a chair in the shade next to his wagon, the sound of Boxer rustling in the tall grass nearby. Sasha had disappeared and was doing her own cat thing. Trader cracked open *The Galaxy and the Ground Within*, slipping right back into the story. He was fascinated by how dramatically different and occasionally warring species could find commonality. They were learning to appreciate one another, judging each other on their actions rather than any preconceived notions. By giving others the time and space to listen and learn, the walls between them were coming down.

It became too dark to read anymore when he was about three quarters of the way through the book. He put everything away and got the wagon sorted for the night. He had to call for Sasha a few times before she came bounding out of the shrubs and into the back of the wagon with a *merf*. Trader picked a few burs out of her fur and checked her for ticks before petting her to get her settled for the night. He laced up the wagon flaps, locking her in to keep her safe. He also haltered Boxer and tied him up close to the wagon.

This high in the foothills, there were all sorts of critters who'd eat Sasha, including great horned owls and coyotes. She would also make a nice snack for a mountain lion, but, for whatever reason, the lions usually steered clear of the main part of Gold Bug. The biggest issue tonight would be the bears. Though grizzlies were rare, black bears were fairly common and had no qualms about tearing apart a wagon to get at the food inside.

They weren't scared of people at all and would often be seen wandering through the settlement.

With everything as secure as possible, Trader headed back to Orko's. He grabbed a jar of honey and peach preserves to share. He followed the dim light from the tallow lamps flickering through the windows to find his way to the house.

With a knock, Helga hollered for him to come in. Orko was at the wood stove, which could be used for both heating the cabin and cooking. He came away with a cast iron pan filled with cooked potatoes, carrots, and wild mushrooms. Steaming sausages already sat on the table. Trader's mouth watered. Orko made the best deer sausage, and he was excited that he was going to get to have some on this trip.

"Dinner smells amazing," Trader said, grabbing a seat. "Thanks again for having me." Helga grunted, a smile on her face and Orko nodded a welcome.

"This is for dessert," he said, placing the peaches on the table. "And this is a gift." He placed the honey jar on the counter behind him.

As soon as the food was served, they dove in. Orko and Helga quickly wolfed down their food and cracked into the peaches. Those were then savored slowly, both of them enjoying the sweetness. After they ate, Orko passed bottles of cider around, and they moved to the more comfortable chairs around the stove. They idly chatted about game counts and sausage recipes.

Feeling that there was no time like the present, Trader asked, "So what's up with my plan for the rest of the circuit? Something I should know about?"

A dark cloud spread across Orko's face again.

"Back at the wagon, I had a feeling there was something you maybe wanted to say but didn't," Trader pressed.

Orko's eyes became hooded and he exchanged a glance with Helga.

"We've done well with the you do you mentality here," Orko started. "We do our own thing and respect other ways of living. Like the Singletons." Orko paused, and Trader could tell he was uncomfortable. "I don't want to be talking bad about no one."

Helga continued to stare at the fire, tense but quiet. Trader waited for Orko to continue.

Orko sighed. "Just hear what I gotta say about Wild Bluff, and you can decide for yourself. I haven't been there recently, mind you. But I trust the Singletons, and the stories coming out of there aren't so hot."

Orko paused again, taking a sip of the cider and stretching his legs out in front of him.

"This is a busy time of year for Singletons. Once the snow melts, they all check in and trade a bit. If it was just one of 'em telling this story, I'd have thought it was bullshit. But they're all saying the same thing in their own way. They say that Wild Bluff has a new leader, an outsider, and it's a very different place now."

Trader felt gooseflesh prickle across his arms for the umpteenth time this season. He knew what Orko was going to say before the words even crossed his lips.

"Word is this preacher showed up at Wild Bluff with a small group about a month ago," Orko continued. "Completely changed everything and severed ties with any outsider. A bunch of the people there were converted. All the Singletons report that some of the original people from the settlement are just gone now. I suspect they decided not to conform; though the stories differ on the why and where all those people went."

Helga grunted.

Trader looked over at her. The room was dark and the firelight danced across her grim face as she stared at the stove. She clearly had her own opinion about what happened to the missing people, but she wasn't going to share it.

"The stories all agree on one thing though. If you go there,

THE BEFORE AND THE AFTER

they try to make you join. I mean, *aggressively* try to make you join. And if you don't, they ask you to leave. Preacher's message encourages conformity and shuts down any questions about the new way of livin'." Orko rubbed his face with a large calloused hand.

"It's gonna be hard for them to survive in these parts with an attitude like that," Orko said gruffly.

Helga nodded in agreement and sipped her cider.

"Did any of them describe what he looked like? Did he have a symbol? Do you know what direction he came from?"

Questions spilled from Trader. He was certain that he'd go to Wild Bluff now, no matter what Orko had to say; he couldn't shake free from Preacher's orbit.

Orko turned to look at him with piercing eyes. "Don't recall me saying Preacher was a 'he' or that he had a symbol. You know this fella, don't you?" Orko's gaze turned accusatory, and Trader felt him mentally pull away.

Trying to explain, Trader told the story from the beginning. He started with the burned-out town in Lodi and wove the tale all the way to seeing Preacher's symbol on the highway in Sacramento. Orko slowly relaxed and seemed to open back up.

"Everyone has their own story about the man," Trader reflected. "I think the bookstore owner in Walnut Creek had the best pulse on the situation. I think what happened in Lodi was a tipping point for Preacher. In his grief and loneliness, he built a belief system…and around that he built a cult as a way to protect himself. A way to feel safe. He preys on the lonely and lost, promising to make those feelings go away if they join him.

"Earl said it was fairly common in the Before for cult leaders to have symbols. This is Preacher's." Trader used his finger to draw the symbol on his leg: three dots arranged in a pyramid with five lines bursting vertically from the top.

Orko nodded. "Yep, all the Singletons drew the same damn thing." He fidgeted a bit with the bottle and said apprehensively,

"I'm a little worried about having that whack job in my backyard."

Feeling magnanimous and slightly inspired by the book he'd put down about an hour before, Trader asked, "Has he ever hurt anybody, though? What did the Singletons say about how the people look in Wild Bluff?"

Orko pursed his lips and tilted his head. He looked over at Helga who shrugged and took another sip of her cider.

"Don't recall them saying anything about that. Just that Preacher gave them the heebie jeebies and that they were essentially told to fuck off." Orko took a sip of cider and stared into the fire a bit before continuing.

"But really, what kinda good can come from running a place like that?" Orko sucked his teeth. "It's either their way or the highway. That place will suffer, even if it's through benign neglect."

Shaking his head, Orko continued, "The world don't work like that now, especially this high in the hills. One rough year and they'll starve to death if they don't work with others. And that's all if a fire doesn't take 'em first. The idiot burned down a town in the middle of winter, and that area around Wild Bluff is ripe for a wildfire."

They sat in silence, all lost in their own thoughts.

Orko's right, he thought. *They'll die without trade.*

A big community like the Machados' might do fine without access to items from other settlements. But even they were at risk and might need help from others at some point. Forming an isolated commune would only hurt the settlement.

"Are you still thinking about heading that way?" Orko asked, breaking the long stretch of silence.

Trader stared into the fire, turning his bottle of cider in a circle on the armrest. It would be easier to just turn back home. Doing so would guarantee that he made it back to Sacramento before the summer temps stretched into the 100s. But part of him felt certain that the entire journey this year was meant to end with Preacher. He felt a pull dragging him in Preacher's footsteps. Even though he wasn't quite sure he wanted to, he knew he *needed* to go. If he didn't, it would itch and burn like a burr in his sock.

Trader sighed. "I think I have to. Can't explain why really. I just feel like…I need to see him…to size him up…for all this to feel finished. Otherwise, I think it'll eat at me like I left something half done."

His words resonated with Orko and Helga. They knew how a job left incomplete could nag at you.

"Be safe, my friend." Orko reached over and clapped Trader on the leg. "We want to see you back next year."

The conversation drifted onto lighter topics until Trader, feeling tired, headed back out to the wagon. The night was pitch black beyond the faint light from the windows and noisy in a wild sort of way. The large redwoods creaked in the breeze. Crickets sang. The croaks of frogs echoed from the creek, and a barn owl made intermittent harsh screeches from a nearby tree.

Trader fumbled his way into the wagon, out of his clothes, and into his bedroll. The evening chill so typical of the foothills settled across the forest, and he rubbed his arms and legs to warm up. Sasha scooted under the covers and nestled in the crook of his arm, purring loudly. With her reassuringly by his side, he fell quickly and deeply asleep.

CHAPTER
THIRTY-ONE

The next morning, Trader was startled awake, his heart pounding in his chest and nose cold from the brisk air. His breath fogged out in front of him. Sasha was still snuggled in the crook of his arm under the covers. He was surprised at how deeply he'd slept and how suddenly he awoke. He sat in his bedroll, eyes wide open, listening intently.

The sun appeared to be fully up, but he didn't hear anything or anyone moving around. Taking quick stock of the wagon, it appeared to have made it unscathed through the night. He crawled out of the bedroll with Sasha glaring at him for disturbing her slumber. Peering out the wagon flaps, he confirmed that Boxer was all right.

What the hell? he thought. *Why am I so antsy?*

He'd slept soundly and felt well-rested, but it wasn't like him to jerk awake. He tried to recall if he had been dreaming before he woke and was met with a wall of fog.

Trader tried to shrug off the foreboding feeling, occupying himself by going through the motions of getting dressed. Outside the wagon, he jumped up and down, rubbing his hands on his thighs trying to warm up. Sasha slowly followed him, looking grumpy. A blue jay screeched at them from up above. Trader turned Boxer loose for a bit before getting him rigged up.

The smell of campfire smoke filled the air, and his stomach rumbled. He'd contemplated a hot breakfast but decided to just get a move on, the anxiety over the looming confrontation with Preacher gnawing at him. There weren't enough hours of daylight to get all the way to Wild Bluff in a single shot. Between the wildlife, the crescent moon, and the uncertainty as to the condition of the road ahead, it wouldn't be safe to travel at night either. He was going to have to suck it up and let one more day pass if he was gonna be smart about it. He promised himself a warm meal tonight to give himself something to look forward to.

Trader grabbed some nuts and dried apricots to snack on as he readied the wagon. Not knowing what to expect at Wild Bluff, Trader went to the small creek to top up his water containers. As he was making his way back to the wagon, he heard the sound of wood being chopped. He meandered over to the cabin and, sure enough, Orko was back at it.

"I'm about to head out. Just topping up." Trader held up the large water containers.

"Travel safe." Orko rested the ax down and wiped his forehead with his arm. "Keep your eyes peeled and make sure you get back here next year."

"Looking forward to it." Trader smiled. 'You take care, too."

Orko nodded in response, sent a quick wave, and went back to chopping wood.

Trader secured everything in the back of the wagon. He called to Sasha, who meowed irritably, peering at him from her bed in the driver's seat.

I'm here already, dumbass, her look said.

As he headed out of Gold Bug and northwest on the 49, he

reflected on the trip so far. He started these journeys every year like an empty cup. At each stop, the people and their stories slowly filled him up, bringing him joy and giving him a sense of community. Wild Bluff would be his last stop on the circuit; his last story. Though his nerves bit at him, he knew this was the natural conclusion of his trip. Like Roland, he was bound on this path. He would need to see Preacher and his followers for himself.

* * *

The 49 was a rolling, two-lane highway that sloped slightly uphill and was surrounded by banks thick with shrubs. When the road dipped back down, small mudslides spilled onto the eroded and cracked asphalt. A mixture of acorn, walnut, sycamore, and evergreens formed variably thick forests that were occasionally separated by native grass fields. When the road rose, hugging the edges of the hills, there were expansive vistas spotted with trees climbing to the peaks of the Sierras in the east. He let Boxer keep a leisurely pace, knowing that they would have to stop in the early afternoon.

On the north end of Coloma, the bridge crossing the south fork of the American River was standing strong. Trader stopped the wagon, pausing to take in the broad expanse of water. Though the river could get mighty powerful and dangerous in some spots, with white crashing waves pounding over large boulders, the river was smoothly speeding along here, making a pleasant rushing sound. A small herd of deer bounded from the banks after being startled by a loud crack from deep in the forest.

As he passed over the western side of the bridge, he noticed a large California king snake, sunning itself on the cement ledge. The snake was pretty brave being out in full view with its bold black and white stripes. King snakes were good critters to have around. They meant less rats, which in turn meant less Weeps. They also kept the poisonous rattlers out of their territory, which was another bonus. Trader had only seen garter snakes and gopher snakes down in Sacramento; both were still useful to have around but not quite as grand as a king snake.

The trio continued north on the 49 until they hit the Magnolia Ranch Trailhead, which was the preferred stop on this route. On one side of the highway, there was a large parking lot, where a fire could be safely lit without burning down the whole damn forest. On the opposite side of the highway, there were the remnants of a vineyard with an old barn. The structure had somehow survived the years, having escaped the wildfires, and provided a safe haven for him to park the wagon overnight.

Trader backed the wagon into the barn, leaving the wide doors open for now. He unhitched Boxer, brushed him down, and turned him out on the grass next to the parking lot. The horse whickered softly and began grazing, tail swishing lazily.

In the middle of the parking lot, there was a well-used, stone firepit that had been built in the After. Set well away from the firepit was a stack of chopped logs. It was a give-a-log, take-a-log kinda thing. Trader, being who he was, always tried to leave more than he took. He brought a bundle of wood from the wagon and collected some fallen branches to build the stack back up. After starting a small fire, he brought over his chair, his book, his hat, and some items to make a warm meal. If he made it hearty enough, a light snack before bed should last him through to the morning.

In a large pot on the grate over the fire, a thick soup of beans, Swiss chard, carrots, and dried herbs bubbled away. He kept one eye on the soup as it slowly simmered, and read his book. Though he couldn't shake the anxious feeling deep in his stomach, the light sunshine, heady smell of the mountains, and rustling of creatures in the forest soothed him just a tad.

When the beans were soft and the broth thick, he ladled it out into a bowl. The soup was rich and hearty. He blew on each spoonful before savoring each bite, careful not to burn his tongue. With the pot practically licked clean, Trader let the fire die down as he finished the book.

In the story, the five strangers had journeyed from understanding, to acceptance, and then to friendship, despite their divergent cultures. The book now finished, he rested it on his lap, his hand on top, and he thought through the story. It had been subtly powerful.

Trader cleaned up from his late lunch, packing everything carefully up in his wagon. Just as dusk started to settle over the hillside, Trader led Boxer into the barn. He checked to make sure Sasha was inside before closing everything up for the night. Gold Bug had enough people moving about it to keep most predators away. But, all alone out here, he needed to lock things up tight.

Since they were tucked away in the barn, he left the flaps of the wagon open and settled into his bedroll. The evening chill swept in fast and furious after the sun tipped over the horizon. Sasha decided his chest was the best place to sleep tonight, rubbing on his chin and purring deep in her throat. Between the sliver of a moon and being holed up in the barn, it was almost entirely black and impossible to see. He was staring into the darkness long into the night before sleep finally took him.

* * *

At some point during the night, Trader woke to Sasha's low growling. He reached to pet her and felt the hair on her tail had poofed up. He could also hear Boxer awake, shifting his weight anxiously. Trader got out of the wagon, grabbing his large walking stick and knife.

Outside the barn, there were sounds of multiple large animals moving, and snuffling noises coming through the crack under the door. They were probably bears or maybe even coyotes based on the number of them. Coyotes didn't worry him, since it was virtually impossible for them to get in the barn. A bear was another story. If it was big enough, it could muscle its way through the flimsy wood.

As he got to the door, the snuffling stopped, and he heard a low, rumbling grunt. Smaller squeals came from slightly further away. That answered his question. It was definitely a bear, and probably a mama with her cubs.

"Fuck," he whispered to himself.

He waited for the bear's next move. The snuffling continued, moving to one side of the barn before circling back. A large thud rattled the door. The bear was probably on her hind legs, pushing on the door to test it out. The door rattled again, as the bear rocked against it, but the old wood held.

Most times, banging two large pots together made enough noise to chase a bear away. Even a mama bear and her cubs would usually decide pickings were better elsewhere when some loud, crazy, two-legged thing came hollering after them. But, if it had been a thin year, they might put up a fight and call the bluff. Sometimes hollering could trigger mama bears into defense mode. Trader decided to play it cool and wait. The door should hold. If not, he could start banging on stuff with his stick and see if he could scare her away.

His patience won him the standoff. After a bit more shaking, he heard the bear return to all fours with a *whump* sound. She circled the barn again, snuffling here and there, before deciding to call it quits, calling her cubs after her. With the river so close, they'd probably have better luck fishing anyway. Plus, the blackberries were coming in, which would be another good source of food for her cubs.

After waiting for a spell to make sure he didn't hear her

anymore, Trader climbed back into the wagon. Boxer was no longer shuffling nervously. He patted around for Sasha, finding her already relaxed and curled back up. Despite being snuggled in the warm bedroll, he tossed and turned before finally falling back to sleep.

* * *

The brisk morning chill woke him in the morning. Trader had slept like shit last night, and his eyes were dry from the lack of good sleep. He decided to stay under the warm covers for a bit, pulling a knit beanie on his head and dragging his clothes into the bedroll to warm them up before he put them on. It was a little over a half-day trip to Wild Bluff. He wanted to be at the top of his game when he met Preacher today and figured a couple of minutes extra in bed wouldn't hurt.

He lay there, nose running from the cold air, uncomfortable and slightly achy. The only way to beat the morning chill would be to get up and start moving around. He pulled his clothes on, still under the covers, before braving the cold. His breath fogged in front of him.

Once out of the wagon, he led Boxer across the street to where he had been grazing yesterday. Deciding to treat himself to a warm breakfast, he grabbed some potatoes, onions, kimchi, and eggs to make a hash. The fire was easy to start, and he was soon feeling warm, with a nice hearty meal digesting away in his stomach.

With his meal finished, Trader poured some water over the fire to put it out and covered it again with dirt. He was always reluctant to make fires and then leave them so quickly. It was a finicky land, and fires were no joke up here. He'd heard enough stories of people being trapped and burned to death from swiftly moving flames. But this fire was solidly out, and the pit was in the middle of a large asphalt island. Everything would be fine.

After checking Boxer's hooves, Trader hitched him up. With his copilot already gracing her bed in the driver's seat, he pulled the wagon out of the barn and continued northwest on the 49. He was curious about Preacher and somewhat inspired by *The Galaxy and the Ground Within* to try to better understand the man. Yet he still felt anxious and was surprised to feel butterflies swarming in his stomach as he turned onto the highway. He wondered if Roland felt like this when Walter was in his sights.

Everyone Trader had crossed paths with to date had warned him about Preacher, advising him to stay away. Trader found himself fretting over what the day would bring. It wasn't a worry like "I wonder what I will wear today?" or "What will the weather be like?". It was a slow, burning apprehension. His mind spun with concern for himself, Sasha, and Boxer. He was even nervous about the wagon and what he had inside. Losing sleep over someone potentially stealing his stuff was a new feeling for him. No one had shared any stories about Preacher hurting anyone or stealing anything. But everyone who'd ever met the guy said he was "off".

What does "off" really mean? he thought.

Trader found himself caught in an anxiety loop as Wild Bluff grew closer with each clop of Boxer's hooves. Even the peaceful views and the occasional wildlife didn't help him get his head back on straight. The miles slowly rolled by as the knot in his stomach clenched.

In the town of Cool, a painting waited for him on the side of an old fire department building like a warning. Three circles arranged in a triangle with five lines bursting from the top filled almost the entire side of the building. Though ash seemed to be part of the paint mixture, some other red liquid had replaced the blood in this rendition of Preacher's symbol. It looked like red clay. The hair on Trader's arms prickled, the knot in his stomach growing tighter.

The 49 cut sharply north before making a hairpin bend south

at the middle fork of the American River. The bridge stood strong as the highway crossed over. The river level here was high from the snowmelt, and the rapids rolling over the thick boulders created loud booming sounds. The angry water only amplified Trader's apprehension.

As he neared their destination, the 49 formed curves that hugged hillsides thick with evergreens. A few small rockslides had spilled onto the road since last season, but they were able to navigate around them. Boxer's hooves echoed loudly as they wound their way closer to the settlement.

Wild Bluff had been a ranger station in the Before and sat perched on the 49, right before the highway crossed into the city of Auburn and intersected the 80. The settlement boasted several pre-existing structures that were used for housing. The sloping hillside around the structures had been intensively trellised and farmed. The harvest from the farms was supplemented with fish and other game they caught themselves or from the Singletons who passed through.

Water was the biggest issue at the settlement. To Trader's eternal befuddlement, they hadn't set up rain catches. Instead, they'd take the steep dirt trail down to the north fork of the American River to wash and get drinking water. The large boulders bordering the river also made perfect perches for fishing while they waited for their clothes to dry.

They didn't have any power at Wild Bluff, using tallow lamps and large pot belly stoves for light, heat, and cooking. Similar to Gold Bug, Trader would almost always hear someone chopping wood whenever he passed through. The last time he had been here, the community had been fairly big, fifteen to twenty people or so. It took quite a few cords of wood to keep that many folks warm through the winter.

Trader wondered what he would find when he arrived. Last year, it was a community similar to Gold Bug: a handful of rural families coming together for survival. They didn't have a defined leader or council. They kept mainly to themselves and helped each other out when needed in a neighborly kinda way. Trader could only assume that Preacher had turned that whole lifestyle upside down. He had no idea what he'd find there this year, and could only hope that folks were being taken care of.

CHAPTER
THIRTY-TWO

The 49 hugged the hillside as it swept back south, taking Trader closer to his final stop. The crashing sound of the north fork of the American River echoed up from the canyon on his left. To the right, Trader could see Wild Bluff hunkered against the hillside through the trees. Situated directly in the center of the road leading into the settlement was the Preacher's symbol, once again painted in the odd red paint mixed with ash.

Trader felt a small dump of adrenaline as the first building came into view. When he turned into the settlement, everything seemed to pause. The few people who were tending the terraced gardens stilled, standing straight and looking at the wagon. Some he recognized, others he didn't. Everyone wore at least one piece of white clothing, dirty from work, but still notable. And every single person had the Preacher's symbol on their forehead. One of the workers walked briskly towards the buildings in the back of the settlement.

Gooseflesh danced on Trader's arms. Sasha, sensing the tension, hunkered down in her bed, ears flat. Even Boxer tripped over his feet, tail nervously swishing. Trader raised his hand in greeting, which was returned with blank stares. A slow, burning dread filled him.

He tried to play it cool, stopping the wagon where he usually would and hopping down to unhitch Boxer. Sasha uncharacteristically stayed put in her bed with her grump-face on. No one approached to greet him or even returned to work. The people he'd passed continued to stare at him blankly, unmoving statues.

Trader was a bit nervous just letting Boxer graze. So he tied the lead rope loose to the wagon and threw a small bundle of native grass down on the ground near his water bucket. The tension was slowly building, and it was becoming increasingly awkward. He had no more idle tasks that he could do without looking like he was faking it. Just as he was getting up the nerve to go speak to one of the workers, a man dressed in pure, unsullied white approached from the back of the settlement. Following about five feet behind were three people, also dressed in all white.

This is it.

Trader swallowed nervously, fear building in his stomach.

His gaze traveled across Preacher and his acolytes. To Trader's surprise, he recognized one of them: it was Bryson, Molimo's boyfriend from the Silvas'. The man's eyes were locked to the ground, hands clasped piously in front. Preacher's symbol blazed on his forehead. Trader tried to make eye connect, but Bryson didn't look up.

Preacher stopped about ten feet away from Trader, his body posture meticulously arranged to look relaxed and his gaze intent. He was an imposing figure. Preacher's followers stopped five feet behind him, in a gentle arc, heads still bowed.

"Welcome, my son." Preacher's voice was steady and commanding.

Trader's palms started to sweat. He considered himself fairly amicable, with an ability to adapt and get along with just about anybody. Preacher was a whole other ball game, and Trader finally understood what people meant when they said the dude felt *off*. There was something about Preacher that made him want to supplicate, and he hated himself for it. He couldn't tell if it was fear or awe.

He took a deep breath, trying to put aside his anxiety, and stepped forward to introduce himself. "I'm Trader. I don't think we've met. What's your name?"

Trader took a chance and reached out to shake. Preacher's eyes widened and he leaned back slightly, shying away from the extended hand, before catching himself. The flinch was just a flicker before a curtain of confidence and peace settled over the man. Preacher smiled softly and gazed down at him.

"Welcome to Lord's Light, my son. Through blood and ash, we've risen into the pure white light of God's love. We are pleased that you have come. Join your brothers and sisters in the sanctuary that is the Lord's Light. Here, you will find safety and succor. Through God, you will also be saved."

Preacher's voice was soft but strong, creating an air of gravitas. Trader could feel himself being drawn in by Preacher's power of influence. There was something about him that demanded attention; it was hypnotizing. After hearing all of the warnings along the circuit, the juxtaposition between the fatherly welcome and the fear Preacher trailed behind him was discomfiting.

"Huh. Place used to be called Wild Bluff last time I was here. Some folks I recognize, but I see a lot of new faces too." Trader's eyes jumped to Bryson, who still had his head bowed. "I also see quite a few people missing."

"God's message is a powerful one, my son. My flock came to Lord's Light about a month ago. My sons and daughters who lived in this place before us saw the beauty in God's way and have joined us."

Trader couldn't help but notice that Preacher refused to use the settlement's previous name. He'd also rewritten the narrative, neglecting to share that not everyone had joined his flock. According to the Singletons, several of the original people from this settlement were now M.I.A. Preacher was damn good at spinning a story of half-truths. Liluye was right; he was selling snake oil.

"All who see the Lord's light are welcome here," Preacher continued. "When you join us, God's love for you will fill the empty well of loneliness that you feel. He will protect you and the ones you love. You will find your purpose here."

Preacher stretched his arms out, singing his siren's song. Trader felt Preacher's magnetic personality start to stretch its tendrils around him. It was disquieting though, like drinking oily water when thirsty. There was a compelling feeling, mixed with a shameful, ickiness. It was difficult to articulate.

Yeah, "off" was right, Trader thought. *I wonder if they'll let us leave.*

The knot in his gut tightened, and he reflexively glanced back to Sasha and Boxer.

Taking a page from *The Galaxy and the Ground Within*, he tried to shake the defensive feeling. Why was he scared of this guy? Though just about everyone on the circuit didn't like him, he hadn't actually hurt anyone.

Jerking him out of his thoughts, Preacher said, "Don the pure white and become one of God. You are welcome here." He clasped his hands in front of him, studying Trader.

Fake it till you make it, he thought. Trader looped his thumbs in his pockets, trying to act relaxed and sure of himself.

"Thanks for inviting me and all. But me, Sasha, and Boxer got our own thing going. I have lots of stuff to trade before I leave though. What're you all looking for? Same as last year?"

Preacher dropped his arms to his sides and pursed his lips. "God provides everything we need," he said brusquely.

Trader chewed the inside of his cheek and tried to roll with it. "I'm sure he does...in fair trades with those who pass through.

Now, I've been trading here for many years, and I know you can't make it through the winter without some of the food that the Singletons and I bring in."

Trader saw a few surprised looks from newbies watching the exchange. He wasn't sure if it was because he challenged their leader or if it was because they didn't realize how rough the winter was going to be. He turned his back on Preacher to start rooting around in the wagon.

"I've got plenty of fruit preserves, dried nuts, nut butter, honey, and some salt. I also have some quilts and knitwear if you are running low. And God has provided you all with some Proxleep too. Gold Bug got hit with Weeps this last season. Never hurts to have some on hand." Trader prattled on nervously and started pulling stuff out of the wagon.

The workers who had been listening in had now moved closer. Some of them knew they legitimately needed some of the items he had. But they were waiting for Preacher's permission. Trader paused before taking more stuff out of the wagon to make eye contact with others in the group.

"I also have books, tools, and other items. Feel free to let me know what you need."

Everyone stood still, not responding, and the silence stretched out. Though Trader was trying to act casual, he had some serious pucker factor going on. He wasn't sure if they would just take all of his shit, beat him, walk away, or what. This was one situation he'd never navigated before, and he felt entirely out of his element. His stomach clenched with the adrenaline dump. A thick and heavy silence built between Trader and the group.

Finally, Preacher turned to the others and said, "God has provided for us, my sons and daughters. Please trade for what may be of use."

He swept his arm towards what Trader had already set out. With hooded eyes, Preacher turned back to frown at him. Trader smiled inwardly, trying not to let the victory show on his face. In that single, bold act of defiance, Trader was fairly certain that he'd done his part to help these people make it through the upcoming winter.

Preacher stepped aside, supervising the hustle and bustle of trading. The community had clearly been short on supplies as the trades often favored the settlement. They cleaned out most of his food and medication. They also took several quilts and some scavenge items, like nails and screws. In exchange, Trader received pelts and furs. He even scored a pair of deer leather moccasins.

Trader watched the group closely as they looked through the wares on offer. The people appeared on the skinny side but otherwise in good shape, with no evidence of abuse or distress. However, two things struck him as odd. The first was that the trades happened in almost virtual silence. The normal idle chatter, pleasantries, and smiles of greeting were completely absent. Second, the books went untouched. Even if he didn't trade any books at a settlement, a few people still picked up a book or two to look at the cover or read the back. The whole thing still felt off.

The more Trader observed them, the more he realized that the silence wasn't an angry or fearful one. It was more of a reflective, relaxed quiet. Preacher didn't appear to be demanding it. Instead, it was just part of the meditative culture of his acolytes.

Throughout the whole thing, Preacher stood quietly and unmoving, hands clasped casually in front of him. He was a looming presence and watched Trader intently. Trader felt Preacher's eyes on him but tried not to let it show how much it gave him the creeps. The leader of Lord's Light wasn't done with him.

CHAPTER
THIRTY-THREE

With trading complete, people retreated to stash their newly acquired items back in their quarters and then returned to work. A few people he recognized from last year made eye contact, but the usual thanks and verbalized appreciation were starkly missing. People just faded away, including the three acolytes who had followed Preacher out. Trader felt a bit empty, missing the casual conversion and feeling of community he typically received when trading.

With a start, he realized that he was alone with Preacher, who was standing with his hands still clasped and his gaze intently focused on him. Trader shuffled around, packing his wagon, trying to look casual. He knew that an invite to stay overnight, or even for lunch, was not at all coming.

Like I'd even want to stay. This place is creepy as fuck, he thought.

Despite Preacher saying he was welcome, he certainly didn't feel like he'd be accepted as his full, authentic self. He was pretty confident that he'd be allowed to simply leave with the trading done. But he still felt that something was unfinished.

Trader got to the point where he simply couldn't shift things around anymore, and he turned to finish this. He slung his thumbs back in his pockets and headed over to Preacher, trying to appear relaxed and maintaining eye contact the entire way. He stopped just a few feet away. Like a Western standoff, the tension built thickly between them.

Preacher broke first. "I invite you to sit and hear the word of God, my son." He gestured over to a stone picnic bench.

Preacher's words sounded like a command more than an invitation. Trader tried to dampen the surge of adrenaline. He didn't want to listen to a sermon, but he knew he had to start somewhere. He shifted the playing field a bit, saying "I've heard some stories about you on the road. I'd be interested in hearing your perspective. Let me grab some lunch."

Preacher tensed a bit as he turned his back on him once again. Trader dug through the wagon, heart pounding with apprehension. He busied himself by grabbing some mixed nuts and a couple of Jasmine's apples. He brought the food items over to the table along with a water jug.

Despite it being Preacher's idea, Trader was still surprised when Preacher joined him at the table. Preacher sat across from him, back straight, hands folded in his lap, and face neutral. His strong presence loomed, even seated. Trader casually opened the jar of nuts, holding it out to share. Preacher didn't respond and continued to study him intently.

Finally, Preacher leaned forward and spoke. "God has brought you here for a reason, my son. He has seen into your heart. He has seen your loneliness and your need for purpose. As part of my flock, you will no longer be alone. God will be your purpose and will fill your heart. Through the blood and ash of the After, you will rise into the Lord's light."

He swept his arm towards the gardens. "Here, God's people have come together. We have found hope through Him. Only under the Lord's light will you find peace and salvation in this world and in heaven. You will never feel alone or lost again."

The certainty in his persuasive tone was hypnotizing. Trader busied himself, pouring a few nuts into his hand, eating them one by one, and trying to act casual as he listened intently. He felt an urge to try to figure Preacher out and see his perspective. But the dude was chafing on him, and he was having a hard time keeping his shit together. Frankly, this guy was freaking him the fuck out.

"Everyone has suffered so much loss," Preacher said, filling the silence. "The world is filled with despair and tragedy. The only path to hope and peace is that laid by God. Thy word is a lamp unto my feet, and a light unto my path. The Lord gives us purpose.

"Each and every person here at Lord's Light has felt the touch of God," he continued, emphasizing each word with a tap of his pointer finger on the table. "They understand that His way is the only way." He paused dramatically to let his words settle and leaned back.

Staring intently at Trader, he pressed, "The people which sat in darkness saw great light; and to them which sat in the region and shadow of death light is sprung up. I am the light of the world: he that followeth me shall not walk in darkness, but shall have the light of life. Through the blood and ash of the After, we have risen into the Lord's light. We are protected."

Passion sparkled in Preacher's eyes.

Wading through the thick sermon, Trader tried to find something that would help him connect with Preacher. What instigated this radical, cultish behavior? Why was he so adamant that there was only one way to do things; that one being his way? Why had Preacher shut his mind off to the wonderful mix of people the world had to offer?

"Join us, my son," Preacher continued, filling the silence. "The Lord's light will protect you. It will ease your suffering and your loss. The Lord is nigh unto them that are of a broken heart; and saveth such as be of a contrite spirit."

Trader continued to silently eat his lunch and tried to keep his posture relaxed. Breathing slowly, he kept himself grounded as wave after wave of proselytizing washed over him. The visceral response to shun this man warred with his intellectual desire to make sense of Preacher. With understanding, he might even reach acceptance. He hoped that Preacher would join him on the journey and become more accepting of others who may pass through. The settlement wouldn't make it through the winter if Preacher severed all ties with the Singletons and Gold Bug.

"Look into your soul, my son. You will see the truth in my words. Those things, which ye have both learned, and received, and heard, and seen in me, do: and the God of Peace shall be with you. Find purpose with us at Lord's Light. With His light, the loneliness will flee into the shadows."

Gaining steam, Preacher wasn't expecting Trader to do anything but listen. He noodled over the best response. When he put his feelings aside and really listened, he noticed the repeating themes of loss and purpose.

He decided to dive right to the root. "What made you so lonely before you found God?"

Preacher visibly flinched, unable to cover his response fast enough. Flustered, he said, "We are all alone before we find God."

Trader hadn't intended to hit a nerve. He rephrased the question with a gentle tone. "Did you feel alone before you found God?"

"Everyone is alone without God," Preacher repeated tersely.

Trader quirked his mouth in doubt. "I respectfully disagree. Plenty of people who don't believe in God don't feel lonely. Sure, the After is a lonely world compared to the Before. But I've met a lot of people on the road. Some are alone and never feel lonely. Some are in large communities and still feel alone. Each person's experience is different."

Preacher's face grew clouded, and Trader felt him withdraw.

"Hey, man, I'm not trying to start any shit. I'm just trying to understand." Trader leaned back and held his hands up, palms out.

Preacher's posture remained stiff, and he squinted his eyes. Trader felt like Preacher was working him like a Rubik's cube, trying to figure him out just as much as Trader was trying to figure Preacher out.

"You must accept God first. Welcome him into your heart. With the acceptance, enlightenment will follow," Preacher finally said. "You must truly believe to see the light. God brought upon us the After, to test us. To find the true believers. Through Him, all will be explained."

Trader noticed he didn't quote the bible this time.

He shrugged noncommittally and said, "We need to take the time to truly understand each other as fellow human beings. You never know; you might end up making a new friend."

He watched Preacher closely. Giving him space to respond, Trader took a bit of his apple and chewed slowly. Preacher stayed silent, hostile gaze locked on him.

After a beat, Trader continued, "See, I've been in your footsteps since Lodi. Something changed there. Now, I do agree that you think you found God and that he filled that hole somehow. But what happened in Lodi to flip that switch?"

Preacher held his body perfectly still, and his lips were pressed in a white line. The muscles in his cheek clenched.

"We all got stories, man. And some of them are fucked up. Those are the scars we carry with us and the burdens we bear. That's what makes us who we are." Trader tapped his chest over his heart. "What happened in Lodi?"

Preacher exploded and slammed his fist down on the table, startling the ever-loving shit out of Trader. He couldn't help but jump.

Preacher stood up quickly, staring down at him, fists balled at his sides and radiating hostility. It was like a switch had been flipped. One minute, he was the strong but welcoming father figure. The next, it felt like he was going to call forth hellfire and brimstone.

His tone was stern and his eyes flashed as he said, "The fining pot is for silver, and the furnace for gold: but the Lord trieth the hearts. Therefore if any man be in the Lord's light, he is a new creature: old things are passed away. Once we are in His light, the past matters not."

"Whoa, whoa," Trader said, not unkindly, holding his hands up again in surrender. "Have a seat. I'm not trying to piss you off. I just want to hear your story." His heart was thudding in his chest.

Preacher remained standing, anger and pain radiating off him. Trader could sense him putting up walls.

"Come on," Trader gently coaxed. "Please sit back down. I wanna listen. Here...have an apple."

Trader set an apple in front of Preacher's spot at the table, unable to hide the slight adrenaline shake in his hand. Preacher ignored the offering and continued to glare at him. Trader took another bite of his apple, trying to look casual and relaxed. However, any self-respecting predator could probably smell how freaked out Trader was from a mile away. Preacher was erratic, and his unpredictability was scary as shit.

"I'm here to listen," he reiterated, gesturing for Preacher to sit back down.

A thousand micro-expressions crossed Preacher's face as he examined Trader. Slowly, Preacher's posture changed, and his hands relaxed to his sides. With intention, Preacher returned to the bench. Trader felt like that was a small win; at least he wasn't being chased out with pitchforks.

"Yes, my son. Listen to the word of God. Through God, you will find the way to community and the way to finding your purpose. I am pleased that you want to find your path."

"I'm interested in *you*," Trader corrected him. "What's your story? What happened in Lodi?" He let the uncomfortable silence build between them.

Preacher took a deep breath, lips pressed in a thin white line, and shifted in his seat.

"Like Job, God purged me of my ties to the earthly plane so that I would find the path to His light," Preacher said, leaning forward. "In his wisdom, he knew that I, like Moses, would lead people to that very same light. To clear that path, He brought down a plague and fires, taking everything I had. And, like a phoenix, I rose from blood and ash into the pure white light of God's love." Preacher's eyes shone with fanaticism as he started to gain steam again.

"What ties did he purge? Do you mean the people you were with in Lodi?" Trader pressed gently.

Anguish flittered across Preacher's face. He could tell that Preacher kept those painful thoughts buried deeply. Sensing him retreating again, he redirected the conversation.

"How did your group end up in Lodi?"

Preacher let out a deep, tormented sigh.

"We had a beautiful settlement in Angel's Camp. We were blessed. And then, God decided to test us. He brought down hellfire, and everything burned away." Preacher's eyes grew distant, and he paused.

Shocked that he'd finally drawn some of the story from Preacher, Trader let the silence stretch between them once again, not even daring to move.

"Our group was tested, and three people died on the journey from the foothills. We found Lodi and thought it was a safe harbor. But, you see, we had not yet proven our faith in God. We had not passed all His trials." Preacher tapped his pointer finger on the table for emphasis.

All Trader could think to do was nod, trying to keep Preacher talking. He couldn't help but wonder how different Preacher's path would've been if the group had stumbled out of the foothills and into Forty Two instead of Lodi. He might not even be "Preacher".

"God sent one last trial to test my faith. To test me as he tested Job. He sent forth a plague, killing my wife, my daughter, and everyone in the group. Never once, did I doubt his wisdom. As I burned the bodies of those I held dear, washing away all earthly attachments, God sent his breath down to raze the city. From the blood and ash of my people, I rose into His light. I knew my purpose was to bring His light to others. It was in the next settlement that I found two lost souls and shined light into them. They are now no longer alone. As I travel, God's light travels with me, saving lost souls."

Trader rolled those words over in his mind, wading through the zealotry to the base facts behind the peroration. Preacher must've lost everything in Lodi. With the people Preacher cared about suddenly dead and the city laid to waste, it was no wonder he felt alone without a sense of purpose. It didn't surprise him that Preacher had reached for anything to fill that emptiness and would cling to that with everything he had. Preacher literally rose out of the ashes, collecting converts along the way to a place he renamed the Lord's Light.

"I am truly sorry you had to go through that, losing everything all at once," Trader replied empathetically. "I can't imagine what that was like. You were part of a big group in Lodi. I've lost people, but not nine all at once. I can see why believing in God may have helped you through that."

Preacher, sensing a victory, enthusiastically cut in, "Yes! God is there for you too, my son. To give unto them beauty for ashes, the oil of joy for mourning, the garment of praise for the spirit of heaviness. Trust in the Lord with all of your heart. His light will give you purpose and ensure that you are never lonely again."

Trader slowly shook his head. "Sorry. I don't think I'm articulating myself right. What I'm trying to say is that I see the pain you've been through. I've never been through anything like that,

THE BEFORE AND THE AFTER

but I understand why you were looking for answers. Looking for a new way of living. Looking for hope. It's a dark world out there. These moments," Trader gestured between them. "These are the times when the true light shines."

Preacher tapped his pointer finger again on the table and said firmly, "No, my son. God's way is the only way to true peace."

Everything about Preacher made him want to throw up his defenses. He tried to tamp those feelings down and shift his frame of thinking. Preacher was a human being who'd been through some real shit. Trader tried to see it from his perspective and was just on the edge of figuring out why Preacher might have found something like religion to fill that empty space.

"I empathize with your situation, and I'm glad you found a way through the pain. We all feel alone sometimes. We all have our own way of coping with that. For some people, it's living in a small community and sharing everything. For someone like me, it's visiting different settlements, sharing meals, and listening to stories. And in the off-season, Sasha and Boxer carry me through. For others, it's a life-long companion. Even the same person may find that what fills a need at one point in their life may be different at another time.

"I am glad you found something to fill that space, especially after what you went through. But your way isn't the *only* way. To quote the bible, 'If it be possible, as much as lieth in you, live peaceably with all'. We need to be open to other ways of thinking. We have to accept others for who they are and the choices they decide to make."

Trying to break the tension, Trader nudged the uneaten apple closer to Preacher. This time, Preacher accepted it but didn't take a bite.

"Some people need a place like this, and it's great you've built that for them. But some people don't, and that's okay too."

He let the silence settle between them as Preacher turned the apple in counterclockwise circles on the table.

"I see your pain." Trader paused again, looking at Preacher.

Preacher's shoulders slumped slightly; his gaze remained on the twirling apple.

Trader sensed that, at his core, Preacher did care about others. The guy just expressed himself in a way that didn't sit right with most people. He also saw that, despite Preacher's heavy-handed leadership of the community, the people still looked to be doing fairly well. There must be a reason why they stayed.

"I also see that you bring these people hope," Trader continued. "You're helping them in a way that you needed back when there was no one left to help you."

Preacher took a deep, audible breath, eyes locked on the apple.

Trader pressed a bit further. "I think you could help more people if you lightened up a bit. Take a moment to see people for who they are and accept them for that."

Preacher's head snapped up. He locked eyes with Trader and hissed, "Who are *you* then, Trader, since you ask me to accept you for who you are? Who are you *really*?" He sat tall, tiling his chin up to stare down at him.

Trader's adrenaline surged at the confrontational tone. Preacher's reactions were all over the place, and he was finding it hard to ride on the emotional roller-coaster with him.

He took three slow breaths before he answered, "I'm someone who likes to be alone with my cat and my horse for three-quarters of the year. I like to have dinner with my neighbor every so often. I like to be on the road the rest of the time, meeting people and hearing their stories. I take those stories with me, and in that way, I'm never alone."

Trader maintained eye contact with Preacher, trying not to break under the heated gaze. Trader did his best to keep his expressions open and relaxed.

"And I find purpose in the people who need me. I connect

people. I spread their stories and their trades, making sure the settlements can make it through another year. It brings me joy to see settlements rise from the shattered remains of the Before. To see them concur Weeps, and floods, and fires, and droughts. I like seeing babies born and bringing books for little kids."

"It makes me happy to wear the first pair of legit brand-new boots and bring leather to the shoemaker at Forty Two to make shoes for others next year. I enjoy seeing people take the time to enjoy art again, like reading books and listening to music at Walnut Creek, or painting murals at the Machados'. I like sharing loom diagrams from the Silvas' with other settlements so that other people can start planting and weaving cotton.

"For me, I don't need a big community. I feel like a part of something when I can link people, pass along their trades, and share their stories. And I don't need God on my journey either. That doesn't make me a bad person. It just makes me who I am.

"Just because I choose to live differently doesn't mean anyone should push their way of life down my throat. Nor does it mean that I should be chased away for not conforming. Differences are important and should be valued. They make us stronger."

Trader stopped there, watching Preacher intently to see how the words landed. Trader had been monologuing, talking more than he usually did with people he visited. He also felt a bit exposed. But he figured that was a fair trade for the bit of insight Preacher had shared into his own past.

Preacher looked out at the gardens with his chin tilted up, the apple ever turning in his fingers. After a long stretch, he said, "You are an interesting person, Trader. God works in mysterious ways. I'm certain he has brought you to me."

Preacher chewed on the inside of his lower lip, a small tell into the anxiety that he tried to keep buried deep within.

"I hear your words and must pray on them."

Preacher startled Trader by abruptly standing up, essentially ending the conversation. Without a goodbye, Preacher headed back to the buildings on the far end of the settlement. The action was so unexpected that Trader sat there dumbfounded. He watched Preacher walk away and noticed that he had taken the apple with him, spinning it in his palm.

Trader was a bit befuddled about what to do next. He'd been dismissed, albeit very awkwardly and without a solid end to the conversation. He intuitively knew that Preacher would not reengage in conversation with him today, and probably not tomorrow either. He suspected Preacher had some serious thinking to do.

Trader figured he'd done what he could for the settlement this season. He'd provided some trades to help them make it through the winter. He'd also engendered a different way of viewing the world that, hopefully, inspired Preacher to be more open to other ways of thinking. And, maybe more importantly, encouraged Preacher to be more welcoming to the Singletons and other people seeking to trade. Leaving those ideas kicking around in Preacher's head was probably Trader's best gift to the community.

He had no clue whether to call the conversation a success or not. All Trader could hope for was that the seeds of acceptance were sown. Even though the tête-à-tête couldn't have lasted more than fifteen or twenty minutes, he felt exhausted and spent. But he also felt *done*; like whatever had drawn him here this season was now finished, and he could move on.

Trader knew he would come back next year, and he was hopeful that he would find a thriving community that had survived through collaboration with others, like the Singletons and the folks at Gold Bug. He also hoped that he could start sharing positive stories of the Preacher, helping others better understand and accept him and his followers at the Lord's Light in turn.

Trader finished up his lunch, packed up the wagon, and hitched Boxer up. Sasha was still grumpily curled in the driver's seat. Though most of the people ignored him as the trio left the settlement, one person looked up quickly and shared a small smile with Trader.

With one more story tucked in his pocket and the last trade of the season done, Trader turned the wagon south on the 49 towards the 80 and home.

ACKNOWLEDGMENTS

Heaps of appreciation go to my family. To Derek Smith, thank you for serving as a sounding board for every step of Trader's journey. Without you, we wouldn't have an apple, and Trader wouldn't have fully embraced acceptance. Thank you to my hubby, Justin Smith, for sticking around when all I could talk about for eight months was this book. I wish I could say we're through the woods, but two other books are cooking on my laptop. (Insert maniacal laughter.) And, to Tyler Dryden, thank you for lending your artist's touch to the design of Preacher's symbol and for all of your hard work on the exterior book design. I know it was like giving birth, and I was frustratingly picky, but the end product is a thing of beauty. I appreciate all of you!

Hoodie, my feline partner in crime and inspiration for Sasha, provided hours of reassuring snuggles as I dug deep to write about loneliness and depression. I was so shattered when he died that I was tempted to rewrite the story to have Sasha die, wanting Trader to feel the same pain. At the end of the day, I couldn't force my grief and loss on Trader and decided that all three of them needed to leave the last settlement together. I wish that all of you find a non-human buddy out there who can bring you as much joy and companionship as Sasha to Trader and as Hoodie to me.

Thank you to my copy editor, Caryn Pine, for dealing with the apostrophe chaos, and, more importantly, helping me weave more of Trader's feelings throughout the book and encouraging me to expand on the final confrontation. Anya Simons proofed the book, saving me from the usual public embarrassment related to my typo-ridden writing. Finally, Gareth Clegg formatted the book for both eBook and paperback formats (GarethClegg.com). Thank you all for polishing everything up.

And to everyone who has read this far through the book, thank you for going on this journey. I hope you find joy in the small things, appreciate differences, and put a little more kindness out into the world.

ABOUT THE AUTHOR

Catherine Sequeira was born and raised in the Bay Area. She obtained her BS and DVM from UC Davis and completed an anatomic pathology residency at Cornell. Throughout her career, she has lived and worked in Switzerland, New York, Oklahoma, and Scotland before returning to California. With over twenty years as a veterinary anatomic pathologist under her belt, she now writes and teaches. In her spare time, she enjoys reading sci-fi and fantasy, playing tabletop games, and gardening. She lives in Northern California with her partner, son, cat, and dragon (the bearded kind, that is).

She can be found online at
https://www.catherinesequeira.com

Made in the USA
Columbia, SC
13 October 2023